# Robert Don Hughes

Broadman
& Holman
Publishers

Nashville, Tennessee

0-8054-6000-4

Published by Broadman & Holman Publishers, Nashville, Tennessee
Editorial Team: Vicki Crumpton, Janis Whipple, Kim Overcash
Typesetting: Leslie Joslin

Dewey Decimal Classification: 813
Subject Heading: FICTION—CHRISTIAN / SCIENCE FICTION—CHRISTIAN
Library of Congress Card Catalog Number: 98-43296

Unless otherwise stated all Scripture citation is from the NIV, the Holy Bible, New International Version, copyright © 1973, 1978, 1984 by International Bible Society; and the King James Version of the Bible.

**Library of Congress Cataloging-in-Publication Data**

Hughes, Robert Don, 1949–
    The eternity gene / Robert Don Hughes.
       p.   cm.
    ISBN 0-8054-6000-4
    I. Title.
    PS3558.U389E85       1999
    813'.54—dc21

                                    98-43296
                                          CIP

1 2 3 4 5  03 02 01 00 99

*This is for Gail. . . .*
*She helped me write it.*

# CONTENTS

# Chapter One

*The tie that binds*

"It's a dream," Jack told himself. "It's all a dream." He thrashed about in the bed, tearing the covers from their moorings and wadding the hateful hotel mattress pad beneath him. He knew he was doing this, even in his sleep. He knew he was uncomfortable and he knew why, yet he also knew that he was asleep, and therefore couldn't rouse himself enough to do anything about it. Couldn't—or wouldn't. He didn't want to awaken because he was terrified, and he knew the reason for that too. He didn't want to see what was in the room with him—and he knew something was.

Outside was New York City—Thirty-third Street and Seventh, across the street from Madison Square Garden, and Penn Station beneath it. He'd booked this hotel because of its close proximity to the railway, and he needed to get up early in the morning to catch the train to Baltimore. Early . . . early . . . needed sleep.

But the real reason he couldn't wake was that presence—that horrible presence that lurked within the shadows somewhere in this tiny room. It was a presence he knew—or thought he knew—a creature like some he'd met before, who had stolen him from his ordered life and taken him to places too hideous to remember. It was a dark thing, demonic in its nature—hungry to eat his stress.

"The sandwich," Jack murmured to no one but himself—that Philly steak sandwich swathed with onions he'd eaten far too late, and against his own better judgment; a late-night sandwich of epic proportions and maximum spiciness, unwisely weighed against the demands of an early travel schedule and a tense meeting at his destination. He thought this, in his dream, and then as dreams will do to onion-flavored thoughts, Jack was the sandwich, and the creature was rising over his bed to eat him. He would have screamed, but he couldn't make his mouth form words, and he longed for Gloria to wake him from this nightmare. She surely would if she were here, but of course she was home in Kentucky. And so the dream continued: Jack the sandwich rolled back to look up at the creature.

It was a creature, after all—God had created everything, demons included. There was nothing that was made that was not, at its worst, a perversion of His creation, no matter how horrible, no matter how fallen. But this thing that loomed above him in black malevolence wore a form of its own design: A horrible mix of stinging insect and soulless, leering eyes. This mask, this costume, had been especially designed to shock the human mind and crush the human spirit. Jack felt the crushing weight of the thing on top of him, smearing him with that acrid insect stench, and he would have screamed if the words had come—indeed, he dreamed he was shouting—but he could force no sound from his sleep-drugged lungs. Again he felt that wadded mattress cover beneath him, felt his legs locked in the grip of entangling sheets, lunged away from the enormous dripping mandibles and—awoke.

"Huh!" he grunted at last. "Ohhh . . ." he groaned. Jack Brennen sat up in the bed, gasping for breath, staring into the darkness before him. The room was dimly illuminated by a strip of light coming from under the bathroom door. Leaving the light on in the hotel bathroom was a longtime habit of his married life. On their honeymoon at a Florida beach, Gloria had left the bathroom light on, to help them make their way through the disorienting darkness of a strange place. He'd done so ever since, even when she didn't travel with him, and now he blessed her for her foresight, for it was enough—enough to see that the room was empty save for himself. The double latch was still on the door, and the single shade was still drawn down over the window.

He hopped out of bed and grabbed his watch. Two-thirty. Three hours before he had to get up. Jack stumbled into the bathroom, eyes adjusting to the light as he checked behind the shower curtain for—whatever. He felt stupid in doing so, but reassured at the same time. He looked at himself in the mirror, rubbed his eyes and looked again, shocked as always at how much older the face looking back at him appeared. His high, Cherokee cheekbones were from his father, the gray-green eyes from his mother, the stubble on his chin a curious gray in contrast to his still-brown hair. He rubbed his hands through that unruly mop as he paced back into the bedroom, turning on the television for company. He was trembling.

It was only a dream, of course. That's what he told himself as he slumped to the carpeted floor at the foot of the bed, fifteen inches from the now glowing screen. CNN took shape before him, and he absently studied the baseball scores at the bottom of the screen, not at all interested in the outcomes, needing only the link to the real world they provided.

He'd never had that dream before. Not that he remembered, in any case. He crawled backward up onto the bed, then swiveled around to pull the shade aside and look out the window. It looked down upon Thirty-fourth and Macy's department store. The street below was still as lighted up as ever, and people still moved about the city as if it were early evening. The city that never slept.

Yes, there were demons at work in New York City—as in every city. "But God is at work here as well," Jack mumbled to himself, aloud. That's why he was here. He was helping to establish an extension seminary to train local pastors. He'd been teaching until late, bantering with a small class drawn from every point on the ethnic compass. Filipinos and Koreans, Jamaicans and New York-born Latin Americans, an Egyptian and an Indian—with a couple of Anglos as well. All were citizens of the modern-day Rome, the "Capital City of the World" as the banners under the streetlights proclaimed. Like the apostle Paul of old they were each seeking to make Jesus Christ known to a world oblivious to that message. There were demons here, yes, but no more demons in New York than there had been in San Francisco, or Los Angeles, or Lusaka, or Lagos, or any other city where he'd ministered.

But they were here. They were everywhere, and they were real. He'd seen them. Talked to them. Recognized them as demonic, done spiritual battle with them, and been terrified by them. And that thing—that monster in his nightmare—had been as real and as present as any he had met. Jack knew it. He released the blind, laid back on the bed, and struggled to control his fear.

"Lord," he muttered silently toward the ceiling, "I realize You know all of this already, but I'm a little shaken here, and I need to feel Your presence."

Almost before he got the words out the phone rang, its red message light flashing in the dim room. Jack sat up with a knowing smile. Gloria. He rolled over and grabbed the receiver from the cradle before the second ring. "Hi," he smiled into it.

"Hi," she said back—fully alert at 2:30 in the morning. She told him she never slept when he traveled. "What's wrong?" she went on, her voice full of concern.

"How do you know something's wrong?" he asked as he eased himself back onto his pillow. He felt himself relaxing, at last.

"I just had this terrible feeling, and I was worried about you."

"I had a bad dream."

"What'd you dream?"

"Oh, you don't need to know."

"Might make you feel better to tell it."

"I don't think so. Had aliens in it."

"Aliens or demons?"

"What's the difference?" Jack yawned. He was already feeling sleepy again.

"Anyone you knew?"

"No," Jack answered, his voice more a rumbling growl than a word.

"Was Ben in it?"

"No. It was really scary. How are you?"

"I'm . . . OK. I miss you."

"One more day, Hon," he soothed. This had been a long trip, and they were both tired of the separation. This was the fourth time they'd spoken today, which was close to average, he guessed, for his travels. When they'd been missionaries in Nigeria he'd been forced to disappear into the bush for weeks at a time, with no way for them to make contact. Once back to the dependable telephone service of the

States, they'd chosen to make good use of all those wires strung between them.

"I didn't tell you," she said, "but you had a nightmare the night before you left. I had to wake you up and turn you over."

"Really?" Jack said, by now feeling fully free of the dread that had shaken him awake, and really needing to go back to sleep.

"Maybe you should talk to Ben about it when you get home—describe your dream to him."

"Maybe I will," Jack mumbled, his eyes closed as the phone lay on the pillow beside him.

"You're going to sleep on me, aren't you."

"I think so . . ."

"OK then. Call me in the morning. I love you."

"Love you," Jack said, and he managed to angle the receiver back into its cradle before dropping off. Morning was only a couple of hours away now. The effects of the dream were gone.

But the dream—and the beast—came back.

* * *

He guessed later that he must have gone on to his meeting the next morning. He must have caught the train to Baltimore in time. He couldn't remember not doing so. He must have functioned in that meeting as if fully present, for he could remember no comments to the contrary. He'd been scheduled to teach following the meeting, and he must have done so, giving a lecture he'd delivered so often he could do it on autopilot. The students would not have realized his mental absence—they'd never heard this before. That's why one of his former deans had often said, "Teaching is a very forgiving profession." In any case he eventually found himself on a plane back to Louisville, seated next to a window, fingering the new tie Gloria had given him for his birthday—and trembling. He was going to be taken again. He knew it.

Jack Brennen had been abducted. Not by aliens—not exactly, although they currently pretended to be such. That's what he'd believed, at first. Eventually he'd come to realize that he'd been abducted by those same creatures who pretended to be gods at history's dawn, the same creatures who had later pretended to be elves and fairies and leprechauns when people had chosen to call them that.

But playing gods and elves was passé for them now. Aliens were now in vogue, so these flexible, adaptable demons now pretended to be visitors from other planets. Jack knew better. They were now what they had always been—fallen angels. Call them demons, call them the devil's minions, call them dark angels, call them the host of Lucifer—whatever you called them they remained what they'd always been—and just as evil as ever. Ageless, deathless coconspirators with legions of evil men, they had perfected deception after deception in order to continue enslaving the human race. They were the principalities, the powers, the rulers of the darkness of this world—and Jack knew several of them personally. The very thought of them gave him chills. Folding his tray table into its fully upright and locked position, he glanced out the window at the clouds. Would they take him off the plane?

They did not. A couple of hours of cramped discomfort later, he was home, giving a blow-by-blow description of the previous night's adventures to his wife.

Gloria's prescription was concise and direct. "Call Ben."

Jack resisted. He hadn't seen Ben for days, which was odd. Usually they met each other in the hallway at least once a day. Was Ben avoiding him? Was he using his "gift" for reading minds again to insure that he didn't cross Jack's path? Certainly not, Jack snorted at himself. It was Ben's psychic ability to read people's thoughts that had caused him to be abducted as a boy by the Fallen, and Ben's exercise of that "gift" had ultimately led to Jack's being taken as well. But Ben no longer read minds. He'd realized many years ago that his mind-reading ability had been more curse than gift— a legacy bequeathed to him by his hippie parents, who had flirted with Satanism. When he had chosen at last to serve Christ, it had departed from him. But if Ben could still read thoughts, he would have read in Jack's mind a steady stream of half-remembered events and vexing questions related to their shared experiences with the Fallen.

It was late. Jack was tired. Ben might be in bed. But the memories stirred up in his brain by his dream wouldn't leave him alone. One thought especially simply wouldn't go away. Were there experiences they had shared with the Fallen that Ben remembered—but that Jack did not? Could Ben shed any light on Jack's vision of these enormous bugs? Giving up at last, Jack picked up the phone and dialed Ben's number.

"Hello?" the young man answered immediately.

"Not reading minds, evidently," Jack began, and he heard the smile at the other end of the line.

"Would be nice if I still could, at least just a little, so I could know what Dr. Jefferson is going to ask on this theology midterm."

"That's easy," Jack smiled. "Think Calvinism."

"Yeah, right," Ben snorted. "I think my *grade* is predestined."

Jack chuckled. "Speaking of predetermination, I've been thinking a lot lately about our 'adventures' together. Having bad dreams too. We traveled in and out of time a lot, Ben, and it all got pretty confusing. For some reason, I'm just wondering—"

"What I remember clearly and you don't," Ben finished his sentence for him.

Jack shivered. Ben's response had been so brusque, so abrupt, it was as if he had read his— "How did you know that?" Jack asked, almost accusingly.

Ben sighed. "Just an educated guess is all. In a way I think I've been expecting your call."

Jack shivered again. "Look," he asked, "could we get together tomorrow? My office—maybe at noon?"

"Right after my midterm," the young man answered, forcing an unfelt smile into his voice. "Sure. I'll be there." But as he hung up the phone Jack had the distinct feeling that Ben really didn't want to meet. Why? The thought plagued him as he wrestled through another sleepless night. The dreams were coming with greater frequency.

The next day at twelve sharp Ben met him at the door of his office. They weren't even inside yet when the student plunged right into the heart of the matter: "It's my tie comment that has you worried, isn't it."

"Your what?"

"My comment about your tie." Jack looked at Ben blankly, so the young man continued. "A couple of weeks ago when I met you in the hall, you had on this tie that had elephants on it. I told you I remembered it, and you said it was new. You got a funny look on your face. I thought my chance comment would start to worry you. I'm sorry, Dr. Brennen. I've been avoiding you ever since."

Now Jack remembered. His birthday tie. Gloria had bought it for him because it had elephants on it, symbolic of their days together in Africa. Never mind that they were Indian elephants. "I . . . hadn't remembered that event, exactly—but I have been having dreams, Ben. Terrible dreams, with huge, bug-like creatures in them."

Ben dropped his head to his chest, and sighed. "UMMO."

"What?"

"We called them the bugs." Ben raised his head and looked Jack in the eye. "You don't remember them?"

"I don't remember *any* insect *that* big. I would think I would . . ."

Ben nodded, and looked away, his face lined with tension. "I was afraid of that."

"And—this thing about the tie? That's related to these—bugs?"

"To UMMO. Yeah. I just happened to remember that you were wearing it the day we—" Ben stopped himself, and heaved a long, deep sigh. "Dr. Brennen, I really don't know what to say. I remember them. You don't. The explanation seems pretty simple, given all our dropping in and out of time—and your new tie. What's happened to me hasn't happened to you. Yet."

Jack stared numbly at Ben. The implications of his words were clear. Ben had already lived through experiences with Jack—and with the Fallen—that Jack had not yet lived through. That was quite conceivable. The Fallen did, after all, have the technology to travel through time. Jack had, himself, visited several eras of human history, and he and Ben had not always been together. Given the way the Fallen shifted back and forth from one time period to another, who could establish—with any certainty—a consistent timeline of events? The logical conclusion of all this was inescapable—Jack *would* be taken again. Apparently while wearing his elephant tie.

"When, Ben?" he asked.

Ben tilted his head and looked back at him. "When? That's a time word, Jack. You and I both know that with the Fallen, time words just don't apply."

True indeed, Jack acknowledged. Even so, the anxiety was churning in his gut, demanding that he ask more, that he learn something, that he make some kind of *preparation. . . .*

Ben spoke evenly, quietly: "You want me to tell you something to get you ready."

"You read my mind," Jack joked—but Ben didn't hear it that way. Come to think of it, maybe it hadn't really been a joke.

"No, but I've read your mind many times in the past, Jack, and I know how it works. You don't look backward, much, but you have an insatiable curiosity to know what's coming, in order to be prepared for it."

"You've pegged me," Jack nodded. "Knowing that about me, what can you tell me, Ben?"

Ben sighed. "I know what I *could* tell you. I don't know what I *should* tell you. I thought we were past all of that—both of us. It never occurred to me until the other day that there might be events I've already witnessed that you haven't yet. So how do we even talk about it? Do I say 'Do you remember the time?' and if you don't then I tell you what I recall?"

"I guess we could try that—"

"But to what end, Jack? Would it help you to know what you're 'predestined' to do, or would it hurt you? Look at this situation. I made a chance comment. You're having dreams of a past *I* remember. We've added things up to realize that you're going to . . . go away again. Does it help to *know* that, Jack? Hasn't it filled you full of dread, instead? Wouldn't it be better not to know, to simply live through the events as they come, and remember that God is sovereign?"

Jack sat back in his chair, exhaling a long, slow breath. "This is the student preaching to the teacher," he murmured. "Go ahead, I'm listening."

"That's really the whole sermon," Ben apologized, dropping his head again.

"And a good one," Jack said, almost under his breath. "But it's a little like preaching in the face of death. People *know* they're going to die—eventually. But what they really want to know is *when*—and if they'll be all right." Jack stood up, and paced around his desk. "I don't guess I really need to know exactly when I'll be taken again. What bothers me—what *does* fill me full of dread—is whether I'll be coming back this time or not."

It wasn't a question, exactly. Still, it did require some response—and it hung somewhere in the room between them for a long time, unanswered. Without the benefit of mind-reading abilities Jack knew what Ben was thinking, and it was exactly what Jack had feared. Ben didn't know.

While his young friend labored to find some proper response, Jack chuckled. "I guess we need to add a new class to the curriculum: 'Pastoral care for the soon-to-be abducted.' Then maybe you'd know what to say."

Ben sighed—a deep, helpless sigh Jack knew the young preacher would breathe many times in his ministry. Time after time Jack had sighed exactly that way, when faced with the imponderable questions that have no answers, but still require some response.

"I understand," Jack murmured. Despite the sudden grip of terror, he tried to reassure his student. "You're not God. How could you know?"

Jack heard Ben swallow. "I guess we *could* go over some events together, just to give you some idea of what to anticipate."

"But as you say, to what end?" Jack shrugged, wishing now he hadn't called Ben, wishing this conversation had never taken place. Wishing he didn't know.

"So you don't remember the bugs at all?"

"You've already said it well, Ben. How can this help?"

"That whole war between UMMO and the Grays? Valhalla? The conclave of the Ultrastructure? The head bug being juiced over our heads?"

"No, no, and no," Jack answered glumly.

Ben sounded truly perplexed. "You don't remember any of those things at all?"

"Not a one. And hearing you mention them only makes me wonder just how long I'll be gone this time. . . ."

Having begun now, Ben couldn't stop himself. "The Nazis? The tower of Babel?"

"Yes," Jack nodded, "and yes."

"Atlantis?"

"Yes," Jack kept nodding.

"The whole genetic experiment thing?"

"I think so," he nodded.

"Running from the Romans in that German castle?"

This one stopped him. "Romans? We were in the first century together?"

"Fourth." Ben muttered. "Were or will be. You make the call."

"All right then. No, I don't remember that. At all." Jack felt like he could almost hear Ben thinking.

"This isn't helping, is it," Ben finally grumbled.

"No," Jack agreed. "You were right about that. I'm far better off to trust in the Lord with all my heart and lean not to my own understanding."

Ben paraphrased the Scripture back to him. "In all your ways acknowledge Him, and He *shall* direct your paths."

"Right," Jack agreed, wanting now for Ben to leave so that he could grieve for his own future in solitude. "God is sovereign."

"As to the other thing, Jack . . ." Ben paused.

"You mean whether I'll return," Jack supplied to help the young man finish his thought.

"Yes, that," Ben said. "I really don't know when, and . . . or if. But I'll be praying."

"And that, Ben, is all any of us who are *not* God can do."

In that moment, Jack felt strangely comforted. Blessed, even. Not because Ben had answered the questions of his heart, for the young man certainly hadn't, any more than he had himself been able to answer the questions asked him over the years by the dying. It was rather the comforting reassurance that *if* he must be taken again, and *should* he not return, he would leave behind young ministers in whose life he had made a difference.

*But I'm not going anywhere,* another part of Jack's mind put in, *because the tie stays in the closet!* As soon as he got home that afternoon he went straight to his tie-rack, grabbed it off, and flipped the offending garment into the dusty darkness. There it rested upon the pile of dead shoes, shoes long ago abandoned but never discarded. What he didn't do was throw it away. After all, he *would* eventually need it— wouldn't he?

\* \* \*

As always, the spring semester lumbered from midterm to break, dragging weary students and faculty along with it. As always, Easter was a glorious, transcendent time . . . followed by the emotional plummet of stacks of end-of-semester papers. Students and faculty alike wondered why these had to be assigned at all—students because they had to write the papers, faculty because they had to then grade them. But such is the curious rhythm of school—post-papers, the semester suddenly rushed headlong into finals and thence to graduation without pausing for breath. Just like that, it was summer. And Jack had not been taken.

"Abduction Experiences! True testimony or fanciful foolishness! Sherry Lynn Ward, one o'clock, here."

Jack glanced up from the paper to catch the tail of the blurb. The woman who gazed back at him from the television wore her trademark enigmatic smile, as if daring him and all other viewers to question her omnipotent wisdom. She was new—one of a whole new pack of talk-show hosts following in the wake of Donahue, Oprah, and Springer—but not so new that Jack didn't already feel overexposed to her. Like most of the talk-show queens and clowns she stayed within a relatively narrow arc of subjects—only the most sensational topics would do. And since somehow the summer had already melted into the ratings sweeps month of July, the afternoon screen screamed constantly about "transvestite drag-queen children of religious parents" and "mothers who dress their children like sluts." Jack generally kept a wide buffer between himself and afternoon talk-show television, but this promo caught him. And, since he was between summer terms, he was free to watch.

He could tell from the first words out of her mouth that Sherry Lynn herself considered UFO abduction stories ridiculous. Arching her eyebrows disdainfully, she taunted one guest after another—subtly, of course. Before asking a belittling question she would cut her colored-contact-enhanced emerald eyes toward her studio audience, as if to ask, "Are you with me on this?" and "Isn't it fun to make people act like idiots?" Then she would start a line of questioning clearly aimed at rendering her guest a fool—and smile ever-so-sweetly while she did it. So charismatic was the woman, so charming in her turn of phrase and twist of lip, that she could skewer her targets effortlessly and still leave them grinning back at her. It wasn't the stories of these publicly-butchered people that intrigued Jack. It was rather the woman's arch, contemptuous attitude. Of course he didn't watch Sherry Lynn regularly, but he'd seen her enough to know she normally endorsed the viewpoint of her most outrageous guest—at least until the inevitable psychiatrist made his or her appearance. But in this particular program she was hacking and cutting from the opening introductions. Why? Jack wondered. Had viewer research indicated that *non*belief in UFOs was now the most outrageous position, and thus the viewpoint she should adopt?

Or did she hide within her some personal agenda toward abduction experiences that rendered her incapable of identifying with this particular cluster of guests? "Then again," Jack wondered aloud to himself, "when did *I* become the guest psychologist?"

"So then you were . . . lifted, you say, off the ground, and floated into the saucer?" Sherry Lynn was asking a dark-haired southern woman with a very earnest, honest expression.

"That's right," the woman nodded.

"Was this with . . . like . . . a tractor beam or something? Like on *Star Trek?*"

"Not exactly," the woman answered warily. She was sharp, Jack thought. She'd clearly caught on to Sherry Lynn's attitude toward this subject and wasn't anxious to make the trip to the slaughterhouse herself.

"Then what was it like—exactly?" Sherry Lynn goaded, smiling.

The southern lady took a deep breath, closed her eyes, then steepled her fingers together over her lips. When she lowered her hands a moment later to speak, she did not open her eyes. It was as if she read her memories off of some personal, internal monitor, speaking of herself in the clinical tones of an impartial observer, rather than a participant: "There was no visible beam, no visible force at all. There was only the sense one moment of being in control of my own body, the next minute not. There was no feeling of vertigo, nor any fear of not remaining upright. There was rather a sense of wonder—of awe—perhaps a question in my mind if this was the rapture, and an elation at being taken—"

"The *rapture*, Elizabeth?" Sherry Lynn sneered—with her voice, not with her lips.

"Yes," Elizabeth responded quietly, but not at all hesitantly. "That's what I thought at first. That Jesus had come for me." She kept her eyes closed as, with a soft, Georgia-born lilt in her voice, she continued: "I was disappointed of course—"

She hadn't intended or expected that as a laugh line, but the audience burst into raucous laughter anyway. When she watched the show herself later, she understood why. Sherry Lynn Ward had done a marvelously well-timed double-take into the camera, her pretty jaw sagging open in mocking incredulity. By the time Elizabeth's eyes fluttered open to look, Sherry Lynn's expression had changed. She now wore the warm, encouraging smile of a sister in the battle against ignorant studio audiences.

"Never mind them, Elizabeth," Sherry Lynn soothed. "Just tell your story."

Elizabeth eyed the audience with a steel magnolia determination, as if weighing in her mind whether it was even worth continuing. Sherry Lynn's hypocritical smile apparently encouraged her, and once again she closed her eyes and went into the mental back room where she'd stored this terrifying experience. "I was floated into the saucer—and yes, it *looked* like a saucer—and around a curving hallway. There was very little light. What light there was seemed to come from glowing apricot-hued letters or something on the walls. Then I was in a room *filled* with light, tipped onto my back and on some kind of table, and for the first time since all of this began, I was really frightened."

"You knew what was coming," Sherry Lynn put in, almost as an aside. But it stopped Elizabeth cold. Once again she opened her eyes, and this time regarded her host with a frankly challenging stare.

"No I did *not* know," she said flatly.

"Well, I just meant that—"

"You meant that somehow I had *seen* what was supposed to happen next on television dramas."

"Well no, I was just meaning that—"

"Because you really believe I've made all of this up, don't you?"

The studio audience was "Ooooouuuu"ing by this time, sniffing at last the fight they'd come to watch. Sherry Lynn Ward once more pulled a face at the camera, this time her "Uh-oh, I'm in for it now, aren't I?" expression. Then she turned back to her guest and waded in:

"Didn't you, Elizabeth? Now *really?* I mean, isn't it a little far-fetched to ask us to believe that people from another planet abduct human beings almost daily, and no national government has been able to find any objective proof?"

There was a burst of supportive applause from the audience. Of course, if Sherry Lynn Ward had taken exactly the opposite viewpoint with this same crisp tone of voice, there would have been an equivalent burst of supportive applause from the audience. Jack was reminded that in the television talk-show universe it really didn't matter whether one said a true thing—only that one said a thing with authority. Unless, of course, one was expressing a Christian perspective. Then one could expect politically correct boos. He found himself cheering mentally for the woman named Elizabeth—not the least because she was describing feelings and events that he had himself experienced.

But she was bound to lose. Instead of responding out of her personal experience, she let Sherry Lynn lead her into a debate about governmental honesty and objectifiable evidence. As the verbal sparring turned into punch and counterpunch, it became clear once again that the person who controlled the microphone and the commercial breaks could steer the program any way she wanted it to go—and make herself appear impartial as she did so.

*Frightening power,* Jack thought to himself, for as the world hurtled toward the twenty-first century, television was both its classroom *and* its courtroom.

". . . but you really didn't ever let me tell my story," Elizabeth was trying to say, a perplexed look on her face.

"Believe me, Elizabeth, we've heard it before," Sherry Lynn Ward said with a pontifical smile, then she whirled toward the camera, pointing her finger into it. "We'll be right back with an Alabama woman who says the *government* is building—get this—*time* machines for the aliens!"

Her pretty face immediately disappeared, replaced by dancing diapers gleefully singing of their dedication to dryness. Jack didn't hear them. He used the break to run up to the kitchen and look for a pencil. His heart was beating hard as he came back down, impatient for the commercial break to end. Jack had *been* to that place in Alabama where the time-boxes had been constructed. Was the true story going to come out at last?

Back from the break, Sherry Lynn Ward introduced her next guest—Carrie Baxter from Huntsville, Alabama. Jack scribbled her name on a sticky note, shaking with excitement, and looked up, waiting to get more information.

What a disappointment. Sherry Lynn Ward never let her tell her story, either. Instead she made the woman look absolutely foolish, twisting her words into traps and then pushing her into them. When Sherry Lynn brought on the guest psychologist for the day, Jack turned it off in frustration.

The story wouldn't be told. The Fallen wouldn't allow it to be told. Jack put the sticky note into the back of his wallet and forgot about it. He knew too much about those flying time boxes already. But the program had made him think—remember—and wonder. He made his way slowly up the stairs, opened his closet, got on his knees, and fished out the tie.

As he beat the dust out of it and held it up next to his chin he felt a shiver of danger rattle through him—a thrill. *What if they took me right now?* he thought to himself, and the very notion made him a little dizzy. It was as if the tie held the key to his own destiny—as if he held his own life in his hands. He'd often used just those words to describe times of decision making to students. There'd been several instances in his life when, at the close of some long-term commitment such as a degree program or in the face of a call to a new ministry position, he felt as if God handed him his life for a moment and said, "Choose."

He looked down at the tie again, perplexed. Was this a choice? Could he actually choose to travel again with the Fallen, or could he choose to have no more direct contact with those hideous creatures? One thing he'd learned about "turning points" was that, once chosen, a pathway could obligate you so deeply that all freedom to choose differently disappeared. There were consequences of every choice; some of them unpleasant. He quickly thrust the tie back into the closet.

But he hung it up this time. He hung it with the other ties on the rack, then walked away. If this was a choice God had given him, he wasn't ready to make it today. At the same time, neither was he ready to close the door on the exciting possibility. Then from somewhere inside him came a grating whisper of doubt that told him what he was really trying to do was play God. "You think holding onto the tie gives you some kind of power over God!" the abusive voice sneered. Jack walked downstairs and out into the summer sun, struggling to ignore the whisperer and to forget the tie was even there.

# Chapter Two

*Whiter than snow*

Sleet started falling during the service. As Jack stood on the platform singing at the top of his lungs, he was calculating how long it would take for the roads to get really nasty: probably half an hour. It wouldn't be much trouble for the few folks who'd decided to come on this morning in the face of the Weather Channel's dire predictions. While their homes were scattered around the county, and some down "holler" roads that could get slippery quickly, they all lived within three or four miles of the church. He, however, had to drive the twenty-five miles back to the city. He could cut his sermon short, but he didn't want to. After all, it had cost all of them something to get here this morning.

It had been a fierce winter, dumping snow after snow upon the region, and each storm seemingly arriving on the weekend. They'd already had to cancel church twice since Christmas. Several viruses were making the circuit as well. The most recent had decimated the choir, which was why he was singing so loudly. Gloria had debated with him this morning the wisdom of going ahead and meeting, as much for his own sake as for the congregation. "After all," she'd argued through a stopped-up nose, "Gabrielle's running a fever and mine's still hanging on, and you're not really over it yet yourself. Why go give your germ to the congregation?"

"I'd only be returning what they so generously bestowed on me," he'd smiled, and she'd rolled her eyes in frustration and given up. She knew there was no arguing with him when he was determined to go to church sick. Instead, she'd blown her nose and asked, "What are you preaching on?"

"Disciples on the road," he'd said as he'd slipped into his coat and shot his cuffs. "What traveling with Jesus must have been like for the disciples, and what that means for us today."

"Jesus would have had the good sense to stay *off* the roads today," Gloria had grumbled pointedly. "It's the Pharisees who would have insisted on going ahead and meeting. It's supposed to be a blizzard, Jack! Six to eight inches!"

"I'll be home before it starts," he'd soothed, leaning over the bed to kiss her good-bye, and she'd hugged him down to her. When he'd stood back up she'd given him her most beautiful smile and said, "*Please* be careful."

He was trying to do exactly that as he angled his van out of the parking lot after the service. Glancing at the clock on the dashboard he saw that it was just now noon. There was already an inch of snow on the church steps, and that on top of a layer of ice. Few folks lingered in the sanctuary. Everyone headed to their cars in a hurry, including the preacher.

The flakes were huge and wet and coming down fast. The shortest way to the main road was straight up a hill, but no one was daring enough to try that route. Though it took him a little longer, he followed the congregation and drove the long, flat way around to it. "Not too bad," he mumbled to himself as he made it to the "New Road" and turned for home. He put eight miles between himself and the church much more quickly than he'd expected to.

The "New Road" was twenty years old by this time. As he drove it carefully he was wondering how long it would take for it to lose that name, if ever—and then he heard it. Something in his engine suddenly sounded very wrong— like a sewing machine. "Oh no," he murmured to no one, taking a tighter grip on the wheel. A chill that had nothing to do with the weather rattled down his spine. "Oh Lord," he added a moment later as the sewing machine sounds grew more frantic. He slowed way down, pleading with God to just let him make it home and wishing he'd paid attention to his wife. He had that sick feeling in the pit of his stomach that he got whenever he encountered "circumstances beyond our control." "Due to circumstances beyond our control," he announced aloud in his best radio voice, "the remainder of today is gonna be a real hassle." In retrospect, Jack realized that was an understatement.

He took a small hill very, very slowly, his engine whining to him all the while to please stop. When he refused, it took matters into its own—pistons. The van began to shimmy, as if it suddenly had two flat tires at once. Then, as they crested the hill together, the sewing machine engine under his hood gave a firecracker BAMMM! and departed this world forever.

Alone in the carcass of his now-dead van, Jack coasted down the far side of the hill. "So," he said to himself philosophically, "*that's* what it feels like to blow an engine." He glanced ruefully into his rearview mirror, then turned all the way around to look back at the plume of blue-black smoke he was leaving in his wake. "A pillar of fire by night, a pillar of cloud by day," he murmured as he watched it, which was probably meaningless, he knew, but certainly better than some things he could say in such an event. He was intrigued in that moment to see how little springs and screws and bits of metal also appeared to be issuing from his tailpipe. Then he turned back forward, and with the little bit of inertia remaining in the old van he battled to get it off the road and onto the shoulder without sliding into the ditch. It stopped. Dead.

Jack sat there a moment before getting out. He guessed there really wasn't any rush. There was no one behind him; indeed, he'd noticed no one else on the New Road at all since he'd left the church. "Should've preached on the wisdom of Solomon this morning," he muttered as he finally opened the door and climbed out. "Should have preached from Ecclesiastes. 'There's a time to have church, and a time to stay home. . . .'" He walked around to the back of the van and gazed back up the hill. The coal-black oil slick he'd left behind him was truly hideous, but the falling snow was doing its best to quickly cover it up. He needed a phone.

He knew right where he was. He'd been up and down this road so many times he could calculate to the minute how long it would take him to get to church from this point. Although he couldn't see them, he knew exactly where the closest houses were in both directions and on either side of the road. He wasted no time thinking about it, but set off walking toward the nearest one. It was a farmhouse back the way he'd come, and about a half-mile off the road across a pasture. It was a good thing he'd worn his boots this morning.

*How silent everything is,* he thought as he started back up the oil-stained hill. It was never this quiet in the city. And how fast the freezing acoustical foam was tumbling from the sky! And how much longer it took to get places when on foot instead of on wheels, especially on foot through two inches of snow, on top of ice. And how few cars were traveling on this road this afternoon. . . . Were there *no* other idiots out today? The back of his throat was beginning to hurt again. Gloria was right, he wasn't completely over the flu yet. Just how high *was* this hill, anyway? How much time was he adding to this trek by going up the road instead of cutting straight across the pasture to his left?

Jack changed course and plunged down off the highway and into that same ditch he'd struggled just moments ago to avoid rolling the van into. That *had* been just moments ago, hadn't it? He leapt across the bottom of the dip and started back up the other side, eyeing the white rail fence above him that would be his next obstacle. At least it wasn't barbed wire. Remembering when he'd been skinny enough to slide between such rails, he clambered over it and dropped to the other side. Then he paused, took a deep breath, and looked back at the van to see how far he'd come.

That was a mistake. He'd managed to get all of twenty yards away. Dismayed, he leaned over the fence and rested a moment. How much time had passed? Glancing at his wrist he remembered he'd left his watch on the pulpit again. Then he whirled around and started on up over the hill. He had to get to a phone. Gloria was already sick, and this would worry her more so. Besides, he was pretty worried himself. Wouldn't do any good, he knew—he was trying not to be—but there it was. Jack was afraid. Despite the fact that he was only a few minutes from his home in one direction and a few minutes from his church in another, and members of his congregation lived all around him, he was in trouble. "Lord," he mumbled in an aside to the Almighty, "I could die out here."

He was trying to keep from berating himself, but it was hard not to. He should have listened to Gloria. He should have had the car checked. He should have pulled off to a farmhouse and called home *before* blowing up his engine. He should have kept on walking up the road instead of heading across this pasture, for it didn't take long to realize this would be even slower going. He shouldn't have even left the van, although he still hadn't heard any traffic pass by. Still, if anyone did, he'd be out here on this hillside instead of down there by the road. "Thou wilt keep him in perfect peace whose mind is stayed on Thee, for he trusteth in Thee," Jack murmured. That was Isaiah 26:3, and it had been his father's favorite Scripture. "Lord," he mumbled breathlessly, "I'm really trying to keep my mind stayed on You. . . ." He glanced back toward the road again, then plunged on toward the farmhouse.

He was almost hoping no traffic *would* pass by—at least that would justify his decision to cut across this field. As he labored to the top of the hill, he paused again and allowed himself the luxury of another look back at the road to measure his progress.

"Where *is* the road?" he muttered. Despite the whiteness falling around him, Jack found himself suddenly in a very black hole. Or rather, a very white hole. He couldn't see the van. He couldn't see the fence he'd just climbed over. And now he was afraid to go on over the hill for fear that he wouldn't be able to see the farmhouse he was certain was somewhere behind him. *God?* he thought, *are You going to get me out of this?* So far he'd managed to keep from whining, but he knew himself pretty well, and figured the "Why me, Lord?"s would come soon if he didn't remain engaged in purposeful action. So Jack once again turned his back on where he *thought* the van was, and plunged onward over the crest of the hill, not allowing himself to expect to see the farmhouse, but hoping he would.

He didn't.

Now he plunged downward, both on foot and in his soul. The going was easier, slightly. It never took as much effort to descend as it did to climb, but it never felt as good either. *There I go,* he thought, *preaching to myself again.* Try as he might, he could never prevent himself from drawing spiritual analogies from practical situations. It was something he'd learned from Jesus. As the incline got a little sharper, his boots threatened to slip out from under him, and he had to splay his feet apart and ski. He guessed this could be fun if it weren't so dangerous—and if he didn't feel so ridiculous. But it was, and he did, and he couldn't see where he was going other than to put one foot in front of another. Jack realized he had entered that mental state he reserved for enduring unpleasant situations: Keep slogging on because this *will* pass. He reached the bottom of this incline and started up another rise.

Though he couldn't see six feet ahead in any case, he *could* at least see his feet. The object, therefore, seemed to leap up in front of him. He slid to a stop and stared up at it, feeling on the one hand incredulous and on the other somehow justified. For Jack knew immediately what it was, even though he'd never seen this particular design. He knew it didn't belong in this pasture. And it caused him, with a shock of recognition, to look down at his tie.

He'd stopped worrying about wearing the elephant tie months before. After all, he'd worn it many times since that summer's day, and nothing had happened. He'd worn it to school when the new semester started, and still nothing had happened. He'd seen Ben several times while wearing it and his young friend had never said anything more about it. It simply stopped being an issue. He'd put it on this morning because it matched his wool suit, which he'd chosen to wear because it was going to be cold. Thus, when the alien ship suddenly appeared out of the snow and loomed up over him, he was dressed and ready to go.

He stood his ground before it, waiting for a hatch or door to open and suck him inside. He'd been through all this before, after all, and figured he knew the drill. He felt very mixed emotions. On the one hand he felt *enormous* sorrow for Gloria and Gabrielle. He loved them so much and would miss them greatly, and he knew they would miss him terribly. This was how people often felt upon realizing they were about to die. On the other hand, what a relief! Here, in a single instant, both the "When will I again be abducted?" and the "How am I going to get out of this blizzard?" questions had been answered! And really, at this moment, he was willing to beg a lift from *anybody*.

He guessed they were going to take him. Weren't they? Wasn't that why the ship was here . . . to pick him up? After a moment of waiting, he stepped back a few feet to try to get a better look at it. This was what he and Ben had come to call a "Fallen flying time craft," wasn't it? It surely wasn't some new type of barn . . . was it? Jack couldn't remember seeing anything resembling this in this field on his way to church. The hull of the vessel bowed out and up over him— he guessed it was twenty feet from where its base sat in a snowdrift up to its outer rim. He took off one glove and touched the nonreflective black surface. Cold metal. He put his glove back on and began to make a circuit of the oddly shaped vehicle, his eyes on that rim. It appeared to be featureless, no seams, no doors, no projections of any kind, a flying saucer of the classical design, the kind he'd seen pictured in comic books and B-movies since he was a child. No, this was definitely not some new type of hay silo. But where was the entrance?

Halfway around the saucer, he stopped and turned around to look behind him, certain that by this time the farmhouse would be in sight. It wasn't. He saw nothing but falling snow and realized that he was freezing. Now this was frustrating: Broken down, cold, sick, out of breath, out of sight of any help, standing next to a flying saucer, and he couldn't even get himself abducted. He wondered if he should try knocking on the thing?

Jack turned back around to the black object and gasped. There was a door after all. It had opened, soundlessly, while his back was turned. A gangway had been helpfully provided. Yet Jack saw no motion within its pitch-black interior. There was no welcoming figure at the top of the ramp. The hatch simply yawned wide, like the mouth of Jonah's whale. A chill shook his shoulders—a chill of fear. Jack was remembering those old nature films about the Venus flytrap. "Come in," the alien-looking vessel seemed to be saying to him. "Come in and be swallowed. . . ."

"Lord . . ." Jack mumbled under his breath, and he pulled his overcoat tight across his chest. He stood trembling—waiting—praying—but there was no coherence to his prayers. They were the prayers of indecisive panic. Jack struggled to focus them—to *think*. In a moment the panic passed. No tentacles reached out and grabbed him. He was not sucked inside the vessel by some giant vacuum cleaner. He was not lifted bodily off the snow by Sherry Lynn Ward's tractor beam. He was just—invited inside. He quickly reviewed his options. Apart from accepting this silent invitation, what choice did he really have? "I'm freezing," he muttered to himself, realizing as he did so that his teeth were chattering. Still clenching his coat tightly around him, he walked up the ramp.

An odd abduction, he thought to himself as he reached the top and stepped into the darkness. He felt very much the fly walking into the spider's web. But by this time he'd convinced himself he had no other choices. Besides, he was curious about this vehicle. It didn't look the same as the one that had abducted him from that small forest near his home on a summer's day years before. It was darker, far darker. While glowing pink signs lettered in strange hieroglyphics had marked the walls in that craft, there were no signs on these bulkheads. There was in fact no light save that streaming in behind him through the entry port, reflected off the white snow. The passageways seemed larger than those in the other craft, as if built for the comfort of much larger creatures. The place smelled differently from that saucer of his memory as well—although now that he thought about it, he couldn't really remember what that space/time craft had smelled like. This walkway had an acrid, caustic smell, like bleach or exploded gunpowder. It was most unpleasant, and he almost turned around to rush back outside to grab a few lungfuls of fresh, snow-crisped air, but he didn't. For it was warm inside this vessel, wonderfully warm. And the further he got from that open hatch the warmer he became. Besides, his eyes were adjusting to the dimness, and he realized that there was indeed some internal illumination coming from somewhere. He'd just been out in the blinding white snow too long to see it immediately. Turning his back to the door he walked further down the passageway. Then he stopped, and pondered.

"I'm choosing this." He said the words aloud, albeit to himself, for they were significant, and he needed to hear them as well as think them. The first time he'd been taken by the demons posing as aliens, he had been kidnapped. He'd been given no choice in the matter, it had happened *to* him, and he'd reacted to it. Now he willingly walked deeper into what was clearly a nonhuman artifact. He didn't have to. And while he could certainly make a case to himself that he had no other choice due to the engine blowout, snowstorm and such, at this present moment Jack knew in his heart that simply wasn't so. In the days ahead when he suffered—and he knew he *would* suffer consequences from this decision—it would be because he had chosen this path, and not because it had been chosen for him.

Then again, does one choose a dream? This all felt so dreamlike, like all those dreams that had plagued him through the summer! He knew it wasn't, of course—the walls of this dim corridor were solid, the engines of this vessel were powerful, the creatures who occupied it could take him places far from home where he did not want to go— but it was all so out of the ordinary! He remembered clearly his first experience with the Fallen, and what it had cost him. Yet long ago those memories, too, had taken on the character of a dream, being filed away in his mind alongside snippets of other experiences, scenes from films, pages from books, and—*real* dreams. From this mental hash of the actual and the imagined, Jack struggled to put together a plan of action, as if—as if he somehow had *control* of this situation. He knew he didn't. Still, to find the courage to go on people often must pretend that they do. . . .

As he crept forward, one gloved hand sliding along the curved surface of the saucer's inner wall, he struggled to clear his mind of these thoughts so that he could listen. He heard nothing—no engine hum, no muffled conversation, nothing. Nor did he see anything save the uniform dimness of this corridor. A chill of fear shook him: This vessel wasn't that big. Had he made a complete circuit of it? If so, the outer door had closed behind him just as soundlessly as it had opened, and he was trapped inside! He had not passed any interior door that he noticed, no portal to take him deeper within the craft. Terrifying thoughts now tumbled through his brain as he suddenly realized how similar was the shape of this object to the ant "motels" he'd put around the house last summer. Panic seized him, and he quickly retraced his steps back toward the door. It wasn't here . . . nor here . . . nor here! Jack began to run, while in his mind two things were happening: He was praying, and he was also shrieking mental imprecations at himself for having been so stupid as to have gotten himself into this mess! There was another layer of thought as well, something he was ashamed to be feeling but nevertheless was. Jack felt anger at God for allowing him to be in this situation, when all he had been trying to do all morning was what he thought was God's will!

So what *was* God's will? Jack stopped running, and as the empty echoes of his footsteps died away he again strained to hear any other sounds within this craft save his own heavy breathing. Nothing. Jack sat down on the floor, his back against the outer bulkhead. Was *this* God's will? Was it in the purpose of the sovereign Lord that he be abducted again? Didn't he believe that all things worked together for good? "All right," he mumbled. "What next?"

A door slipped open in the interior wall right in front of him. Jack eyed it suspiciously. He was not in a hurry to get himself mired any deeper into this situation. "Now," he said to himself—or to whomever else might be listening—"did that open because I spoke?" He watched the opening for another minute, half expecting it to close back up and not wanting it to close on *him*. It didn't seem to be a door, actually—more a section of the wall that had been temporarily removed. *What a maze this place could make,* he was thinking as he got back to his feet. He walked purposefully through the gap and looked back to see what happened. Sure enough, the wall closed. "OK," he sighed hopelessly. "So I'm being herded. Where next?"

This room was as dimly lit as the corridor and was completely devoid of furniture, like a new apartment on moving day. "Somebody new moving in?" Jack mumbled. "Me, perhaps?" The wall on the far side of the empty room now opened, and Jack ambled through it without hesitation. Why should he hesitate? His course was fixed. He had donned his "I can handle anything if I take it moment by moment" expression, and the attitude that went along with it. Jack was prepared.

Then he staggered backward. And turned around to run. And slammed face-first into one of these maze walls that seemed to be gone one minute and here the next. It absorbed the blow for his forehead like foam rubber, something Jack would have felt thankful for had he not been so terrified. His passage blocked, he whirled around again to face the center of this circular chamber, which was obviously the control room of the craft. And there they were, still, looking back at him. Bugs. The creatures of his nightmares.

He had once done battle with carpenter ants—huge black ants almost an inch long that had begun to appear singly here and there around his house. He'd pursued them to an attic crawl space. Flashlight in hand on a hot, hot day he'd wormed his way on his belly across the beams and pink insulation to the tiny wedge of space where the rafters joined the roof. Pushing himself along he'd finally pulled his flashlight up under his chin to see . . . the nest. A foot from his face, they stood at attention, silent sentinels in shining black armor, watching him. And he'd crabbed backward in such a hurry that he'd nearly stuck his elbow down through the ceiling of the kitchen.

Jack had seen all of the *Alien* movies. He'd felt with Sigourney Weaver's character the terror and revulsion of those glistening black exoskeletons and the utterly inhuman minds that occupied them. Now Jack trembled in horror as he beheld something very like those special effects creations—and realized that they had trapped him. He knew then: This craft was an ant motel for *humans*.

All people battle bugs. It's an ingrained reaction, a human survival skill in the face of inhuman competition for space and safety. He'd taught his world religion students of the Hindu—Jain, really—practice of *ahimsa*, of those monks who swept the pathway before them with a whisk broom to

33

keep from stepping on any little creatures. Jack didn't buy it himself. When he saw a spider, he squashed it.

Now he was squashing himself against the wall. And though the strange material yielded, it did not open again to let him flee. Soundlessly one of the horrible beings rose from the oddly shaped furnishing upon which it had been resting and moved toward him. Jack screamed, but the walls drank the noise away, leaving him feeling even voiceless in his helplessness. The thing rose up on its hind legs and extended its huge abdomen toward him, wasplike. In the instant before it plunged its huge stinger into Jack's belly, he looked down . . . and saw his tie.

# Chapter Three

*Blackness*

When Jack came to consciousness and realized where he was, he immediately passed out again.

Then he dreamed. When he was a boy he'd had an operation. Coming out of the anesthetic in the recovery room had been traumatic. He had been bound to the table, evidently because in his sleep he'd been struggling to pull out the tubes and IVs. He remembered it only dimly, but it had been horrible. He'd been crying and fighting his bonds, and someone—a nurse, someone—had been scolding him. "Johnny," the voice had been saying sternly, "Quit!" A scolding voice—an angry voice—a voice that in that drugged state had seemed to him devoid of love, a terrifying voice. "Johnny! Quit!" the voice had commanded, and in fear and shame he had stopped struggling and gone back to sleep. When he had awakened again in his hospital bed, he had shivered to remember the cruel coldness of that voice. The memory of it still chilled him.

Jack now relived that terror. He woke to find himself struggling, once again fighting his bonds, and crying. But there was no voice this time. Only a dreadful, loveless silence. And when he saw once again where he was, he wept—loudly, helplessly, hopelessly. In the mercy of God, he once again passed out.

The third time Jack awoke, a verse of Scripture was spinning over and over in his mind. First Thessalonians 5:18: "Give thanks in all circumstances, for this is the will of God in Christ Jesus concerning you." *The will of God!* Jack shouted silently inside his head, scolding himself as that voice had scolded so long ago. *How is this the will of God, when it's all your own fault!* But this time as the shock threatened to engulf him, he beat it back with that same Scripture. "Give thanks in all circumstances," he recited, running the verse through his mind again—and again—and again. And he managed to stay awake. Not that he was actually *giving* thanks, not yet. But he was trying. "Give thanks in all circumstances," he murmured, surprised that he could hear his voice, glad of that bit of comfort. He was fighting now not only the physical bonds that held him captive, but the spiritual noose that had tightened around his heart, the hopelessness, the anguish, the terror that threatened to consume him. "This is not hell," he told himself aloud, once again comforted by the noise. Finding encouragement in his own voice, he spoke his thoughts aloud. "You cannot be in hell, for you have been saved by the grace of God in Christ Jesus. And you are not dead, obviously, since you can feel and see and talk. Although," he added, "this sure does *look* like hell, and I *feel* horrible. . . ."

He began to list in his mind what he saw and felt, looking for distraction in that mental exercise. But the task of overwhelming this dread was enormous, and his view didn't help him at all. What Jack saw was a huge empty space, very dark, yet illuminated enough to be visible. It was a cavernous, regularly shaped cone of empty space that dropped well below the limit of his vision and rose high above him. What he felt was the bondage of a cocoon of webbing that held him helpless, like spider-silk holds a fly. It did not wrap around his face, leaving him free to see and speak, but it did rise behind him above his head. There it attached him—he assumed—to the curving wall. He assumed so for he could see other figures hanging across the well of darkness on the far side of the cone, so-webbed and so-attached. His legs and arms were bound tightly together and had gone to sleep. He wiggled them to awaken them, steeling himself against the fierce prickling of nerve endings coming to life. He couldn't really feel his stomach. "Maybe that's not a bad thing," he mumbled, remembering the way that huge, needle-sharp stinger had plunged into him. Maybe his mind had awakened out of the sting-induced paralysis before his body had, for surely a stinger that enormous would *hurt*—wouldn't it? He couldn't remember anything beyond that point, couldn't recall being wrapped up in this netting, couldn't remember being brought to this place, couldn't remember any other interaction with the insectlike being that had stung him. All Jack knew was that, like an idiot, he'd walked into an alien-looking vessel, discovered it held a wasplike crew, and been stung by one of the things into unconsciousness. "All right," he said "so the bugs have got me. Us," he added, including himself in this helpless group that hung by threads down a cavernous well.

Jack struggled to organize his thoughts. The bugs. Ben had spoken of "the bugs" in that hallway at school so long ago. UMMO he had called them. No doubt these were the creatures Ben had meant. So: What were they? Were they real aliens this time? Or had Jack instead run into a very different set of the Fallen, a group of demons that had chosen to wrap themselves in the terrifying forms of "creeping-things" just as the first group that had abducted him had enfleshed themselves as "Grays"?

Ignoring the burning, tingling discomfort in his awakening limbs, Jack focused his thoughts on his own experience. He had once been abducted by creatures claiming to be aliens. These beings had taken him on a round-trip tour of the moon that had turned out to be no more than a highly effective Disneyland-style illusion. He had every reason to believe that this was more of the same. He was hanging from the wall in an empty cavern. This was obviously intended to make him believe he'd been taken aboard the "mother" ship after having been trapped aboard the flying saucer and—stung. But could this not be the same cavern under the New Mexico desert that the first demon he'd met had tried to convince him was another world? After all, he and all those he could see around him were hanging; that is, he felt the force of gravity, and his own weight clearly was dragging him down deep into this silken bag. If they were on some mother ship, would they not be floating freely away from the wall, even if tethered to it? As for those other captives hanging in the distance—wasn't it just as likely that they weren't people at all, but illusions, dummies, or projections intended to make him *believe* he was aboard an alien vessel? After all, he couldn't exactly go over and check on—

"Hello?"

The voice chilled him, for it wasn't his own. It was male. It quavered with terror. And while it appeared to prove that he wasn't alone, Jack didn't really *want* that proven to him at the moment. It made their predicament more real and made him feel even more helpless. "Hello?" he shouted back, filling his own voice with authority and strength—a habit of long years of pastoring, when people required peace from him when he didn't feel at all peaceful inside.

"You can talk!" the man sang, sounding exultant. "You're alive!"

"Yes, I am," Jack agreed firmly, "and so are you!" He waited for an answer but heard none—none but the sound of the man's weeping. In relief? In despair? He spoke again—stupid words, he realized as he said them, but nevertheless he heard them coming out of his mouth: "Are you all right?"

"What?" the man stopped his weeping to snarl back, "Oh, yes. Sure. I'm *fine.*" Then he subsided back into weeping.

Jack almost said, "Don't cry." *Almost.* He thought through the proper thing to say, and came up pretty empty. What do you say to a fellow captive hanging helplessly in a spider's web? "Do you know anything?"

"What?" the man snarled through his obvious despair.

"Do you know anything?" Jack repeated. "Anything about where we are, why we're here, what's going to happen next? I'm just asking for information." He monitored his own tone of voice as he spoke. It was even, measured—almost normal, as if he was asking directions of a stranger.

"I know as much as you do. Or as little," the man growled.

"Can you remember how you got here? I walked onto a flying saucer in a snowstorm and got stung in the stomach by a huge bug."

The other man laughed—a mirthless, hopeless laugh, but laughter nevertheless.

"Sounds stupid, doesn't it."

"Pretty stupid."

"It's just that . . . I've been abducted before," Jack said, realizing as he said it how much *more* stupid that must have sounded.

"Oh really," the man answered sardonically. "Then I guess you can show this rookie abductee the ropes, hunh?"

"Terrible, isn't it?" Jack said after a moment, with purposeful self-deprecation, "to find out the one person in the world you can talk to is a nutcase?"

"I didn't call you a nutcase," the other voice answered unconvincingly. "But if you've really been through this before then tell me: What happens next? What are these things? Where are they taking us?"

"I don't know what happens next. I've been abducted before, but by the so-called Grays, not by bugs. As to what they are? Well, let's just say I don't yet believe they're aliens—"

"You think they're people in bug suits?"

No, Jack really didn't believe there were people inside these creatures, but neither did he feel ready to talk of demons to this stranger. Not just yet. "You know, it just occurred to me that this is sort of like being trapped in an elevator."

"Trapped in an elevator! Buddy, I have to say this. You really are weird!"

"No, think about it. You're trapped, you're helpless, hanging in space, passing the time talking with strangers, making stupid jokes, trying to be hopeful, wondering— when."

"OK. But here's the problem, my friend. When they get you out of an elevator, you're *out*—free to go, you know? When they get us out of these webs—*if* they get us out of these webs—what then?"

Jack reviewed his brief conversation with Ben about the bugs and remembered no details. "I don't know," he finally confessed. Ben had told him they would meet again—somewhere amongst the bugs—and that meant *he,* at least, would get out of this situation. But what was this situation, exactly? If these were Fallen, what were they after? Those he'd met and battled before had been seeking some means to get off the planet. But if these were of the Fallen, then what was *this* all about? He was suddenly recalling the spectacular sky battles he'd witnessed over the tower of Babel. Who, exactly, had been fighting whom? It seemed like Ben had said something about a war between the bugs and the Grays. He tried to remember, but it was all fuzzy—dream-like.

His conversation with the nearby stranger had paused—like airplane conversations that don't really end but just sort of fade away. Suddenly his new colleague spoke up.

"I've got a question for you. Are you hungry?"

Jack considered that. "Not a bit."

"Me either," the man called. "I'm wondering if that sting they gave us shut down our digestive processes." Jack heard a catch in the man's voice and feared he was about to start crying again. "What if that stinger was planting *eggs* inside? What if we can't feel our stomachs because there's aliens hatching out *inside* us, eating on us, like we're all a lot of cocoons or something?"

Jack couldn't help but be shaken by the thought. Still, he was convinced these things were no more aliens than Gork and Astra and the rest of the so-called Grays that he'd learned were demons. "Hang on there, friend. I don't know, but I don't think so."

"So what are they then?" the man yelled back at him belligerently. "What do they want of us?"

Jack started to answer, then realized what he was thinking wasn't much more encouraging than the other man's idea. He did know, after all, that the Fallen were deeply interested in genetic experimentation, and had been ever since the beginning of life on Earth. Not that they were creative at it. They were much more practiced at destroying creation—a lot like people in that way.

Instead of answering, Jack prayed for the man. He prayed for himself, too, and for all of those hanging silently around them inside man-sized baggies. He prayed for his family, he prayed for his church, he prayed for forgiveness for being so stupid as to get himself into this mess, then he prayed that God would use him somehow now that he was here. But how could God use him? What did that mean, exactly? Jack had no question that God worked through people; he'd preached that over and over. But exactly what people could do in given situations was a question that required new answers in every new instance. That was hard to teach, of course. His congregation wanted quick, easy, painless prescriptions for living that could be noted in the margins of their Bibles. That wasn't how he viewed the application of Scripture to Christian living. He viewed discipleship as a daily regimen of spiritual exercise, designed to prepare a person for any eventuality. But an eventuality like *this* one? What help did his faith provide in the face of the horror all around him? What could he say that could lend hope and courage to this unseen stranger—or to himself— or to any of the other hundred or so people these creatures had harvested out of their daily routines and warehoused here in this horrible hive? Suddenly Jack was himself teetering again on the edge of despair. All the awful possibilities now nibbled at his own mind. *Could* these be real aliens this time? *Could* they be using his body as a food sack for their young? *Could* it be that this was the vanguard of an invasion force that—

NO. He was doing it! He was letting himself be consumed by his own dread, giving an opening to fear! Exactly what the Fallen would wish. If he gave them opportunity they would flood his mind with fears, drowning his hope in terror and despair. And he recalled another lesson he'd learned long ago, in that previous brush with the demonic powers that manipulate the world, seeking to rule it: the

Fallen feed on fear. That is their food, their drug, the elixir that gives them ecstasy!

Faith. That was it. The faith of David in the face of Goliath, the faith of Daniel among the lions, and the faith of Daniel's three friends at the mouth of the fiery furnace, the faith of Paul awaiting execution in Rome. Faith Jack had. Words of faith he could share—if he would. And words are contagious, whether they be words of faith or words of fear. He was, himself, feeling the contagion of the other man's terror. Maybe he could spread a little infection himself? "Even though I walk through the valley of the shadow of death, I will fear no evil, for you are with me. . . ."

"Bible verses?" the other man snorted contemptuously. "Are you quoting *Bible* verses now? Look, the Bible's not going to get you out of this mess, or me either."

"Can't hurt."

"Can't help either. Look, you said you've been through something like this before. How about giving me something I can *use* against these things?"

A sharp response jumped to Jack's lips, but he caught the words before they were said. He was silent for a moment, then said, "Maybe that's what I'm trying to do, my friend."

"Well, try something else," the man snarled.

The man. Jack had been thinking of him simply as "the other person." He finally decided to ask, "What's your name?"

The other man's immediate reaction was automatic. "I'm Randolph Donaldson." Then he added acidly, "But what difference does it make? I'm not ever going to need it again, am I? You and me are just part of the food chain now, buddy. And we can talk all we want to, as if what we think matters and one day we'll get together for an abductee reunion and laugh about all this. But the fact is, food doesn't need a name. And that's all we are. Just food."

"How do you know?" Jack asked.

"I don't know anything. Food doesn't need to know any-thing."

"Why do you think we're food? Have you been here long enough to see that? Have you seen anything that makes you certain that's all we are to them?"

"You mean have I seen a bug fly in here and chew somebody's head off? No. But I do know this. We shouldn't be talking so much. I *have* seen the bugs react to *that.*"

"What do they do?" Jack asked.

"Fly back in here and sting us again. So if you don't have any real *help* to offer, then if you don't mind, I'd just like to hang here really quietly and try to keep from getting another one of those stingers in my belly."

It wasn't a feeling—Jack could really feel nothing at all in the region of his stomach—yet it seemed to crawl up from inside him. The fear again. The dread. The horror of captiv-ity, the loss of control, the sense of powerlessness—the fear. The power of words, hopeless words, once again revealed. He was overwhelmed. Jack began to ask God to send an angel.

He'd seen angels. He'd been visibly surrounded by them in times past, in moments of utter glory when he'd been cer-tain of the presence of God and His power in the universe. Jack had talked to an angel—one who looked so much like his wife Gloria that he'd called her that. During his previous experience with the Fallen she'd never seemed to be more than a wing-tip away—not that she had wings. The angel Gloria had explained to him the nature of the Fallen. She'd rescued him from drowning in the Flood. He now began to long to see her again, to feel the comfort of her presence.

*Why?* Jack asked himself silently, so as not to bring the wrath of their captors down upon himself and his neigh-bors—why did he need to see an angel? He had himself questioned American culture's recent fascination with angels, feeling that focus somehow drew people's eyes off of God and onto his servants. He'd seen an "I love my guardian angel" bumper sticker one day in traffic that had him wondering if the owner of the car loved the God who *sent* guardian angels as much. Yet here he was wanting to see his again. To be able, Jack guessed, to objectify the power of God. This despite the fact he'd had many life experiences that had made God's power abundantly real to him that had nothing to do with any vision of a heavenly being. Why, then, did he need an angel's visit now? What he *needed,* Jack preached to himself, was to refocus his attention on the God who had revealed Himself in the Scriptures. If angels revealed themselves it would be because God had seen Jack's need and met it, not because Jack had asked for such a revelation. Once again, Jack prayed. He was still praying when the winged demons flew into the cone.

Terror. Randolph screaming. A rush of air stirred by hundreds of powerful wings, as huge creatures with black enameled bodies swooped down from above them, carrying bagged-up humans in their enormous mandibles. Jack watched in abject revulsion as they stuck these new victims to the walls, like a boy pinning butterflies to cork board. A touch of irony there, Jack thought, wanting to be sick. There were other voices screaming around him now—for all he knew, Jack may have been screaming himself—and now the bugs began methodically to plunge their stingers into these, rendering them voiceless again, anesthetizing them once again into nightmare sleep. With a loud whoosh of beating wings a bug flew straight at Randolph Donaldson and extended its pointed abdomen at the place where the screaming man hung. Jack smelled and felt the total evil of the thing, the utter absence in it of any good or gracious quality, and suddenly his fear was gone, replaced by righteous fury. He heard himself utter words totally out of character for the "normal" Jack Brennen, but which seemed absolutely appropriate in this hideous setting: "By the blood of Jesus Christ the crucified and the resurrected, be *gone* from here!"

A very odd moment followed. The bug at whom he'd hurled these words just seemed to freeze in midair. Its wings stopped whirling. Then, like Wile E. Coyote over a canyon, it suddenly plummeted out of sight. Several unseen captives around him gasped at the sight, and Jack felt a momentary thrill of triumph. It was swiftly chased away by a new terror as a half-dozen bugs zeroed in and shot toward him, stingers spiking toward the target of his belly like enormous darts.

Pain. Followed by blackness.

# Chapter Four

*Truly alien*

*There's no way out of this,* Jack thought, and he chose not to open his eyes.

The thought came the instant Jack regained consciousness—perhaps before. Perhaps it was the thought that woke him. It was not a despairing thought, particularly. More a matter-of-fact admission that he was helpless. He was in the grip of the darkest evil he had ever encountered. Yes, he had been abducted before, and those creatures had been both powerful and evil. Yet that encounter had been manageable somehow—perhaps because of the presence of Ben and his gift, perhaps because Jack had not known at the start what he was facing, perhaps because of the visitations of the angel who looked like Gloria. Or perhaps it was because those beings—demonic as they were—at least communicated with him. The demon he'd nicknamed Gork—worshiped as Baal in biblical times and by many other names down through the centuries—had sought to win him. These inhuman creatures had stung him, tacked him to a wall, and kept on stinging him. They seemed to regard him as worthless.

*Then why haven't they killed me?* Jack argued silently, still not opening his eyes. Surely that meant he had some value to them, or why would they bother? He wasn't altogether sure he wanted to know what that value was, but they obviously had to have some purpose in all of this. *What was this place?* Jack thought, and he opened his eyes at last.

*Surprise,* he thought. And quiet elation too. He was no longer hanging on a wall. Instead he was lying in some kind of tube, a hollowed gray cylinder of a material that might have been plastic or might have been something else. He was sealed into it, stretched on his back. There was a dim light within this shell, a phosphorescent greenish aura like that of a glow-in-the-dark toy. Surely he was no better off than he had been when bagged up in the web.

But it felt better. For some reason that he really couldn't explain, lying on his back in a sealed tube appeared hopeful. It felt like—progress. There seemed purpose in this where he'd seen none before. And though his mind easily could have imagined himself entombed, instead he imagined himself in one of those tiny tube hotels in Japan that he'd read about. He felt—private.

That was a big part of his sudden comfort, Jack realized. Instead of being hung in a huge room with other sufferers, here he at least appeared to be by himself. He'd always been a private person, preferring to be alone in his own space. This felt like a cocoon, and he imagined himself as a chrysalis in a state of metamorphosis. "Oops—" he muttered, making the unpleasant connection between cocoons and bugs. He immediately decided he needed to try, at least, to get out of here. He moved his arms and legs, discovering he was still clothed. That was a plus. He wiggled his toes to be certain he still had his boots on, and found he did. They weren't comfortable, but he was still glad. If he had any hopes of escaping from this place, he needed shoes. He struggled to turn over, and with great effort he managed. There was space to do that—barely. Still, he relished this little bit of control over his own circumstance. He felt some freedom, some room to breathe!

What about his stomach? As his hands felt around down there he tried to twist around inside his chrysalis to see—no luck. There wasn't room for that. Nor could his fingers really tell anything about his stomach. It was numb, still. All of his bodily functions seemed frozen. That made sense, he guessed, for if the creatures were taking them someplace it certainly minimized any need for care. He wondered about Randolph and his other fellow captives. They could be within inches of him on either side, squirming within their own private tubes. Was Randolph still terrified? How was the man interpreting this?

Now that he'd opened the floodgates, the questions poured back in. Where was this place? Had they been transported to a "mother ship"? How long had he been in blackness? Had they passed through interstellar space? Was it years, perhaps centuries since he'd last been conscious? Was he even, by chance, on another planet? Who were these hideous captors? Visiting anthropologists? Space invaders? The mutant results of some government experiment?

"No," Jack said aloud. These were the bugs Ben had told him about—and they were demons. Demons in a different form from the Grays, but demons still. He'd smelled the evil on them when they'd stung him. He'd seen their helplessness in the face of the name of Jesus. And if they were demons, then they were fallen angels, creatures doomed to

Earth by their own rebellion, locked upon the planet's surface just as Baal and his consort and all the other Fallen had been. Of this he felt certain. And they were still somewhere on Earth. What time period he didn't know, for he knew this could be almost anytime.

All these questions made Jack anxious. He was really far more interested in answers. He glanced around at his tube again—and wondered. The bugs could have kept him helpless in his bag. This was different. Could it be these UMMO creatures expected them to work their way out of their tubes when they awoke?

Jack wormed his body down in the direction of his feet until they rested upon the flat surface at that end of the cylinder. Then he pulled back his knees as far as the cramped space would allow and kicked. He was not disappointed when that wall didn't immediately fly outward. Nothing in this adventure had been easy for him; why should it begin to be so now? In any case, it felt good to kick, whatever the outcome, so Jack kicked the wall again and again and again.

When his feet began to sting he held off and caught his breath. *So, maybe the door's on the other end.* Once again Jack was squirming, this time the other direction, not yet allowing himself to feel the panic of being trapped. Instead, he imagined himself as a chick in the throes of hatching, or a butterfly looking for a way out. *No wonder those creatures look so exhausted when they finally emerge,* he thought. Without traction or any projection to push against, this was hard work.

At last he managed to press his forehead up against the wall at the "head" end of the cylinder. Wiggling and grunting he finally got his arms above his head, elbows out, his hands under his chin. He'd been a running back in high school, and all through the season had borne a huge black bruise on his forearm from "ripping" would-be tacklers. With that same determination, he aimed his elbows at the circular surface before him and lunged.

The cap popped out like the top of a can of tennis balls. Fresh air filled his tube and his lungs, and he suddenly realized how much his body had needed oxygen. Despite feeling terribly vulnerable, and despite his wish to leap out of this place and sprint to safety, he had no choice but to hang his head out of the opening and gasp for breath. He used the time to glance around, searching out the quickest way of escape. What he saw assured him that he didn't need to rush: There was gravity, at least. Jack was pleased by that. It felt like Earth's gravity, too—not too heavy, not too light. On the other hand, gravity had its downside. It appeared that his tube was at least a hundred feet above a dimly-lit stone walkway.

"I guess I could jump. . . ." he mumbled, but not seriously. Could he climb down? he wondered. Risky. Jack decided just to wait. He was feeling oddly cheerful. True, he was still a captive to demons who had left him trapped in a hollow tube, high up a veritable cliff face. On the other hand, he'd made it out of the tube on his own power. He was alive. They'd left him here for a reason and would doubtless be back for him. And he was a child of God. In a situation like this, that meant everything.

He eased his torso further out and rolled to look to both sides. The rows of tubes extended endlessly in both directions down this corridor. He twisted onto his back to look above him, and saw then that the lid of his tube had flipped upward, held in place by some hidden hinge. Beyond it he could now see that the stack of tubes extended at least another hundred feet upward, and probably further still. He'd not by any means been stuck on the top row. The wall across from him mirrored this one—row upon row of cylindrical tubes stacked upward, downward, and across. *How many people are stored in this place?* he wondered, both amazed and horrified. "And why?" he added to himself, aloud.

Jack watched the darkened corridor far below him for some time, searching up and down this endless hive of stacked tubes for some other sign of hatching life. No one appeared. He thought of shouting, to try to waken those around him and tell them how to break out. It wouldn't be hard now to reach out and knock on the lids of his neighbors. If enough tubes were opened below him, perhaps he could climb down after all. . . .

Finally, however, he decided just to slip back inside his own private bunk bed, pull the lid almost closed, and wait. His mind overflowed with questions that only the bugs could answer. Mysteries without solutions grew tedious after a time, and he had no wish to swap more misinformation with his fellows. He knew that none of the sleeping souls around him had a clue. When the bugs came back, Jack was resolved to start asking *them*.

* * *

It didn't make the evening news—except in Des Moines. There, the anchorwoman recited in suitably somber tones that a plumber had been killed in an automobile accident. She called her viewers' attention to the fact that he had been active in local affairs, having served as a leader in the local trade union. File footage of strike negotiations some years before identified the man and his role in society, and a member at the local union was interviewed on camera. "Fred was a fine man. Really fine. Couldn't do enough for you. Really a shame." But while the event was never reported outside of the state, a chill of uncertainty shivered throughout the Dark Lord's realm. This unassuming labor leader had also been the Ultrarch of the Ultrastructure. His body had been inhabited by the Overlord.

He'd been taken by the Fallen early in his life and had worked hard at pleasing them. He'd played his part patiently and loyally, keeping their secrets, delivering what was required to those who required it. He'd reveled in being on the inside—in the know. He had learned all the secrets, heard all the mysteries, seen all the hidden places under the earth—and he'd enjoyed it. As he'd steadily advanced through that hidden organization that ruled the world, he'd been included in the decision making, allowed to give his opinions at the highest levels. His opinions had mattered. It had been enough for him. He had never had wealth, although he and his wife lived comfortably enough. He had something better: power. He'd always been the one who laughed the loudest at those idiots on the tube who claimed they'd seen flying saucers or been abducted by aliens. This had been a cover but an easy one to maintain—because he'd known the truth: There are no aliens, he had been told at last by those he served. There are only the Dark Powers that rule the world—and he could rule it with them.

Then he'd been chosen.

At a worldwide conclave so clandestine no member of the press had gotten a whiff of it, he had been selected to rule the world. After all, somebody had to. Someone had to be the vehicle, the living shell through which the Overlord moved among humans. Whether this creature was the devil himself or just one of his minions, Fred didn't know. He just knew he had to do his duty, and he accepted it. After that meeting Fred was no longer the same. Everyone noticed it. He'd walked with more confidence, spoken with more authority, dictated what would be done—and it was. Those who knew him best said Fred was a different person. Not that that was bad, they'd quickly added. He no longer practiced his trade—he couldn't, really, for he was gone too much. Nobody ever knew where, not even Fred's wife, but the money started pouring in. Fred had been "doing all right!" his friends had said.

But now he was dead. Now, with Fred gone, it would be somebody else's turn to be the vehicle of the Overlord—some other poor soul.

Throughout the Fallen there was a renewed sense of dismay that they could do no better job of protecting their own. The demons raged amongst themselves. This was happening too often! The unfortunates who had been appointed to protect the Ultrarch swore in fury at those so-called "guardian angels"—who never seemed to guard those humans pledged to their Satanic Lord's cause. Those appointed to punish these for their failure screamed back in accusation, "It was *you* who were to be his guardians!"—and began extracting the terrible penalty. For the moment, the Overlord was missing. He would be back, of course. But in the leaderless chaos the UMMO made their well-planned move against their hated rivals, the Grays. And it was a master stroke, so carefully timed that some among the Grays wondered if it had been UMMO itself that had staged the unfortunate plumber's death. . . .

\* \* \*

When the bugs came back, Jack was dozing. He'd fallen asleep praying—something that often happened when he was thoroughly weary. Early in his ministry he had felt guilty about this, scourging himself with Jesus' words to His disciples when they could not watch and pray with Him in the garden. But Jack no longer felt any censure from the Lord. Times of dozing prayer had frequently been blessed with new insights. So often was this true that he sometimes set his clock to wake him early on Sunday mornings. He would then meditate on his sermon for a while, then lay back down to "sleep on it" for another hour. He would frequently dream that he was preaching, and wake again refreshed and fully prepared to do just that.

This was such a moment. As soon as he heard the sound of their wings, Jack was alert and ready to deal with whatever came, for the Lord was present with him. Having awakened many times like Samson, who "knew not that the Lord had departed from him," Jack was much comforted by this awareness. He certainly knew the difference.

He had many more minutes to contemplate the closeness of God before they finally got to him. He heard the drone of their wings beyond his lid, moving up and down the face of the hive. He assumed they were fetching out the sleepers and carrying them down to the floor, but he really had no way of knowing. He heard no human voices, just the hypnotic buzz of those thousands of beating wings.

Then it was Jack's turn. The lid popped outward, huge mandibles reached in to grab him by the head, and Jack shrank backward in the tube. That was a mistake. Pure pain suddenly radiated outward from his belly, so fierce that had the tube's space permitted it he would have doubled up. Instead he pressed his feet against the back wall and shoved himself forward, allowing those terrifying jaws to close around his head and drag him on out. If this hurt his head at all Jack didn't notice, for his pain receptors were too busy reacting to the horrible stinging in his gut. His abdomen felt like it was about to explode.

Once Jack was halfway out of the tube, the bug changed its grip, and the stomach pain stopped. The thing had caught him now around his waist, and jerked his legs free. Huge filmy wings flapped furiously around his face as they plummeted down the face of the hive, then he was deposited on the stone floor with an abrupt drop. The fall banged his head backward on the hard surface with a sickening CRACK. Jack was very grateful now that he hadn't tried to jump this distance. *That* would have been a mistake. He allowed himself a brief groan, then tried to stagger to his feet.

It wasn't easy. The hours—days? weeks?—of suspension in the webbed bag, coupled with however long he'd been held in the tube, had already caused the muscles of his legs to atrophy. That didn't take long, he knew. He also knew there was no way to get strength back into the muscles without using them. He sagged against one of the walls, catching his breath, and looked around.

Everywhere he looked, the view was the same: people pushing themselves to stand up, some falling, some groaning, many others holding their stomachs and rolling on the stone floor. The whole scene was dimly illuminated by the greenish light emanating from the honeycomb of tubes above them. It was a hellish vision.

*Hellish, yes, but not hell,* Jack thought. They may be in the grip of hell's minions, but they were human, still—and could still help one another, if they chose. He saw a man near him struggling to find his feet and went to lift him. The man at first jerked around to peer up at him in terror, then his eyes softened, and he nodded in mute thanks. Jack helped him lean against one wall and looked for someone else to assist. Then he just stood still for a moment, surveying the crowded corridor in dismay.

They were all clothed but clothed differently. Some of these people appeared to be dressed in costumes from eighteenth-century Europe, while others wore clothing more fitting for a Polynesian island. The variety was astounding—and fearful. New questions bubbled to attention in Jack's mind, questions of time as well as place. He knelt beside the groaning form of a woman wearing a peasant dirndl that was clearly homemade. While it didn't look like anything made in this almost-elapsed century, it also looked relatively new. Had she been plucked from some nineteenth-century Russian steppe just days ago by bugs traveling through time?

Why? He then began to notice the frequent appearance of white lab coats, far too many to be random. Were the UMMO embarking on some gigantic research project, and kidnapping scientists to staff it? He was certainly no scientist. Then again, maybe he'd just been selected to replace a laboratory rat.

As the flying bugs continued to harvest the hive, Jack became aware that the crowd was thinning. He looked down the gallery in the direction from which the bugs had come and saw that those captives who could stand had been formed into a column and were shuffling that way. He quickly saw why. One of the creatures hovered almost motionless in the air above them, its wings a blur, its soulless eyes directed downward. Those in front of him who hadn't caught on to the order apparently got a new jolt of pain in the belly, for they would suddenly double over, then quickly start walking. Jack didn't wait for the cattle-prod. He joined the rear of the column and passed under the sinister warden's watchful gaze, feeling the breeze off the creature's buzzing wings.

The corridor between the two hive walls was about eight feet across, and the group shuffled forward, five or six people abreast. Nobody spoke. Two new images—completely different from each other—popped unbidden into Jack's mind. On the one hand, this felt like waiting in line at Disney World to ride the Pirates of the Caribbean. The other image was far more sinister. He was reminded of films he'd seen of Jews at Auschwitz being "processed" before being gassed. He shivered but kept on walking.

Weary of unanswered questions, Jack's imagination began offering unwanted conclusions. This was a vast group of people—many thousands—and how many saucer-jumps back into time had it taken to assemble such an enormous throng? It was truly a monumental undertaking. How long had it taken for them to—but that was a time question.

Possessed of the technology to render time meaningless, UMMO could have done it all in what appeared to be an instant. Jack's head spun. . . .

Why? The vast crowd had obviously been collected from many different places and times for some purpose. That purpose was not death, surely—why go to all this trouble for that? The demons who had collected them possessed technology for destruction far superior to that of the Holocaust—Jack even had reason to believe some of that Nazi technology had been provided to them *by* the Fallen. Apparently the demons needed them alive, and some kind of genetic experimentation seemed the most likely explanation. Some, perhaps most of them, might well be killed in that process, but that would be a by-product. They'd been kept alive because the bugs somehow *needed* them alive.

The column had bunched up together now—evidently making its way through a bottleneck. Slowed to a stop, Jack did what he often did in traffic—he lost himself in thought. He was remembering that day in ancient Atlantis when the rain began to fall, and the way Astra, consort of Baal, had sought to seduce him by taking on his wife's appearance. Bodies. The Fallen had needed bodies to inhabit. The technology had been there in Atlantis before the flood—and had been drowned. Now, in this period upon the earth, the technology had come again. Because of a Scottish sheep named Dolly, cloning was on the front of every news magazine and a subject on every talk show. *And, of course,* Jack thought, *if they can publicly announce they've cloned a sheep, then somebody, somewhere, is working on cloning people. Perfect people. Which takes a huge genetic sample.* Jack looked around him and muttered aloud, "People like us."

Several heads swiveled to look his way, shocked that he'd actually broken the silence. "You speak English?" a voice behind him whispered, and he looked over his shoulder to see who spoke. An earnest-looking man in fashionable wire-framed glasses peered through them at him.

"I do. And you obviously do. But I'm guessing not everyone around us does."

"Shh!" another voice said, and a woman was looking at them reprovingly and pointing upward toward the bug. She obviously didn't want to be punished for their apparent misbehavior.

Jack frowned. "How do you know they won't allow us to talk?" The moment the words were out of his mouth, Jack knew. As he clutched his stomach and crumpled to his knees, he caught the smug look on the woman's face. *How unkind,* he thought as the pain swelled his stomach. *You'd think people in this common plight would be for one another.* The moment of agony quickly passed, and he got back to his feet. He didn't search out Wire-rim's face again, nor Smug-lady's either. Jack just did as he was supposed to do: faced front, closed his mouth, and waited.

As he waited his turn to go—wherever—Jack thought of the virtue of patience. He considered himself a patient man. He also realized that he rarely thought about patience except when he was impatiently being forced to practice it. He'd lived long enough to recognize that some situations were simply not under his control. That never seemed to stop him, however, from trying to find ways to *exert* some control, to try to steer situations in the direction he thought they should go. So while he waited he watched; studying the bizarre setting, gazing back up over his shoulder at the hovering bug who monitored them, or glancing around at his fellow captives. He was struck by their expressions—or rather, their single expression, for all the faces seemed to wear the same one: terror, masked by bland acceptance. It was the look children wear when they're being scolded and don't know yet how they'll be punished.

He thought of Jesus' words about those He had come to save—like sheep having no shepherd. That made sense in this context, of course. As far as any of them knew, they were being led like lambs to the slaughter. He doubted if any of those around him shared his experience of interaction with the Fallen, apart from their horrifying abduction by these armor-plated creatures. He knew more than they, he realized—or at least, Jack *believed* he knew more. That awareness of the truth, that hope based in experience, became to him an obligation. Jack needed to do what he could to save these people, these lost sheep from many different places and times gathered up by spiritual wolves.

And, he reflected, there was time. The ability of the Fallen to move to and fro throughout various time periods in human history had taught Jack two things: The first was that *if* you can travel through it, the concept of "time" is meaningless. The second was that nothing *in* time could be changed—at least, not without the permission of the sovereign God. The angels defended certain critical events in history by limiting the demon's access to them. It seemed to Jack that all the Fallen ever managed to accomplish in those time periods to which they *were* given access was to further the Plan of the Ages. Not without cost, certainly, to persons: The Age of the Church had always been a time of spiritual warfare, and the reality of humanity's sinfulness gave the Evil One and his cohorts plenty of raw material to pervert and destroy. But the ultimate end of things was fixed forever. The victory was already won. Whatever the demons did for sport they did with the terrible awareness that their own destruction *would* come, and they could do nothing to thwart it. No wonder they played in time, going back again and again into human history. They were like condemned felons filing one groundless appeal after another, struggling constantly to stave off the inevitable. *And this,* Jack thought, *is just one more hopeless attempt. . . .* He turned back to face the head of the column and saw at last what was holding up the line. Each person was being filed in turn through a single door. Above the door was some writing, and Jack strained now to read it. When he finally could, he realized what this was all about—and laughed out loud.

# Chapter Five

*Abandon all hope?*

He couldn't help himself. Despite the shocked looks and warning glares he received from his new comrades, despite the threat of more pain from the stinger in his stomach, Jack couldn't help but cackle at the hokiness of the sign. In English, in German, in French, and in Italian, the ponderous words read the same: "ABANDON HOPE, ALL WHO ENTER HERE." Inscriptions in dozens of other languages he couldn't read appeared around these, but Jack was certain they all read the same. It was the sign over the doorway to Dante's inferno. The demons wanted them all to believe they were on their way into hell.

He managed to choke down his laughter before the buzzing guardian stung him back into obedience, but he didn't try to stifle his scornful smile. Those who looked at him received an "Isn't this ridiculous?" shake of the head—and quickly turned away lest they, too, should be punished. Looking back up at the multicultural greeting, he thought again of Disneyland, and quietly began to whistle "It's a Small World after All" under his breath. This drew more looks—and even a few embarrassed chuckles. People from his own time period, certainly, who would get the joke.

Once again a basketball was being blown up in Jack's stomach, choking off his breath and with it his whistling. But it didn't break his smile. He shut up, but he grinned through the fierce pain at all who looked at him. Of this one thing Jack was certain: He had been saved by the grace of God through Christ Jesus, and he was definitely not going to hell. This appeared to be the only way he could encourage those around him that they weren't either.

By this time Jack and his fellow travelers could see what was taking place beyond the narrow door, and everyone's terrified attention focused in that direction. Groups were being loaded into rooms about twenty at a time. Then the door would close, silent wheels would turn, and a new empty room would open to them. He thought immediately of the Nazi boxcars, but these were well-lighted rooms with formed-plastic seats—more like a monorail cabin without windows. When it was his turn Jack stepped through and took a seat, the muscles of his rubbery legs feeling grateful for the rest. Because he boarded with those who'd been standing nearest to him, all eyes immediately turned to him as others took their seats. Most glared disapprovingly. Jack was obviously a troublemaker, one likely to cause them all pain. He was a marked man.

So when the door slid shut behind them and the cabin began to move, Jack smiled all the way around the circle, meeting every gaze. This was certainly out of character. On planes and subways he always sought to blend in with the background, to be the person-who-wasn't-there. Now, however, he feel keenly that same obligation that had struck him back in the line—the obligation to share the truth. He took a deep breath, and announced, "This is not what you think it is."

"What is it, then?" the man with the wire-rim glasses asked, at last feeling emboldened to speak.

"It's certainly not hell, I can tell you that."

"Then where *is* it?" the man demanded, and Jack recognized the voice.

"Randolph Donaldson?" he asked, and the man frowned behind his wire-rims.

"You know me?"

"We've spoken," Jack replied, smiling. "We were tacked to the wall next to each other."

"Oh," Donaldson grunted, not at all impressed with this news. "You're the loudmouth that got me stung again. Thanks a lot," he caustically added.

"You don't look anything like I pictured you!" Jack offered in a friendly tone.

"And you look exactly like I pictured you," Donaldson snapped. Then he announced to the group, "This guy says he's been abducted a dozen times before. So tell us, from your *vast* experience, how you know that we're not in the grip of all the demons of hell."

"From my *vast* experience," Jack answered softly, throwing the man's mockery back at him, "I can tell you that's *exactly* who we're in the grip of. We're just not in hell, that's all."

"Demons?" Donaldson responded, peering intensely at him. "You really believe they're demons?"

"That's ridiculous!" a new voice put in—with a distinctly British accent. Jack turned to see it was a middle-aged man with brilliant blue eyes and a professorial air. "There are no such things as demons, as the two of you know perfectly

65

well. Now stop making fools of yourselves, the both of you, and quiet down lest you get all of us in trouble."

"Yes! Please!" said a woman seated across the aisle from the man, and Jack recognized her as the smug-faced woman in the line who had seemed to take some satisfaction in his being punished before.

"I'll talk to who I want to, buddy," Donaldson snapped, "and you can keep your long English nose out of it!"

"Oh come on now!" the brittle professor scolded. "You certainly can't believe the notion that this alien species is really a lot of demons in disguise?"

"I don't know that I believe it," said Donaldson. "What I do know is that we're in the grip of something horribly evil, and that these beings certainly want to make us *believe* we're in hell." He looked back at Jack. "If you really believe they're demons, how do you know we're not in hell?"

"Because I'm a Christian, and I'm here with you," Jack answered flatly.

"Oh, please!" the smug woman groaned. Donaldson hooted, then grabbed his nose and chortled into his hand, pushing his wire-rim glasses up over his forehead. Several others in the cabin also laughed or shook their heads. The professor merely rolled his eyes.

Jack wasn't surprised. He'd had a pretty good idea what response his comment would draw before he said it, but he'd said it anyway because it was true. He glanced around the cabin again, still smiling, and noted that at least a dozen faces stared back at him without any comprehension what-ever. Non-English speakers. Several of these were dressed from another century. But there were a couple of faces there that watched his attentively, seemingly with comprehension, who weren't laughing. One was an Asian man whose almond-shaped eyes studied Jack's intently. Another was a rather thin fellow—the only person in this car wearing a white lab coat. Jack certainly had their attention. He leaned back against the bulkhead of this vehicle and spoke to those who could understand him.

"All right, assume if you wish that we are in hell—as they want us to believe. Doesn't this all seem awfully *physical* for that?"

"I don't assume that at all," Donaldson answered evenly, a hint of challenge in his voice. "I agree with you that's what they want us to believe. But I think that the most obvious conclusion is what this Englishman thinks: That we have, indeed, been abducted by some alien race, and that we're being transported somewhere for their purposes. You say you've been abducted before, right? Look, I normally wouldn't give a moment's thought to what a person like you might say, but then again I never believed in UFOs before, either. And you don't seem to be taking any of this too seriously—like you really do know something we don't. Is that because you've been through all of this before?"

"Not exactly," said Jack. "The ones who took me before—aliens, demons, whatever—looked like what the movies call 'Grays.' But one feature *is* very similar between them." He reached back over his shoulder to pat the formed-plastic backrest of the seat he occupied. "They both tend to favor *very* human technology."

"At the moment, perhaps," Donaldson acknowledged. "This does feel a lot like riding Atlanta's MARTA or the Bay area's BART. But there was nothing human about that saucer-craft that picked me up."

"You're sure of that?" Jack asked, raising an eyebrow.

"Ridiculous," the professor snorted quietly, folding his arms and looking away from them.

"I'm sure of *nothing*," Donaldson grunted, his face hard with frustration. Another person accustomed to being in control, Jack thought. A lawyer? he wondered. A business executive? The man peered at him again, his eyes demanding answers: "You think they're working in conspiracy with the government, then?"

"I think they're working with persons whom they've carefully placed in *all* governments," Jack answered. "I don't think they need to deal with governments directly. Conspiracy works best when it's based on persons and not institutions." *Persons like you,* he thought to himself as he looked at Donaldson. The thought chilled him.

"This is *X-Files* stuff," the smug woman chimed in peevishly.

Donaldson whirled on her. "Lady, in case you didn't notice it, we're in a very *weird* situation, well worthy of an *X-Files* episode. So unless you have some answers, why don't you just plug it up?"

Jack winced and held up both of his palms in a plea for peace. "Listen, we've all got a perfect right to be angry, and we can take it out on one another if we choose. Not that it'll do us any *good.* . . ." His tone was pleading, not scolding—an appeal for peace rather than a scornful rebuke. Donaldson looked back at him sullenly, but also seemed to cool down. Jack suddenly felt like a jury foreman and plunged ahead accordingly. He looked around at the other faces who watched. "We've dominated the conversation. Some of you understand English. Has anyone else been through this before?" No one spoke, but several shook their heads in a mute no. Others raised their eyebrows in confusion, not understanding his question. Still others—including the smug lady and the Englishman—avoided his gaze, drawing into themselves as if wishing to be left alone. They didn't want to be identified with these people who kept breaking the rules by talking. *And who could blame them?* Jack thought. Maybe he was getting them all into trouble. . . .

But the majority of those in the car now looked expectantly at him, waiting for his story. "All right, I'll tell you what I know. I was indeed abducted by creatures posing as aliens but who are in fact demonic beings. Now that's not so hard to accept, is it? You've all seen these—bugs. Don't they look like gargoyles from a cathedral, or like Hollywood monsters? They can look like a host of things, for they can inhabit various bodies. Early in our history they posed as gods, and our ancestors worshiped them. But they are not gods. They are in a desperate battle *with* God, and while they constantly scheme against Him they constantly fail."

"Save the theology and tell the story," Donaldson demanded flatly. He was looking at the floor.

Jack addressed himself to the man's shining bald spot. "What I'm trying to say is that these things are not new to our race. They didn't suddenly arrive with the dawn of the space age. They've been with us since the beginning—here—on the earth. Yes, this *is* Earth. We've not been carried aboard some alien space vessel by visiting anthropologists."

"How do you know that?" a new voice interrupted—the young Asian male, who had not until this point shown interest, joined the debate. Jack welcomed this newcomer to the conversation by leaning toward him and smiling grimly:

"The technology of this cabin, for one thing." This really wasn't how he knew, of course. He knew the truth by his own experience, confirmed by the clear witness of the Holy Spirit in his heart. But he also knew he would need to convince these others on the basis of their *own* experience. "Think of the technology of the tubes they placed us inside. Consider the human languages of that melodramatic sign we walked under. Look at this—this amusement park ride they've loaded us onto. All of these were obviously designed for humans, and all are conceivable and thus achievable by state-of-the-art Earth technology."

"Which could just as easily have been transported to another world," the Asian man responded evenly.

Jack nodded and asked, "But why? Why transport these things—and us—elsewhere, when it would be far easier to simply construct them beneath our home planet? If we've been transported to another planet for some purpose known only to the bugs, why does it match so perfectly Earth's gravity? Have you noticed feeling any heavier or lighter than normal? Have you experienced any weightlessness since your abduction began?"

"So tell us, why *are* we here?" Donaldson demanded, his cold blue eyes now looking up to meet Jack's. "Why are these 'bugs' here? What do they want from us?"

"We're probably here for many different reasons," Jack sighed, looking away. He glanced toward the man in the lab coat, still silently watching. "Some among this group may be scientists or researchers—" He stopped and looked back at Donaldson, asking "Is that what *you* do?" When Donaldson didn't answer, Jack glanced over at the Asian. "Or you? Or any of this group?" Jack looked toward the man in the lab coat, as did several others, but he didn't respond. Jack guessed that at the moment that might seem threatening to admit to, since the others might presume some complicity with their abductors.

"Clear up for me why they need *our* technology," Donaldson asked. "I mean, if they're demons they've got magical powers, right?"

"Because they're trapped on this world, and they are without the creativity to invent for themselves a way off of it. For them, the 'ABANDON HOPE' signs are true. For them, this world *is* hell. They want a way to get off of it, and they're hoping our science will ultimately provide a way for them to do that. In the meantime—throughout the whole course of human history—they've tried to make this world hell for all of us too. They have no inventiveness of their own—apart from knowing how to manipulate each of us through our own desires." Jack held up a hand to Donaldson to avert another interruption, adding, "I'm just telling what I know. The ships they abducted us all in were built by human ingenuity. This *is* a human-made cabin, built to the specifications of some engineer somewhere who was well-paid to design it. They have the best of our scientists working for them, for the same reason that we all work for somebody: because it's a living. Ultimately, what their researchers produce is marketed to the rest of society, while the creatures ride the crest of still newer technological breakthroughs. For all we know," Jack added, "this may be their recruitment process."

After a brief pause the smug woman murmured, "That is a ridiculous story."

Jack looked down the aisle at her and nodded his head in dismay. "I agree. But this is a ridiculous situation."

No one else spoke for a minute, then Donaldson took a deep breath, leaned back in his seat, and crossed his legs. "So why are you here? If you know all of this already, why are they taking you?"

Jack had had plenty of time to ponder that question. He just didn't know the answer. "*Because* I know all this, perhaps? I don't know. Because I'm a Christian and have no credibility with anyone who doesn't believe? Because they revel in our confusion and take joy in our faithlessness and our fear? Look, the lady down the aisle there isn't going to believe what I've seen because of what I am. But maybe others of you will, given your own experience." Jack leaned forward and spoke with quiet intensity. "You can believe me if you want. And while I'm telling you all this, let me tell you something even more unbelievable: While our captors cannot travel through space, the flying vehicles that abducted each one of us *can* travel through time. I've been there and done that."

Now Donaldson stroked his jaw with one hand and let a slow smile stretch across his face. "Oh, really."

He was into it now. No turning back. Jack plunged on, ignoring the incredulous stares and muttered mockery that greeted each of his revelations. It was, after all, the truth. "Really. I've seen Atlantis and watched the flood drown it. I've seen other creatures, different in shape, as odd-looking as these bugs or even more so. I've been deceived by their illusions, for they are liars. I've watched these creatures battle in their time ships over the tower of Babel. More important, I've seen angels and seen the power of God visited upon the—"

The rolling cabin suddenly jerked to a stop, and the door slid open.

One of the huge insects stepped aboard, and Jack was forgotten in the corporate terror. The thing turned to Jack and then shuffled toward him—a bit awkwardly, Jack thought. It seemed to have all its eyes focused directly on him.

"You want me?" Jack asked. The creature just looked back at him, expectantly. Now Jack was once more the focus of every person on board. He stood up, gave a tiny smile and a wave at those watching in horror, and walked out the door. He was followed wordlessly by the bug. The door hissed shut behind them, and the train of monorail cars rolled forward again, leaving him behind with his escort.

"So," Jack mumbled aloud to himself. "I guess I said too much." He glanced behind him and was not surprised to see three dark-suited men waiting for him up a lighted corridor. Men in black. He walked toward them confidently, wondering if he was about to meet Ben again. He knew, after all, that eventually he would. Ben had told him as much. But his thoughts quickly returned to the group he'd just left behind. What would become of Donaldson, and the professor, and the smug woman, and the silent lab guy, and all the others who now rolled off down the seemingly endless tunnel? Were any of them feeling as sorry for him as he was for them?

His waiting escort parted to let him pass, then fell in beside him, those on either side gripping his arms. They marched him up this sloping access corridor at an even pace, then abruptly steered him to the left and through a door into a well-lit chamber. This was furnished with a single table and several chairs: an interrogation room.

The bug didn't join them—if it *was* a bug. Something about the way the men in black related to the supposed creature convinced him it was only another man in black in a creature costume, worn to terrorize the others within the cabin and maintain the illusion. Jack was sure it had succeeded. He doubted if there had been much more conversation in the car following his abrupt removal. "Where'd your friend go?" he asked as he took a seat at the interrogation table. "Down the hallway to molt out of his disguise?"

The men in black made no response, verbal or visual, to his question. They just took their places: Two standing behind him, one—the team leader, he guessed—sitting at the table across from him. Jack tried again: "Are you three from Atlantis?"

At this, the team leader did flick his gaze past Jack's head to look at one of the others, but his eyes quickly came back to lock hard into Jack's. He was dark-haired but fair-skinned, and Jack guessed Hollywood would have found him attractive. When he spoke, it was with precise English that bore no trace of any recognizable accent. "You are both talkative and knowledgeable, Dr. Brennen. We found your exposition in the transport vehicle quite entertaining—but ultimately disruptive. Rather than allow you to inflict it any further on your co-riders, we thought you might be willing to share it directly with us."

Jack smiled and looked down to see he was fingering his ring, turning it around and around on his finger. He didn't *feel* nervous, but he guessed he must be. "If you know my name, you certainly know my story."

"We may seem to you to be omnipresent, Dr. Brennen, but we're certainly not omniscient. You appear to have a perspective on our enemies that might prove useful to us. Please. Tell us more."

"Who are your enemies?"

"You spoke of watching a battle in the sky above the tower of Babel. You're aware of the war in the heavens, which has been waged inside and outside of the time-stream. You've obviously been aboard the enemy craft. You might possess information that would be helpful to us in our battle against them. For example, we find your mention of Atlantis most intriguing. Who took you there, and how, and for what purpose?"

Now this was interesting, Jack thought to himself. His interrogators obviously knew about the battle at Babel. But did they not yet know *where* in time Baal and his cohorts had gone to hide after losing that exchange?

His head began to spin as he considered the implications of this conversation. Could it be that he had just revealed to Baal's enemies where in time they might find Baal? When time becomes meaningless, the apparent sequence of events becomes totally relative. Baal had known that his enemies would ultimately find him, for they had all the time in the world to do so. Jack had been in Atlantis *with* Baal at that time. But could he conceivably have been—was about to become—the person who gave away that location to the "enemy"? Could *this* be why he had been taken again?

"Whatever," he sighed to himself. Whatever happens, happens. And Baal's enemies had indeed found them in Atlantis, so Jack would be giving nothing away to tell them his story. Besides, these were wars *between* demons. He leaned back in the straight-backed chair, laced his hands behind his head, and began to tell them all he knew.

\* \* \*

The snow continued to tumble from the sky—great, huge clumps of the stuff. The weather forecasters had missed it again, Gloria thought grimly. This was clearly no six-to-eight inches, but a record-breaking blizzard. And Jack wasn't home yet!

"I don't want to be angry, Lord," she prayed aloud—but she was, and she knew it. *Why* had he gone! Because it was Sunday, of course—and neither snow nor sleet nor fear of death could stay the dogged preacher from going to church! And now he was out there in the snow somewhere, maybe stuck in a snowdrift, maybe flipped over, maybe—

"Lord," she prayed again, "please keep my imagination from thinking the worst. And please, Lord, *please* help him get home!"

She felt her forehead, still hot despite the aspirin, and added, "And if you could take away this fever, it would sure help me to handle this crisis better. . . ."

She glanced at the clock. It was well after two o'clock, and services were over at noon. "Time to start calling," she sighed. She hated to have to roust the church folk out of their warm homes on a day like this, but she needed help. She dialed a number, confident there would be an answer. Who besides her husband would be out in weather like this?

"Hello?"

"George," she said quickly, "this is Gloria." George would have no trouble hearing her concern. Her voice was laden with it.

"What's up? Brother Jack not home yet?" George was a quick thinker. He was immediately worried with her.

"I was hoping maybe he'd gone home with you."

"Ah—he would've called you, wouldn't he?" George answered, trying not to allow too much concern to tell in his own voice.

"Yes," she said flatly. George knew their telephone habits.

"Ah—I'm pretty sure he started toward home just as soon as church let out. Let us out a little early, actually."

"That would have been two hours ago," said Gloria, telling him nothing he didn't already know, but needing to say it in any case.

"Well—it's coming down pretty hard out there. Maybe he just pulled over to the side of the road until it slowed down some?"

"That's not Jack," she sighed. "He would plow right through it. Why wait if it's only going to get deeper?"

George chuckled despite himself. "Yep. I'm that way myself."

"Can you help me, George?"

"I'll try," he said honestly, "but the fact is I may not be able to get out my own road. If he's broken down somewhere, it'd be closer to Brother Henry's house. I'll call him first, and see if he can get over to the new road and check it out. Meanwhile I think you might call the county sheriff and see if they know anything about the van."

"Thank you, George," Gloria murmured, fighting her frustration and her fear.

"Try not to worry. He may walk in any minute. Henry and I'll call you just as soon as we've checked out the road."

"Let's pray before you go," she said, and she heard George smile reassuringly into the phone.

"I think that'd be a good idea," he said, and Gloria led them in a brief prayer. When she'd finished, he said soothingly, "Now don't you go getting any ideas about wrapping up in a robe and trying to come look for him yourself. We'll take care of this."

"Thank you again, George. I can't thank you enough."

"You just stay put. We'll call you." Then he was gone, and Gloria dropped the phone back into its cradle. She stood up and wandered around the room for a minute, not knowing what to do next. Then a thought occurred to her. She sat back down on the bed and called Ben.

* * *

They fed him coffee and croissants. And they asked him questions. Jack answered to the best of his ability, feeling somewhat strange to be doing so. He could almost imagine the large, gray face of Gork bobbing like a balloon in the corner of the room, gazing at him accusingly, looking betrayed. How could he be giving away all their secrets?

He owed no loyalty to those who had first abducted him. They were demons. He resisted the impulse to consider them "good" demons, and these who now held him some-how "badder." Jack's loyalties needed to be to the Lord who had allowed Himself to live among these creatures for an earthly lifetime—and suffered death at the hands of people and institutions they had manipulated. Jack's loyalties needed to be to the world of people whom the Lord had come to save—people like those riding in silence in the sub-way cars down the ramp. He had no idea what impact the information he shared would have on his fellow captives—nor *could* he know, he guessed. So he told the truth as he saw it. Why not? Jesus had said the truth would make peo-ple free.

His granite-faced interrogators listened in rapt attention, coming and going in the room in a round-robin of tag-team questioning, never leaving less than two men with him at all times. When he seemed to tire of his chair, bending and twisting to stretch his stiff muscles, they invited him to take a walk with them, and Jack went willingly. They led him through room after room in this subterranean complex, some spartan like the interrogation chamber, others sump-tuously furnished, apparently for their comfort. He began to ask them questions concerning their recruitment for their task and their lands of origin. These they ignored, almost as if they never even heard Jack voice them, directing the conversation instead back to what he had seen.

How long this went on Jack didn't know—nor did he really care. Time was meaningless, so what difference did it make how long things took? He did grow weary after a while, however, and they recognized it and took him to a room to rest. It was like a thoroughly stocked hotel suite, except that the rooms had no windows. As he laid back on the bed he wondered to himself if this was how a mob informant was treated. Smiling at the thought of being in the "witness protection program," he reviewed his own witness. He had made no secret during the long conversation of what he believed—both about himself and his faith, and the apparent absence of faith in his interrogators. He'd told the truth as he understood it. Jack certainly hadn't abandoned all hope. In fact, he found himself wondering with some excitement just where he might be sharing his witness next, and with whom. As his thoughts trailed off into sleep, he was praying that something he had said or would say might somehow bring glory to God—here in the tastefully-decorated caverns of pseudo-hell.

# Chapter Six

*Prisoner exchange*

Once again they were moving him. Their crisp, determined steps conveyed the concern they each clearly felt, but which they refused to show on their faces. He'd told them things they did not know, which obviously needed to be reported up the chain of command. And who was in this chain of command? Jack wondered as they climbed the wide, concrete ramp. To whom did these men report? How many layers up did the hierarchy climb?

They wouldn't tell him, of course. They'd answered his questions only with more of their own, sticking strictly to the prescribed agenda while revealing nothing to him. They were adept. Well-trained. He was impressed with their professionalism, even as he wondered about their souls.

An old word, *soul,* Jack thought. Not frequently used anymore. Modern language had replaced it with a number of others: psyche, personality, awareness, self-perception, or, simply, self—yet none of those seemed to get at what Jack understood by the old word. Had these men in black "sold their souls to the devil," in that now clichéd term of Bret Harte and Charlie Daniels? Had they *known* that's what they were doing when they did it? Or had they slipped so naturally and gradually into the service of these evil beings that they hadn't taken note of their souls at all? Jack guessed the latter, as he struggled to keep pace with these well-exercised warriors-in-suits. Perhaps they counted themselves patriots. He would never know. They would never tell him.

Now sweating with exertion, Jack was relieved to see an elevator awaiting them at the top of the ramp. He was ushered aboard, buttons were pushed, the door closed, and they ascended to—somewhere. He turned around to face the front, obeying the unspoken rules of elevator behavior. No one spoke. Then again, he was really the only person among them who'd been doing much speaking at all over the last few hours. To what end, he did not know. He had, at least, told the truth.

The elevator opened on a garden—an indoor garden, lit by artificial lamps from high above, but a much more pleasant place than any he'd been in lately. It had the feel of the lobby of an upscale luxury hotel: elegant, attractive, perfectly designed, yet ultimately so tightly controlled as to appear dead. It was to a real garden what a robot would be to a man. It had no . . . soul.

As the quintet of soulless men marched him through a soulless subterranean garden, Jack worried about Gloria. He wished he could call her. The reflex was so natural he actually scanned the walls beside the elevators for banks of glistening chrome phones. There were none, of course.

Marching briskly again, the knot of men burst through a pair of doors, passed under a vaulted ceiling washed with still more artificial light and by an immaculately clean, carefully sequenced fountain, and passed through another set of double doors into an enormous living area filled with couches, chairs, tables, and lamps—all very tasteful and decorative. Jack guessed a few interior designers had been abducted through the years along with the scientists and engineers. But he couldn't get it out of his head that it all appeared to be an elaborate set, the kind that showed up often in James Bond movies. Larger than life. Too much larger than life to be real.

"Welcome, Dr. Brennen," said a voice off to his left. He turned to see a casually attired gentleman with close-cut silver hair and an equally well-trimmed beard approaching him through the maze of couches, a drink in each hand. "You'll be wanting cola, I think," the man said, extending one of the glasses to him. Jack took it gratefully and immediately tipped it back, draining half of it, almost in a single gulp. When he lowered the glass with a thankful smile, the men in black had disappeared and the silver-haired man was settling backward into the nearest couch. "Please, Dr. Brennen, do be seated. These couches are far more comfortable than those hard seats down below."

Jack took the place the man had indicated, at the other end of the blue-dyed leather sofa, and found it was most comfortable. Indeed, it seemed to swallow him whole and to relax him at once. "Nice," he smiled. "Thanks for the drink. That was a hot walk."

"Likely more a trot than a walk, if I know my men," the man responded warmly, his large smile, framed by that beard, revealing perfect white teeth. "But let's cut these opening formalities short and get to the point, shall we? A clever man like yourself will have assumed that I've been listening to everything you've said. A fascinating story too—fascinating. For us, it's like a glimpse into that other—that 'rival' culture, one might say. You can call me Wesley, Dr. Brennen, though of course you'll guess that isn't my real name. And while I know it's forward of me, since you're an American and generally of a casual mind-set, may I call you Jack? It will speed things along."

"What things—Wesley?" Jack asked, determined not to be intimidated by this man's brusque style—and feeling foolish about even worrying over such. After all, what did it matter what this man thought of him? Was there ever any point to all the games of power and dominance that people play against each other?

"It will speed our conversation," Wesley said casually. "My decision about what we do with you next. Whether to kill you or not. Matters like that."

Jack just nodded, woodenly. What else could he be but cooperative? "In that case, by all means, call me Jack. In fact, let's become the best of friends!" he added with an exaggerated smile.

Wesley acknowledged the joking tone with another large smile. Then he added, "Don't worry, Jack. It's not my intent to dispose of you. You have value to us—although I'm sure you can understand why we needed to separate you from the others down in the tram?"

Jack shrugged. "I was probably telling them too much."

"They didn't believe you. Most did not, in any case. That simply wasn't a helpful conversation for them. Too confusing. You teach communication, I believe?"

"Yes . . ." How much did these people know about him? Not that it was difficult for anyone to find out anything they wanted to about anyone else in this day of the almighty Internet. . . .

"I'm certain you teach about the importance of finding the right audience for whatever you have to say. I myself have been an excellent audience for your message. As a matter of fact, I found your story *most* helpful, and we're act-ing already on some of the information you provided. Besides, it was a good tale, and I do love a rousing story."

"I imagine you do get bored down here," Jack said. It was a cocky statement, he guessed—perhaps not a wise one—but then he was feeling rather cocky at the moment. He didn't like being a captive and didn't like the overbear-ing menace of "Wesley's" attitude.

Wesley's smile turned to a sneer. "I do quite well 'down here,' as you put it. But I have no intention of wasting time describing my life to you. You appear to be well aware that presently—whatever *that* word means to those of us with the power to travel through time—we are at war with a competing race of beings, the group you apparently choose to call 'the Fallen.' Your relationship to this rival group appears to us to be so close that we have come to count you as one of their leaders. From this point on, then, you should consider yourself a prisoner of that war."

Jack was laughing. "You perceive me to be a *leader* in that crowd? For a group so obviously skilled in intelligence gathering, that's an amazing misperception!"

"How you view yourself doesn't concern us—Jack. How you are viewed within that group—your influence upon their attitudes and decisions—concerns us very much. We are most of all interested in how much they might want you back. You see, they're holding a few of our own whom we would very much like to have returned to us."

Jack frowned. "You're working on a prisoner exchange?"

"Exactly!" Wesley smiled, reaching out to pat Jack on the shoulder. "A prisoner exchange."

Jack frowned thoughtfully. "I'm afraid that's a waste of your time, Wesley. I really doubt they'd be excited to have me back."

"It's worth a try, right? And it seems we've gotten as much useful information from you as we can gather, so I can't see much use of keeping you here. Your evident willingness to share your experience with anyone, regardless of the appropriateness of the moment, means you would undoubtedly poison the attitudes of those whom we have collected for our service. We obviously can't put you back in among them. So let's both hope that your former colleagues do want to trade for you. Otherwise, you're quite useless to us—apart from perhaps making use of your brain and other body parts in genetic research. Several of our scientists are quite intrigued with the study of 'religious' brains. You are bright enough to get my meaning?"

Jack was indeed. He licked his lips, then took another long swallow of his drink. It didn't taste nearly as good now. "You have no conscience, do you?" he observed.

Wesley laughed. It was a genuine laugh of delighted surprise. "A conscience! What an archaic notion! Tell me, Jack. With all you've seen, do you actually believe there is such a thing? Or a universal system of ethics and morality to which it relates?"

"We both know that I believe in God," Jack answered quietly. "Why else would your scientists want to slice up my brain?"

Wesley smiled reflectively. "Yes, of course. I mean, I'm quite aware of your religious affiliations—it's your job, after all. Right? But I've met plenty of churchmen who recognize organized religion for the scam that it is and have no compunctions about simply acting the part and taking the money. It's rare that I've ever had a conversation with anyone who actually believes the stuff."

"I'm sorry about that, Wesley," Jack said honestly. "I think you've been talking to the wrong people."

"Maybe so," Wesley sighed, a look of contentment on his face. As he settled back into the couch and crossed his legs, Jack felt that the man was enjoying this conversation—that he found it entertaining, somehow. "I just think it remarkable that a person who has seen what we've seen would hold onto such an incredible view."

To hold onto? Had Wesley once believed and found he couldn't hold onto such a faith? "What have we seen, you and I?" Jack asked. "I mean, really *seen?* Things we can verify from our own experience?"

Wesley looked at him sharply, as if to ask, "Are you probing me for information?" Then his face softened, and once again those sparkling teeth revealed themselves in a friendly grin. He loved philosophical speculation. "I have seen the underpinnings of all life on this earth, Jack. And so have you. I know the truth, and the truth has made me free."

"Now you're quoting Jesus."

"And he was right, of course!" Wesley cackled. "He was an alien, Jack. Surely you know that by now? A member of one of the competing races who have sought to colonize this planet, and still wrestle for control of it. You've seen them, Jack! How can you disbelieve?"

"That's interesting," Jack answered quietly. "Now it's you who are talking about beliefs." Wesley laughed derisively— hooted, really—but Jack went on. "Don't you see that what you believe is no more verifiable than what I believe? You see these creatures as aliens, for that's what they've told you they are, and that's what your scientific worldview and your humanistic internal measuring stick have predetermined you *will* believe. But can you prove it, Wesley? Our forefathers recognized these creatures as demonic forces, and I believe they were right. Your scientists may cross-section my brain to find some evidence of a spirit and find nothing. Will that prove I didn't have one? Or merely that science has a limited capacity to see beyond the material?"

"Oh, come on," Wesley snarled. "You hold onto your faith because it's convenient, nothing more. If what we've witnessed in our lifetimes has proved nothing else, surely it's proved there is no loving God watching out for you and me,

nor any invisible guardian angels hovering near us on imma-
terial wings." The man's bitterness showed through. Jack
remembered when his philosophy professor had said,
"Scratch a cynic and you'll find a disillusioned idealist lurk-
ing beneath." Whom he'd been quoting Jack couldn't
remember, but it had proved true over and over in his life.
Even Wesley had been a little boy once—in England, perhaps, or South Africa? Had his grandmother taken him to
church with her and showed him how to pray? What
"churchmen" had he met since then that had taught him the
Church was a con?

"*I've* seen angels," Jack said softly.

Wesley's eyes flew wide. "What?"

"I've seen them. Talked to them. Sorry, Wesley, but I
have. Not often. Not nearly as often as I've wished. I'd love
to see one now, for example, as you talk about severing my
body parts for study or trading me back to creatures I know
with certainty are just as demonic as your bosses. You base
what you believe on what you've seen? So do I. I've just
seen different things. As I said before—maybe you've been
talking to the wrong people."

Wesley stared at him, incredulity freezing his expression.
There was that moment—Jack had seen it many times
before—when a person decides either to ask a deeper question or to close the conversation. Wesley finally snorted and
drew himself backward, and Jack knew: case closed, witness
dismissed, discussion over. Given this, Wesley's next statement was totally predictable: "You're crazy."

Jack shrugged. He was thinking about how Festus had
said the same thing to Paul. "I'm a believer. You nonbelievers have never been able to tell the difference."

Wesley stood up, swirling his drink in his hand. "All of
this is fascinating, my friend, but it's really quite beside the
point, isn't it? From what we both can verify, we're sitting
here waiting to hear from a group of aliens—you can call

them whatever you choose, but that is what they call themselves—to determine if you are worth enough to them to swap you for one of my best crews. Not that it makes any material difference to your future if they do come and get you. Our technology has surpassed theirs, and they're doomed. They've been running from us—hiding in time, as you yourself have said. We've just not been able to locate them. But given what we already knew, and adding to it what you've told us, we shall quickly dispose of this rival race—and you along with it. Sorry about that, Jack." Wesley sneered, and added, "But I guess, from your viewpoint, that just means you'll see Jesus sooner, right?"

"Right," Jack answered, with a conviction in his voice he didn't really feel. He wished he had Paul's attitude of "to live is Christ, to die is gain." The truth was, he wanted to continue living—and to be reunited with his wife and daughter—and to be returned to his primary ministry. He loved to teach. His mind brushed across the courses he was currently teaching. Had they canceled classes due to the blizzard? Unlikely, he thought. Classes had only been canceled three times in the school's history due to weather, and one of those times had been to pick up after a tornado! What day was it? Were they even in the twentieth century still? Jack realized Wesley had been saying something to him he hadn't heard. He tuned back in. . . .

"Has it ever occurred to you, Jack, that your creatures might actually be demons—but mine are not?"

"What?" Jack blinked.

"Ah," Wesley gloated, "so it hasn't! Think of this, then. Suppose your creatures—the ubiquitous 'Grays,' let's call them, since that's what the media prefer—really are indeed the earthbound demons you want to believe them to be. Let's say they are indeed trying to get off this miserable little planet, and riding the back of human technological advance to do so. Leaving aside all of this God-talk, we've been doing—out of sight, out of mind, right?—then what do you suppose they would do if another, equally superhuman race were to arrive in the neighborhood? Fight, perhaps? We've certainly seen evidence of that. Panic? Hide in history? We've both seen evidence of that too. Think of it, Jack! Makes sense, doesn't it? The little gray creatures who've been hiding in the bushes throughout mankind's history, playing at being elves and fairies and whatever else, are now under the terrible pressure of an invasion from outside this solar system! Wouldn't they act exactly as your friends are acting?"

"Interesting," Jack shrugged.

"It's more than interesting, Jack; it's the case. You talk of my 'bosses'? I've been to their world—to UMMO itself! I've seen their ships! And believe me, my friend, if you thought the contrived ending of *Independence Day* was stretching credibility a bit, I can assure you that I *know* it was. My . . . masters—let's call them—do indeed have the technology to destroy this world. But what a waste! So much easier to simply assume control over a world of beings already enslaved to hosts of little gray creatures—these who have styled themselves 'gods' to keep us in check. We're simply tiny cogs in the greatest corporate takeover in history! And I, for one, am glad I'm on the right side of the merger." Wesley finished this speech with a self-satisfied smirk that seemed to Jack rather childish. Then again, he had his own understanding of an attempted corporate takeover in the heavens and had read in Revelation what would be the eventual outcome. He pondered all of this for a moment.

"Silent now?" Wesley asked, flashing his beautiful teeth. "Are you seeing my point at last?"

"Oh, I see your point," Jack shrugged.

"But . . ." Wesley prompted.

"It just seems to me as I hear you explain it that the same wicked spirit is ultimate master over *both* of our supposed sets of aliens."

# Prisoner exchange

Wesley just peered at him a moment, then sighed grandly. "Why bother. Your mind is totally closed, isn't it?"

"We're back full circle, Wesley. I believe in what I believe. You believe in this." Jack gestured around them at this huge hall. He looked up as he did so, thinking that it really was huge. You could clear out the couches and play a basketball game in here, and have seating for at least three thousand—

The thought had barely crossed his mind when a black box materialized at the other end of the hall, hovering two feet over the tops of the furniture—jumping into this time from some other. Both he and Wesley gaped at it a moment, utterly stunned—during which time part of one side dropped open and three men in black leapt out and ran toward them. Wesley scrambled backward, shouting something into a microphone Jack now noticed he was wearing. Jack just sat and watched as the three men hurdled couches as they raced toward him, followed by the flying black box, which was gliding swiftly up behind. As they grabbed Jack bodily—one by the legs and two by the arms—and hurled him through the gaping opening into the box, he heard gunfire from the door. Bullets whizzed about him but he could do nothing to dodge them. He was more worried about landing on the steel grid flooring that rose up to meet his forehead. His reflexes finally worked enough for his hands to shoot up to his face and cushion his fall. At that same moment boots were hitting the floor around him, and the bay of the black box was closing behind his three rescuers. He glanced back over his shoulder to see that Wesley and his own men in black were now rushing toward them, their guns still blazing. Jack took this all in with the open-mouthed curiosity that only shock affords, then the bay door was shut and the box was dropping into the black void of time.

*Ah, this again,* Jack thought, rolling onto his back. *More time travel.* He couldn't help but think to himself, *Been there, done that.* Apparently he was going to do it again.

# Chapter Seven

*Lord of pride*

As these new men in black who had rescued him hoisted Jack to his feet, the lights came back on. During his previous travels with the Fallen, light after blackness had always meant that they were dropping back into the stream of time somewhere—or rather somewhen. He guessed the same would be true of this flying box. He looked at one of his rescuers and asked, "What time are we in now?"

The man just shrugged. "What difference does it make?"

"None, I suppose," Jack acknowledged, and he swiveled his head to survey the squad who surrounded him. They looked no different from the men who had spent the morning—he guessed it had been the morning—grilling him for information. Oh, they each had different features. One was slightly taller than the others, another was bald—but they all had that same veiled expression that he'd come to expect from these human functionaries of the Fallen: expressionless faces, and hawklike eyes that missed nothing, yet nevertheless seemed dead.

Were these Jeffrey's men? The last he remembered, his old college friend had been heading a "security" detail of these inhuman humans in Atlantis, hoping to get out before its inevitable cataclysmic end. This was after a falling-out between Baal—or Gork, or Ruzagnon, or whatever name the demon who'd first abducted him was going by in this century—and a creature Jack had come to know as Kundas. Jeffrey had been working for Kundas by that time. An odd occurrence, Jack remembered, for Kundas hated people. Was it Kundas' party who had snatched him from Wesley's underground hotel? Jack shivered at the thought. That particular demon had suggested more than once that he be executed. After divulging all he knew about the activities of the Fallen in Atlantis, what tortures would Kundas devise for him? If this was—

"Come on," the man he'd spoken to urged him gruffly, and Jack realized they were clustered around in formation to march him someplace. Didn't these people ever tire of marching to and fro? He didn't argue. He just started moving his feet.

A door slid open and they steered him through it into a larger, more finished room at the other end of the box. There a delegation awaited him, in a form to which he'd long ago grown accustomed. They were "Grays," that supposed alien race popularized by the twentieth-century media in *E.T.* and dozens of *X-Files* episodes. Could Kundas be among them? For all of his close encounters, they all still looked the same to him—

"Welcome, Jack!" one of these spoke in his head, and he was immediately—relieved? "We've found you again at last!"

The Grays had no voices, communicating with him by projecting thoughts into his head. They had the power to control human thoughts—or rather to "steer" them—through which, Jack reasoned, they had tempted humankind from the beginning. But they couldn't read his mind, as Ben could. They *did,* apparently, have ears. This made for strange sounding encounters with humans, rather like listening to one side of a telephone conversation. But while they did not voice their thoughts, Jack had nevertheless found it possible to "hear" a difference in inflection from one Gray to another—an accent, almost, that allowed him to recognize them as different entities.

He was therefore—yes, the word was relieved—to hear this particular demon's "voice." This was old Gork—or Baal, as Jack had at last begun to think of him. This creature had boasted of being the Baal of the Old Testament Philistines—along with playing the roles of dozens of other "gods" down through time. Jack had termed him Gork from their first meeting, for the creature had always seemed somewhat foolish to him then, for all his menace and bluster. Gork never seemed quite able to carry it off. Not surprising, perhaps. Jack reminded himself that as a god Baal had always been a lover, not a fighter. Still, he was a formidable adversary. He was no god, of course, but he was certainly what Scripture would call a principality, a *power.* He'd obviously wielded enormous influence among the Fallen for centuries, and he was—despite his occasional charm—utterly evil. Jack determined that he would not again fall into the mental trap of dismissing his adversary through assigning him a ridiculous nickname. He would give the demon his due and call him Baal.

"Were you looking for me, Baal?"

The creature seemed to smile inside Jack's mind, clearly pleased at the title. "You know, I've always liked that name," the creature thought to him. "That was a good period for me—before those desert tribes swooped in, of course."

"Ah, yes," Jack smiled slightly. "Those Jews."

"Difficult people to work with," Baal communicated in a friendly tone of thought. "Hard headed. Difficult to get them to believe *anything*."

"Maybe that's why the Lord chose them," Jack wondered aloud. "If He could get the stubborn Jews to believe and obey, then through them He could reach any tribe on Earth. . . ."

The next thought out of the Gray's head was cold and formal—a clear rebuke, Jack knew, to his mention of the *real* God: "Let's not waste time." He gestured curtly with his spindly arm for Jack to follow him and led him to a tiny elevator in the corner of the room. These boxes, Jack knew, had been designed to fit into the bay of the American space shuttles—although to his knowledge none of them had ever actually made it into space. They looked like one of the modules for the orbiting space station, and like them had been designed to make maximum use of space. Baal squeezed himself into the corner of the triangular lift, evidently expecting Jack to get into it with him. Jack took a deep breath and complied, although the feeling of his own skin pressed up against the false flesh of the demon made his stomach churn. The ride was blessedly brief.

The upper level, while clearly designed for economy of space, nevertheless also had a feeling of luxury. Baal liked to surround himself with the symbols of power, and luxury was certainly one of those symbols. He was curious, however, to see no sign of the controls that guided the craft. He guessed there was yet another room at the other end of the box, over the entry bay where he'd been tossed aboard. Jack guessed that was where the other Grays went, for they did not follow Baal and himself up into this room.

Baal sauntered across the carpeted floor to a large chair, and folded his spindly body into it. He gestured toward another. "Sit down, Jack," Baal said, and his thoughts seemed tinged with weariness. "You've been with my enemies, and I'd like to know what they said."

Or what he had said to them, Jack thought—to himself alone, thank goodness. "I see," he answered. "Is that why you rescued me, to find out what I know?"

"Why else?" Baal asked, his almond-shaped obsidian eyes regarding Jack with apparent indifference. "You know me well, Jack. We've traveled far and wide in this world together, and deep into the well of time. Would I risk my security, my ship, and my crew to do such a thing out of some ridiculous human emotion such as loyalty or love? Meaningless human fictions. I do what I do out of simple self-interest—as *you* do, Jack, whether you admit that to yourself or not. Oh, I realize this love business has a powerful hold upon you." Jack felt Baal's mocking smile inside his brain. "I'm Baal, after all, one of the most successful fertility gods in all your history! I've been selling 'love' to you humans ever since we made you. But it's really all self-interest, Jack, and you needn't be ashamed of looking at it that way. All humans act out of narrow self-interest, nothing more. Now tell me about my enemies."

"And is this in *my* best interest?" Jack asked. He was only half-serious, but it did gall him whenever Baal made such sweeping statements about his motivations. What did demons know of loyalty? Disloyalty had plunged them into these circumstances! And what did they know about love, apart from how to pervert it into lust?

Baal laughed inside his head. "If you have any desire to continue living, Dr. Brennen, you will do exactly as I say. I think that's in your self-interest, don't you?" This was an oily threat, dripping with menace.

Jack simply wasn't buying what Baal was trying so hard to sell. "You know, for all the fact that I know you're a demon, I've never been convinced by any of your threats.

You obviously could have killed me many times over, and yet you haven't. You could have left me with those flying insects and with Wesley, or whatever his name is. They appeared quite ready to sacrifice my brain to their perverse science. And yet, you rescued me. You say yourself that you act only out of self-interest, and I'm fully convinced that's true. So I can't figure why you'd kill me now, after going to all this trouble to get me, since I obviously have something you need or want. And since I have a hard time believing I have any information you couldn't get some other way, I really can't seem to take your threats seriously. Sorry," Jack added, and he folded his hands in his lap.

Baal's shining black eyes looked away then, scanning the rich decor of this tiny room as if seeking some new way to put his thoughts into—thoughts. "You are most disrespectful, Dr. Brennen," Jack heard at last. "You always have been."

"And yet you welcome me back, as if you've been hunting for me. I don't understand that. I've been safely at home with my family for years—and very happy that you've left me alone, by the way. Why this sudden interest now?"

Baal's eyes came back to gaze into Jack's as the demon thought toward him, "What is now, Dr. Brennen? I really don't know what 'now' means to you at all. My comrades and I have been in and out of time so often that I'm afraid I haven't much confidence in the whole concept. And to be totally honest, I've not exactly been looking for you. It was Ben who brought you again to my attention, and—"

Jack suddenly sat up. "Ben? Is he here?"

"—and I suspect that's only because he saw you were in trouble. He has a great fondness for you, Dr. Brennen. Quite inexplicable, from my view."

"Because you know nothing about love," Jack shrugged. "Is he here?" Jack repeated. "Can I see him?"

"Currently young Ben is involved in . . . certain tasks I've set for him. He is quite gifted, as you know, thus I'm obliged to keep him busy. Of course, if you choose to be noncooperative in sharing what you've seen and heard I suppose I'll be forced to call upon Ben to pick what I need out of your mind—"

Jack nodded curtly. "Fine. Why not do that." He needed to see Ben—how old was the boy now? Had he admitted his faith to himself yet? Evidently not, for he still possessed this "gift" that made him so valuable to these creatures. He guessed that their first meeting would be rather awkward. What would Ben think when he plucked his own future from Jack's mind and realized what he was to become? If denying Baal's request could put him in direct contact with Ben, then Baal could expect his full uncooperation.

"Still resistant," Baal grumbled, communicating enough of his frustration to give Jack a slight headache. He could do far worse, Jack remembered. "That's disappointing. I had hoped that we might put the past behind us, Jack—perhaps even build a relationship of mutual self-interest that would be of immediate help to me and provide lasting rewards to you."

This line of thought suddenly seemed so ludicrous that Jack erupted, "Baal, you're a demon! And I'm a servant of Christ!"

"Unnh—!"

Jack heard Baal's mental grunt at his mention of the Lord's name but didn't let the demon's obvious discomfort interrupt him. "Since you *know* this, surely you comprehend something of how I must feel about helping you!"

"Why must you always bring these extraneous concerns into the conversation?" Baal countered fiercely. "I'm not asking you to betray your—that One. I'm at war here with an alien race, and while you persist in using that outdated religious terminology to describe me, I assure you that 'tempting' you to sin is the least of my concerns! I am in grave difficulty, Dr. Brennen, in a desperate struggle. And so are you! For unless I'm badly mistaken, one of my enemies has implanted a device in your belly that can inflict upon you great pain! Indeed, the only reason you're not in utter misery at the moment is because they haven't found you—yet. They will, Jack. And when they finally do, they'll activate such agony in your stomach that you'll think you're going to die. Rather, you'll *wish* that you could die! Now understand, dear Jack, that your suffering will not bother me in the least. In fact, I might regard it as somewhat justified, given your stubbornness. I may even take the time to enjoy watching you writhe. . . ." Baal's tone of thought turned decidedly ugly. Jack had no doubt that Baal would not only enjoy his pain—the demon would relish it.

He could hardly be surprised by this. He'd learned long ago that the Fallen feasted on suffering—that they consumed people's pain, and snacked on their fears. And while Baal was far and away the most charming demon Jack had ever dealt with directly, he was, nevertheless, a demon. "I . . . forget, sometimes, when talking to you, just what it is I'm dealing with."

"You have no *idea* what you're dealing with," Baal told him contemptuously. "You think you know, with all your pompous religious notions that amount to nothing more than childish superstitions! You think you have control over your petty little life, don't you? But you are powerless, Jack. Utterly at my mercy." While his alien body remained totally still, Baal thought a sordid cackle into Jack's brain—an icy snicker of sadistic glee that froze Jack's spirit with humiliation. He swiveled away from Baal and gasped for breath, struggling to clear his mind of the shock of this soul-bruising thought. The only spiritual self-defense that came to him was the thought, *Greater is He that is in you than he that is in the world.*

It was enough. With a refreshing breath of insight—or true inspiration—he suddenly realized the nexus of this particular demon's power and appeal. While Kundas radiated the rage of hatred, and Astra seduced the body with lust, the focus of all of Baal's attentions and concerns was pride. Power, dominance, position, honor, esteem, recognition—and humiliation—these were Baal's favorite toys and tools. No wonder the creature struggled so mightily to be the first among his kind. And, Jack thought ruefully, no wonder he found himself in *this* particular demon's presence, for pride was so often at the center of his own disobedience. Realizing all this, Jack took a deep breath and turned back to face his oppressor. "You really don't have to tell me I'm nothing, Baal. I know that already."

The huge head on the skinny neck regarded him balefully, silently. Then, "Did a little spiritual rain dance in your heart, did you, Jack? Summoned down 'the Great Spirit' to give you a little shower of blessing? That's not going to do your guts any good when the bugs start twisting on them. You can pray all you want to, but I assure you that thing they planted in you *will* hurt just the same."

Jack's fingers found their way to his stomach almost of their own accord. He looked down at them, and began to hunt for some tear in his shirt where that stinger, or needle, or *whatever* they'd stuck him with had gone through. He could find none—but he remembered well enough what it felt like. He needed no further demonstrations.

"No surgeon in this century can successfully remove that stinger, Jack. It's so tiny they wouldn't even be able to find it! But I can, of course. And I *will* remove it, so long as you are willing to give me a simple level of cooperation that will benefit us both! Now have I made my point clearly enough?"

Baal was indeed beginning to get through to him. "How do you know they'll find us?" he asked—then it came to him. "*Through* the stinger? Is it some kind of tracking device as well?"

"They have ways," Baal communicated, endeavoring to sound mystical and mysterious, but mostly seeming smug.

"If so," Jack answered frankly, "then it seems ridding me and this ship of that device should be your first priority." The fear was back, setting Jack's stomach on fire without need of the stinger's assistance.

"It does seem so, yes," Baal responded coolly. "Now. Will you be cooperative? It seems like such a tiny thing to ask, under the circumstances."

"I'll try to be," Jack nodded. "As much as I'm able. If you'll remove it first."

"Ah!" Baal's thoughts smiled. "Now we're bargaining, are we? That's a good sign, Jack. I can appreciate the barter. But I'm going to have some difficulty meeting your request."

"What difficulty?" Jack asked, his mouth feeling dry.

Baal's skinny little arms gestured around them. "This little ship, marvelously constructed as it is, is terribly cramped. My surgery is aboard the old saucer. You do remember my surgery, don't you, Jack?"

"I do." It was in the surgery of the old saucer that this creature had tried to fool him into believing there were multiple races of aliens struggling for control of the planet by donning the body of a so-called "White." At least, he had come to believe he was being misled, and that all reported alien encounters were in fact demons masquerading for a science-bewitched society. That meant the bugs were demonic creatures, too—didn't it? Wasn't that what the angel who looked like Gloria had told him? Was Baal trying again to convince him that there really were aliens competing for this planet?

"Unfortunately for you, Jack, the saucer—and the surgery—is elsewhere at the moment. It's safely tucked away somewhere none of the other factions can find it. At the moment we're fairly well-hidden ourselves, but I'm afraid we'll need to show ourselves to get to where we need to go. And make no mistake: we'll be fired on in the process. I can guarantee that tiny little misery-maker inside you will be activated during the fight. The pain might cause you to do almost anything, maybe even to try to cause me harm. So I think it would be in both our best interests for you to tell me everything you can of your recent experience, so that I can take measures to avoid our flying insect friends as much as possible. Do you understand, Dr. Brennen? Tell me you do. . . ."

"I understand. It's just that . . . I don't know what of my experience might be helpful to you—"

"Start by describing where you were. Ben told me a little as he plucked it from your mind—only enough, really, to allow us to get into that large cavern and out again. I know its location, now—no surprise, really, but still that's helpful. What I *don't* know is what UMMO is doing or why they're doing it."

"UMMO," Jack murmured. The bugs again.

"That's what they call themselves to people, yes. Their real name is utterly unpronounceable by the human tongue. They're a bad lot, Jack. Have been ever since they arrived on this tiny rock."

This sounded like Wesley's story. "Are you trying to convince me they're different from you, that they really are some invading race from another planet?"

"Does that surprise you so much, Jack? Haven't I told you that from the very beginning? You've become so convinced that my colleagues and I are demons that you've quite disregarded any other explanation I've given! Of course they're from another planet, from a whole system of planets in the region of the sky you know as the Southern Cross. And yes, we've been battling them for a long time—forever, as far as you're concerned. We've kept them isolated to South America, mostly, and held them in check easily until that renegade Kundas divided our forces and squandered our weapons on a senseless internal struggle. Seeing our weakness, all the other factions jumped into the fray, and now UMMO appears to be gaining the upper hand."

Jack shook his head in amazement. "You'll pardon my saying this, but what you're describing sounds like the gang war of some immortal, infernal Mafia."

Baal cackled in Jack's brain—long, hideous laugh. "And whom do you suppose really *controls* the Mafia? Whom do you suppose invented the Mob and empowered it? Who exactly do you think set up the structure of the Five Families to manage the ruthless activities of otherwise lawless hoodlums? Why do you think they've been so difficult to root out? Oh, we're letting them fade away now. We have other, more powerful organizations through which to work—richer, less 'civilized' agencies in the hills of Columbia and the streets of Los Angeles, and well-positioned in high places in Moscow. But those have long been UMMO's strongholds, you see, and it's indicative of their emerging strength. The Mafia allowed itself to become too visible, enjoying all the attention from Hollywood. It's more useful now as a diversion. All the old 'godfathers' are gone." Baal snickered inside Jack's mind as he added, "Don't you just love that name? God and father, rolled together into a soulless, hidden authority figure who orders 'hits' on the unsuspecting! A nice touch, don't you think? How very like that supposed Being you waste your time worshiping!"

Jack refused to be baited, saying instead, "And now you work through governments."

"We've always worked through governments. They're the epitome of organized crime. But you know all of this, Jack! Why waste our time going over it again? UMMO could find us any minute, and then where will we be? You'll be in agony, and I'll be scrambling to hide us again with UMMO on our tail! Give me some information. Start with telling me how they picked you up, and why."

"I don't know why," Jack grumbled, as much to himself as to Baal. "I can tell you *how*." Then he proceeded to relate all he'd experienced since the Sunday morning when his engine blew up during a blizzard. Baal listened avidly and actively, mocking Jack's stupidity for walking naively aboard UMMO's craft, probing for details about the interior of the horrible black cone, jerking with shock at the description of the hive of bodies and the huge numbers of abductees being processed. But it was Jack's mention of the numbers of people in lab coats that caused Baal to erupt into fury.

"Our people!" Baal thundered inside Jack's mind. Jack grabbed his head and doubled over in his chair. "They're harvesting *our* workers," the demon raged on, either oblivious to the pain he was causing or unconcerned by it—or both. "That's what they're doing! These are people *we've* developed! Years of careful toil in developing hidden networks laced through the whole of human science, and now these heavy-handed idiots are ruining it! That's how these insects are, Jack! No subtlety! Where we use a scalpel they use a club! How are we going to explain this sudden flood of disappearances? *That's* why they took you, Jack! UMMO smelled us on you! This has to be stopped right now!"

As Baal leapt out of his chair and started toward the far end of the box, he added almost as an aside, "Hurting, are you, Jack? Perhaps that'll be a helpful reminder of just whose presence you stand in!"

Jack was really not standing at all, at the moment. He'd rolled out of his seat onto the floor, and now curled himself into a ball, barely able to think for the migraine-like flashes that ripped at his brain. Once Baal left the room the fiercest agony began to recede, leaving a throbbing ache behind as a residue. Which was worse, he wondered—having his abdomen inflated like a football or his head crushed in a vise? "Lord," he murmured. That was all the prayer he could manage.

The box dropped into the black of timelessness once again, and Jack rolled onto his back and stretched his arms and legs out to brace himself. From what Baal had described to him, this was going to be a terrible trip.

If anything, it proved to be worse than he'd imagined.

# Chapter Eight

*Ben again*

Surfacing somewhere in time, dodging fire from an UMMO craft in pursuit, plummeting back down into the black time void—again and again. Jack felt certain this must be much like being in a submarine diving to escape a destroyer. And as if the vertigo of these time drops weren't enough to cause him to lurch with nausea, it appeared that regardless of when they resurfaced in the time-stream, the enemy immediately locked onto the stinger buried in Jack's stomach, and turned up the volume on the pain. It was like the unbearable agony of a kidney stone, only in the upper stomach instead of the back. It had to be worse than any knife— each time he was certain that his stomach would literally explode and blow out his sternum. It pressed on his lungs, cutting off his breath. It pressed on his heart, making that muscle flounder and flip. Jack did what anyone would do. He screamed. That quickly got him into the control room.

His screaming had attracted Baal's attention. Two Grays he did not recognize flung open the door and dragged him through it, into a room filled with plastic-clad machines, digital readouts, dials, keyboards, and switches. They dropped him again to the floor, for which Jack was grateful when they plunged once again into the time void. At least he had the floor to hold onto. This ungainly craft seemed to waddle more than it flew, and he felt certain he was going to be sick.

Baal sat only a few feet away in a large chair, facing a bank of monitors that gave the control deck the appearance of a video-editing suite. During the firefight with the UMMO ship, Baal's rage was boundless. He shouted inside Jack's mind the filthiest curses imaginable, which produced more vise-like miseries. Once into the sudden blackness, these mental imprecations would drop off to an obscene mutter, which made Baal seem so crass, so—stupid. In these brief, gasping moments between stabs of pain Jack had to wonder: how could this vile creature have contributed so much to the monumental mushrooming of evil in this world? Baal seemed so helpless in his frustration—so human. Or was it that humans, enraged by their own limitations, unconsciously aped the wrath of the demons? He thought no more about this, for once again the craft broke someplace into the time-stream, and within moments UMMO had again jabbed its long tentacle into Jack's stomach.

"That's it, Jack," Baal mocked him. "Scream. That's why I brought you in here. When you quit screaming, I'll know we've lost them."

An explosion nearby—*very* nearby—rocked them. They left time and the explosion behind them, and the pain eased. Jack used this brief respite to roll onto his back and gasp. "Can . . . we . . . not . . . stay here?" he managed to get out.

"Stay where, Jack?" Baal thought into his head. "We're nowhere. Nowhen. Flying blind. What good is that? No, I'm afraid our best chance is to keep looking for a place and time where they're not looking for us. That—or toss you overboard."

Jack had thought of that already. He made no comment, concentrating on simply breathing.

"It may come to that, of course," Baal continued. "Although I hope not. That would feel like losing, and I do hate to lose. Besides, who knows what new information UMMO would wring from you if they managed to take you alive? You're certainly talkative, Jack. So if I do have to jettison you after all of this in order to get away, it'll be your corpse I throw out. You understand, I'm sure."

That wasn't going to happen, Jack knew. Not, at least, until he saw Ben. He heard Baal tap a key. The lights came back on. He steeled himself for what was to come. . . .

"You're not screaming," he heard Baal think to him after a moment.

"I'm not hurting."

Baal swiveled around to look at him—obviously waiting. Jack rolled his head to the side and looked back. They waited together now—expectantly. After a minute Jack shrugged. "Nothing," he said.

Baal turned back to his monitors and examined them thoughtfully. "Just like that? They've got us again and again, and then suddenly nothing? I'm wondering. Suppose they're tracking us now *without* hurting you—undetected. Waiting for us to presume we're safe and return to our base, revealing it to them." He looked back at Jack. "They're shrewd, these UMMO. They've proved that."

Jack took a long, deep breath—a sweet, unhindered breath. "Or maybe the Lord's just taken mercy on me."

He expected a snide response from the demon but was surprised. The demon's attention was focused so intently on his controls that he didn't seem to notice. "Just to be safe I think I'll take us through a few more time zones. You don't mind, do you Jack?" he added sarcastically.

Jack didn't mind—so long as those side trips didn't bring them back into contact with the bugs. He had never liked bugs. Now he loathed them. He laid on his back looking at the plastic ceiling above him, grateful for the momentary absence of pain—and for the promise of the protection of God, even in the presence of his enemies.

*   *   *

Ben was not at home—not in the dorm, anyway. But Gloria's giftedness with a telephone was a family legend. She could find anyone, anywhere. Through conversations with three of Ben's friends she found out that he was serving some church out in one of the counties as youth minister, which church he was serving, and the name of the family there that had "adopted" him. Jack and Gloria had been so adopted by a family in each church where they had ministered—laypeople who saw it as part of their service to God to take special care of young preachers and their wives. She knew without thinking that was where she would find Ben on a day like this. She was right.

"Hello?" said the tentative, surprised voice.

"Ben?"

"Mrs. Brennen! Hello!" Was there a hint of tension in his words? Perhaps an anticipation of this call, and of its purpose?

"Call me Gloria, please!" she smiled into the mouthpiece.

"Uh—OK, Gloria," Ben responded, although he clearly was not comfortable using it. For all of his intimacy with various world figures in his youth—or perhaps because of it—Ben had become an extremely formal young man.

Gloria struggled to put him at ease. "Trapped by the snow?" she sympathized, still smiling.

"Uh . . . yes, ma'am. I'm staying with some folks in my church."

"I'm glad to hear it. I wish Jack had done that."

"Is . . . something wrong?" Ben asked quietly. He knew the answer already, of course, and without having to read her mind. There was no other reason she would track him down.

"Jack is missing," she said at last—with such worry that it seemed to take all the breath she had just to get it out.

"Dr. Brennen?"

"Yes. He started home from the church before noon but he's not here yet. It's normally a half-hour drive. . . ."

"I'm sorry," Ben murmured, knowing immediately what she feared and fearing it himself, but not wanting to add to her anxiety. "Maybe his car broke down?"

"I'm guessing so. I've got the deacons out hunting him."

"Anything I can do?" he asked sincerely. "I'll come and look with them if you think that might—"

"You just stay put," she interrupted. "They'll find him— if he's there to be found. . . ." She let the end of the sentence dangle.

Ben waited for a moment. "Are you thinking . . . ?"

"I'm thinking everything, Ben," she said quickly and quietly. "I'm thinking anything."

"I see." Ben glanced up at Mary Filkens, who was obviously listening in on his conversation from the living room without really wanting to. She could hear the tone of concern in his voice and was trying to guess the circumstances as Gloria went on.

"And among the things I'm wondering . . . well . . . he's told me a lot about your time together—I mean, when you were a teenager."

"Right," Ben nodded. "Ah . . . could you hang on a minute?" He covered the mouthpiece and called across the room, "Mary, is there another phone somewhere? This is kind of—"

"Personal?" Mary filled in for him, embarrassed that she'd been listening. "There's one in the basement, down by Phil's workbench."

"Right. Mrs. Brennen?"

"Gloria," she reminded him.

"Right. Gloria. I'm going to change phones. Just a minute."

Gloria waited, finding herself relaxing a bit, comforted just to have someone to talk to who would understand her real fears in this situation. She walked once more to the window and looked out—hopelessly, really—and noticed that the flurries had momentarily paused. The neighborhood looked silently beautiful, muffled by the downy comforter of snow the winter had pulled up tightly around it. The sight made her ache with sadness. Strange, she mused, how depressing such beauty can make you feel when the right person isn't there to share it with you.

Ben's voice broke in on the thought. "OK, now I can talk. I didn't want to—well, you understand. That's a time in my life I don't talk about much."

"I understand. But Jack told me you and he had a conversation about it some months back?"

"We did. He wanted to know if—" Ben stopped himself, took a deep breath, and plunged into the heart of the matter. "Gloria, I know Dr. Brennen tells you everything, so I'm really not surprised to hear from you. In fact, I guess I was expecting to, eventually."

"He's gone again, isn't he," she said flatly—not a question but a statement. "They've taken him again."

"Maybe. Or maybe he just ran into a snowbank, or something like that, and will be walking in any minute."

"I don't think so. I have a feeling about this, Ben—a burden. I'm an intercessory pray-er, and I'm usually right about those things."

"I understand," Ben said—and he did. He'd lived too many years of his life knowing things that those around him didn't know to question the spiritual gifts of others. Though he hated the implications and feared the consequences, he felt certain she was right.

"Can you tell me anything?" she asked plaintively. "I mean, I know he told you that you remember things he doesn't—events that you shared in—in time—that he doesn't recall."

"I'm afraid I do. Found that out by accident, really. Although in retrospect I realized that there were periods in our—adventures—together when he appeared older."

"The age he is now . . ."

"Yes."

"So you knew he was going to be taken again?"

"I did. It's just difficult to piece together the timing of these things—impossible, really. It sounds crazy, I know, but we slipped around through time so much that I can't tell you with certainty when any particular event happened. Maybe Dr. Brennen explained that to you?"

"He did. He tried. But it's all really so hard to comprehend or—or to believe—that I've tried not to think about it much. I just accepted what he said and went on, you know?"

"Yeah."

"You need to understand, Ben, that while it seemed months to the two of you, to me he was only gone for one afternoon!"

"Right," Ben answered confidently. "And maybe—*if* he's gone again—he'll be back again before nightfall!"

"Hmm," Gloria smiled. "A comforting thought. You're an encourager, aren't you?"

"I know Dr. Brennen is. I know those are the kinds of things he would say to you if he could."

"You're right." She paused a moment, then asked, "But can you give me any idea of where he might be right now? Just a guess."

Ben grunted and pondered. "Hard to say. Nevada. New Mexico, maybe. Guyana."

"Guyana!" she gasped. "You mean where Jim Jones and his followers committed suicide?"

Ben heard the shock in her voice and realized his words had slipped from being encouraging to being fearful—but he was into it now, and she clearly wanted details. He figured he might as well tell her the facts. "Not far from that exact cite, if he is there—and moving back and forth between the present and that exact date as well. Or he could be in Nigeria."

"Nigeria!"

"You see," he said apologetically, "it really isn't all that helpful to know. That's what I told Jack."

"I—I recognize that," Gloria answered, clearly shaken. "But I'm just not the kind of person who can sit and wait for news without trying to do something about it."

"I know. I understand completely. It's just that I can't think of anything to suggest. If he's in a different time then the question 'Where is he *now*?' is meaningless. He's completely unreachable—at least by us. I can't really think of anything you can do to help him—or *did* do, if you want to think of it in those terms."

"Other than pray."

"Other than that. And I'll certainly be praying along with you, Mrs.—Gloria."

There was a moment of silence between them, and even though Ben no longer read minds, he felt like he knew what was going through hers. She was deciding whether to ask him if—

"Does he come back to me, Ben?"

—to ask him that most important question. The one he'd been expecting since he first heard her voice. The one he couldn't answer. Ben sighed. "I wish I knew, Gloria. I'd tell you if I did. We were kept separated a lot of the time—I was busy doing a lot of things for the Fallen, and he was doing his best to try to prevent their success. Then he was just gone. I assumed he did return to you—or rather that he *will*."

Gloria groaned at the complexity of it all, and Ben went on quickly. "This is all so confusing, I know! That's why I try never to talk about it. I can tell you with certainty that I did see him again at about this stage in his life—after I'd enrolled in seminary—and it scared me out of my wits. I couldn't *believe* the things I read in his mind about myself!"

"Anything that hasn't happened to you yet?"

Again Ben sighed. "Gloria, I'm sorry, but I really can't remember. We were in the midst of a war at the time, and—"

"A war!"

"Yes, and a pretty fierce one. It seems logical to me that the *real* time of that war is the present we're living through *now*—although as I said, the word now is pretty meaningless. But look, *I* survived it, and I have every reason to believe Jack survived it too."

"That's—comforting," said Gloria, trying hard to make it so.

"Not very," Ben admitted. "But I'll remind you of something that should be. . . ."

"I know. God is in control."

"He is. And though Jack argued a lot with himself about it in his head—remember, in those days I could listen in on those conversations—he always ultimately believed that he was only there because that's where God had *put* him."

"I'll try to remember that."

113

"I'm afraid that's the only thing you can do, Mrs. Brennen. Believe that, and pray. By the way, I don't think prayers are anymore bound by time than the angels are."

Gloria nodded into the phone. "I agree. And I will keep remembering what you've said. Can I call again if I need to?"

"Please! I want you to! As soon as you know anything, call me. Just glancing out the window, it looks like I'm going to be at this number for quite a while. And while I certainly can't tell the family I'm staying with the details, I assure you we'll spend the afternoon praying along with you!"

"Thank you, Ben. It's been *good* to talk to you. Really helpful. I'll call you later."

"Good-bye, Mrs. Brennen."

*"Gloria!"* they said together and laughed. It was a brief, ultimately empty laugh, and as soon as the link between them broke Gloria again felt terribly lonely. She put her favorite gospel CD on the stereo, but she couldn't get it out of her mind that she needed to *do* something. God was sovereign, she didn't doubt that for a moment. But she knew, too, that God uses human agency to accomplish His sovereign design. Otherwise what was the purpose of prayer? Why would Jack be needed? She had some other resources she could call on, she realized—and a half a second after that realization the telephone was back in her hand.

\* \* \*

After the second pain-free time jump, Baal swiveled to peer at Jack again. "Still no pain?"

"More an ache," Jack answered, his fingers rubbing his shirt under his tie—the spot where a tie tack would go if he still wore such things. He glanced down at the tie, amazed that it had weathered the trip so well. He was determined to wear it faithfully until he saw Ben. It was his last link with certainty.

"Let's try an experiment, shall we, Jack? Let's assume young Ben is currently reading your mind. Let's tell him that we shall meet at exactly 3:32 P.M. on January 5, 1974, under the jungle."

"Under the jungle?"

"Ben will understand," Baal replied, the words sounding smug in Jack's mind. "You just hold that date clearly in your mind for me, will you?"

"January 5, 1974, 3:32 P.M. Why that date, in particular?"

"No reason. It's just a date. And believe me, we'll not be there long. Ben, if you are listening, we'll need the surgery prepped and a carrier."

"What's a carrier?" Jack asked.

"I'm talking to Ben, Dr. Brennen. Please try not to let your own thoughts interfere with the message. Your life may depend on it."

"Fine," Jack shrugged, and he was silent. Although he did wonder if a message borne by his mind to Ben's might not be garbled if he did not himself understand it.

"Hold on—" They went black again, just for a flicker of an instant. Then suddenly there was a burst of activity around him. The door to the conference room flew open. Two men in black grabbed him up off the floor and into another of those corner elevators. Squeezed together like packed meat they rode down it quickly and exited on the run, Jack scrambling to move his legs under him so that he could help in his own transportation.

The craft was open again—the hatch yawning wide—and beyond it he saw a familiar old sight: the saucer-shaped vehicle that had first abducted him, which had come to stand for "home" for a chunk of his life. There was no time to glance around at this location to determine what "under the jungle" meant. The men in black carried him under the saucer without his feet touching the tarmac—if that was indeed what was beneath them—and he floated upward into it a moment later, pulled by that same power that had first picked him up off the meadow near his house years ago.

Grays guided his body, rather than carried it, around familiar-looking curved hallways, then pushed him into the cabin he had known as the surgery. Baal was already waiting for him, which seemed incredible given the brief amount of time that had elapsed since they'd touched down. He held in his hand a long, pointed instrument which darted and retracted with an almost lifelike agility—a terrifying thing Jack didn't like the look of at all.

"How else are we going to get the stinger out of you?" said a voice behind him.

"Ben!" Jack shouted, trying to twist around and look that direction. It was no use. He was not moving under his own power. They slid him onto the steel-topped table and leaned him backward, standing him at a forty-five-degree angle to the floor. Once strapped aboard it Jack felt the freedom of his limbs again and twisted his head to look for Ben.

"We'll have plenty of time to talk," Ben told him. "We've got to dispose of this device right now. Lie still."

Jack did as he was told. He wanted this thing out of him, and he would do whatever they told him to enable that.

"Good for you, Jack. Good for you," Ben said from somewhere behind him, still out of his line of sight. But there was no question that this was once again the young Ben. The voice was higher-pitched than that of the young man he now knew so well—and the caustic, bitter inflection of the young Ben's words were far different from the calm, measured musings of Ben, the seminary student.

"*Seminary* student!" Ben shouted, and suddenly the boy's head rounded the table and thrust up next to Jack's face. "What are you talking about!"

Jack had to smile. "I didn't say a thing." And of course, he hadn't.

"Out of the way, Ben," Baal ordered sharply, and the boy dodged back behind the slanted table. Jack turned his head to face Baal and that approaching instrument—and saw beyond the gray figure another steel table in a position mirroring his own. Strapped to it was a wild-eyed young African man with duct tape stretched across his mouth. He, too, was strapped down, and was watching these proceedings with terror. Who was this? Jack wondered, and why . . .

Then it struck him. This was the carrier—the one who would bear his pain in his place. Baal was about to remove the stinger from him and plunge it into this poor captive.

Ben laughed—a childishly brutal laugh so out of character with the grown Ben's spirit as to send a shiver down Jack's angled spine. "You didn't think we'd just throw it away, did you?" Ben mocked with all the unconscious sadism of a teenager. "Maybe put it in a specimen bottle and let you keep it in your pocket?" Reacting to Jack's unspoken disapproval of his attitude, Ben's voice turned harsh. "We're in a war here, Jack, or have you forgotten? We're doing this for your own good!"

At that moment Baal plunged the needle-like tip of his instrument right through Jack's shirt and T-shirt—just as the bugs had done. All Jack could think of at the moment was why they'd given him no anesthetic! It was like probing for a splinter, but much deeper, and he would have cried out if the shock of the stick hadn't completely knocked out his breath. This was exactly like it had felt when the first bug had stung him back aboard the dark craft he'd found sitting in the snowstorm—how long ago? And like the second time as well, when he'd hung suspended in a webbed baggie from the side of the cone—

"He's been stung twice!" Ben blurted out suddenly.

"Twice?" Baal thought aloud to everyone present. He appeared incredulous.

"Twice in his memory," Ben answered, and Jack—silent on the table, stiffened against the pain, had to agree.

The instrument retracted, and Baal whirled away from him and—without benefit of either anesthetic or sterilization—slammed the pointer into the bound African's sternum. Through his tape he screamed—and Jack felt such an enormous sense of guilt that he rolled his head back onto the table and wept.

Baal pivoted again to face him, once again waving the instrument over Jack's chest.

"Sterilize it," Ben ordered firmly, and Baal paused and looked at the boy. He apparently said something directly into Ben's mind, for Ben was clearly answering when he said, "I don't care. With that disease you've loosed into this region we can't afford to take the risk!" Baal twisted aside as Ben went on: "Don't worry, Jack." Ben leaned his face around into Jack's field of view. "I'm taking care of you." Once again Ben spoke back to Baal. "I know that. But he clearly remembers being stung twice! What good is all of this if we don't remove them both?"

"No, please," Jack tried to say as he saw Baal coming toward him again with that pseudo-stinger.

"We've got to get it out, Jack. It's the only way." By that time Baal was again probing below Jack's chest cavity in search of an UMMO stinger. Jack's fingernails scrabbled at the surface of the steel table, then his fists clenched—and the instrument retracted. Baal held up the point and peered at it, then turned once more to plunge it into the sobbing African. Jack heard the man's muffled cries and rolled his head helplessly from side to side, grief-stricken at what the suffering he was causing this innocent stranger. *My pain,* he was thinking. *He's got to bear my pain.*

Ben read his thoughts and spat out contemptuously, "It's *his* pain now, Jack, and you ought to be *thanking* me for it!

# Ben again

Instead . . . ? Leave it to you to turn a simple operation into a theological event!"

The men in black were already unstrapping the carrier from the table and floating him out of the room. Where to? Jack wondered, and Ben answered swiftly: "He's going back into the time box in your place. They'll take him where we know UMMO is watching for us and dump him. With any luck the kid'll get an education and a place in the Ultrastructure out of this, so quit feeling so guilty!"

Baal had tossed the instrument aside and moved up to loom over Jack. Now he thrust his thoughts once more into Jack's mind. "I wonder why I do these things for you, Jack Brennen. Maybe it's because I still have hope we can make something useful out of you. In any case—you're welcome." Then he whirled away and darted out of the surgery, his thoughts obviously on more pressing matters.

It was left for Ben to unstrap Jack from the leaning table and to help him to stand up. Jack's knees buckled under him, and Ben crouched to catch his weight and hold him. Jack put his arm around the boy's shoulders and hugged him.

"What are you doing?" Ben snarled, already knowing and embarrassed by it.

"I'm just glad to see you," Jack murmured weakly.

"Shut up," the boy grumbled. "Save your breath. You'll need it to get to your room."

"I still have a room?"

"Of course you have a room! You were only gone for five hours, Jack! You think we changed the sheets for you?"

"Five hours?" Wasn't it closer to five years? It might as well be twenty centuries. "I hope there's something to eat. I feel like I haven't eaten for months." And, Jack reasoned, that could quite literally be true.

# Chapter Nine

*Like old times*

Trisha Paulson sat curled up on the couch, watching the television over the head of her husband. He'd fallen asleep in her lap, a pretty regular occurrence when he was watching football and the game got dull. This game had been exceptionally dull—although a little strange. The Colts were playing the Packers at home in Indianapolis, and it was very hard to see the field through the drifting snow. In the sloppy cold, the teams had traded the ball back and forth a dozen times, and all either offense could do was try to run. Sometime deep in the third quarter Larry had faded out, leaving her in charge of the remote control.

If it was a dull game to him, it was deadly boring to her. But this was, at least, something they did together, an oasis at the end of the weeks they both spent primarily on the road, and apart. He was a salesman—and a good one—marketing products on a loop that took him regularly down to New Orleans, across Mobile and through Dothan, then down into Florida.

Trisha was a federal marshal. She never knew where exactly she would be sent—and that was OK. She was an easy-going person with a good sense of humor and a ready smile. She was also a tall woman and could be deadly calm when tested by those she was called upon to guard. It was her job. She did it without a lot of fanfare—and she did it well.

She flipped the channels, seeking anything that might grab her interest. Nothing did. She came back around to the ballgame—and the snow. Trisha liked snow. She wished it would snow here in Montgomery, but it rarely did.

She'd stopped her channel surfing on the Weather Channel long enough to see that the southern edge of the blizzard had tracked just north of Cullman, all but closing I-65. She was glad she wasn't on the road tonight, that she was sitting here in sweat pants and socks with her snoozing husband. Still, she was bored. She was thinking about turning off the tube and picking up the closest magazine when the phone rang. She leaned down the length of Larry to fish the cordless receiver out of the cushions and pressed the button. "Hello?"

"Trisha?"

She knew the voice immediately—would always know it. Suddenly the late afternoon was no longer boring. "Gloria! How *are* you, Hon!"

"Oh, I'm all right—"

"I haven't heard from you in so long! How's Jack!"

"I'm—not sure." Now she could hear the heaviness in her friend's voice, and she immediately got up, maneuvering a pillow under Larry's head in the process.

"Uh-oh. That doesn't sound good." Maybe it was the investigator in her, she didn't know, but she immediately heard herself probing: "Are the two of you having problems?"

"It's not that," Gloria said quickly, and Trisha was relieved. But it was something bad. That was immediately clear from her tone of voice.

Trisha's own voice dropped an octave into her serious range as she asked, "What is it?"

Gloria pulled in a long, deep sigh and answered, "Trisha, Jack's missing."

"Missing? You mean, like in the snow?"

"Well, yeah—"

"I saw on the Weather Channel that it's been dumping a couple of inches on you per hour—"

"Yes, and he *had* to go to church in it—"

"Well of course," Trisha shrugged, smiling slightly. "He's Jack." Serious again: "And he didn't come home, I guess."

"He hasn't yet."

"Maybe he's broken down—"

"That's what I'm hoping. I mean, I *hope* it's only that."

"What else could it be?" Trisha was on full alert now, standing up in the middle of the living room, weight balanced on both feet, the phone cradled lightly in both hands.

"He may just be stuck out in the snow, and if that's all it is, I've got the deacons out looking for him. But I don't think so, Trish. I think he's been taken."

"Taken?" Trisha winced. "You mean kidnapped?"

"I mean something like that."

"But—why? Who would kidnap a preacher?"

"Trisha, you're a *good* friend, and we've known each other a long, *long* time."

"You know it. And I'm right here with you, Hon."

"But I'm about to tell you a story that you're going to think is crazy, and I just need you to listen and hold judgment until I finish it. OK?"

Trisha took a long breath, then glanced down at Larry sleeping peacefully and moved into the bedroom. "Well, let me get comfortable." She dropped across the bed, rolled onto her back, propped two pillows under her head, and said, "Shoot."

"OK. But it really is going to sound crazy."

"Yeah, well, I've seen some pretty crazy things myself. Go ahead."

Gloria took another long, deep breath, then muttered, "Here goes." And she began telling Trisha all she could remember of the stories Jack had told her of his travels with the Fallen. And for the next hour and half, Trisha said nothing except an occasional, "Wow." Gloria was right. It did sound crazy.

* * *

Jack walked hunched over, clutching the spot where Baal had removed the two stingers. It wasn't that it hurt exactly—in fact he was already feeling far better than he had in . . . what? Days? No, it was rather the gravity of the situation, the shock of these circumstances that had left him drained of energy. He felt such a mixture of relief and guilt that he really didn't want to walk at all. If Ben had let him he would have slumped down against one of the curving walls of the corridor and just stared across at the other one. Ben, however, was determined to get him into his room and out of Baal's sight. So Jack crept along, eyes to the floor, helping all he was able.

Once inside his cabin, Ben walked him to his bed and gave him a push, saying, "Here. Lie down," as Jack toppled over.

"Not much choice," Jack mumbled, curling himself into a fetal ball, protecting his stomach. That was reflex by now. His mind was busy sorting through the shambles of his thoughts. "Five hours?" he said at last, twisting over to look up at Ben.

"From my perspective," the boy responded.

*The boy!* Jack thought. Still only about fifteen years old—the same age he'd been when Jack had first met him in San Francisco more than twenty years before. "Five hours? That's all?"

Ben made a face—something of a cross between disdain and love. "I can tell by the lines on your face and your growing bald spot it's been a *lot* longer for you. You're *old,* Jack!"

"And you're still a boy . . ." he said in wonder. Then he shook his head, as if to clear it. "It's been four or five years, at least, for me. And actually, a lot longer for you." He thought of the mannerly seminary student he'd talked to in the hallway the Friday before—

"What *is* it with this *seminary* student thing?" Ben blurted out. "You were thinking about that on the table!" Ben began pacing around the room. By now he'd read both the image and its significance in Jack's mind, and the whole incredible notion set him reeling.

Jack allowed himself the luxury of a smile—something he couldn't remember doing in a while. "That's right. That's what you become." He tried hard not to sound smug, but he wasn't certain if he was really successful.

"But—" Ben protested, his eyes now wide with evident frustration. "But I don't believe in God! What am I doing taking classes at a seminary?"

Jack shrugged his shoulders. "You do believe, now. Maybe I'd better say, you *will.*"

"But this is incredible!" Ben shouted, frowning fiercely. "How did it happen?"

Jack started to respond—but just couldn't. Instead he grunted and said, "I'm having trouble talking. Weak, I guess. You mind if I just run what I know to be true through my mind and let you read it?" He didn't wait for Ben to answer.

He just closed his eyes and began to recall the experiences the two of them had shared since his explosive encounter with the boyhood Ben in Atlantis.

Ben read his thoughts, the pain and distaste growing more and more apparent on his face. "I find you?" he snarled, wrinkling his nose.

"You did. Do," Jack murmured, then continued on in thought alone: *You were hitchhiking on a road not far from where this saucer first abducted me. You'll remember the place*—and Jack visualized the road, and the sight of Ben waiting for him there on the roadside, knowing he would pass that way. Not that Ben knew that by reading Jack's mind—

"Why not?" Ben pleaded anxiously. "You mean I lose my gift?"

*No,* Jack thought to his young friend, surprised at how easily he was slipping back into this mode of simply thinking his replies. *You choose to sacrifice it for the sake of your own freedom.*

"Whose freedom? Mine?" Ben seemed to ponder this a moment, as if unable to comprehend such a state. "Freedom," he murmured. "Why do they let me go? I didn't think they'd ever let me go. . . ."

*Maybe they don't. Maybe God sets you free. For you shall know the truth, and the truth will make you free. . . . I'm not trying to preach to you, Ben,* Jack thought on. *Scripture just happens to be a part of my thoughts.*

"And I'm happy there?"

*In seminary? Most of the time, I think. You seem happy to me—fulfilled. You seem especially happy when you talk about your youth. . . .* As he thought of this, Jack visualized the church where Ben was serving and the group of teenagers surrounding him who clearly loved him—

*"Me?"* Ben blurted out in disgust. "With a bunch of screaming teenagers?"

"Well," Jack said apologetically, "it seems to me you've spent a long time being one. Maybe it gives you a special insight into how to help them." His thoughts began to move on to the way Ben related to the young people in his charge, but Ben stopped him with a hand to his arm.

"Just . . . just hold up for a minute, Jack. This is my future you're showing me, remember? I'm going to have to have some time to digest all of this. And don't be so smug!" he added, clearly reading that thought Jack never intended to convey. "As far as I'm concerned *none* of this is ever going to happen!"

"It's OK, Ben. I'm not pushing." His eyes still closed, Jack allowed himself a little smile, and voiced what Ben already saw anyway. "It *is* kind of interesting, though, after all these years when you've always had the advantage of knowing exactly what I was thinking, to know something about you that you don't know. . . ."

"I don't like it much. Stop laughing!"

"I'm not laughing at you, Ben. I'm just amused by the situation, that's all. I'm your friend, Ben. I've always been your friend. You know that."

"Then why do you betray me?"

Jack's eyes flew open. "What do you mean?"

"I've read that memory, too, Jack. Somehow you betray me. How? When? Why?"

Jack slowly sat up, this sudden change in the tone of the conversation pumping adrenaline into his system. "You think I betray you?"

"It's there in your mind, Jack. A conversation we had— or will have—in Atlantis."

Jack gazed at Ben steadily. He remembered that day clearly—remembered the anger and hurt in the boy's eyes, remembered the harsh words—and remembered the eyes of the evil one, gazing back at him through Ben's. He felt a chill rake down his shoulders. "That hasn't happened yet?"

He twisted his head around to peer at Ben—and saw those eyes again.

A change had come over the boy—a drastic, disfiguring change. Jack had gotten too close, he guessed—too close to the fears and terrors that Ben kept locked up tight. Too close to the truth. And in his fear, the boy had turned inside to his master.

"Come on, Jack!" Ben cackled. "You think we actually go to *Atlantis?* You've got to be kidding! Or dreaming. You're kidding, aren't you?"

Now Jack was confused. Though the saucer hadn't moved, it seemed like the ground had shifted beneath him. He'd been so relaxed a moment ago, for the first time since being taken. Now the fear flooded back in a rush: "What *has* happened, then? Where *are* we, in time and space? This is . . . so . . . confusing!"

"It is to me too," Ben grumbled, turning his back.

Jack got up off the bed and circled it so that he could watch Ben's eyes. "You have to help me catch up, Ben. I know time is meaningless but surely sequence isn't! Have we escaped and run to California yet?"

"Of course," Ben growled, turning away again.

"Been picked up by Jeffrey in the mountains?"

"Yes." Ben made the word carry incredible boredom.

Jack kept trying: "Experienced the witches' Sabbath?"

"And you spent your time with the angels. Or *thought* you did."

*Oh, I did all right,* Jack thought, still trying to get Ben to look him in the eye. He remembered that night vividly. Standing in the dark watching screaming drunks trying to lose themselves in an empty, self-consumed ritual, he had suddenly been transported—or so it seemed—into heaven itself. He'd seen angels—a glorious ring of shining beings whose glory made the raucous party disappear. He'd spoken with Gloria then—not his Gloria, but the angel who had taken her form to encourage and comfort him. Ben could say it had all been in Jack's mind if he chose. But it had been as real as any experience of Jack's life—perhaps *more* real than any, for in those moments he had seen the world for what it truly is.

"Whatever," Ben shrugged. "I just know that I was there, and *I* didn't see them."

"When did that happen, Ben? To you I mean? Have we already gone deep backward in time together? Seen the tower of Babel?"

Ben nodded. "We just this morning fought a major battle with UMMO over a tower Baal was building in the Middle East. We left you down on the plain, safe. That's where I assumed you still were. Then while I was scanning for UMMO's location I heard your thoughts, told the Boss, and we set up the plan to come and get you. Now that's what *I* remember, Jack. So what's all this about Atlantis?"

Jack scanned his memories. It had been so long ago and seemed more dream than reality. In the intervening years he'd forgotten so much of it. And yet—it seemed—that this was simply untrue. "Ben!" he said at last, rubbing his forehead in concentration. "That's not the way it happened! You were *with* me all the time I was at Babel!"

"Was I?" Ben challenged, arching a mocking eyebrow. "*All* the time? You're absolutely certain?"

"Absolutely! So was Jeffrey—until he left us, and went to work for Kundas. . . ."

"Oh?" Ben said, pretending surprise. "Jeffrey's with Kundas now? The Boss will want to know that."

"But before he left us, you were telling us that you had begun to read the minds of the demons themselves, and that—" Jack stopped himself. Ben had picked up a sandwich off the dining tray and turned to look at him. There they were again. Lucifer's eyes. And Ben could read his horror.

129

The boy took a bite of his sandwich, chewed, and swallowed. Then he looked back at Jack and said, "So?"

*Why continue?* Jack thought. But he did anyway, as if trying to reach through the being controlling Ben to the boy trapped somewhere inside. "You told us that they were all crazy."

"Mmmmm," the boy grunted, chewing another bite. "Could be."

Jack no longer felt the energy to speak. He knew with whom he was dealing now. *You're lying to me,* he thought.

"Why would you think that?" Ben shrugged, playing the cool teenager perfectly. And behind it was that puppet master who was unredeemably evil.

*Because I can see you in there, behind Ben's eyes. You're the father of lies.*

Ben snorted a laugh. "A little melodramatic, don't you think, Jack?"

*It's after Atlantis, isn't it?* Jack asked through his silent thoughts. *You remember all of that, and Ben does too. You held him then. I saw you.*

"Who's crazy now, Jack? You suddenly think I'm the boogie man?"

*Are you planning on trying it all again?* Jack wondered wearily. *Over and over, again and again, infinitely replaying the past until for once you get it right? One of my faculty buddies told me that the mark of insanity is doing the same thing again and again while expecting a different result.*

"Cute," Ben grunted, finishing the sandwich. Then he wiped his hands and reached out toward Jack expansively, saying, "Jack, I'm Ben, remember? Your friend?"

But it wasn't Ben. Once again Jack quoted Scripture in his mind, knowing that it would be read: *Greater is He that is in me than he that is in the world.*

Ben wheeled around and started for the door. "I've had enough of this suspicion. You're just confused, Jack. And who could blame you, with all the pain you've suffered? Get some rest. I'll come back later."

Jack spoke aloud. "Where are we? And what time period are we in?"

Ben stopped and looked back. "Baal told you that. 1974. We're under Nigeria. You've been here, I think. Later in time, of course . . ."

*Nigeria,* Jack thought, marveling at the coincidence. Yes, he'd been to Nigeria—had lived and worked here as a missionary. But that period in his life seemed almost more dreamlike than his first abduction. It was not an altogether pleasant memory, for while he had loved the people, Nigeria had been a hard place to live. It was also, however, a place he knew—or parts of it, anyway. "Where in Nigeria?"

"Can't tell you exactly—wouldn't if I could, since the Boss thinks you already know too much and talk too much about it. I will say it's a complex, constructed somewhere under the jungle, near the border between the old Biafra and the ancient kingdom of Benin."

"Under the bush," Jack corrected.

"The what? Oh," Ben nodded, reading from Jack's mind the information that Nigerian's rarely referred to any place in their nation as "jungle." "Under the bush then." Reading Jack's thoughts, Ben chuckled. "Trying to place it, Jack? I don't think you will. I can read from your mind that there are dozens of such 'enchanted forests' in various parts of the country. The important thing is that people avoid them— and therefore don't bother us."

That was true. All over Africa there were enchanted woods or "sacred groves" that local people avoided. They were believed to have "too much magic," and if people wandered into them without protection, terrible things might happen. They might come upon the enormous web of a gigantic spider, or fall into a meeting place of snakes, or— worst of all—be taken by the peeled-skinned spirits to their home beneath the ground and be tortured for their intrusion. Jack felt another stab of grief at the plight of the poor young man who'd been made a scapegoat to carry away UMMO's stingers. If the man survived at all, it would only be to enlarge upon the reputation of this particular enchanted grove, and to further warn people away.

"You're getting the picture," Ben nodded, avoiding any mention of the African's unwilling sacrifice. "It's a very convenient fiction, Jack. It keeps prying eyes far away. And a close relationship with the army—links formed during the Biafran War and reinforced by frequent 'gifts' to the local commanders—means that we can operate out of here with little government interference."

Jack nodded, understanding only too well. The second mention of the Biafran conflict had deepened his grief. He had talked with combatants from both sides of that nation-rending war, when the Southeastern section of the former British colony had sought to secede. It had been a horrible conflict, leaving thousands dead and thousands more homeless and starving. Many more had simply disappeared—

His eyes suddenly flew wide, and he peered intently at Ben. "The disappearances?" he demanded. "Were they—"

"*All* wars are brutal, Jack. You know that. And wars in nations where official records are haphazardly kept simply do provide opportunity for a wholesale collection of specimens."

"Specimens!" Jack spat, revolted. "You sound like you're collecting insects here, Ben, not human beings!"

Ben—or whomever it was who currently controlled the boy—smiled enigmatically. "Interesting choice of words, Jack, since it's really UMMO that does most of the harvesting of bodies. You see the irony there? Huge bugs collecting *people* for a change?"

Jack frowned fiercely. "They're not insects, anymore than Baal is a Gray. I've been with them, remember? They may be wearing a different disguise but they're still your fallen angels, masquerading in a hideous shape to scare human beings into serving you! Tell me, did they invent the bug form themselves, or did Hollywood invent it for them, and they just adopted the shape when they saw how much it terrified us?"

Ben chuckled—whether as a demon or simply as a cynical teen taking none of this seriously, Jack didn't know. Either way, the inappropriate laugh chilled him as Ben said, "That's really a time question, isn't it Jack? 'When?' As you say, you've been with them. You've seen their harvest— been harvested yourself! What difference does it make 'when' they got the idea to become bugs? Oh, I know," Ben continued, more soberly. "I can read your disgust at me for not 'caring' more about the plight of the human race. But really, when I look at history I have to wonder: Does your *God* care, Jack? Aren't all wars just as horrible as the Biafran War, or Vietnam, or Korea, and what has your God done to stop them?"

It was a terribly old argument, one Jack had heard many times—making God responsible for all evil because He had made creatures *capable* of evil actions. He knew the intellectual dead end it led to and didn't feel like wasting the time on it at the moment. "But what's the *purpose* of the harvest? What are they doing with these 'specimens' they've collected?"

The false Ben gazed back at him, an unfeeling smile still in place. "Guess."

"Genetic experiments?"

Ben snorted. "Well now *that's* obvious. C'mon, Jack. You're surely more creative than that!"

Jack looked back at the boy, hardly recognizing the person the evil one's presence had made him. With distaste he let his mind speculate on the extent of evil's interest in genetic manipulation. He remembered the laboratory in the palace basement in Atlantis—all the disfigured bodies pre-served in huge glass jars—and said, "To make new forms for themselves."

"Obviously," Ben said wearily. "But your bias against them prevents you from seeing any *positive* outcomes for the human race from the continued experiments. Come on, Jack, what's the one thing people want most, the thing that makes death so fearful?"

That was easy. "They want to live forever."

"Bingo," Lucifer said from behind Ben's eyes—and smiled.

*Eternal life,* Jack thought, of course. It was the key to the vampire legend—the chance to live forever, even if it did mean drinking the blood of others and never seeing the sun. It was the unstated—if currently impossible—goal of all of modern medicine, to preserve the organic functioning of the body as long as possible, keeping brain-dead patients alive and breathing far past the point where they could ever hope to recover anything like normal life—short of a miracle. And of course, it was the heart of the gospel—the gift of God made possible through the sacrifice of Jesus Christ. But that was not an *organic* human life. The gospel promised a glo-rified body, not a perpetuation of the existence of these aging flesh-sacks called bodies. "I see," Jack said at last. "You're still playing God—and still tempting people to do the same."

"I'm not surprised you'd see it that way, Jack. You are so biased! In any case, it *will* happen. The secret of eternal life *will* be found—in fact, may have been already—"

"Isn't that a 'time' statement?" Jack mocked. "'Already'? When is already? Are you talking about 1974, or the day these UMMO things plopped a time craft in my path and res-cued me from the blizzard, or some time way in the future? Is there an 'event horizon,' a point in time that means 'now' to heaven and earth, beyond which even Satan himself fears to venture for fear of triggering the end-time?"

Ben just smiled back at him.

"Otherwise," Jack continued, "all of time turns into a single present tense, all one single eternal 'now' in the mind of God—in which, as we both already know, you and the Fallen are eternal losers."

This creature who had been Ben peered back at Jack, then raised his eyebrows and made a face. "Oh, Jack!" he scolded good-naturedly. "What an idea! You think you're going to escape?"

Jack's face fell. That was, indeed, the direction his thoughts had turned.

"Come on now!" Ben continued, still cackling. "We've gone to all this trouble to rescue you from UMMO and you're already planning to leave us? You think you know your way around Nigeria well enough to hide? You don't even know the *language,* Jack! You have less knowledge of Yoruba than a local village infant!"

*All true,* Jack thought. This was the terrible disadvantage of being with a mind reader—especially a mind reader who could no longer be trusted.

"Why don't you trust me, Jack?" Ben asked—sounding quite sincere and a little hurt. "I'm your friend. From what I read in your memories we're going to be friends for a long time. Why not just relax? You're safe here, Jack. *I'm* the one who got you away from UMMO. Haven't I always taken care of you in the past?"

Jack said nothing. What could he say? He thought of the uncertainty of his continued existence. His memories assured Ben of a future, but Ben couldn't provide him with the same assurance. Ben *would* grow up, but would Jack live to grow old?

"You can't know," Ben grunted—trying, Jack guessed, to be comforting. "It's better just to play your assigned part and let the future take care of itself. Most people live that way, right Jack?"

*What is my assigned part?* Jack countered. *And who assigned it?* This was the "why me?" question, and Jack hated himself for asking it. It sounded so whining. And even though he didn't voice it, he couldn't hide the self-pitying feeling from Ben, or from the thing that rode inside of him.

"You know, you're always asking the same questions. Why fight this? You're here. You already know why Baal needs you. He can dip further into the past when you're aboard."

"But why is that?" Jack argued. "Didn't you once tell me he keeps me aboard because he's afraid the angelic Guardians will zap this time machine to the ground if I'm not aboard? Like they did to that saucer above Roswell, New Mexico? If that's so, isn't it admitting that Baal and his buddies are under the ultimate *control* of those guardians? If it's true, doesn't that make Baal wonder if I'm not a sort of 'Trojan horse,' here on assignment from the *Lord* of those angelic beings? After all, you—and Baal—know my true loyalties!"

Ben stepped back a bit and took a deep sigh. "How certain are those loyalties, Jack? I mean, really? With all you've seen, how can you cling so tenaciously to the mythology of some all-powerful God?"

Jack thought his response, still trying to speak through Ben's gift to the frightened boy he knew was hidden somewhere behind this malevolent presence. *With all you have seen, Ben, how can you continue to let yourself be manipulated by these who have no hope? Break free of this creature that holds you! Trust the God this creature so fears!* He would eventually, Jack knew, and thus Ben knew it too. *Ultimately, you will confess your faith in that God and be transformed.*

"Because I'm 'predestined,' Jack?" Ben snarled, truly angry. "If you really think Satan is inside me, don't you think he might possibly read from your mind an antidote to prevent my eventual salvation?"

*Is that it?* Jack thought. *Is that the point of this whole exercise?*

"I'm only speculating, Jack," the boy said bitterly. "After all—I can only read minds. You're the one who knows my future."

Again it came, as it had so often this day: grief. Ben was no longer the boy he had been. But along with the grief came hope, for Jack was secure in the knowledge that Ben *was* a child of God—or would be. *No,* he thought toward the devil in Ben, *you know as well as I do that there's nothing you can do that will ever change that.*

"Don't be so sure, Jack," Ben muttered between his teeth. "Don't I have something to say about my own destiny?"

"Yes," Jack answered. "And you say it. You eventually exercise the freedom you have inside you to refuse to work with these creatures. I've known you a long time, Ben, and without having to read your mind, I know this about you: *freedom* is the one thing you want most. And you're going to get it."

"Maybe. Maybe not. Times change, Jack."

"True. But you'll not change time, regardless of how many passes you make at doing so."

"So we each follow the script written for us in heaven? That sounds so boring! So very restrictive! So very un-free!"

"More restrictive than following a script written for you by Baal? Or Kundas, should he manage to get hold of you? Or Astra? Where is Astra? Is she here?"

Ben—or the creature steering him—jumped at the chance to change the subject, especially to one that could throw Jack off balance. "Why do you want to know? She is a very seductive presence, isn't she! You want to spend some private time with her?"

"That was *not* what I was thinking about," Jack protested—but now he was. He'd been deflected by his own mention of Astra into remembering his time with her in Atlantis, not that he'd known at the time it was that she-demon. Pretending to be a woman of Atlantis she'd taken on the face and figure of Gloria to confuse and seduce him. He could feel angry about those memories, or guilty, or—*Or I can just admit those thoughts honestly, Ben, and go on beyond them to honestly reaffirm my faith. One thing about you, Ben: your gift does require from me the utmost honesty. You know, in some ways that's liberating—kind of like talking to a counselor who can see through every lie.* As he thought this toward Ben, Jack was reminded that this truth applied in any setting. God was always far more conscious of his thoughts and feelings than Ben could ever be—and of the thoughts of everyone else, Ben included. "We just manage to hide that from ourselves, Ben," Jack said aloud. "So let me just agree that, yes, Astra is indeed lovely—for a demon. I was just wondering what the relationship between Baal and Astra is right now, and what role if any she's playing in this current war."

"The part she's always played, I guess. Whatever suits her self-interest at the moment. But what do you mean by the 'current' war, Jack? This is the constant war, the never-ended, never-ending war. We're in 1974. If you've been liv-ing in the late 1990s, what's current about that?"

"Why this date?" Jack asked, still trying to make sense of their date and location against his knowledge of Nigeria. In 1974 the oil boom was making the country rich—a situation that wouldn't last. Was there something in the free flow of oil money and expatriates that made this time particularly—

"It's just a time, Jack. As good as any other. An innocu-ous period in which to hide. We'll be found eventually. Until then it's a convenient place to plot strategy."

"Aren't you needed in those meetings?"

"Why? They don't need me there to read one another's minds. . . . Oh," he finished, understanding Jack's thought.

Jack made it clear to him. "I wasn't talking to Ben just then. I meant—you. You there *inside* of Ben."

The boy—or whatever—sighed and fixed Jack with a hard glare. "Are you going to be like this from now on? Constantly doubting me? Looking for Lucifer behind my eyes?"

"I don't know *how* I'm going to be, from now on," Jack responded. "When is now, and how much more 'on' do I have? How can I plan ahead when I have no control over where I am or whom I'm with? How can I plot strategy when you can read and counter any plan I might make before it's fully formed? I think I see how I'm going to have to live, and I guess it's really how I ought to live always: on the crest of the moment, following instantly and without question the guidance of the Holy Spirit. You can't read His mind, can you?"

Was the one within Ben startled? Nonplussed? Repelled? Somehow blocked? A strange expression played across Ben's features, and he quickly turned to start out of the cabin, saying, "You've had a difficult trip. Despite what you think, you're safe here. Get some rest." With that he was out the door.

Jack flopped back on the bed, his mind whirling. He'd never been so confused in his life. He didn't know where he was bound or what he could expect when he got there. He couldn't trust anyone now, not even Ben. And there was a war raging among the demons, a war that had always been and would continue to be until God sealed up this age and started afresh with His chosen ones. But for all of his confusion, of this he felt certain: God had ordained that he be here at this moment—for whatever reason. Despite the daily fiction of personal control over his life that he shared in common with all people, he knew that his actions were really under the control of a sovereign God. No other explanation for the twists and turns of life made sense to him. This, apparently, was his destiny. He had been sent. But to do what? What could he do about anything that he had seen and heard?

*Does it matter?* Jack thought. Having seen inside a mystery, he felt strangely relaxed. He'd been reminded again of his finite creatureliness, as well as of the fact that he wrestled "not against flesh and blood, but against principalities, against powers"—against wicked spiritual beings far beyond his strength to subdue, or even effectively counter. He *did* know something about spiritual warfare. He knew if God's people trusted in their own strength and power, they would only fail. "Did we in our own strength confide," went the words of Luther's ancient hymn, "our striving would be losing." That was him, all right. Through Ben, the Fallen could read his thoughts and counter his every plan. Only by letting God steer—by living each moment on constant alert to the guidance of the Spirit of God, and acting immediately upon those impulses—could he hope to effectively serve God's purpose. It *must* be in God's purpose that he was here, not merely Ben's or Baal's. As to why? Why should he presume that he could even know?

He missed Gloria's counsel. They'd been through a rough year. She'd been diagnosed with a serious illness. During that interminable waiting for test results she'd had an experience of walking three days with a constant sense of God's presence. God had promised her that He was before her, behind her, and on either side of her, and that anywhere she looked or walked He would be there. That had been the case. Her face had shined with the heavenly presence, and her prayers rang with the truth of that promise. It had been a fiery furnace—and God had walked her through it. Jack could only hope to walk through this one with the same resolve.

With the extraction of the stingers, normal functions were returning to his body. He was hungry. He was exhausted. He was uncomfortable. He still had this stupid tie around his neck! He slipped the knot loose, pulled it off, and held it up to look more closely at those little elephants. Then he chuckled. How ridiculous to think that a tie could somehow control the actions of God! In any case, Ben had seen it now. That particular time loop was closed. Jack tossed it across the cabin, pulled off his shoes, and reached out to the food tray to grab a slice of bread and a slice of ham. He ate quickly, half-wondering if he would manage to get it eaten before sleep claimed him. As he gobbled the sandwich he thought to himself that, even though God was meeting his needs, he *would* like to see an angel again.

"Why?" the voice of the Holy Spirit said within him, "when I am with you always?"

"Right," he said aloud. Or maybe he dreamed that he said it, for Jack Brennen finally slept in peace, the half-eaten sandwich in his hand.

# Chapter Ten

*The valhalla gambit*

Trisha actually looked forward to Mondays. She loved the diversity of her job. As a federal marshal she couldn't predict where a week might take her. She might be assigned to protect a federal judge who'd received a threatening phone call, or escort someone in the witness protection program to make an appearance in court, or track down a fugitive who'd violated parole and dropped out of sight. But this particular Monday was different. She'd been completely unprepared for Gloria's story of abductions and alien demons and Jack's disappearance. She wanted to help, but she was at a total loss where to start.

She kept hoping Gloria would call with the news that Jack had been found, but it was now mid-morning and that call hadn't come. If he had indeed been kidnapped then the case really belonged to the FBI—but *alien* abduction? As far as she knew there was no real "X-files" department at the Bureau, and she didn't much feel like calling those guys and asking if there *was*. The U.S. Marshal's office had a love/hate relationship with the FBI, born out of the Bureau's "favored child" status with the government. The engrained arrogance of its agents was legendary among law-enforcement professionals. She didn't like the thought of giving those people over there an excuse to laugh at her—and she was pretty certain they would.

Nevertheless, if it came to that she wouldn't hesitate to call. She worked with all of the agencies regularly—FBI, DEA, ATF, and the rest of the alphabet soup of law-enforcement—all but the CIA. And who knows, maybe she'd worked with them as well, without really knowing it. The Marshals had dispatched a detail to Panama to arrest Noriega and transport him back to the States for trial, so she guessed she might have been working with CIA operatives. But aliens? And Gloria had told her that Jack didn't believe they were really aliens at all. Was she really going to call the FBI and ask if they had a special unit assigned to battling *demons?*

It seemed the wisest course was to wait through the day and see if Jack turned up. If he didn't, then she would make contact with this Ben person Gloria had mentioned and try to piece together a composite of places he might have been taken. New Mexico? Someplace called Area 51? Trisha sighed and slumped down into her chair. Her badge wouldn't be of any help in getting into those places. She'd need a higher security clearance and a really good excuse. She gazed into her computer screen as if it was some crystal ball that would suddenly light up with a solution to her questions.

"Hard at work?" her chief said, coming up behind her.

"Sort of stumped, really," she mumbled back over her shoulder. Her chief was a woman and a very good friend.

Trisha felt like she worked *with* Andrea more than for her. "You got something for me?"

"Warrant detail. Got word from the Northern District office that John Brockman might be in Huntsville. You remember that one?"

"Drug bust coming into Mobile? Made bail and disappeared?"

"That's him. I thought you must be working on it already."

Trisha was surprised. "Me? Why?"

"You're not?" Andrea frowned, for now she was surprised. "Hmm. That's odd. This fax was waiting for you this morning, and I just assumed it was related. You can see why . . . ." She passed the fax to Trisha, along with a file labeled CS.NO.84722/33 07-03-97 BROCKMAN, JOHN G. "Brockman's got several aliases. I figured it was an anonymous tip on the guy from one of your sources."

That slight frown still creasing her forehead, Trisha read the one-sentence fax—and her frown deepened.

*re: Jack Brennen*
*Ms. Carrie Baxter in Huntsville may have help.*

It was handwritten and unsigned, with no stationary imprint nor identifying features that might give a clue as to its source. The fax number of the initiation point was listed, and she would check that out first, but experience told her that would turn out to be a public phone/fax and would provide little direct information about the sender. There was really little here to go on other than the tip contained in that one line. And given the story Gloria had told her, to receive such a fax was both confusing and a little frightening. Still, it did give her a place to begin.

"You think it's related?" Andrea asked.

"Hmm?" said Trisha, coming out of her reverie.

"Look at that name. Don't you think that might be this guy Brockman?"

"Oh. No, Chief. I know what this is about, and it's a completely different thing."

Andrea shrugged. "Oh well. Two birds with one stone. You can check that out in Huntsville when you go up this afternoon to try to locate Brockman."

"This afternoon?"

"Can you make it? We've got a con-air Lear leaving at three to take a prisoner up. I figured you could catch a ride. You don't want to be driving the interstate today, it's a mess."

"I heard. Twelve-car pile-up. Yeah, I can run home and get ready. Have to let Larry know and grab some things."

"Dress warm, Trish. It's cold."

"I'll bundle up."

"And that fax really doesn't have anything to do with the Brockman case?"

"Not that *I* know of."

"Weird," Andrea murmured, shaking her head as she walked back into her office.

It was weird. And down in her gut Trisha had the feeling things were only going to get weirder.

\* \* \*

Ben shook him.

"What? Honey?"

"Sorry," Ben snickered, "but I'm not your Honey."

"Uuunh," Jack moaned, sitting up. *And what a pity that is,* he was thinking, dreading whatever this day would bring. For he was back in a room he had long thought himself free of—a prison he'd managed to relegate to the status of a bad dream. But here it was—*his* cabin aboard the saucer. He sighed and rolled over.

"How'd you sleep?" asked the boy who knew the answer without asking.

"Fine, I guess. I don't remember." Jack looked down to see that he was under the covers, dressed only in his underwear. "Who put me to bed?"

"I did. You don't remember that either?"

"Nothing," Jack answered—chewing. He swallowed with some distaste and muttered, "It's a wonder I didn't choke. I seem to have a bite of sandwich still in my mouth. I was really weary, Ben." *Still am,* he added in his thoughts.

"I knew that. While I was getting you out of your shirt you were telling me something about there being night shrimps in the bathroom, and not to step on them barefooted or I would get glass in my foot."

"Night shrimps?"

"You were dreaming."

"I guess so." Jack rolled out from under the covers to sit on the edge of the bed and yawned. "Did you read my dreams?" he asked, curious. He rarely remembered them, and sometimes wondered if he was missing something because he didn't.

"I try not to do that much. People's dreams are pretty surreal. You don't want to go there."

"Do the demons dream?" Jack asked. He was growing more alert—and along with that came a renewal of his revulsion for this place and for his captors.

"They don't sleep. Besides, you *really* wouldn't want to go there."

One thought led to another. "Do you sleep, Ben?" In his mind, Jack's question was really *Are you* you *today? Or something else?*

Ben snarled his response to the thought. "I was me *yesterday,* Jack." Then he made a point of changing the subject. "Look, they brought breakfast. You need to eat and change clothes."

"Why, am I going—"

The lights went off and the saucer shivered. Another time drop. Jack grabbed the edge of the bed and waited, his head spinning. "I guess I'd better change that question to 'Where are we going?'"

"Don't you mean when?" Ben grinned—and Jack saw that he did, for the lights came back on and they where *there*—wherever, whenever.

"Whatever," he shrugged. "I'm sure you know."

"I am now. I wasn't sure before. Didn't know if the Guardians would let us through."

"They let you back to 1974. Or so you tell me. . . ."

"This is deep time."

"As far back as Atlantis?"

"I told you, Jack," Ben said with exaggerated frustration. "I don't know anything about Atlantis, even if your head is filled with memories of the place."

Jack still didn't believe him, and there was no way to veil that disbelief from Ben. He didn't try, but neither did he push it. "So where are we, then?"

"You'll see. But first you'll need to change. So will I."

"I'll be glad not to have to wear that suit anymore. . . ."

Ben laughed—and not at all pleasantly. "You're certain of that? Your new clothes will be laid out when you get out of the shower. If you can call them that." He cackled again and left the cabin.

*That was cryptic,* Jack thought as he stood up and stretched. He glanced at the breakfast tray and was reminded again that while this *was* a prison, at least he ate well. Still hungry, he sat down and devoured a plateful, drank some good, fresh coffee, then found his way into the shower—a luxury he'd missed terribly without actually thinking about it until now. The water was warm, and that was wonderful, for he was beginning to feel a little chilly. In fact, it was downright cold when he got out, and he toweled off quickly, glancing around as he did so for a razor. Just as his other bodily functions had returned with the removal of the UMMO stingers, his beard had started to grow back. He saw none and dismissed it, for he needed to put something on.

"That?" he said aloud to himself as he gazed with dismay at the bed. He saw no underwear, no pants—just a roughly-woven robe and a kind of coat made with skins stitched together. Skins! He glanced around for his discarded T-shirt, but it was gone—a thought that gave him another chill. *Who came in and took it?* he wondered. *Who took my suit and shirt as well and left this—garb—on the bed?* "Oh, no," he moaned. But by now he was freezing. He quickly put the stuff on.

"Hey, Conan!" Ben said as he came back into the cabin through the sliding door. "Like it?" he asked wryly.

"You know what I think," Jack growled. "Not even a T-shirt? I don't wear anything without a T-shirt under it! This itches like crazy!" He whiffed the hide cloaking one shoulder and screwed up his face. "It stinks too!"

"Gotta look—and smell—the part, Jack."

"What part? Where are we?" he said, slipping his feet into equally foul-smelling fur boots.

Ben didn't answer, instead reaching down to pick up another strip of leather that Jack hadn't noticed. It was a rough belt, to which was attached a sheath—and a knife. "Don't forget this. You may need it."

Jack pulled out the knife and examined the blade. It was very real—eighteen inches long and honed to keen edge. Its haft was ornately carved of bone—easily of museum quality. And from what little Jack knew about such things, it was perfectly balanced for his hand. Even so, he felt ridiculous strapping it on.

"Get into the spirit, Jack! Enjoy the experience!"

"Like this is some adventure game or something? Grown men shooting paint balls at one another in the forest?"

"Potentially more dangerous. But safe enough for us. Come on."

Jack reluctantly followed Ben out of the room and out of the saucer, and felt immediately the necessity of the hair-covered skins wrapped around him. His breath turned to frost as they walked together across the straw-covered flag-stones of an enormous great room. Jack turned and looked back.

The saucer sat in the middle of the huge room, crushed tables splintered beneath it. It looked incongruous in this setting—but then again, it looked incongruous in every setting. Several inhabitants of this fortress stood gawking at it, and gawking too at Jack. Not wishing to be engaged in conversation—not wishing to be here at all—Jack turned and followed Ben, who had raced up a stone stairway with all the excitement of a kid—which, Jack reminded himself, Ben was. The staircase led to a balcony which opened through an archway onto the sky—and there Jack stopped, gazing out on the majestic spectacle of the surrounding mountains.

The flat roof of the fortress stretched out before them, the size of a football field and frosted with fresh snow. Battlements rose up on all three sides, with tile-topped square towers on both of the far corners. Beyond the walls, the mountains jutted up sharply, snow coating them down well below the treeline. They were in a mountaintop fortress somewhere in the distant past—and they were under attack.

Ben had rushed ahead of him to lean over the parapet and look down. Now he jerked his head out of the way as a javelin arched upward over it and fell, silent and harmless, into the snow. The boy grinned back at him gleefully. Jack thought immediately, *Ben, you're crazy!*

"No, I'm not. I could see it coming before it was thrown. Come look!"

"What is this place?" Jack shouted, keeping his distance from the wall.

"Valhalla! We're in the fortress of the gods!"

"Which gods?" Jack frowned. If this was supposedly Valhalla then he thought he knew. . . .

"You do," Ben grinned. "The gods of the frozen north! Odin, Thor, Loki. Baal is Loki here—the trickster!"

More evidence of the Fallen's deception of mankind down through the ages. Jack's mind flashed back to an unpleasant encounter with Druidic priests in ancient Britain, and he shook his head wearily. "Oh, no," he murmured. "Look, Ben, I don't think I can do this again."

"But we're gods here, Jack! We're worshiped!"

"Right. By those warriors hurling javelins at us? I'm not a god, Ben, and I'll not pretend to be one. I'm going back to the saucer to hunt for my real clothes." He'd just started to retrace his tracks toward the archway when he heard a sharp *crack!* directly in front of him and a blast of over-heated air threw him backward into the snow. Ben rushed over to help him scramble to his feet as he gazed with shock at the object that had materialized before him. One of the flying boxes had suddenly arrived in this time and place.

"UMMO!" he gasped, truly terrified, struggling to get out of Ben's grasp.

"No," Ben soothed him. "It's ours. Listen, you've got to stay with me. Things are going to get dangerous in a minute."

"I think they already have!"

"We're fine! Look! Come here and look!"

Shaken, Jack allowed himself to be led to the parapet and peered carefully over the edge. Despite Ben's assurances he was not at all comforted by the sight. A legion of warriors—Roman, by the look of their helmets and standards, but wrapped up as warmly as he—advanced up the steep side of the mountain toward them. Jack stepped back immediately to avoid being seen, and looked at Ben, his eyes huge.

"Like something out of a movie, huh?" the boy grinned. He was obviously loving this.

"Are you going to tell me what's going on?"

"Figure it out, Jack."

"You haven't told me the time!"

"A.D. 300."

"Why 300?"

"It's a nice round number. And yes, those are Romans. Roman mercenaries, anyway. Their minds are clogged with words sounding vaguely Germanic."

"Diocletian is the emperor, then," Jack mumbled to himself, struggling to find some piece of information to place these events in context. What was all this about? Was UMMO supporting Diocletian in this time period? Against Germanic chieftains backed by the Grays they'd been taught to worship? Was this just another senseless conflict sponsored by demonic superpowers to produce still more dead bodies?

"That's why I like traveling with you Jack, you know so much. So what kind of emperor was he?"

"Strong," Jack remembered. "After a series of weak emperors. Reasserted Roman control along the Rhine. Thought he was a god."

"Don't they all, Jack. Don't they all."

"He also persecuted the Christians." That was why Jack knew him.

"Well there, you see?" Ben teased with the utter lack of taste of a teen. "A man like that can't be all bad!"

Jack made no response. He was missing the grown Ben. That spiritual change of heart couldn't come soon enough.

Suddenly the flying box behind them burst open and out jumped a squadron of men in black—men in skins, in this case, for they too had dressed for the occasion. Jack noticed as they raced to positions around the rooftop that regardless of their costume they had the same inhuman look about them of every MIB he'd met. And they had not bothered to

152

exchange their weapons for the swords and spears of the period. They carried AK-47s, clips already in place, and as soon as they reached the ramparts they began to pour down fire on the advancing legion. Jack backed away, not wanting to see the carnage. *Why did they even bother to change clothes?* he thought.

"They're the warriors of the gods, Jack. Of course they'd be armed with thunderbolts!" Ben smiled, and added proudly, "You remember Loki, don't you? The bringer of fire. The starter of quarrels. The god of fraud."

"How fitting. And now hundreds of Roman warriors will die to demonstrate his godhood. I'm sorry, Ben, but this is just not fun to me."

Once again Jack started toward the staircase that led to the interior of the fortress, giving a wide berth to the black time box.

Ben chased after him shouting, "You've got to stay with me, Jack. The Boss doesn't want to lose you again!"

"Then you go with me to find a fire someplace. It's cold out here, and we both already know how this battle is going to turn out." He noticed flakes of snow had begun to tumble into his face, and glanced up.

*Crack!* Another box burst into view right above the first—and this one *was* UMMO. It immediately opened fire all around them.

Suddenly the men in skins were scrambling back to cover, their defense of the fortress forgotten in their haste to get away. Some actually made it into their own box before its ramp swung shut and it leapt skyward to avoid being destroyed right there on the rooftop. Others raced toward the same archway Jack sprinted for, urged onward by Ben's now terrified yelps: "Inside, Jack! Get inside!"

Cannon fire now blasted the stone walls of the fortress as the UMMO ship raked the rooftop, chasing its ascending twin. Jack hesitated just inside the arch, looking back to watch the firefight, thinking that at least now the battle was balanced again, and the mercenaries might have a chance to survive. "Time to go, Jack, time to go!" Ben shouted, shoving him on inside.

The balcony over the great room was slippery now with the tracked-in snow of a dozen pairs of boots. Jack walked down the stone stairs carefully, holding onto the wall as he said, "I have a question, Ben. If the Guardians won't let you travel into deep time without me along, then why did they allow UMMO?" Because this was the best way of protecting the inhabitants of this age from the foolishness of the feuding demons? He was more convinced than ever that, despite Baal's lies, the bugs were indeed just another branch of the Fallen.

"We've got to get out of here, Jack!" Ben shouted, pressing on his shoulders to hurry him downward. They made it at last to the floor of the great hall, which looked now like a command room about to be taken. Warriors—some of them carrying automatic rifles, others more primitively armed—raced back up the steps as Baal stood in the doorway, gesturing madly and doubtless directing commands into minds all around them. Jack heard nothing but the boom of the cannon, the chatter of rifle fire, and the whining of aircraft as the boxes above them wheeled around in deadly pursuit of one another.

*But why do they allow it all?* Jack wondered as Ben pushed him into a corridor at the bottom of the stairs. Behind them there was an ear-splitting clap as a missile blasted through the arch and into the wall across from it. The castle rocked, the great hall filled with smoke, and in all the confusion Ben was suddenly no longer nearby. . . .

Jack stopped running and looked back the way he'd come. Smoke and dust choked his lungs, and he really had no wish to backtrack. But he also had no wish to be separated from Ben. He fought his way back into the huge room in time to see the saucer disappear.

"Are they leaving us again?" Jack shouted in anguish to Ben, but Ben wasn't there to answer. Terrible memories of being abandoned in deep time surged through Jack's mind, and he issued a silent plea: *Ben, if you're listening, please don't let them leave me here. . . .* Then he heard shouts from the top of the stairway and looked up. Through the smoke, silhouetted against the gray sky, Jack saw that the Romans had taken the rooftop and were now pouring down inside.

He ran. Back down the corridor he raced, trying to move his legs the way he had when he was a halfback, dodging obstacles as he put distance between himself and the center of the battle. But he'd been seen, and he heard pursuers grunting and shouting behind him. The corridor branched, then branched again, then he wasn't sure if he might not actually be running back toward those who chased him. Instead, he heaved open a heavy oaken door and stepped into the room beyond, shoving the door closed behind him and leaning against it to gasp for breath.

The room was large—either a master bedroom or well-furnished guest room—with a fire burning in the grate on the far wall. He could quickly see that there was nothing nearby to block the door, nor any other way out. If they had spotted him, he was trapped. He heard footsteps in the hallway behind him, and circled the bed, looking for space to hide beneath it. With a heavy kick the door flew open, and three Roman mercenaries bounded inside. The lead warrior grunted with satisfaction when he saw Jack and cocked his javelin back behind his head.

Jack grabbed for the knife and out it came—then he stopped. This was ridiculous. What was he going to do—throw it at this first warrior like Indiana Jones, then kick-box his way past the other two? Jack was no warrior. He was no longer even an athlete. He was a sedentary seminary professor who

155

got most of his exercise running late to class—and he was about to be killed. He thought sadly of Gloria, dropped the knife to the floor, and told God he was ready.

But the javelin didn't split him. It was never thrown. The three warriors froze, their eyes wide with sudden terror. Then they fell backward, scrambling to their knees to crawl desperately out the door. They'd seen something—someone—behind him. Before he even turned around Jack knew who it was. He wondered if she'd let *him* see her. . . .

She did. It was the Guardian who had protected him in the past—who protected him always, he guessed. "Gloria!" he sang—for she looked exactly like his wife.

"So you seem to have named me," the angel replied sedately.

"I thought you'd abandoned me."

"I've never left you. You just don't always see."

"Why?" Jack asked, eager to get all the information he could during this brief encounter—for he knew he would not see her for long. "Is there something wrong with my faith, with my spiritual vision—"

"You're not often permitted to see. No one is."

"But why not?" Jack pleaded. "I see Baal. Too often! I see the Fallen. I hear the voice of the evil one regularly! Don't you realize how encouraging that would be to us, to be able to see Elisha's vision of the encircling angels whenever we're facing the armies that surround us?"

"You believe that would strengthen your faith, Jack?" Her tone was not scolding, but neither was it approving.

"Of course!"

"But then you would be living by sight, not by faith."

"Is that so bad? You don't understand how much people long for such a vision, for such assurance of God's presence! People wear angel pins on their lapels, buy books about angels, watch television shows about angels—"

"Ah, yes," she replied, smiling slightly. "The one with the red-haired girl with the Irish accent." Then her smile faded. Her brilliant eyes narrowed, piercing him. "What do you find so fascinating about us, Jack?"

"Everything! How many there are of you, how you're organized, how you do battle with the evil one and his fallen comrades, how you protect us—"

"And the outcome of all this is—what? Worship, Jack? The very thing that despicable liar craves?"

"No . . ."

"It's a tool he uses often: demonstrations of supernatural power to win human dependence upon himself. All of them do it, for it goes to the source of their lust—to be 'as gods.' It's the first lie of the garden. Do you think we who made the choice to serve and obey actually *enjoy* your adoring attention? We, whose focus is only on directing your faith to the One who truly deserves it, to that One Most High? No. We watch—we guard—we obey. And when we must, we unveil our presence to reveal His glory."

It seemed then to Jack that a window opened behind her through the rock wall of that fortress—opening into glory. Her own radiance faded by comparison, as if she stood outlined against all eternity. It didn't blind him, although he thought it should have. Instead the light poured in through his eyes and down into his soul, illuminating his whole dim being, washing over his imperfections and searing away the darkness that didn't belong within a child of God. It was both inviting and cauterizing, enveloping him with warmth and covering him with truth. Against the backdrop of that grandeur the angel almost seemed dark. He thought he understood far better what Paul described as moving from glory into glory—that he was seeing past the messenger of God to the message itself. Then the heavenly vision was gone, and Jack stood facing an angel. Only an angel. And he felt deprived.

Jack took a long, deep breath, understanding at last the steady calm in this radiant creature's eyes. It was humility— the confident humility of an obedient servant, content with her place in the heavenly order. "Are you here to take me home?" he said at last.

"I'm here because He is here—and He is in you. To remind you that wherever you are, He has let you be. To remind you that your ultimate purpose is the same as mine—to bring honor and glory to Him. Isn't that reason enough for my presence?"

Jack stepped backward and felt the bed behind his legs. He slumped down to sit on it, sinking deep into its feather-filled mattress. "I don't know," he murmured honestly, still filled with a sense of loss. "Why am *I* here?"

"They brought you." There was no question who "they" were.

"But why? What's their purpose in all this? What can they possibly hope to accomplish?"

"They have no hope, Jack. And why do you assume evil needs any purpose other than selfishness?"

"Surely *they* think they have purpose."

"All lies. The lies of power. The lies of control. The lies of the little gods the Betrayer tempted them into believing they could become. They are hopeless fools, Jack. They have no purpose."

"Then why do you let them in and out of time? Why do you permit this?"

"I don't permit. I only guard."

"But are you just going to let them destroy history?"

"You speak as if it's something sacred," the angel responded evenly. "It's not. They have always been destroying history. And history is the record of their own destruction. What could they further ruin that they've not already perverted beyond all rescue?"

Jack thought on that, then shook his head, still confused. "But can they change anything by their interference?"

"Nothing that cannot ultimately be set right. All things will be. But that time has not yet come."

"Which time? The time of the end? Is the end coming soon?"

"It's not in my authority to know that, Jack. How could it be in yours?"

Jack sighed wearily. "I wish it would come soon."

"Is the world ready for His coming?"

"No," he answered honestly.

"If the Holy One is in no hurry, why are you?"

Jack pondered her words, then tried to give the most honest response he could think of: "I guess—when I look around, I just wonder how much more He can stand."

Once again, she smiled. "Do you think it's only you humans who wonder that?"

"That's right," he remembered. "You told me before that the angels wonder about that too."

"We have marveled at His patience from the very beginning. It's a mystery to us why He loves. But I've told you much of this before . . . do you not remember?"

"It's—been a long time."

"You do remember, at least, your own purpose?"

"I do. It's to trust—to serve—to love—to be obedient. . . ."

"Even if that means being where you don't want to be."

Jack nodded. "Or when."

"You've had some difficult experiences, Jack. I'm here to tell you that they're not over. Remember your resolve to live every moment listening to the Spirit—and be prepared to act courageously."

Sensing she was about to leave him, Jack reached out toward her. "Will you be nearby?"

"The Spirit is with you always."

"But will I see you aga—"

"Your friend comes to find you," said the angel who looked like Gloria. Then she was gone.

The room was dark now, by contrast. He looked at the fire in the grate and waited, listening for footsteps in the hallway behind him.

"Jack!" Ben shouted, stepping cautiously into the room. "There you are!" There was a nervousness in his voice Jack thought he understood. He was certain when the boy said with forced lightness, "Who have you been talking to?"

Jack shifted around on the bed to look back at Ben. "You know."

"I . . . I don't."

"You saw her in my mind. Just like the last time."

"All right," Ben agreed, his voice dropping lower. "You're right. I saw her in your *mind*, Jack. I didn't see *her*." He was clearly troubled.

"But I did. I saw her—and I saw beyond her." He spoke with a confident faith he knew Ben would find more troubling still. "Why can't you just believe that, Ben? You know of the Guardians; you speak of them freely. Why can't you accept it when a Guardian speaks with me?"

Ben hesitated a moment, then said, "Let's get out of here, Jack. This place is spooky!"

Jack shook his head in quiet dismay. "You deal with demons everyday, and you find *this* place spooky?"

"Come on, Jack, please! They're waiting for us. We've got to go!"

Jack didn't move. He just turned his head back to that place where the angel Gloria had stood and shown him heaven. "Go where? Somewhere deeper back into time, where UMMO can find us again and more lives can be lost? Are we late for yet another failed attempt to change the inevitable outcome?"

"I'm trying to tell you, Jack. The war is over. The Boss and UMMO have been summoned to appear before the entire Council of the Ultrastructure."

Jack turned his head to look back at Ben. "Summoned by whom?"

The boy looked back at him anxiously. "The Overlord is back. And is he ever angry!"

# Chapter Eleven

*Previous attempts*

The Lear jet that flew Trisha to Huntsville was one of nearly thirty planes operated by the U.S. Marshal's Office to convey federal prisoners across the country. It didn't have "Con-Air" painted on the side, but that's what its unwilling passengers had come to call it—so frequently that the slang name had stuck and eventually found its way into a movie title. It was a comfortable plane, and Trisha had spent the time resting her eyes and reflecting on the strange events of the last twenty-four hours.

Who had sent the fax? She doubted she'd have any answer to that until she managed to speak to this Ms. Carrie Baxter. She resolved to do that as soon as she checked out the tip on Brockman being in Huntsville. At the moment it seemed no real coincidence that her job would take her to the same city—just a chance assignment based on Andrea's misinterpretation of the fax.

They bounced down onto a frosted runway without problem at ten after three. By four she had linked up with the source of the tip—an addict and sometime courier for Brockman who kept trying to straighten out. "He got his tail up this morning and took off," the man said, grinning apologetically. "I tried . . ." he shrugged, and Trisha nodded.

"Where was he going?"

"Ah—north, he said. I couldn't just come out and ask him, could I?"

"Friends up there? Any family you know of?"

"He's got a sister someplace close to Chicago, I think. Rockman? Rockford? Yeah, Rockford! Like the *Rockford Files*. You remember that show?"

By five she'd checked in with Andrea and gotten the order to go on to Chicago and follow up the lead. There was a flight leaving for Atlanta at 7:50 to connect on to Chicago, and Trisha would be on it. That gave her about two hours to track down the woman in the cryptic fax and see what she might know of Jack Brennen's disappearance. It wasn't hard. There was only one C. Baxter listed in the local directory, residing in an apartment close to the university. Sitting in Huntsville rush-hour traffic, she was scolding herself for not first calling Gloria and seeing if this trip was absolutely necessary, if Jack had been found or called in. Still, she had the time—and this was clearly a mystery that intrigued her. Maybe she hadn't called because she didn't want to know.

She found the place easily enough—there were directions to the huge complex in the phone book, probably due to a constant turnover of student renters. When she knocked on the door, a small, quiet-looking woman with a sunken chin answered.

"Ms. Baxter?" Trisha said, readying her wallet to flash her badge.

"Yes . . . ?"

"I'm Trisha Paulson with the Federal Marshal's office." She flipped open her wallet. Trisha recognized immediately the alarmed expression that flashed across the woman's face. Something to hide.

"Oh." Carrie Baxter peered at the badge carefully, as if to be certain it was legitimate.

"May I come in?"

"Of course. Sorry." Carrie Baxter stepped aside to admit her, then closed the door behind her and locked it carefully. "I . . . I guess I knew you'd come for me eventually," she said apologetically, which immediately put Trisha on her guard. But the next question took her completely by surprise. "That television show was a mistake, wasn't it?"

"What?"

"I knew I shouldn't go on it. But after the congressman wouldn't take any action on the information I gave him . . . well, I just wanted to try somehow to get the story out. Then she wouldn't let me. I guess I won't have a chance now, will I?"

Trisha peered at her, both perplexed and curious. "Ms. Baxter, I'm sorry, but I really don't know what you're talking about."

"You don't?"

"I don't," Trish admitted, risking a slight smile.

"But you're from the government, aren't you?" It was Carrie Baxter's turn to look perplexed.

"I'm a federal marshal, yes. But I only came looking for information about a Dr. Jack Brennen."

Carrie put a hand to her face. "I'm so embarrassed. Umm—would you like to sit down?"

"Sure," Trish said, glancing around for a place. The woman was obviously either just moving in or about to move out. There were half-packed boxes strewn everywhere, and only one chair and part of the couch had nothing stacked on them. Trisha chose the chair. "Do you know Jack Brennen or know anything about him?"

Carrie Baxter carefully moved a box to the floor and sat on the couch. "Not to my knowledge," she said, and for the first time Trisha saw in her eyes the woman's sharp intelligence. "I mean, he may be connected to—I mean, no. I don't. I've never heard the name, that I recall."

"Umm-hmm. Does this handwriting look at all familiar to you?" Trisha pulled the fax out of her pocket, unfolded it and passed it across the box to Carrie. The woman studied it carefully, her face twisting with concern as she read her own name there.

"No."

Trisha tried again. "Can you imagine any reason why someone would fax my office suggesting that you know anything about this case?"

"Is—is he an aerospace engineer or something like that?"

"No. He's a seminary professor."

"A seminary professor?" Carrie said, frowning with surprise. "You mean he's a Christian?"

"Most of them are, I think," Trisha said, smiling mildly. "In fact, he's a preacher."

"Well then," said Carrie, clearly at a loss, "I guess our pastor might know him. Maybe he preached in our church or something?"

"Ah . . . no, I don't think that would be it," Trisha responded, taking the fax back. "This man disappeared last night. His wife is a very good friend, and she thinks he was—now this is going to sound very strange, I know—but she believes he was abducted."

Carrie said nothing for a moment. She just sat studying Trisha's face. "Then this is about the television show."

"What show was that, Ms. Baxter?"

"The *Sherry Lynn Ward Show*. I was on it several months ago."

Of course Trisha knew who Sherry Lynn Ward was. She'd watched the show a few times, enough to know its format. "What was the show about, Ms. Baxter?"

Carrie sighed deeply, looking down at the fingers she had knitted together in her lap. "You talk about strange! Have you got some time, Officer . . . ?"

"Paulson," Trisha supplied, adding, "but just call me Trisha. And I have plenty of time." She didn't even glance at her watch. Of this she was certain: there would always be another flight to Atlanta.

Carrie examined her face again, this time with a knowing look. "You look like you know Jesus, Trisha."

It was a surprising statement—but a complimentary one. "I do."

"And you look like someone I could trust—and believe me, I don't think that about many people anymore."

"Thank you." Trisha nodded, waiting for the woman to go on.

"Now, I'm about to tell you the strangest story you ever heard."

"I don't know about that," Trisha answered softly. "I heard a pretty weird one last night—"

"Well, you're really going to think this one sounds crazy."

"—and that story began exactly the same way!"

"Really?"

"It did."

Carrie Baxter shrugged and wrung her hands together from the elbows. "I guess it could all be part of the same one. They're all over the country. All over the world. I told it all to the congressman, but he just kept my documentation and covered it up. I guess they got to him."

There was a flood of information in that statement, Trisha knew. She just didn't know what any of it meant. "Who did, Ms. Baxter?"

Carrie sighed again. "The aliens."

*Yep,* Trisha said to herself, *this is going to be the same story.* "Go on."

"I used to work at General Aeronautics Industries here in Huntsville. It's a government contractor working on components for the space shuttle. At least that's what I thought they were doing, what everyone thinks they do. But I discovered that some of the products we were developing were not being made for the government at all—at least not with public government knowledge. And although I knew what I was doing was illegal, immoral, and unethical, I began to gather documentation of all this and make copies of it. Stupid, huh?" she asked, raising her eyebrows.

"If you felt you had good reason—" Trisha prompted.

"I did! I thought at first it was a conspiracy to defraud the government, and I figured that had to be *more* immoral and illegal. To tell the truth—I felt like I was *supposed* to do this. I'd never thought of myself as a whistle-blower type. But then who does? I mean, you see something happening and you react to it, and if it's wrong, you tell someone, right? There were tremendous sums of money being poured into this project—I mean enormous amounts, from unnamed sources, and I thought it must be coming from other nations trying to steal our technology. And so I—well, I just kept collecting and kept searching, and no one stopped me, and then I began to feel that somehow the Lord Himself was *empowering* me to do all this without being caught. Like I had been purposely placed in just this position to do just this thing, and I would be disobedient not to. I really wanted to talk to my pastor about it all, but I couldn't, you know? That would have implicated him, and since all of this was so secret and so . . . so dirty, I realized pretty early on that somebody could get killed. I figured if anybody got killed it should be me alone. Can you understand that?"

"Completely, Ms. Baxter."

"Call me Carrie, OK? I already feel like I know you and—anyway, the more I pieced together the more I realized that these vehicles weren't being constructed for another government at all . . . that we were building these things for aliens."

That seemed to be a pretty big jump in logic, so Trisha interrupted: "How? Did you see any aliens or see pictures or have any evidence?"

"Not at first," Carrie said, shaking her head. "I really don't know exactly how I came to that conclusion. Intuition, maybe? The locations we were dealing with all seemed connected to flying saucer sightings you'd read about in the paper, and—well, eventually, it just seemed the only thing that made sense, even if it did sound utterly ridiculous at the same time. The technology being included in these things was way beyond anything I knew we were *supposed* to have. I didn't find out for certain they were aliens until later on."

"How?"

"When I was almost abducted myself."

Trisha nodded, unblinking, trying very successfully not to register any expression other than alert interest. "Almost?"

"I'll get to that. While I was collecting evidence, we managed to get a new congressman elected from this district. Ralph Wilkenson?" she said, and Trisha nodded. "I say we because I worked in his campaign. I thought if we could get a Christian elected it would make a difference in Washington, you know? I really believed in him." Carrie Baxter sighed deeply—the sigh of betrayed confidence. "You just can't place your trust in people, Trisha. I sure proved that."

"How?"

"Once we got him elected, I bundled up all the information I had and took off for Washington. Gave it all to him. Left it right there in his office. He seemed so *nice*, so *believing!*

He even prayed with me. I left there that day feeling so relieved, like I'd finally finished my task and could forget about it. Oh, I was expecting repercussions, of course, but I figured they'd all be out in the open. Testimony before Congress and that sort of thing. I thought I was ready for all that. What I wasn't ready for was to be attacked by two flying saucers while I was driving home." Carrie paused in her story and looked over at Trisha. "You're wondering why I'm still here to tell you all this, aren't you."

"I'm just listening."

"OK," Carrie said, watching Trisha carefully for her reaction as she said, "I was rescued by angels."

When she didn't go right on, Trisha asked, "You saw them?"

"Yes I did," Carrie answered confidently. "And they were beautiful. They grabbed up those spacecraft—I'm talking about real flying saucers, here, big things!—and just made them disappear. Just like that." Again Carrie paused, waiting for Trisha's reaction.

"And then?"

Carrie shrugged. "I went home. My mother's house, really. I stayed away from my own apartment for weeks. And I waited. Nothing else happened. No more flying saucers—and no more angels, either. And no congressional committees or public statements from Congressman Wilkenson. I didn't go back to GAI. I hadn't planned to in any case; I'd already cleaned out my desk. After a couple of weeks I got a job with a temp agency in town and stayed on with a company I temped for. I've been there ever since. Have moved around town a lot. I start to get suspicious that someone's coming for me, start getting up at odd hours of the night to look out the windows. I was just getting ready to move again. . . ." She gestured around at the boxes.

"And the congressman? Nothing? No help?"

"He never even returned my phone calls. Didn't return my documentation, either. I was so stupid! I should have made copies of everything, but I was trying to get the burden off of myself, you know? Once I gave the materials to him I figured *everyone* would eventually have copies, that it would be in all the papers. It didn't happen. It was like *nothing* had ever happened—although once I realized Wilkenson had been silenced, I did expect to see government officials at my door any day, come to arrest me for industrial spying. That's why I got so nervous when you showed me your badge." Carrie smiled wanly.

"And—the Sherry Lynn Ward program? How did that happen."

"Oh. That." Carrie gave an exasperated grunt. "My sister watches that show, and she'd seen them advertise for anyone who had been abducted by flying saucers to come on and tell their story. After all those months of nothing, I'd finally told my sister what had happened, so she called me and asked if I wanted to go on this program, tell the world what I'd seen, expose it all. I asked her if she was nuts, but I did pray about it, and finally decided that I should call them and go on. Boy, was *that* a mistake! That woman is a real witch!"

"A witch?" Trisha asked.

"Oh, I don't mean like a 'witch' witch—although who knows!" Carrie shrugged. "What I mean is, she talked to me before the show, really serious and sweet, patting me on the knee, telling me I would do fine, just to tell what I'd seen, etc. Did the same with the two other women who were on with me. But then when we were actually on the stage and the cameras were running, she wouldn't let me tell my own story. Instead, she just asked questions and made statements that would make me look like an idiot. She made fun of me and got the audience laughing at me, all the time pretending to be a kindly, right-thinking person who was trying to

171

help me see how foolish I was to believe in such things. She had a psychiatrist on the show to 'analyze' why we women were having these 'experiences,' as she called them. It was awful. I wanted to choke my sister."

Trisha had listened to all this carefully. "But you said you felt like God had wanted you to go on?"

"I did. I guess I missed the signal there, didn't I?"

"I don't know," Trisha said, glancing down at her watch as she added, "you did what you thought you should."

"That's true. It's just that . . ."

"Yes?" Trisha prompted as she seemed to falter.

"I just wonder what it was all for. I mean, if God was leading me to explore all this, and if He was leading me to turn the information over to the congressman, and if He *did* intend for me to go on that show—then why hasn't anything worthwhile come out of it all?"

Trisha looked back at her blankly. She'd been gauging the time to the airport, realizing she *could* make that flight to Atlanta. She'd not really anticipated the question. Still, she tried to answer it, not as a U.S. marshal, but as a Christian sister. "Who knows how God might have used it—right? Maybe there was someone else out there that needed to hear what you had to say, even if Sherry Lynn *did* just want to use you."

Carrie smiled, rather sadly. "You're very kind. I really wish I could have helped you with what you're looking for. . . ."

"You have helped," Trisha said, standing up. "A lot." And that was true. She'd certainly verified some things Jack had told Gloria. The trouble was—what could she do about any of this? Right now she had to catch a plane to Atlanta.

* * *

Jack had no idea which direction to go to return to the saucer. He'd run down these hallways in terror, not watching where he was going. As Ben escorted him back through the castle, his mind was still filled with the heavenly vision—much to Ben's chagrin.

"You've got to put it out of your mind, Jack."

"Why?"

"Just . . . pretend that it never happened."

"But it did."

"I said *pretend!*"

"I don't know why you're worried about it," Jack responded as they stepped back out into the great hall. It was still filled with dust and smoke, and part of the roof was missing, letting snow drift in as well. Jack eyed the walls above them with distrust; they looked like they could collapse any time. He saw no Romans, however.

"They've been taken back to their camp. We won."

"Who's we?" Jack snorted.

"Just . . . be cool, Jack," Ben whispered as they climbed the saucer gangplank. "That's all I ask—"

"But why should—" The words froze on his lips as he stepped inside. The rest of his body froze too. Three UMMO, their black shells glistening in the unnatural light, stood five feet away from him, staring at him. A visceral revulsion shuddered through him, triggering his gag reflex. Nausea seized his gut. Were they about to sting him again?

"This way," Ben muttered, dragging him backward, for the three UMMO blocked the corridor to their cabins. Ben was pulling him the other way, taking the long way around the craft to reach their rooms—and to avoid the malevolent bugs. "That's why," the boy snarled at him under his breath when they were on the far side of the ship.

"What are they—"

"—doing here?" Ben finished for him. "They're here to plan strategy with the Boss. They're here for a premeeting to plan their defense. We've all been summoned to appear, to give account for this war they started in the Overlord's absence."

"Who is this Overlord?" Jack whispered. "Satan himself?"

"I don't think so. One of his closest captains, I think. He's the one who possesses the Ultrarch of the Ultrastructure. He got disembodied when the latest Ultrarch was killed, and now he's back. Ah, could we talk about this later?" By this time they'd reached the doors to their cabins—and come back into sight of the bugs. The three UMMO now faced this way, staring at Jack as if they wanted to devour him. He ducked quickly inside his door, with Ben right behind him.

He stood beside his bed, trying to still the pounding of his heart. From angels to demons in a matter of moments. Why was he here? "Because they brought you," Angel Gloria had told him. And God had permitted it.

"Calm down, Jack. They're not here for you."

But he couldn't be calm. Despite his awareness of the Spirit's presence, despite his assurance of angelic guardians watching over his shoulder, the feel of naked evil pervaded the place. "There's terrible evil aboard this ship, Ben. Enormous evil."

"So what else is new? I don't like them either, Jack, but we'll have to get used to them. There's a new alliance now."

"I thought these two groups were mortal enemies!"

"It's what I've been trying to tell you! They've been summoned before the high council of the Ultrastructure. They're in deep trouble, and they're trying to cover their backsides! And would you *please* stop thinking about her?"

Jack's thoughts had shifted back to his encounter with the angel. "You saw her, Ben. You know what's true!"

"I'm telling you, Jack, they can sense her on you! That's why they were staring at us, so just, please, put her out of your mind!"

"Can *they* read minds?" Jack asked, his knees growing weak.

"They can read Guardian influence, of *that* you may be certain! Now be quiet, I'm trying to concentrate." Ben closed his eyes—and immediately began to writhe on the bed as if in pain.

Jack shook his head. "Why, Ben? Why fill your mind with their garbage? Don't you realize the more time you spend in the thoughts of these creatures the more like them you become?"

"Shut up! They're arguing over what to do with you!"

Jack shut up.

The conversation between demons took place on the control deck, a floor above Jack's cabin and on the far side of the ship. Nevertheless, Ben could hear the conversation as if he sat in the midst of the creatures. He began to relay to Jack what he heard, like a UN staff member on a head-phone doing simultaneous translation. One of the UMMO spoke for all of them.

"We shall all be punished. I, for one, do not relish that experience again—do you?"

Baal responded for the Grays. "I do not. So let's reason together, and quickly! There must be a way we can show that our past competition can benefit all!"

"You have suggestions?"

"That depends. What have we accomplished?" Baal was asking.

"*We* have collected genetic specimens from every strata of history," the UMMO spokesman said. "We have collected scientists—"

"*Our* scientists!" Baal exploded.

"They belong to all of us. Or had you forgotten?"

"We groomed them. . . ." a more subdued Baal responded bitterly.

175

"For what?" the UMMO taunted. "To build yourself a better shell? To make yourself 'pretty' for your human slaves? Look at us! We are terrifying to these creatures, as terrifying in form today as we once were to their great-grandfathers who called us monsters! They belong to us, not we to them—or have you forgotten that, too, in your haste to please! *We* have no need to win their applause. We need only to humble them in terror, and they will do what we demand without question!"

"You're fools if you really believe that," Baal snarled back. "This generation of humans mocks at terror regularly. They don't believe in you. And if they *did* they'd think they could battle you. They constantly make movies about fighting your hideous form—and in their movies, they always win."

"UMMO does not like being called fools."

"Then wise up! The Overlord will call you that himself unless you listen to me and think clearly! Perhaps the peasants you deal with are greatly impressed with your shiny black shells, but the North Americans and Europeans must be *won*. They serve their own interests alone. They don't even believe the Exalted One exists, much less us! And we have the power to feed their self-interests, to give them whatever they think they want. But listen—all you UMMO, listen to me! *Everything* in that society depends on appearance! That's why we've sought to make ourselves attractive to them!"

"Is that why you harbor among you those who talk to Guardians? Because you're seeking the long lost beauty?"

Jack shivered as Ben relayed this to him.

Baal answered sharply. "There's a reason for that one's presence. We began to find it difficult to make use of the time travel technology. The Guardians blocked us. They destroyed one of our disks over New Mexico, even allowing humans to recover the body of Kundas. We wanted no repeat of that! So we carry that one with us in order to be permitted to penetrate deep time."

"*We* had no trouble finding you. We had no trouble coming here. Do you think we carry with us such a one? Are you saying the Guardians permitted *us?*"

"I have no explanation for that. I'm telling you what I know."

"But you know the Guardians have been here, in this place, in palpable form! We could smell it coming aboard this saucer. Perhaps you think to win some advantage with the other side? How do you think the Overlord will regard such a practice? We UMMO know. He's going to rip you out of that sack of gray flesh and chew you slowly." There was laughter from the UMMO after that statement, laughter so maliciously savage Ben could barely stand to relate it to Jack.

"You think *you'll* escape their vengeance?" Baal was arguing in the face of their glee. "We had four of these new craft built, at tremendous expense! It was you that stole one, blew another to wreckage, and lost the third! You think the Overlord won't punish you for that?"

"Apparently you forget: drug profits helped pay for those craft. Our profits. It was *you* who stole them, thinking to monopolize their use. You started this war with your greediness!"

"And *you* destroyed one of the vessels with your stupid violence!"

"UMMO does not like to be called stupid."

There was a face-off then in the room above them, in which both sides caucused and planned horrible vengeance upon the other. Ben just rolled his eyes as he described this and propped his head up on one elbow. Jack realized his legs were aching. He'd been standing stiff as a board throughout this exchange. Now he found the edge of the bed with his hand and sat down. "The UMMO are worried that Baal will outsmart them," Ben explained to him in a whisper. "He's had far more dealings with the technological mind-set in recent centuries."

UMMO broke the deadlock at last. "UMMO must consider all options," the speaker for UMMO began. "What do you suggest we say together to the High Council?"

"We'll tell them we've been scouring time for genetic material," Baal responded. "You've been doing that, right? And we Grays say that we've been grooming scientists to manipulate that material, not just to give us the more appealing forms we need to control these creatures, but to realize the ultimate goal itself—"

"We have all been blocked from that goal!" UMMO interrupted. "We've been unable to get these boxes off the planet! *You* control the government of the United States; why can't you steal us a shuttle? That was the plan!"

"That was *not* the plan! The plan was to maneuver the boxes aboard successive shuttles with the full cooperation of the military authorities! Besides, there are other space programs! Ask the Osiris group why *they* can't provide a vehicle."

"Theirs keep blowing up."

"So would ours if we tried to take one by force! Be reasonable! The Guardians will blow up any shuttle we steal! They may blow up any of our time boxes whenever they choose! That's why we have to use them while we have them to accomplish that *other* goal. . . ."

"To render this rock eternally our own? A tiny prison . . ."

"But once it is ours, and ours alone, then we will be free to develop our own spacecraft free of any Guardian interference!"

"And how do you propose to do that?"

"Those scientists of ours that you just plucked out of time? They were happily working on the genetic keys that will allow *us* to furnish what only the . . . the . . . the other side has been able to offer. But since you've snatched them away from their homes and laboratories, the lost productivity may never be made up! The human outrage at their disappearance may bring the Guardians down upon us all! You must return them all without any memory of their abduction, as soon after their moment of disappearance as you can! Otherwise, who knows how the human element in the Ultrastructure might respond!"

"This worries you, does it?" UMMO sneered. "You're afraid of what the little creatures might think?"

"I'm afraid of *failure,* and what it will cost us all! I'm afraid of the Overlord! I'm afraid of the Exalted One above him! I'm afraid of the Guardians! I'm afraid of the end time! And unless you truly are fools then you fear these things too!"

Once again there was a discussion among UMMO. Ben waited it by rolling on his back and peering absently at the ceiling. Jack used the silence to pray.

"Watch that, Jack," Ben snapped, whirling around and pointing a warning finger. "I'm telling you—they *will* come and get you—" He broke off, listening, then glanced at Jack. "They're talking again," he murmured, and began again to relay the conversation.

"UMMO will tell the Overlord what you suggest," UMMO agreed. "But can't we do more, as well? Consider. We are here in a time period that proved so miserable in its outcome. Oh, you and your cohorts were up here in the European forests, happily sending bands of savages down against UMMO's world empire. It was UMMO who had the technological advantage then, UMMO that prodded these creatures toward civilization. And for what? The other side used *our* roads to spread their message! Our emperors kept trying to stamp them out, but they kept spreading their 'good news' like a contagion! While you were taking advantage of our internal weakness, they kept skulking around the catacombs beneath the city, meeting, plotting—expanding. Infecting us!"

"And whose fault was that?" Baal roared. "You were the gods of Rome! You had the responsibility to stamp it out!"

"And you could have helped! Instead, you laughed at UMMO and played at being gods up here in the northern forests until they infected you too!"

"We never thought it would survive your purges. You failed!"

"And we were punished for it! Centuries of suffering, which UMMO does not want to repeat."

"What are you suggesting?"

"That we finish that task now, together, before returning to face the Overlord! We know where their pockets of believers clustered. Why not simply remove them from the stream of time—dispose of them early? Make *them* a genetic research project! Allow the Guardians to claim their souls before they have the chance to spread this contagion any further—"

"As if the Guardians will permit *that!*" Baal interrupted, livid at UMMO's stupidity. "If we could, why not simply go backward in time another three hundred years and stop the debacle in Bethlehem before it starts!"

"You mean prevent the birth entirely?" the speaker for UMMO responded, pondering the thought as if it were new.

"Idiots! We tried all that, don't you remember? You think *He* would permit *that?*"

"No . . . but perhaps . . . going further back still."

"We tried that, too, at Babel, and *you* shot down our tower!"

"A different time. A different plan . . ."

"We tried to destroy His chosen ones in Egypt when we held the whole nation of them enslaved, but we failed there too!"

"You failed. That was your operation—yours and the Osiris group. But we had our own warriors at the time, and they were nearly invincible. Why not make them completely so now?"

"What are you suggesting?" Baal was screaming at the stupid bugs. "You want to give cannons to the Assyrians?"

As Ben relayed this statement, Jack couldn't help himself. He burst out laughing. Ben leapt across the bed to grab both sides of Jack's head and jerk it around to face his, but it was too late. Shock, bewilderment—resignation played across the boy's features. Jack just stared at him, his own heart once again beginning to pound.

The cabin door slid open with a bang.

# Chapter Twelve

*Summoned to appear*

It happened so quickly. One moment they were both sitting on the bed in Jack's room, the next they were being dragged into the corridor, around the curving hallway and up into the control deck, being pummeled, kicked, shaken, and hammered at each step. Jack felt the itchy, insectoid claws of an UMMO wrapped around his neck—smelled the sulfurous stench of the thing's shell. Then he was thrown to the floor of the control room, Ben hitting it right beside him, as Baal loomed fiercely above them both. A spear of pain jabbed into the base of Jack's neck just above his spine, causing him to writhe onto his back and look up at the circle of demons closing around them. Baal thrust his furious thoughts into both his head and Ben's.

"So, young Ben," Baal seethed. "So you can read *us* now, too, can you?"

"UMMO does not like being mocked," Jack heard—and the *feel* of these words in his brain, the first that any UMMO had pointed directly into him, was unlike any communication he'd ever received. The thoughts themselves were almost metallic—knifelike, totally devoid of any hint of human warmth. By contrast Baal's pronouncements seemed like those of an angry uncle, as he raged on.

"How long have you been reading us, Ben? All this time? Ever since I brought you aboard, befriended you, made you what you are? And what have you been *doing* with this information? Revealing it to your confidante here, obviously, for his entertainment. No—" He interrupted himself, speaking to one of the UMMO who was tipping back up onto its hind legs and thrusting its abdomen forward to sting. "These two belong to me. I'll deal with them."

The UMMO had reached out to grasp Jack's head in its stinking pincers and was saying, "This one was ours until you stole him from us."

Baal thrust the claws away and got between them. "He was mine first. I simply took him back."

"With the boy's help. Yet the boy seeks to make fools of *all* of us."

"An oversight," Baal argued with a dismissive flip of his hand. "I didn't know until now that Ben had enlarged his gift."

"UMMO will take them both."

"They belong to *me*. I'll deal with them."

Jack watched this battle over his body with an odd sense of detachment. Shock and pain rendered him unable to react as anything other than an observer. The terrifying implications of this nightmarish debate were beyond belief. He was denying to himself that any of this was happening.

But it was. "You'll answer for this," the UMMO threatened Baal.

"Then let me answer."

"They both must die."

"Now that would be a rather swift and painless resolution for both of them, wouldn't it?" Baal sneered—and Jack shivered at the icy cruelty that glistened behind the demon's thoughts. "The man goes straight into the hands of the Guardians, and thence to . . . ?" Baal left that destination dangling, implied but unvoiced, and turned to Ben. "And the boy's gift—which is obviously considerable, even more so than I'd realized—would be lost to all of us. Is that wise thinking? Leave them to me. I'll take immense pleasure in punishing them both."

"UMMO will have our piece of them."

"Very well," Baal said expansively, diplomatically. "You shall have a piece of each—but I'll have mine first. And they will not be killed. The boy is too valuable to lose—even if he *does* need a lesson in manners." Baal turned his black, almond-shaped eyes to gaze down coldly at Jack. "And I can think of *many* ways to make the man suffer for his arrogance—well, short of the blissful release his death would provide him—and they shall be applied."

The invisible vice on the back of Jack's neck suddenly clamped tighter, and he grunted. His forehead suddenly seemed to swell. Ice picks jabbed in at both temples. "Does your head hurt, Dr. Brennen?" Baal asked solicitously. "Ah, that marvelous professorial brain. Is it feeling—*full?*" Baal turned around to face him squarely and directed all his sadistic savagery down into Jack's aching face. "Are you so certain you have friends in high places? Where are they now? Your 'angel,' your personal guardian? Where is *she* now? You think she would dare show her face in the midst of"—Baal swept his arms wide to include the others—"such a gathering?"

Baal shook a long, slender finger before Jack's nose. "I've warned you many times before not to take me lightly. And yet you laugh at us? Your masters? Isn't that foolish, Dr. Brennen? You've been reading too much C. S. Lewis, I fear. Wasn't it he who wrote 'The best way to chase the devil away is to laugh at him'—or some such nonsense? Feel like laughing now, Dr. Brennen? Come on. Laugh for us!" Though Jack didn't believe it could, the cramping in his head grew in intensity. "Can't?" Baal teased. "Are we 'devils' no longer hilarious?" Just as Jack thought his eyeballs would pop out from the inner pressure being exerted on their sockets, Baal rounded about to jerk Ben up off the floor.

"And you, my boy, are the cause of this, of course. You were the one who brought him aboard. Foolish of me, to indulge your whim. Ah, but you were so gifted, I thought! In need of diversion from the difficult task of living inside other people's minds. Was I being—how shall I say this delicately—too *kind?*" Jack couldn't tear his gaze away from Baal's obsidian eyes. His own pain was easing off into mere soreness—but what was happening inside Ben's head? For the boy stared upward, a look of utter anguish on his face, as Baal obviously did something—*awful* to him.

"How is *this* then, Ben? Are you reading my mind? Are you reading all our minds? What do you see there, hmmm? We can crush your soul, Ben—crush your talented mind to worthlessness, simply by thinking of the most commonplace things—commonplace to *us*—things that give us pleasure. Read our minds, Ben, go ahead! What do you see in *my* mind? Didn't know I was capable of such hatred? Or did you? Have you read it there, Ben, my hatred of you? How I despise your childish conceit, how I loathe your fragile body? Did you know I can stop your heart?" Baal reached out a hand in a sudden gesture, and Ben grabbed his chest and gave a plaintive little squeak—then a gasp. "There," Baal cackled. "Terrified? Felt death's cold fingers scrabbling at your chest, didn't you? Or did you know that I can stop your breathing?" Hoisting Ben high with one hand, Baal turned his other gray palm upward, his bony hand a gripping claw, and Ben choked and grabbed for his throat. For a few seconds he froze, both hands clasped around his neck, his tongue lolling forward—then Baal dropped him to his knees. Again Ben gasped for breath and flopping back on his heels wheezed in three quick breaths and rolled down to the floor again, panting.

"Yes," Baal snarled, stooping over him, thrusting his face down into Ben's, closer with every shouted thought. "Go ahead and suck the air into your lungs, you stupid boy, and listen to my thinking! Can you see in my mind how I mock your feeble hope to be free of me? You'll never be free of me, Ben. I own your soul. I will chew it in eternity, and you'll long for a body with lungs and a voice just to be able to scream! You are worthless to me, Ben. Your *gift*—now *that* has value. Look into my demon mind, Ben, and see how I intend to wring every possible advantage I can out of you, every stolen thought, every borrowed experience you can glean from the minds of others for my purposes, and when at last I need it no more, see here in my mind how I will drop you, screaming, into the void!" Ben was rolling on the floor now, whimpering, his hands laced together and clamped onto the top of his head.

Baal straightened up then and backed away, gesturing downward. "Look at him writhing there, you of UMMO. You want your piece of him? Push your thoughts into his tiny human brain! Let him *truly* read us!" Baal stooped again, his face back into Ben's. "You want to sample our thoughts, boy? You want to sample madness?" Ben screamed as Baal continued. "Do you read, here in my mind, that I have the power to leave you tottering on the brink of this mental pit for as long as your tiny life endures—and that I shall enjoy every moment of doing so? Here, Ben! Gorge yourself on our madness!"

And Jack could take no more. He suddenly sprang upward, like a crouching tackle firing out on a linebacker, and slammed Baal backward shouting, "Stop it! Stop hurting him!" For such a powerful presence, Baal's gray body was incredibly light and fragile. Jack was surprised to see he had knocked it airborne across the room. Surprised—and a little embarrassed.

The UMMO surged toward him en masse, but Baal rebounded off a wall and back onto his feet, and rushed back toward Jack, again thrusting the UMMO aside. His words were gleeful inside Jack's brain. They tumbled out in a torrent. "Ah, *here* is the warrior at last! Rising to rescue the lad, are we? Ready finally to do 'spiritual warfare' with we 'minions of hell'? How very brave, how very *sacrificial* of you! Ever do battle with demons, Dr. Brennen? Think you know the tricks? Go ahead. Try them. Battle us. Exorcise us from this ship! Or do you need a bell, book, and candle? That's a quaint little ritual; do you know it? Do they still teach that one in seminary? Or are you of a more modern sort? 'The something something rebuke you,' isn't that how it goes? What's the matter, Dr. Brennen? Are we too many for you, is that it? Are we 'legion,' perhaps?" Baal stepped back into the center of the control room and spread his long arms wide in invitation. "Come, Brethren! I offer you a *feast* of this weakling spiritual warrior!"

All the adrenaline of his spontaneous rescue attempt had now drained away. Jack stared into the faces of the creatures ranged before him and saw only one face reflected there upon all of them—the face he'd seen on Ben—the accusing, advancing, attacking face of the Adversary. He mumbled the only words of defense that came to mind. "Touch not the Lord's anointed. . . ." He said it without conviction, almost with embarrassment. He remembered watching a charlatan evangelist on television defend himself from an investigative reporter's allegations with this phrase. He'd thought it sounded phony then. It sounded phony on his own lips now.

And not just to himself. The demons howled with delight. Inside his head he heard the shrieking guffaws of ridicule, direct from the fire-red rim of the demon pit. Humiliation flushed over him. Scorn poured down upon him. Shame welled up inside him. Accusation thundered down upon him. Confusion jolted through him like an earthquake of the heart, rocking his soul's foundations. . . .

One night in Africa, when he was still an unmarried missionary, his spirit tiptoed along the edge of this same pit of despair. He sought to count his blessings and counted curses instead. He thought of his misery, of his loneliness, of his frustrations and his failures. And he doubted. He let himself doubt. He'd never done that before. He had *always* believed, from the very first moment he knew that Jesus' sufferings on the cross had been intended for *him,* and not just for grown-ups. In the moment he'd understood, at seven years of age, that he, too, was a sinner in need of Christ's salvation, he had believed. He had never before doubted the existence of God, nor God's love for him, nor his own salvation, nor the accuracy of Scripture, nor the promise of heaven. But on this night, as an African who lived just over the wall from him played a nerve-fraying record over and over and over while he struggled to pray—Jack had doubted. He was laying on his back on his bed—and in that moment it was as if the bed gave way and he tumbled, dizzily, backward into the pit. What if it wasn't true? What if it was all a lie? What if Jesus was just a very good man, as Schweitzer and some other so-called Christians wrote? What if there was no God? What if he'd lost his faith? What if he'd wasted these years spent telling others about Jesus, what if there was nothing to it? All these things he thought and felt in those seemingly endless moments of spiritual deadfall. And then—he was caught. Like some tightrope walker who had lost his balance and fallen from the wire, only to be snagged near ground level by the safety net furled beneath him—God had caught him. And the Spirit of God said—almost audibly—"I've got you."

Now, once again, Jack fell into the net. "The Spirit is with you always," Angel Gloria had reminded him. And in this moment, under assault by supernatural specters who loathed him, it was the Spirit that spoke from Jack's depths, from that place inside him "too deep for words," to trumpet, as if from Gabriel's own horn, a thunderous, faith-filled "Touch not the Lord's anointed!" Jack could not defend himself. Then again—he didn't have to.

And the demons were stopped. At that very moment they stopped. Jack opened his eyes—he hadn't even really known they were closed—and looked around the control room. He really expected to see angels filling the place. There were none. Only the demons looking back at him—hateful, spite-filled, furious—but muzzled.

Then, before any of them could take full measure of what had just happened, there was another presence in the room—a dark, horrible presence far more menacing than any Gray or UMMO could ever aspire to be—that said, "Now this is an interesting tableau." It was peering at Jack with something like a distasteful respect—or rather, at the Spirit in Jack. Jack gazed back.

This was clearly a being far more powerful—and more evil—than any Jack had ever encountered. And from the way the other demons fawned on him, struggled to get near him, to explain themselves to him, almost slobbering on him in sloppy adulation, Jack knew. This was the Overlord.

The being almost smiled in grim acceptance of Jack's recognition—then began to brush off the demons struggling to cling to him. "Stop that," he commanded, and they did.

Immediately. Then he looked again at Jack. "Why is this reeking creature aboard this ship? The stench on him is unbearable! Who's responsible for this?"

As one, all the rest of the assembled horde, Grays and UMMO alike, pointed claws or fingers at Baal, who was trying to shrink himself into the wall.

"Of course," the being snarled, with a glare at Baal that would have toasted rocks. Then he turned regally, surveying everyone in the room. "You were all summoned to appear. We're waiting. Why the delay?"

No one dared speak at first. At last one of the UMMO responded: "We have been—blocked."

"Blocked?" said the dark presence with a fierce smile, and his burning eyes came back to Jack. "By this little fellow? Or the one there on the floor?" Then it looked back at the UMMO that clustered together in apprehension. "Or were you rather blocked by your fear of answering the charges laid before you? You have kept us waiting!" The thing chuckled wickedly and added, "I think you're all going to be very sorry about that. . . ." Then the being's eyes blazed hot, and he snarled, "The Exalted himself has sent me to fetch you, and *I'm* not happy about *that*. When the Exalted is finished with you, then I will take my piece. And the longer you delay, the more I'll be entitled to take. . . ."

Though it didn't actually lick its lips—it had no lips, that Jack could actually see—there was that *feeling* from the dark presence, as if it contemplated these that quailed before him as delicious morsels to be slowly savored. Then the thing briskly finished delivering his message: "I think you'd best busy yourselves with your little controls there, and see if you can't beat me back." As instantaneously as he'd come, he was gone.

The whole room leapt into feverish activity. The Grays present dashed to positions at control panels. The UMMO lurched for the door—but were very careful to give Jack a wide berth. They skirted him cautiously, as a recently burned child might avoid a fire, keeping a wary eye upon it. Not until they were out of the room did Jack become conscious that Ben was clutching him around the legs. He reached down and pulled the teenager to his feet.

"Leave the boy!" Baal shouted, and he blocked the door, his immense rage once more in evidence.

Jack ignored Baal's command as he slung one of Ben's arms over his shoulder and bent to grab the boy behind the knees. He lifted him off of his feet and started forward, saying only, "I'm taking him to his room." As he walked toward Baal he was praying, moving his feet by confident faith, and at the last moment Baal stepped aside, making no move to stop him.

Once back into Ben's cabin, Jack laid Ben on the bed and sat there holding him as the boy sobbed and sobbed. What Ben had seen in the minds of the demons Jack could only imagine—and he didn't choose to try. There was nothing he could say, and he knew it. Instead he just gave the comfort of his presence and his closeness, and Ben took it from him. Gradually the sobbing lessened as Ben read the peace in Jack's mind and absorbed it. Finally he was able to speak and muttered through hoarse gasps, "Promise you won't ever leave me!"

"I promise," Jack said—and he meant it.

At that moment he meant it. When at last the boy slept, exhausted by his ordeal, Jack had time to reflect on that promise—and regret it. He realized he hadn't been thinking. For Jack had made other promises in the past. He had other obligations—responsibilities that took precedence over his promise to Ben. And it came to him as he sat there watching over Ben that he may have just planted the seed for Ben's betrayal. . . .

\* \* \*

Henry Ritter sat in the cockpit of his private plane with his pilot, cursing at the weather, the delays, the DEA, the city fathers of Tampa Bay, and everything else that came to mind. They'd been delayed on the ground for an hour, and he knew there would be still longer delays in the sky over Atlanta. And he was late. He had a deal to close, and drug dealers were notoriously time-conscious. "This could get us both killed, you realize that?" he snapped at the pilot, who had heard this all before a dozen times and just gazed stolidly out the window. Henry ran his hand through his thick red hair and fired off another string of four-letter observations, there being nothing else he could do in the situation. Then suddenly he shut up, his eyes staring out over the right wing of the aircraft. "Uh-oh," he muttered ominously. This finally drew his pilot's attention.

"What?"

"Set her down."

"What?" the pilot said again, his voice rising on the end of the word this time in astonishment.

"I said set her down. Now."

"Why? Where?" the pilot frowned, dipping the left wing to glimpse the wintry farmland below.

"Anywhere! I don't care! Just get us down!"

"But—" the pilot started to protest again—then gasped.

"And *that's* why," Henry Ritter growled as a saucer pulled into formation with them twenty feet from the pilot's left wing. The man gasped again. "There's another one over on this side," Henry added casually, looking out his own window again.

The small jet began dropping quickly as the pilot searched the ground before him for a possible landing strip. "Dirt road?"

"Dirt road, farm road, interstate for all I care. Surely you've made enough jungle landings to handle a touchdown in south Georgia!"

In moments the pilot was angling toward a country road, hoping they weren't about to meet some farmer on a tractor coming the other way. He was suddenly grateful it was winter instead of the time of spring plowing. He was *very* aware that the saucers on either side of him were matching his moves perfectly, as if they'd flown in precision formation with him for years. He bounced the wheels twice, making sure he kept right between the fencerows on either side. The saucers split, one shooting forward to hover before him, the other dropping out of sight behind. "Boss," he asked as they rolled to a stop. "Are you dealing with *those* guys?"

"In this business," Henry Ritter observed philosophically, "you deal with whoever's got the product and got the money." Then he snapped out instructions for the pilot to fly on to Atlanta, tell the driver at the airport to warn of the waiting clients, and then to fly on to New Mexico and wait. "You know. That place in the desert where you've picked me up before—near Santa Fe? Let me get outta here," he added to himself as he hopped out of the now motionless plane and dropped heavily to the asphalt. The pilot heard Henry cursing as he limped rapidly under the hovering saucer. A moment later the thing shot skyward, and Henry Ritter was gone.

\* \* \*

Ronald Pearson adjusted his tie as he walked out of the elevator and through the columned lobby of the University Club of New York. Everyone had to wear a tie at all times in this stuffy old place, and Ron always checked his at this point to insure it was straight. He didn't like people looking at him, and if you didn't dress correctly in here they would stare at you in disapproval. As he walked toward the door that opened onto Fifty-fourth Street, the doorman—a friendly gray-haired Irishman with a large red nose—smiled at him and said, "Your car is waiting, Mr. Pearson."

Ron stopped, and looked at him. "But I didn't order a car—"

The doorman raised a puzzled eyebrow, shrugged, and pointed out the glass door. Beyond the awning and the sidewalk Ron saw a black limousine—and felt a quiver of nervousness in his belly. He was scheduled to meet a trio of well-connected Sicilians at Sparks, a few blocks away. He didn't like the idea of them sending a car to get him—

The chauffeur stepped out and opened the back door with a flourish, and Ron's whole perspective shifted. This was not a mob driver, and he knew now that he would not be making his luncheon date after all. He'd seen the man before, of course. His name was Jeffrey, and he'd long been Pearson's contact inside the Ultrastructure. Jeffrey had picked him up many times before, always dressed in this same black suit. The chauffeur's cap, however, was a ridiculous touch.

He tipped the doorman with a false smile, then walked briskly out and got into the back seat. "Right *now?*" he leaned forward and murmured as Jeffrey got back in the car.

"Right now," he heard as the limousine turned right on Fifth Avenue and started the tortuous process of getting out of the city at noon. Ron Pearson knew this for certain: they would *not* be going to LaGuardia.

\* \* \*

In her Burbank studio, Sherry Lynn Ward was barking orders at her coproducers. She impatiently endured the fussy attention of her makeup man as she reviewed the notes for the coming show. Child molestation. She hated shows on child molestation; they were so—dull. But they did rend hearts and light up the switchboard, and that was the name of the ratings game: audience participation.

Suddenly her cell phone rang, and she grabbed it off the dressing table and snapped, "I'm about to go on! What?"

The line was dead—and her cell phone was still ringing. That *other* cell phone, always kept in her purse. She dived under the makeup man's arm, grabbed her purse, and fished it out as fast as she could. "Ruth!" she bellowed as loudly as she could, then flipped it open and answered breathlessly, "Yes?" her whole demeanor entirely changed. As she listened, her eyes grew wide, then she frowned at the makeup man and fluttered her hand furiously as she mouthed, "Get Ruth now!" He dashed out, and her producer dashed in, just as Sherry Lynn Ward said, "You've gotta be kidding! NOW? The audience is already in place, they're being warmed up, I'm about to go on!"

Ruth waited, watched, and listened as Sherry Lynn said, "Yes. . . . Right. . . . Five minutes, on the roof."

She snapped the phone shut, her face gone white under the makeup. Then she looked at Ruth, who was pointing at her watch and waving her toward the set and the audience beyond. "Can't do it, Ruth. Gotta go. Tell them I just got violently ill."

"But Sherry Lynn, you can't do this! The network—"

"Can't you see I'm sick!" Sherry Lynn screamed, scooping a hairbrush up off the table and throwing it against the wall. "Run a backup tomorrow! We've got, what? Six in the can? That one with the male strippers." She was already grabbing up her purse, coat, and filofax and heading out toward the back of the soundstage.

"But you said you wanted to fix the part where you—"

"Run it as is! The audience'll love it!" Her heels clattered as she trotted up a metal-grid staircase toward the lighting booth and the doorway out to the roof.

Ruth was still protesting. "What are we gonna do with this slate of guests—?"

Sherry Lynn stopped on the walkway above and leaned over the bare rail. "Listen, Ruth," she called down with a charming smile. "I'll bring a terrific show back with me, I promise." Then she was out the fire-exit door with a bang.

Ruth stared up at where her star had just disappeared. Then she blinked twice, murmured, *"Hard Copy* will have a field day with this one," and turned her attention to the unenviable task of canceling a major taping.

There were cancellations all around the globe that day—and people rousted out of their beds in Sidney, in Tokyo, in Kazakistan, and Iran. The Ultrastructure had been summoned to appear.

# Chapter Thirteen

*The ultrastructure*

Jack woke with a jerk and was immediately alert. He was in his own cabin, on his own bed, still dressed in the robe, skins, and boots of Valhalla. Something, however, was different.

He bounded off the bed and quickly walked to the closet—still no clothes. *Have to find some soon,* he thought, then forgot about that as he moved quickly out his door and into Ben's cabin.

Ben was gone. Jack paced around the room a moment, thinking what to do next—just then he realized what had changed. The saucer was still. There was no hum of whatever esoteric engine powered the craft. He bolted out the door and into the corridor, quickly making the circuit of the craft and seeing no one: no Grays, no men in black. He stepped into the elevator and rose quickly to the control deck, finding it, too, was empty.

Jack scanned the control panel, suddenly impelled to try to take off while he had the chance. *Ridiculous,* he thought to himself immediately. He had no idea how to fly a plane, much less such a sophisticated piece of equipment that navigated not only in space, but in time. *Still,* he thought as he looked down at the range of dials and levers, *perhaps I need to watch more closely the next time I'm in here.*

Where had everyone gone? He ducked back into the elevator and down a deck, then in toward the center of the craft and the entry bay. It was open, the gangplank down, and he walked out to find that the saucer was parked in a huge hanger—underground, no doubt. He stopped to have a look around, chilled to see not just this saucer but a dozen others like it ranged beside it. Nor was this the only design. Across the way he saw an even greater number of UMMO craft—bulkier, darker, squarer-shaped vessels, including perhaps the one he'd walked into during that fateful blizzard. There were still other models lined up down the way, including three of the time boxes—the three remaining time boxes of those he'd first seen years ago near Huntsville. Years ago in his time. How old were they in actual use? Months? Or centuries?

This was some in-gathering. Jack guessed the whole gang must be here. He'd noticed immediately that the ships were being guarded by men in black—who had in turn noticed him. But none accosted him. They just watched him, all of them, as he strolled past these silent, waiting vehicles, wondering where he was supposed to go.

At last one of the dark-suited guards caught his eye and gestured to a distant corner of the hanger, back the other way. Jack smiled his thanks but received no acknowledgment as he walked past the man in that direction. A door opened onto a corridor that looked strangely familiar, which led through a series of double doors to a place he recognized immediately. He was in that huge, subterranean hotel-like structure above the honeycombed tubes and tram-trains of UMMO.

UMMO. He had faced the UMMO in the power of the Holy Spirit, and they had kept their distance from him. Jack paused where he was and made sure that he was in the presence of the Spirit before taking another step. *Here I am, Lord,* he prayed silently. *Wherever this is.*

Somewhere on the northern coast of South America, wasn't it? Either Ben or Baal had told him that. He glanced around. There was the fountain. Above was the artificial sunlight. Over there were the walls beside the elevators where there *should* be telephones, but weren't. As he looked back around he saw a familiar face—although not a particularly friendly one. It was the man who had called himself Wesley, and he was gesturing toward Jack to come.

Walking that way, he began to hear sounds coming from beyond the doors—the noises of a large number of people engaged in many private conversations. He nodded at Wesley as he stepped past him, and Wesley smiled back coldly.

The cavernous lounge where he had been rescued was now filled to capacity with people. Easily a thousand, Jack guessed, of all races—all *human* races, he added to himself. As he walked cautiously into the room he began to recognize celebrities sitting and talking with nobodies. They wore all manner of dress, from black-tie and cummerbund to caftan and turban, and even a few agbada and dainsiki, the customary dress of West Africa. They wore skirts and saris as well, for about a quarter of those present were female. All were merrily eating and drinking, as if this were some immense cocktail party. Buffet tables lined the walls—as did more of the ubiquitous men in black, who ringed the room and watched.

Feeling terribly out of place, Jack began to circle the center of the crowd, searching for Ben. Suddenly a woman planted herself in front of him and demanded "Who are you? John the Baptist?"

He was shocked, first, to be so accosted when up to that point he'd been so totally ignored. He was shocked, second, to realize who this was, and he had trouble organizing his thoughts to respond. "Well, my name *is* John," he blurted out, "and I *am* a—Oh!" He suddenly understood and glanced downward at his outlandish-looking skins.

"Where *did* you get that outfit?" she giggled—not unkindly. "The animal rights people would eat you up. Eat you up? A little joke!"

Jack still couldn't make his tongue work, for this was Sherry Lynn Ward. And while he didn't like her show, to be standing next to her under the intense focus of her famous gaze was—disconcerting. Especially when dressed like an idiot. Or a prophet.

She was apparently accustomed to having this effect on people, for she carried on the conversation despite his lack of response. "I've had them on my show many times. The animal rights people. They are very passionate. So—where were you when you got your summons? Filming some biblical epic? Were you on location?"

"I . . . in a way," Jack stammered. "I was somewhere in Europe at the beginning of the fourth century."

Sherry Lynn laughed. "Really? What movie?"

"No movie," Jack answered honestly. "I really was somewhere in Europe at the beginning of the fourth century."

She looked puzzled—then her eyes lidded in understanding, and her voice dropped. "Time travel? You were *with* them?" Sherry Lynn Ward was impressed.

"Yeah," Jack nodded, wishing this conversation wasn't happening as she grabbed his arm and drew him further away from the heart of the crowd.

"And that's how you were dressed?" she whispered conspiratorially.

"How everyone was dressed," Jack shrugged. "Now I can't seem to find my pants. . . ." It was an honest enough statement, but it came out sounding like a joke. Sherry Lynn bent double, covering her mouth with her hand to stifle her mirth. Jack just blushed.

She straightened back up, still grinning, and said, "You're funny. C'mon, let's get something to drink." She grabbed him by the hand and led him to the nearest buffet table, scooped up a glass of wine and tried to hand it to him.

"Ah . . . just water," he said, stepping away from her to pick up a bottle of water and a glass.

"Oh, I remember. Nothing but locusts and wild honey, right?" she said, arching an eyebrow and sipping the wine herself. "Time travel!" she murmured, examining more closely Jack's stitched-skin coat. "I mean, I knew we had the technology now, and I knew that outfit looked awfully authentic. Wish I could do a show about *that*. Wild." She glanced back up into his eyes and demanded, "So what were they doing there?"

This was a formidable woman, Jack was realizing, accustomed to getting whatever she sought. She had that gift of being able to make whatever person she was with at the moment feel like the most special person in the world. With such enormous charisma, no wonder she was able to convince all kinds of people to spill their secrets merely for the entertainment of her viewing audience. Jack forced himself to be wary but answered, "They were trying to change history. Didn't work. Never does."

"You've been to the past with them *before?*" she whined, envious of his adventures.

"Many times," Jack said somberly.

"You're kidding!"

"I wish I was." He poured his water and took a drink.

"Which group?" she asked—demanded to know, really.

Jack didn't understand the question. "Uh . . . umm . . . what do you mean?"

*Stupid,* said her expression, but her lips said, "The Ku? Grays? Osiris?"

"Oh. Grays, I guess."

"You *guess?*" she frowned, now doubting his veracity.

"And UMMO," he added.

Sherry Lynn took a step back. "UMMO," she said respectfully. "They're scary."

"They certainly are that."

She stepped back closer and explained, "But I understand that it has something to do with the environmental conditions on their home world. You see, they evolved from the insect life of a planet much like ours that had been so polluted by its humanoid inhabitants that the humans all died off! The Space Siblings are simply helping us see what will happen to us if we don't clean up our act! A real warning to *us* from Gaia, don't you think?"

She had bought it: the "Kindly Space Siblings" line. Just like Jeffrey had, before he got too close to them and saw the truth. And this was coming from a woman who publicly mocked UFO sightings and taunted those who claimed they'd been abducted! "I've never heard you talk like this on your show," Jack said.

"You recognized me?" she said, obviously pleased.

"Of course. But I saw you once last summer doing a program on UFO abductions, and you were ridiculing the young women you had on your—"

"Well, of course I was," she preened, looking at Jack like he was crazy. "What do you *think* I'm going to do? Go on and announce 'I belong to the Ultrastructure, and we control your lives'? Not likely!"

"Why not? I mean, it's true—"

"Oh, I understand," she said suddenly, nodding. "You're one of the 'announce now' faction. OK, I see your argument: 'They're here, everybody knows, we're in charge, so let's get onto the business of fixing this planet.' But it's not like the timing is really good at the moment—do you think? With the Millennium 'End of the World' jitters and all, the whole planet would go crazy! The Genome Project alone would cause them to come after us from every side of the political spectrum. And then there's the AIDS mess to explain. No, I think we're a lot better off to get well into the next century before we announce. Give us another decade to get a lot firmer control of the emerging government structures. Although, I'd *love* to do it now too! I'm in a perfect position right now to air that announcement! Of course if I can keep the ratings up as long as Phil and Oprah did, then I'll be in an even better position to be the chosen one later. Can't you see *that* going out on the airwaves? What's the matter?" she asked Jack, noticing at last that he was staring at her with a strange expression. "You're looking at me funny. Is it my lip-stick?" She started to reach into her purse for her mirror but stopped when Jack shook his head.

"Don't you know what these things really *are?*"

Sherry Lynn Ward eyed him carefully, and a slow smile spread over her face. "Of course I do." Then her eyes narrowed, and she asked, "Don't you?"

"I know they're not benevolent space brothers from another planet, I can tell you that."

"Oh, really?" she said regally. "What *are* they, then?"

Jack didn't hesitate to say it. "They're demons."

Sherry Lynn blinked—then laughed aloud, once more doubling over and covering her mouth, then straightening up to peer at him from under a dipped eyebrow. "You *are* funny! You're either terribly funny or terribly deranged!"

"I don't think I'm either one."

"Well in either case you would make a *great* guest! What are you anyway? A . . . a prophet of doom?" She pointed again at his robe.

"I'm a teacher," he answered quietly.

"What do you teach?"

"Theology."

She examined him anew, then burst out, "That explains it! Of *course* you would put a theological slant on all of this; that's your job! Fascinating! Really, I have to have you on my show." She pulled her huge daily planner out of her purse and unzipped it.

"To do what?" Jack asked.

"To talk about the space angels!" she said without looking up. She was writing furiously.

"I said they were demons, not angels. Believe me, I know the difference, and you would to if you'd actually been in their presence—"

*Now* she looked up. "You've seen *angels?* I've done some *wonderful* shows about angels. Have you ever seen any of those?"

*I'm getting deeper and deeper into this,* thought Jack. *Too deep.* So he lied. "No."

"But I can see your angle now!" she said, scribbling excitedly. "Old idea of course—extraterrestrials as angels and devils. It's been done so many times, but it's a *wonderful* cover for a theologian to maintain, and you'd be *perfect!*"

"For what?" Jack said. His impulse was to walk away from her, but he knew by now that she would just dance after him and grab him by the robe.

"For a show that discusses 'Demons from the Stars—The Theology of . . . of . . .' Oh I'll come up with something. Or Ruth can. I'll get the Mars rock guy, too—you know, the one who found signs of life in a Martian rock? He's over across the room; I've had him on the show before. And we need a psychiatrist to analyze humankind's need to believe in something. Oh, this is great!" she said, still scribbling. "We may have to shoot it live Wednesday since I figure I'll miss tomorrow's taping too. OK: Wednesday morning, LAX, I'll have a car to meet you and we'll put you in the Beverly Hills Hotel. I'll get you tickets from wherever you live—or if this thing drags on for a couple of days, maybe we can get them to fly us there together." Suddenly she looked up, as if embarrassed at what she'd said. "Not that I'm not thrilled to be here, of course! Look at this room, these people! This is spectacular!" Suddenly she was back down into her pages, pen ready to write, demanding, "Where do you live? Oh! What's your *name,* first!"

Jack felt sick to his stomach. But he also had a thought: Perhaps through Sherry Lynn he could get some word to Gloria. "Dr. Jack Brennen," he said at last.

"Earned doctorate, of course?"

"Yes . . ."

"That's just so much more credible. And you live in—?"

"Louisville."

"Lovely town," she offered as she scribbled, "especially at Derby time. Phone number?"

Jack gulped, then told himself, *If she calls, at least Gloria will know I'm alive.* Not wanting to do it—not at all—he gave Sherry Lynn Ward his home number.

"Got it. I've gotta run over here and grab the rock guy real quick before they start. . . ." And with that she was off, running in her high heels across the crowded lounge.

Jack stared after her, bemused. Then someone touched him on the back, and he turned around.

"Hey there," the man said. He looked vaguely familiar. "Didn't want to interrupt you when you were talking with Sherry Lynn, but I just wanted to tell you, I really figured you for bug-food when they took you off that train. But you were sure right."

Now Jack recognized him. It was the man in wire-rimmed glasses who had shared a tram with him in the caverns below. Randolph something . . . Randolph Donaldson.

"Ye . . . yes," Jack said. "How long ago was that?"

"You don't remember? Why?" the man grinned unpleasantly. "Did they sting you back to sleep?"

"No. I've just been—out of touch."

Donaldson glanced down at his robe and raised his eyebrows. "I guess so. It was three weeks. You really don't remember?"

Jack shrugged. "Time flies . . ." Or rather, the black boxes fly while time just sits there. And he certainly hadn't been having fun.

"I could tell that wasn't a real UMMO taking you off. I think all of us could. Even so, nobody talked again for a *long* time after you left."

"What happened to you?"

"Oh, the usual, I guess. Tested me. Talked to me." A grin swept wide across the man's features as he finished, "Invited me to join! I tell you. I don't know what game you all were playing with us down there in the tunnels, but this is utterly *incredible!* You can forget the Senate. This is, by far, the most exclusive club in the world!"

Jack glanced around. "Yes . . . probably so. . . ." He nodded.

Donaldson clapped him on the shoulder—one of those manly gestures of false friendship between strangers—and said, "Good to see you! Gotta get inside, get a good seat. . . ." Then he took off for the far doors of the lounge, which Jack now saw were open. This crowd was just beginning to thin out as people headed through them.

Jack glanced down at his water glass and realized he was hungry. He wasn't far from the table so he grabbed a plate and a snack, then turned to watch the crowd as he ate.

There was Ben. He was on the far side of the room, walking toward the doors between two dark-suited guards, his eyes glassy, his jaw fixed. As soon as Jack caught sight of him, Ben turned to look back over his shoulder at him. Then the guards pushed him on through. Jack tossed his plate onto the table and rushed that way, but it was as if that very moment the entire herd finally sensed it was time to move, and everyone else began moving toward the doors. Jack was blocked, pushing against the flow of traffic. He let himself be carried inside the meeting room by the crush, and stood on tiptoe trying to peer over heads to see where Ben was seated.

"There you are!" Sherry Lynn Ward was suddenly beside him again, grabbing him by the hand and jerking him into one of the rows. "Thought I'd lost you," she scolded as she pulled him to the middle of it and plopped herself down in one of the seats. "Sit down," she ordered, jerking on his arm.

Jack complied obediently, without thinking. His total attention was riveted in disbelief upon the dais atop the stage. The conclave of the Ultrastructure was about to commence, and *everyone* was here. . . .

* * *

Whatever day it was, whatever time zone or century Jack was in, for Gloria it was still an endless Sunday afternoon, locked in by drifts of snow and locked up by an anguished heart. She had prayed. She had called all those she knew would pray. She had wept. She had raged. She had argued with God, then pleaded with God. She had slept—briefly— but when she woke Jack was still not home, she had still heard no word, and the tears of frustration had come again. Gabrielle, just as worried, had come down to spend a couple of hours with her, but the tension and worry and grief in the room had grown too much for her and she'd gone back up to seek solace with her books. And for Gloria, time—that time the saucers danced through, that made time meaningless to Jack—simply dragged on.

On the first ring, the phone was in her hand. "Yes?"

"Gloria?"

"George! Yes?"

His tone of voice was measured—warm and strong enough to lend her courage, but not light enough to raise her hopes. "We found the van. It was broken down on the side of the road—spread an oil slick half a mile. Looks like a blown engine—"

"Jack?" she asked quickly, cutting him off.

"Haven't found Brother Jack yet," he said, slowly and carefully, "but I'm certain he's just walked to one of these farmhouses around here."

"Where are you?"

"Well, that's just it," he admitted. "I'm in the closest house to where he broke down, and these folks haven't seen him. But we're out checking," he went on earnestly. "Brother Henry is over on the other side of the road, the ladies are calling around. Unless he caught a ride he's around here somewhere, and we'll find him."

"I'm coming," Gloria snapped, jumping to her feet.

"Now Gloria, wait," George pleaded calmly. "There's no good reason for you to do that and plenty of good ones for you not to. I know the shape that other car of yours is in; it's got a bad oil leak and the tires are bald. Believe me, you wouldn't make it out here; you'd get hung up some place yourself. You don't want us to be out looking for you, too—right?"

She groaned in reply. Just groaned.

"I know," he murmured. "I know. But really, listen. We've got this whole end of the county out looking for him; the sheriff is here, so—just, please, wait there and pray.

That's the best thing you can do, I promise you. We'll find him soon."

"But it's getting dark!" she pleaded, as if somehow George could control that.

"We've all got flashlights," he said, his voice soothing. "Here. I just turned this one on. Looks real good. Put new batteries in it just a week ago. OK?" She said nothing. "All right?" he tried.

Gloria sighed—a long, deep sigh that summed up all of her feelings with no need for words. Then she grumbled, "All right."

"I promised you I would call, and I called. Right?" She could hear his gentle smile.

"Right."

"So, I'll call again soon—soon as we find him."

"All right," she said, allowing herself to be comforted by his calm. "I can't thank you enough, George."

"Oh, you don't need to thank me, Gloria. He's your husband, but he's my preacher."

"I know," she said, managing a smile. "Be careful."

"I will do that. I'll call soon. Jason, did you check down by the—" The phone went dead with a click. Gloria just held it to her ear until the dial tone began, then slowly lowered it and placed it in its cradle.

So. Some news, anyway. "Jack," she scolded him aloud, "why didn't you just stay with the van!" Of course she knew why. Then he wouldn't be Jack. Always rushing ahead, always trying to fix things right now whether he knew how to or not. But at least this information eliminated some possibilities. He wasn't upside down in a ditch, hadn't slid off a bridge into a frozen creek. But it still didn't eliminate the one she most feared. Gloria stretched out across the bed, head buried in her pillows, and returned to the business of serious prayer.

* * *

This conclave of the Ultrastructure resembled nothing so much as an annual stockholder's meeting for a huge multi-national corporation—which, Jack thought upon reflection, he guessed this was. *The* Corporation. The rulers of the darkness of this world. . . .

Due to Sherry Lynn Ward's adroit maneuvering, they were seated in the very middle of the house, not more than twenty-five feet from center stage. Ben was on the front row down to his right, seated with a cluster of black suits. Among them he recognized Jeffrey, his college friend turned man in black, as unlikely an outcome as any he could ever imagine. Then again, how likely had it been that *he* would be sitting here? The last time he'd seen Jeffrey had been on a rooftop in Atlantis, with the water rising. But was that the last time Jeffrey had seen *him?* His friend's hair looked darker—less streaked with gray. Could be colored, of course, but his small-eyed, round-faced friend had never seemed the least bit vain. Had Jeffrey not yet lived through his seven-year Atlantean mission?

There were many other notables in the crowd around him—people he'd read about, seen on the news, some whom he'd been thrown together with during his previous abduction. But his eyes were drawn back again and again to the well-lighted figures seated on the dais—five representatives, one for each of the five "races" the Fallen play-acted at being. There was a sixth chair as well, at the moment vacant. Or in any case, Jack couldn't see anyone seated there. The whole room, however, seemed permeated with the sinister presence of that dark being, that disembodied Overlord who had issued the summons to Baal. Was that *his* chair?

Where was Baal? He was not the Gray seated on the dais. Jack thought he could easily be wrong since all Grays looked so much alike, but to him this creature looked like Kundas, that dour demon who hated all humans and made no secret of it.

There were scores of other Grays seated in the audience—one was just down the row from him to the left, another in the row ahead to the right, a whole row of them seated together down close to the front. But there were other "alien" forms in the mix as well. He found his attention drawn back again and again to those "races" new to him, the ones he'd never seen. One of these, seated in the center of the dais next to the empty chair, now rose to address the crowd. Unlike the Grays, this type had mouths, and this particular creature had a deep, booming voice.

"Welcome, all of you!" he thundered, without benefit of a microphone. He needed none. Jack slumped down in his chair, rolled his head toward Sherry Lynn, and waited until she turned her head toward his.

"What kind is he?"

"You've traveled in time and you don't know?" she whispered mockingly.

"Never seen one like that."

"He's one of the Ku," she said into his ear. "The Far East is their territory—China, Tibet, Japan, the Philippines. They're almost as powerful as the Grays but much less social." The Gray in the row in front of them turned around and gave Sherry Lynn a hard look. Jack figured it also must have told her, mind-to-mind, to shut up and listen, for she looked at it with surprise, then gave it a charming smile and sat up straight in her seat.

Jack studied the Ku in wonder. Despite knowing what it was that animated the body, he was still fascinated to watch it in action. The Ku was more like the Grays than any other race appearing on the dais—about the same height, equally slender, with long, graceful arms. But its fingers were webbed, looking something like bat wings, and its skin color was quite different: almost orange. The most striking difference, however, was that mouth that all Grays lacked and the rows and rows of sharp, triangular teeth inside it. Like shark teeth, Jack thought, as he listened to this initial speech.

"You are the chosen! You are the elite. You have ruled in the past—you rule now—and you *will* rule your peoples and nations in a visible way, as soon as the announcement is made. Today, you are the invisible government of the world, the invisible United Nations. Please! Give yourselves a hand!" The Ku made a smile that to Jack looked more like a grimace and began to slap his webbed palms together. The crowd responded warmly with thunderous applause, some so moved by his words that they even cheered.

Jack applauded automatically, if with restraint. He really didn't want to draw any more attention to himself. Why, he was wondering, were they letting him see this? He could hardly believe that he'd become lost in the crowd.

The Ku was ready to speak again, and the audience fell silent. "You have come on command. That is good. You had no choice, of course, given your duty to this universal enterprise. Even so, some of you came at great personal sacrifice. That will be remembered to your credit. We cannot do this without you."

"Do what," Jack murmured under his breath, not meaning to say it aloud.

"Hush!" Sherry Lynn whispered, then smiled again brightly at the Gray, who had once more turned his head to look back.

The Ku continued. "But there is tragic news to report. The Ultrarch is dead—"

"Again?" someone near Jack whispered in shock, and he heard other such whispers rustle through the room.

"An automobile accident," the Ku explained mournfully. "Just one more indication of the dangers inherent in this world your forebears have created—dangers we will all work together to correct. As always, we who sit on this panel—along with the millions of others we represent—affirm our promise to assist you, our younger sisters and brothers, in reshaping this planet into a safe, sane, and secure one for you and your children. It falls to us, then, to tap yet another of your number to fill this vacant chair, to represent the *human* race in this six-member panel. It could be any one of you. We shall make that announcement in a moment." Jack felt Sherry Lynn Ward sit up straight next to him. Without Ben's gift he could still read her mind. She was thinking *Me! Me! Choose me!*

"Before we come to that, however, there are progress reports to be heard. The first is a report on current market conditions, for which I recognize my brother from Osiris."

The Ku sat down as a creature to the left of him stood. As the leader of Osiris launched into a dense, near unintelligible monologue filled with facts and figures, Jack noticed that Sherry Lynn had opened up her fat diary and was writing something. He ignored her, intent on studying this so-called life-form.

He'd seen this shape before, and heard them called the Whites. Baal had once put on one of these bodies to mislead him. He'd seen others floating in giant jars under the palace in Atlantis. But this was the first time he'd seen a "real" White in action, and despite the boring drone, Jack had to admit the creature was impressive. Much taller than any Gray, the White was also bulkier—almost fat by comparison. Multiple chins under his face added to this impression. His most notable feature, however, was a huge, pointed nose. A shade darker than the rest of its skin, the White's nose looked almost like a beak. Jack remembered pictures he'd seen of Osiris painted on the walls of Egyptian tombs. He could easily understand why such images might be painted if this creature had been playing god in the time of the pyramids. His bearing was certainly regal enough. He looked—and sounded—like a thoroughly self-confident aristocrat.

Jack was mildly amused at the way the White illustrated his speech with charts and graphs, projected on a diamond-vision screen that spanned the stage behind him. He was still thinking about this as Sherry Lynn passed her diary to him, and he realized she'd been writing him a note.

*Osiris: the race that governed ancient Egypt and, before that, Sumer. Home planet is Marduk, or Nemesis. Also called the Whites, the Talls, Nibirians, and the "Big-nose Aliens." Still controls all of the Middle East and parts of Europe, as well as India. Believed to be the oldest race on the planet and the maker of mankind.*

As Jack read the last line he shook his head and wrote her a note back.

*Why would "the maker of mankind" need to use Microsoft PowerPoint to illustrate a speech?*

She scribbled her response in seconds.

*Why would a demon?*

Jack shrugged, and she smiled triumphantly. He went back to listening to the White's drone. He gathered from the convoluted report that the Ultrastructure had its long fingers in everything—manipulating all the world's stock markets, controlling all cartels, massaging the currency markets, encouraging and discouraging various industries and innovations, juggling relations between labor and management, enriching the haves and impoverishing the have-nots to exacerbate political turmoil, stoking racial hatreds to generate wars and massacres in order to provide bodies for further genetic research, and all the while generating huge cash reserves by robbing themselves through the Sicilian Mafia, the new Russian "Mafia," the Japanese Yakuza, the Chinese Triads, the Colombian drug lords, and the independent street gangs of a hundred great cities. It made Jack sick.

When the White finished he was given a polite round of applause, which he appeared not to notice at all as he sat down. At that point Kundas rose—Jack was almost certain it was Kundas—who proceeded to telepathically communicate with the entire audience on the status of the current genetic research. He made several complimentary references to UMMO's excellent efforts at specimen collection and the need for that "harvest" to continue. Jack reached over to take Sherry Lynn's notebook and wrote.

*What do you know about the Grays?*

She took it back and began writing, passing the book back to him as Kundas was concluding.

*Don't you know this? Home planet Zeta Reticulli. Wide-spread in this quadrant of the galaxy, controlling many other planets. Once highly competitive with the Whites. Technologists and anthropologists. Prompted the Renaissance. Territories include USA, Western Europe, parts of Africa. Largest population on the planet—next to us, of course!*

Jack read this, nodded, and wrote back.

*You sure know your aliens.*

*I study this stuff!* Sherry Lynn scribbled, and passed the notebook back to him as the representative of yet another type unknown to Jack stood up to speak. Climbed up was really more accurate, for this creature was half the size of a Gray or a Ku, standing only about two feet high. It had to stand up on its chair to be seen. With only one large eye, big, floppy ears, three-fingered claws in the place of hands and bright green skin, this was by far the most alien-*looking* species on the dais. Apart from UMMO, of course. Jack wrote.

*The proverbial little green men?*

*Your gender bias is showing!* Sherry Lynn wrote back. *She's female!*

217

Jack wrinkled his forehead. *How can you tell?* he wrote, then added *Describe?* and turned back to listen to the little green woman as she spoke. That wasn't easy. Her speech was a series of unpleasant grunts and growls, barely understandable as English. That brought another question to mind: did everyone in the Ultrastructure speak English? But Sherry Lynn still had the notebook. He craned his neck to read what she was writing:

*Manisolas: Home planet in the Sirus system. Sometimes called Sirians, also known to human history as gremlins, leprechauns, fairies, dwarves—you name it. Prefer cold climates, so mostly found in Northern Europe or Southern South America, especially Argentina. Also Australia. Make crop circles. Extreme ecologists, very protective of mother Gaia. The original Greens!*

From what Jack could make out of the grunts and snorts, the diminutive green creature was indeed addressing ecological concerns. But she was so tiresome to listen to that no one seemed sorry when she finally climbed down from her chair and sat on it. Jack thought the applause she received was less for her speech than for the fact that it was over. His eyes turned then to the representative of UMMO, expecting that he—she?—would have the last say.

Instead, the Ku stood back up and raised his webbed hands for silence. "It is time at last to call forward the new Ultrarch—the new leader of the human race."

# Chapter Fourteen

*The ultrarch disposes*

As soon as he heard these words, Sherry Lynn Ward shoved her diary into Jack's stomach and gave the stage her full attention. A hush fell over the rest of the audience as well, which had steadily grown more and more restless during the preceding reports. It reminded Jack of Oscar night when it finally came time to present the *real* awards.

"As all of you know," the Ku leader continued, "this is not a volunteer position. Nor is it an honorary position, to be rotated in some politically correct manner through all races, nationalities, and genders. There are no nominations to be made, nor ballots to be counted, nor any provision for declining the nomination. Once the Ultrarch is *chosen,* he is chosen. There is no debate.

"Be it known to all assembled, then, that the chosen Ultrarch is once again a North American, who has been instrumental in making our recent technological advances in time travel possible. Ron Pearson of New York City, USA, you will advance to the dais and take the vacant chair."

There was a smattering of applause, but it quickly died away when it became apparent that this was to be a somber moment. The elected man looked somber indeed—bewildered, even—as the men in black under Jeffrey's command filed up the aisle to escort him forward. He had been seated behind Jack and to the right, and as all eyes turned that way he seemed almost unwilling to get up. He came, however—Jeffrey's stern countenance made it clear that he would have to—and so he slipped out into the aisle, nervously straightening his tie, and led the little parade to the dais.

Sherry Lynn looked at Jack, her nose wrinkling in chagrin. "Who's that?" she whispered. "Do you know him?"

As a matter of fact, Jack did. He'd met him on the saucer during his first abduction. Pearson had struck Jack then as an ambitious but insecure man who knew he was caught in something far larger than he could handle. As he walked past them, that impression lingered. It was clear that Pearson did not want to be doing this.

Jeffrey and another MIB marched him up onstage, guiding him toward the chair while the Ku pulled it out for him. Jack saw the man give Jeffrey one last imploring look as his two escorts placed their hands on his shoulders. Then, with a downward push from both of them, he sat.

The transformation was instantaneous—and chilling. A sulfurous stench filled the theater. The man's face grew rigid—then wild—then, suddenly, he gave the entire audience a cold smile. And Jack knew: Ron Pearson was no longer Ron Pearson. The dark presence that had hovered over this meeting from its beginning was now riding him. This was true demonic possession. Ron Pearson was not the

Ultrarch. The Overlord was the Ultrarch, and he now owned and operated Ron Pearson.

Now the creature rose from the chair he'd apparently occupied from the beginning and took complete command of the meeting.

"I think I need a microphone," he said flatly, using Pearson's voice. His black-clad attendants leapt to obey him. "Thank you," he said smoothly, once it was in his hand. "It is my great honor to accept the nomination of this panel to serve the planet in this vital way. Yes, I have been intimately involved in the time-travel project. I was thrilled to be in a position to make the contributions I have made to our forward progress as a race. The technology of time travel is still so new that none of us know, as yet, how to make correct use of it. There have already been some mistakes made. My first commitment to you all is that we shall continue to experiment with the technology, finding ways to cooperate with history rather than seeking to interfere in it."

Jack glanced around, wondering if no one else saw the utter transformation of this man's persona. Wasn't it obvious to all?

"But that is only a means to an end!" the creature went on, his voice rising—hardening. "The *first* priority must, of course, be continued forward progress in the vital area of genetic research. Our joint task is nothing less than the quest for eternal life! Only through achieving immortality will we humans at last be allowed to join our partner races in the further seeding of the galaxy! Nothing short of everlasting life will permit us to leap the vast distances between the stars! We must thank our Star Siblings, seated here to my left and right, for their contributions to our growth and progress, for through their efforts that goal is now tantalizingly close! And so, I hereby charge you, Kundas, and the Gray Zetans you now lead, to focus your *full* attention upon this task."

Suddenly the Ultrarch's voice dripped acid, as he turned to face Kundas directly. "As some of us know, that has *not* been the total focus of your group in recent days. You have apparently been—distracted. You Grays have become sloppy! I now publicly call your race to account for a horribly destructive failure in viral manipulation! I speak, of course, of the AIDS epidemic." Murmuring could be heard throughout the room, but it stopped as soon as he continued.

"I shouldn't have to remind you that unauthorized testing upon uncontrolled population groups is absolutely forbidden! We have hurt ourselves—badly—with this AIDS infestation! It has taken in its wake hundreds of our *own,* useful participants in our cause! How clumsy," the Ultrarch snarled. "How utterly pointless! Before all assembled, I challenge you to address this failure!"

Jack watched with rapt attention as Kundas stood, bowing slightly to the Ultrarch before turning to address the crowd. "I rise on behalf of *all* my race to apologize, to you and all present, for this incredible miscalculation. As you know, I was not the chief administrator of the Zetan population at the time this infamous act was perpetrated upon humanity. There is one who stands accused today for other equally serious crimes who made that decision—against my counsel! The result has been indiscriminate loss of life, when as you yourself know, the ultimate purpose of the project was targeted *infection* of a particularly resistant demographic group—a group far too rigid in adherence to their archaic belief system to be able to accept with equanimity the announcement of our presence."

As he parsed the long sentences, Jack felt a burning in his stomach and a weakness in his legs. Was he saying . . . ?

"Our difficulty," Kundas continued, "has always been in finding a delivery system that would effectively target this group. Sexual transmission of the virus proved to be precisely the *wrong* choice. This religio-political sub-set of the world population is particularly insistent upon sexual chastity."

Incredulous, Jack tossed a quick look at the back of Ben's head. *Christians?* he thought at the boy. As unobtrusively as he could, Ben turned his head and looked back at him. The boy shrugged apologetically, and nodded. Jack's head was reeling as he heard Kundas continue. . . .

". . . promise to continue to make every effort to help stem this brutalizing epidemic—which is only just, given our culpability in the matter. But let me add one last note: It does seem only proper that this matter, among others, should be laid at the feet of the administrator who perpetrated the fiasco! His headstrong negligence has smeared the entire Zetan race!"

*That would be Baal,* Jack thought. Then again, Baal always had been a sex-focused demon.

The Ultrarch was speaking again, with a controlled authority completely foreign to that of the man whose body he controlled. "Your explanation is lucid, Kundas. I accept your apology on behalf of the whole assembly. And I promise: The responsible party *will* be punished. Let us turn our attention now, however, to the continued collection of specimens and tissue samples essential to the great leap toward immortality. UMMO has been particularly helpful in this phase of the project, experimenting with time travel to procure the necessary living materials for unhindered experimentation. UMMO has recently fetched from their studies scholars who are, even now, reviewing historical texts for the best possible sources in time for the pickup of sample tissue. We will, of course, continue to press on with collection of aborted fetuses, regardless of the current interference of government in my own country and others. UMMO, you are of course assisting the Grays in this project and will continue to support them in it by transporting both live and

223

dead specimens currently held in the vaults below us to the center appointed for that research.

"But this raises yet another problem that must be resolved. Since the death of the last Ultrarch, there has been unnecessary friction between UMMO and the Zetans, resulting in human loss of life not only in this present century but in the past as well. This conflict has already cost us all incredible sums, due to the destruction of one of the six time ships only recently constructed by my own company! As Ultrarch of humankind, I demand that both UMMO and Zetans account for this!"

Kundas glanced at the representative UMMO, then stood up again. "Once again I rise to apologize on the behalf of my kindred. The history of all our relationships on this planet has proved nothing, if not the futility of such internecine quarrels. We have nothing to gain by them, and everything to lose, for we weaken ourselves in the face of our true enemies—the . . . the human keepers of the status quo!"

*He almost said "the Guardians,"* Jack thought. He knew Kundas was certainly *thinking* of the Guardians.

"However," the sour-tempered Gray continued, "I must again lay this charge at the feet of a previous administrator and strongly request that he be held to individual account!" Kundas sat down and looked toward the UMMO on the stage.

"UMMO?" the Ultrarch said pleasantly. But in that word there was imbedded a command that the UMMO could not refuse.

The speaker for UMMO rose up on his hind legs, light from spotlights flashing off his black shell. "I am the new speaker for UMMO. The previous speaker for UMMO awaits execution for the stated crimes," he said, projecting his thoughts to the whole crowd. He then turned to look to his right, to a row of UMMO seated together in front of the stage. Haltingly, he added, "UMMO will carry out all injunctions of this Council."

The Ultrarch continued to gaze toward the new speaker of UMMO, at last saying menacingly, "Is that *all* that UMMO has to say?"

The speaker for UMMO looked back at him, then moved around to the edge of the stage. He was met there by a cluster of other UMMO, and they quickly conferred. After this UMMO consultation, the speaker stood up and announced, "UMMO is sorry."

The Ultrarch gazed sternly down at the cluster of insects at the stage's edge. "It is the judgment of this Council that UMMO will provide all moneys necessary to replace the destroyed vessel—a sum in excess of two billion U.S. dollars!"

The speaker bent down again for another quick conversation with his fellow bugs, then raised back up. "UMMO agrees."

The Ultrarch smiled grimly. "UMMO will also return to their appropriate places and times all scientists, scholars, laboratory technicians, and researchers recently collected in a coordinated hostile action against the Zetans. They are to be returned to a time and place as close to their point of abduction as feasible, with all memories of this experience blanked."

Kundas spoke up. "Stingers removed?" he urged.

The Ultrarch pondered this. "No need to go that far," he said, and Kundas looked away in frustration. "UMMO, do you accept this instruction?"

This time the UMMO conference was brief. "UMMO accepts."

"Very well," said the Ultrarch. "Let this be UMMO's first priority at the close of this meeting. We all understand, however, that due to the nature of time travel, this task need not be rushed. Therefore, let a complete examination first be made of the mind of each thinker taken. All contributions and potential contributions shall be recorded. I believe, Kundas, that you have a staff member admirably gifted for this task."

"He will be set to it immediately," said Kundas. Jack glanced at Ben. The teenager's head slumped forward in dismay. They would be keeping him very busy for a while.

The Ultrarch rose up to Ron Pearson's full height and proclaimed, "Finally, it is to be understood that no more friction between the UMMO and the Zetans will be tolerated! At the first signs of such, the other races shall be obligated to step in and discipline *both* sides in the conflict! And since such an event would be terribly wasteful of energies much needed elsewhere, it seems valuable to provide a demonstration of such discipline to all present. This should serve as a deterrent to anyone who might contemplate breaking the peace. It should also serve as a reminder that this Council *means* what it says. In order to seal this cessation of hostilities while providing some measure, at least, of final vengeance, each race will be privileged to execute its chief antagonist. Prepare the stage, and bring out the two failed leaders."

His command was instantly obeyed. The men in black cleared away the tables that sat upon the rostrum. The panel rose as a group and stepped to the side of the stage where the men in black had placed their chairs. As they took their seats, a group of UMMO walked onto the stage from the right, carrying above their heads their bound and wiggling former speaker. At the same moment a group of Grays walked on from stage left, rolling a huge, fluid-filled glass jar, in which floated the body—and trapped spirit—of Baal.

Jack knew it was Baal, for as soon as he was pulled out of the tank Baal addressed him directly. *Jack!* he cried inside Jack's mind, *please help me! This is unfair, so unfair! You're*

*the only one who can help me, Jack! Pray for me! They're
going to hurt me so badly!*

Jack sat up, shocked. And then he did what he assumed
anyone would do in the face of such a request, regardless
of the source. Jack prayed. And the Ultrarch saw it happen.

At the center of the stage the two groups exchanged
prisoners. All eyes in the auditorium focused upon their dif-
fering preparations for execution. All eyes, that is, save
Jack's—and the Ultrarch's. For the Ultrarch had risen once
more from his seat, and now fixed Jack with a stare so hateful, so malicious that Jack had no choice but to stare back.
He was thus spared the sight of dozens of UMMO encircling
Baal and stinging him again and again—over and over and
over. He heard the end, however. Everyone in the audience
heard the end, for as Baal was ripped from the body that
had sheltered him he shrieked in agony and rage. He was
still a most powerful spirit—a ruler of the darkness—and he
did not go gently into the torment the others had prepared
for him. Jack assumed everyone in the place had felt the
final stab to the back of the head that he'd felt, for all around
him people were suddenly rubbing their necks.

Where had Baal's spirit been taken? Into hell? Inside the
other demons? How did they metabolize misery? It was a
question he'd often pondered, wondering how, exactly, the
fiends partook of human suffering. Now it took on a new
dimension, as he tried to imagine how they devoured one
another.

Back up on the stage, UMMO shredded the now inani-
mate body and consumed it on the spot. The Grays who now
held their own struggling victim just watched, apparently
amused. *How pitiful,* Jack thought, *to exist utterly outside of
any care.*

At last nothing remained of Baal's body but scraps. It
was the turn of the Grays to exact their own revenge on the
former speaker for UMMO. The UMMO's six legs had been

bound together with steel cables. Another cable encircled his midsection, pinning his wings inside his shell. At the Grays' signal yet another steel cable was dropped from above the stage, and the creature was suspended from it. He struggled and jerked at the end of that line as a Gray drilled a hole through the exoskeleton of his back and inserted a small device.

Jack had seen *The Phantom of the Opera* performed live. He had gasped with the rest of the audience as a crystal chandelier suddenly swung up off the stage and out over the heads of the crowd. He heard that same unison gasp now, as the huge bug was hurtled up toward the high ceiling above them. The house lights came on, heads tilted back, necks craned, and chairs rocked backward as everyone followed the huge insect's unwilling flight. Then the Grays detonated the bomb inside its body, and the UMMO exploded like a disgusting piñata. Bug juice sprayed everywhere, covering everybody and everything. This meeting was definitely adjourned.

"Now *that* was interesting!" Sherry Lynn Ward snarled, standing up to shake the slime off of her. "And this was a new outfit! I wish now I'd come dressed like you!"

Jack wasn't listening. He was watching the new Ultrarch watch him. The Ultrarch had turned to Kundas and whispered something, and Kundas had in turn summoned Jeffrey to the apron of the stage. As the crowd began to filter out of the theater, Jeffrey barked directions to his people. Evidently Wesley was doing the same, for before Sherry Lynn had finished her sentence there were men in black blocking either side of their row—all gazing expressionlessly at Jack.

Wesley and his group were to Jack's left, Jeffrey and his unit to the right. Jack decided to take his chances with an old friend. He pushed Sherry Lynn toward the right. "What are you—" she started to ask, then she saw Jeffrey's tight smile, and shut up.

"Jack!" Jeffrey said jovially. "I thought we'd lost you at Babel! Here we are again. How long's it been?"

"That all depends," Jack answered, ignoring Sherry Lynn's look backward at him over her shoulder. "Do *you* remember Atlantis?"

"Remember what?" said Jeffrey.

"Never mind," Jack murmured, stepping out of the row and starting up the aisle toward the exit. Jeffrey fell in step beside him, while other MIBs ringed them both behind and ahead.

Sherry Lynn was prodded forward and out of the circle as Jeffrey muttered, "You'll need to go with me, Jack. Kundas has a job for us and says you're needed."

Sherry Lynn Ward looked *most* impressed this time as she turned around to back up the aisle in front of the tight formation. "You're taking him back into time?" she called to Jeffrey.

"Or he's taking us," Jeffrey answered, pushing others aside as the group rushed Jack toward the door. "Excuse me—get out of the way—" Jeffrey was muttering. His eyes were directed across the middle section of seats at Wesley, whose identically dressed group was also rushing to their respective exit.

"Then that means you can bring him back to any time, right?" Sherry Lynn called out as they pushed by her.

"Guess so," Jeffrey mumbled. "Step aside . . ."

She was behind them now, jumping up on her toes to shout, "Then remember! He needs to be in Los Angeles by 2:00—no, make that 1:00—this coming Wednesday! You got that?"

"Right!" Jeffrey shouted without looking back, then shot Jack a pinched-face grin. "What does she really know about you?"

"Not enough," Jack answered, keeping pace with his escort. There was no chance Kundas would let him on that show, he thought—with true relief. But he did hope Sherry Lynn would place that call to Gloria.

They were out through the door into the large lounge now, walking quickly. Wesley and his group met them coming out the door, and Jeffrey angled toward him. "We're working together now. No trouble."

"No trouble," Wesley smiled. "We just have direct orders to escort you out of this place and see you safely into your ship."

"We're on our way," Jeffrey growled as the now larger group pushed their way through the crowd out the door of the lounge and into the lobby.

"Where are we going?" Jack asked.

"We have some errands to run," Jeffrey said evasively. "Don't worry, you'll feel right at home. We've been assigned Baal's old saucer. You'll have your own cabin back, your own bed."

"I'll go on one condition," said Jack.

"You'll go, regardless," Jeffrey chuckled, "but just out of curiosity, what do you want?"

"I want my clothes."

Jeffrey glanced down at Jack's robe, still smiling. "What's the matter with what you've got on?"

"Besides the fact that it stinks, itches, and it has bug juice all over it?"

Jeffrey laughed again, this time out loud, and Jack began to relax. Despite all he'd seen, all the places he'd been, Jeffrey still appeared, at least, to be his friend. "We'll see what we can find."

By this time they were through the lobby and marching down the corridor into the hanger. Some of the vessels were already gone. Others were thundering to life. The conclave was breaking up in a hurry.

"You don't appear to be very popular with the new big chief," Jeffrey murmured.

"You know what he is, Jeffrey, so you also know why."

"Of course I know. I've been ridden myself—*by* Kundas. Do you remember?"

Jack did indeed. "It's as if the man disappeared, replaced by—"

"Exactly," Jeffrey cut him off. "This Ron Pearson fellow? He was my hire. You may remember that I ran him. Always nervous as a cat, a spineless whiner. When I picked him up in New York this afternoon, he was pleading with me to set things right with some Mafiosi he was standing up. Scared to death. Out of his league, and he knew it. So then they announce his name, we sit him down in that chair, and suddenly he's Hitler reborn. Happens every time."

"Every time?"

"Every time there's a new Ultrarch. And that happens way too often. Nobody should want that job, Jack. Ultrarch's have the life expectancy of a mayfly."

"The Guardians," Jack murmured.

"Maybe," Jeffrey shrugged as they neared the rampway up into the saucer. "Maybe the Overlord just burns them out. May I never have occasion to learn firsthand. Inside," he said, gesturing to the men behind him, and Jack waited with him as they boarded.

Wesley and his people had shadowed them every step, and now Wesley stepped up to smile unpleasantly at both of them. "Glad to see you again, Jeffrey. We'll talk."

"I'm sure we will."

"And Dr. Brennen. It's good to see you. It's especially good to see you go."

"We're on our way," Jeffrey snorted as he turned to head up into the saucer, but Wesley and his group did not leave. They just stood in place, arms folded, until Jeffrey and Jack were both inside and the rampway closed up behind them.

Jeffrey stepped onto the elevator up to the flight deck, but when Jack started to follow him in, Jeffrey pushed him back out. "Not in the control room, Jack. Sorry, but Ben told us earlier you were contemplating leaving without us."

"It was a passing thought," Jack explained, but Jeffrey just shrugged and smiled.

"It was a thought. Enough reason to insure you have no chance to act on it. Why don't you go get cleaned up, Jack. Get some rest."

"My clothes—?"

"There'll be something waiting for you when you get out of the shower. I may even be able to locate a clean T-shirt." The elevator door closed, and Jack was left alone. He wandered around the corridor to his room, relieved to at last have some time to himself. He stripped of the stinking robe and the skins, and started to toss them into the hall in disgust—but stopped. He really didn't know why. Instead he took them into the bathroom with him, washed them out, and hung them up to dry.

He took a long reflective shower with plenty of warm water and soap. He prayed as he washed, thinking of Gloria, of his daughter, of Ben, of his students, of the people in his church—of Jeffrey. When he stepped out and dried off, he was elated to see on the bed stacks of fresh underwear, alongside the contents of his pockets: his wallet, his comb, his keys. *My keys,* he thought sadly, picking them up and dangling before him. Keys to a house he couldn't get to, a cluttered office he might never see again, and a dead van. Even so, they warmed him. *Odd,* he thought, *the things that give us comfort.*

He stepped to the closet and opened it, expecting to see his suit and the elephant tie he'd worn so faithfully. Instead he found a half-dozen starched white shirts, a rack full of anonymous ties, and three identical black suits. On the shelf above were two black fedoras and several pairs of dark sunglasses. Jack had just become a man in black.

\* \* \*

Trisha missed the flight to Atlanta after all. People in Huntsville weren't accustomed to driving in the snow, and accidents had snarled traffic all over the city. After a quarter of an hour of anxious frustration, she finally leaned back in the seat of her rented car and told herself, "Relax, Trisha. It's just as well." She pulled into a motel near the airport. It had been a long day, and she needed the rest.

She plugged in her laptop once she checked in and saw she had E-mail from Andrea. There were several other leads on the Joseph Brockman case that she was to follow up in the morning. Good thing she hadn't made the flight. She worked with the phone book and the list of contacts for an hour, then ordered room service and began searching the Internet for UFO websites. There were plenty available, and she surfed through them, shaking her head at all the eccentricity out there: Roswell, Area 51, MJ-12, Milton William Cooper, Dulche, Groom Lake, Robert Lazar, Taos, Mount Shasta, S-4, Catalina Island, the Philadelphia Experiment, Montauk, the Mothmen of Ohio, the Allagash abductions, dolphin channeling, Zacharia Sitchen—whew! At the same time, she had to confess that none were any stranger than the stories she'd heard in the last twenty-four hours from people she knew believed every word they'd told her.

Finally she turned off her computer, went outside, and built a snowman. It cleared her head. Trisha loved the snow.

\* \* \*

There was a knock on his door, and Jack called out, "Come in."

Jeffrey walked inside—and laughed.

233

Jack stood up, modeling the hat and dark glasses. "So, Jeffrey! You've finally made a man in black out of me."

"You look more like a Blues Brother," Jeffrey cackled, plopping himself down on the bed and propping up his head with his hand.

"That *is* the idea though, isn't it?"

Jeffrey rolled over on his back, completely relaxed. "You asked for clothes, Jack. I just figured you wouldn't want to stand out in the crowd."

"Maybe I don't *want* to be identified with this crowd."

"It's not a bad life, Jack," Jeffrey said quietly.

"How can you *say* that? After all you've seen!"

"*Because* of all I've seen," Jeffrey argued good-naturedly. "I've been a firsthand witness to events that have changed the world. I've seen ancient civilizations at their peak. You remember my interests in college, Jack, how I always had my nose in some esoteric book of ancient mystic wisdom. Now I could write those books—if I chose to reveal the secrets."

"Yes, you were always into secrets. I always thought you'd make a great librarian. I *never* figured you for a spy."

"Intelligence, Jack. That's the key word here. The calculated acquisition and use of classified information. And you could make a good one yourself if you weren't so obsessed with your celestial safety valve."

"God, you mean."

"Whatever you want to call it. Look, you can wear the uniform without being on the team. And you'll be spending some time with us. Maybe a lot of time. Maybe you'll change your mind."

"You already tried to recruit me once, remember?"

"When?"

"Oh, that's right," Jack said. "You wouldn't remember. It was a conversation I had with you in Atlantis. Apparently you haven't had that conversation with me yet."

Jeffrey rolled back up onto his elbow and peered at Jack. "That's the second time you've mentioned Atlantis. Are you talking about *the* Atlantis? As in the mythical land of Plato?"

"Guess what," Jack said, dropping the glasses into the hat and the hat on the bed. "It isn't mythical. You'll see for yourself."

Jeffrey pursed his lips and narrowed his already close-set eyes. "You want to tell me more about this?"

"It's these time ships, Jeffrey. They ruin relationships. Oh, believe me, I understand what you're feeling. When Ben told me I'd be taken by you people again, I asked the same kind of questions you're about to ask me. Trying to 'be prepared for what comes.' He wouldn't tell me anything, and he was right not to. The best way to be prepared is just to live each day as it comes."

"Very philosophical, Jack," Jeffrey nodded, "but garbage. Tell me what we do together in Atlantis."

Jack ignored Jeffrey's demand, instead continuing, "These ships rip us loose from the anchor of our shared experiences. Time is an anchor, Jeffrey. It's a universal standard, an objective measuring stick we can all trust."

"Everything's relative, Jack. Atlantis?"

"No. Everything is *not* relative. But that's certainly what the demons have taught us to believe. And these time-travel devices, and the lies, and the genetic manipulation, and the conspiracies—all these things confuse our values."

"Maybe there are no values."

"You know better than that, Jeffrey. You already know these things are not benevolent space brothers—and you know who they're up against. They're fighting God, Jeffrey. They know they're eventually going to lose. That's why they keep circling back—hopelessly looping again and again through time—prolonging the agony. Why try to recruit me to join you? Why not join me instead?"

"Now you're preaching," Jeffrey chuckled.

"Every chance I get. It isn't too late, you know. . . ."

"You forget," Jeffrey said, still smiling. "I'm Jewish."

"So was Jesus."

Jeffrey got up off the bed and stretched. "Look. You're going to be with us for awhile. That's a nice, innocuous, nonspecific word, isn't it? *Awhile*. I'll try to make it as comfortable for you as I can because you're my friend. And you're welcome to come out with us if you want, to see the sights—but you may not want to."

"Why? What are these errands you're running for Kundas?"

"Weren't you listening to what was said in that meeting? We're off to the past to harvest bodies."

# Chapter Fifteen

*Harvesting bodies*

It happened over and over. The lights would go out as they dropped into time. Then the saucer would land, and he would hear the rampway descend. There would be footsteps in the corridor, muttered conversations, things being carried aboard. Bodies. Then the rampway would be retracted, and the lights would again go out.

Jack kept to his cabin. For days—if days they were—he did nothing but eat, sleep, think, and pray. The food was excellent, if a bit rich. The bed was comfortably firm. There were books to read if he'd felt like reading, but he did not. He felt like thinking—turning over in his mind the things he'd seen and experienced, the memories of his previous voyage upon this ship, which flooded back now as if they'd only happened yesterday. *Which,* he thought to himself, *they might have. . . .*

He was plagued by questions: many questions, with enormous implications, which led to still more questions. He asked for and received from Jeffrey a notebook to write them down—to try to separate them out from one another and try to make sense of them all. At the top of the page he wrote his first question in the tight, Koine-flavored print he'd adopted during his first semester of Greek:

WHY HAVEN'T THEY KILLED ME?

It didn't seem reasonable to Jack that the Fallen would let him live. They knew who he was, *what* he was. At the very least, his prayers aggravated them, perhaps even somehow hurt them. If his presence—or rather in the presence of the Holy Spirit within him—somehow blocked their plans, then why not permanently dispose of him?

*Permanently.* There was another time word. The Fallen could not permanently destroy him. Death would only free him. And in a sense, had they not already disposed of him by locking him inside this flying prison of time and space? Wasn't Jeffrey ultimately just his warden? Jack finally concluded that the demons could *not* kill him—not by themselves, anyway, despite their demonstrable supernatural power. But they could surely prompt people to kill him, couldn't they? They'd killed Jesus through the rage of the Pharisees. They'd killed Paul, and Peter, and thousands of other martyrs down through the ages. Jeffrey, or Wesley, or one of their nameless, empty-faced soldiers could walk into this cabin and put a bullet through his head.

Perhaps that would eventually come. But they hadn't done it yet, despite manifold opportunities. Maybe he still held some usefulness to them in allowing them to penetrate deep time without interference from the Guardians. Once the harvesting was over—once they'd paid a visit to every scene of carnage in human history and collected all the leftover human scraps—perhaps then they'd be done with him. Meanwhile, the Fallen had effectively put him out of their way—away from Ben, away from the family he loved, away from his ministry, and away from heaven.

Jack determined, therefore, that in the meantime he would be an irritant, like that grain of sand that somehow gets into an oyster shell and is transformed into a pearl by the oyster's discomfort. Jesus had been the Pearl of Great Price in the oyster of this demonic world. That's what Jack would be: a constant source of irritation to the Fallen's worldwide conspiracy.

AREN'T THEY TERRIFIED? Jack wrote.

For despite the Fallen's apparent success in manipulating the world's social systems, there was one social structure that continued to grow, surviving their every attempt to stamp it out. The Church continued to spread through the world like a wildfire through prairie grass. The very technologies that made the Fallen's demonic illusions so powerful also provided the means for freely communicating the truth of the gospel. If they still viewed this as a contest rather than an accomplished fact, then the Fallen were losing, for more and more missionaries were pouring themselves out in service. People groups who had never had the opportunity to hear the story of Jesus were hearing it. Wherever they seemed to have successfully stamped out the fires of faith, the flames sprang up again nearby, burning hotter still through the zeal of the persecuted. If history was any gauge, then their attempts to kill the Church had to be considered totally ineffective. They'd been more successful by letting it grow fat and rich and complacent. The demons' best defense remained what it had always been: neutralizing the effective witness of Christians by tempting them—one by one—to compromise their faith. And yet, the Church still continued to grow. No wonder they were using every means available to try to kill off the body of Christ. As the ranks of evangelical

Christians continued to swell into a third millennium of faith, the Fallen must be surely terrified that they were running out of time.

Time.

WHERE DOES MY EXPERIENCE FIT IN THE FLOW OF EVENTS BEN AND JEFFREY REMEMBER?

Jack puzzled over this at length. The three of them had shared a conversation one afternoon in the shadow of the tower of Babel. Sometime soon thereafter their different time streams had diverged. It was easy to figure out when with Jeffrey: he had left them to go it alone and had eventually enlisted in Kundas' rebellion. But when had Jack and Ben broken continuity? Sometime soon after the fall of the tower, a very different-acting Baal had picked up the two of them, speaking riddles about the long period of separation and telling of the wonders they would both soon see in Atlantis. When had his own time and Ben's become separated? Had Ben somehow disappeared and returned during that . . . time?

Jack sighed in frustration. Without the anchor of shared events there was such *confusion!*—Jack suddenly thought of the way modern computer technology could cast long dead movie stars in modern television commercials. Jack mumbled to himself, "Postmodernism is a pretty good strategy for destroying linear thought. You can convince society that history is infinitely revisable. . . ." Which was exactly what the Fallen had been trying to do, Jack realized with a shudder. But that raised another question, and Jack scrawled it on his pad.

SINCE THEY CAN NOW TRAVEL IN TIME, WHY ARE THEY SEEKING ETERNAL LIFE FOR HUMANS?

Once he got it down, that one seemed self-evident. The Ultrarch had answered it in his speech to the Council. While they could certainly confuse people's perceptions of the past, they'd evidently learned by now they couldn't change the past itself. Now they were trying to alter their future instead, by lengthening the lives of their human slaves indefinitely. While pretending to be aiding humankind's "leap to the stars," they were still trying to get off this rock themselves. But why?

WHAT DO THEY THINK THEY CAN ACCOMPLISH BY GETTING OFF THE PLANET?

It wasn't as if God would suddenly forget them! Wherever people went, the Church would go with them. This was *all* God's universe. But he guessed the Fallen were like the prisoner who fantasizes about escape and examines every opportunity to get away. Evidently they clung to the notion that somewhere, away from this planet, they might at last find a hiding place from judgment. They wanted to ride humanity to the distant refuge of the stars and to ultimately dominate the galaxy as they had dominated this planet.

BUT WHY ALL THE DIFFERENT ALIEN DISGUISES?

Why not just one? Because they had always been in competition with one another? They had long played at being gods—in different forms with different races. Had the knitting together of God's world through the Great Commission finally forced them to cooperate with one another, even as they competed? They certainly weren't doing so out of any love for one another, despite their saccharine appeals for universal tolerance.

WHERE DOES THIS OVERLORD FIT IN THE INFERNAL HIERARCHY? he wondered.

The creature wasn't the evil one himself. He'd spoken to Baal and the UMMO of "The Exalted." Was this global conspiracy only one of Satan's continuing projects? That had to be the case. While Lucifer certainly dominated the activities of the Ultrastructure, he wasn't limited by it. The Overlord was only a lieutenant—albeit a powerful one. He was just as afraid of the one he called "The Exalted" as the lesser demons were of him. Jack assumed that, if he failed, the

Overlord could himself be replaced, just as he'd replaced Baal. Meanwhile the evil one continued to be busy elsewhere. No, everywhere.

Jack reviewed what he'd written and was depressed. The situation of this world looked totally hopeless. He started to write down WHY DOESN'T THE LORD COME NOW? but he scratched through that. The angel had told him why. The mission of the Church was not yet complete. And suddenly, Jack realized with a shudder what might be the *real* reason the Fallen seemed so interested in eternally prolonging human life.

IF NO ONE IS EVER ALLOWED TO DIE, THEN NO ONE COULD EVER GO TO BE WITH GOD! THEY'RE TRYING TO LOCK HEAVEN'S DOOR FROM THE OUTSIDE!

That was it. Jack sighed and put down his pencil, finally understanding. It all made perverse sense to him now. The Fallen wanted to kill off the present-day Church, replacing it with a New Age mish-mash of religions focused on worship of themselves. Meanwhile, they were pushing human creativity to give them the universe. They would then seed the stars with their own wickedness, turning the heavens into a vast, sprawling hell. Every demon could have his own planet—and his own subject population of eternally living, eternally miserable human slaves. Then they would finally be able to "be as gods." "Lord?" Jack muttered in the silence of his cabin, "just how far are You going to let them go with this?"

He stood up and paced his room—his cell. Other questions tumbled through his mind—more temporal, personal questions. What was the Lord's purpose for him here? How and why would he betray Ben? And why was it that Jeffrey could not bring himself to believe? That last one had stumped him as long as he and Jeffrey had been friends. It had always seemed that Jeffrey wanted so desperately to believe in *something*. Why couldn't he simply believe in God? Why couldn't everybody?

The lights went out again, and Jack knelt where he was to weather the bouncing of the saucer. When they came back on he went to the closet and got out a pair of sunglasses and a hat. Enough of this brooding. Jack was ready to do something.

He waited at his door until he heard the rampway drop and the footsteps pound down it. Then he stepped into the corridor and followed them.

Jack's first breath of fresh air in days filled him with euphoria. His first glimpse of where he stood made him stumble with vertigo. Then he gasped at the breathtaking landscape that stretched out, quite literally, at his feet.

He knew immediately where they were. He'd seen these square-cut, salmon-colored stones every time they'd ever watched the family slides. When he was only two his father had made a trip to the Mayan ruins in the Yucatan peninsula and had come home with plenty of pictures. The saucer was perched atop one of those steep Mayan pyramids—only this one wasn't yet in ruins. It was very active.

A dense rain forest of jungle extended for miles into the distance, but a highly developed civilization clustered at the foot of this pyramid. Thousands of its citizens were gathered in the paved square 150 feet below, gazing upward in rapt silence. Jack didn't want to turn around to see what they were watching. He already knew. But at last he did.

The stone altar itself was shaped like a curved saddle or a chopping block. His dad had taken a picture of it and had always said the heads carved in each raised end were of birds. Jack knew, now, they were not. They were the heads of Osirins—big-nosed Whites. It was easy to make the comparison, for a White stood beyond the altar, watching as the human sacrifice was offered to him. A Mayan priest in towering headdress stood over the victim, who was being held faceup across the dip in the carved rock. As the priest raised his ornate stone knife, preparing to plunge it down into the man's gut, something surprising happened—surprising to Jack as much as it was to anyone who witnessed it. Jack heard himself shout "No!" then felt himself make a dash for the altar.

He never got there. Three alert men in black cut him off, grabbing him by his arms and waist and slinging him around to slam him up against the side of the saucer. The victim had heard him and turned his imploring pleas Jack's way, but it was far too late. There was nothing Jack could do. The knife was flashing down, the blood was spurting from the impaled stomach, the priest was raising his red-smeared weapon above his head in religious ecstasy, and the crowd below had broken into a hymn of joy.

That was all Jack saw, and far more than he'd wanted to see. He was wrestled into the saucer, thrown onto the floor of the entry bay, and booted twice in the ribs. One of them must have kicked him in the head. . . .

\* \* \*

"That was quite a display," Jeffrey said sardonically.

"Where am I," Jack groaned.

"The surgery. Don't try to get up. You're strapped down."

"Are you going to kill me now?"

"Oh, Jack, come on," Jeffrey snarled. "If we'd been planning to kill you, we would have done it already. Could have just thrown you off the pyramid. Now that would have made an interesting spectacle for the congregation, wouldn't it!"

"Why didn't you?" Jack murmured, trying to raise his hand to his aching head. He found it was strapped down too. "I'd be another body . . ."

"Well, now, that's just the thing. We don't need *your* body. We've got plenty of bodies—and there are plenty more where they came from. Your contribution won't be necessary. Thank you, though, for your generous offering."

"What *are* you going to do with me?"

"Hmm," Jeffrey murmured. "Really haven't given it much thought. Put you back in your cabin, I suppose. Lock the door this time."

"Why are you doing this, Jeffrey?"

"Doing what? Keeping you alive?"

"Working for these creatures." Jack had closed his eyes. The light overhead was blinding, and strapped as he was, he couldn't turn away from it.

"Very simple, old friend. I want to live forever."

"You call this living?"

"I already told you," Jeffrey answered Jack calmly. "I find my life incredibly interesting. The places I've visited, the things I've seen—"

"The blood you've spilled . . ."

"Blood really doesn't bother me, Jack. In any case, I didn't spill it."

"You caused it—"

"No, no, Jack, I didn't cause it at all. This all happened a long time ago, don't you see? I'm just the black-suited mortician in the silvery sky chariot, come to bear the body away to heaven."

"The Whites caused it."

"Closer to the truth, but still not quite accurate. These *people* caused it. Their religious sensibilities demanded it. You know something about religious sensibilities, I think?"

"How can you compare—"

"It's all the same thing! The lamb's blood on the altar in my Jewish heritage? The sacrificed Son of God in yours? All religions are obviously the same. They all want your blood. How's your head?"

245

"It hurts."

"Good. Maybe next time you won't try to change history."

"Change history?"

"These sacrifices happened, Jack. Historical fact. Ruined the Mayan civilization, true, but we didn't do that. They did it to themselves. Generated enormous numbers of bodies, which we're disposing for them. It's part of our new policy of cooperating with history, rather than interfering in it. We're collecting *these* samples while I understand another crew is collecting from the period of the Black Plague, and still others are working the Inquisition, Auschwitz, places like that. I would think you'd be relieved, Jack! After all, we're making use of long-dead corpses for research rather than kidnapping living people off the street. That's *something* at least, isn't it?"

Jack tried to think of some response, but could only shake his aching head.

Jeffrey paused a moment, then added, "I did warn you."

That was it. Despite his attempt to interfere, nothing happened to him. Jeffrey had him put back in his cabin, locking the door to insure Jack didn't surprise them again. And the harvest of bodies continued.

Eventually the hold was full, and Jack felt the saucer actually fly again. The drop through time at the end of the journey felt just the same, but soon thereafter Jeffrey came through his door and announced, "We're here."

"Where's 'here'?"

"Back home. I call it home, anyway. It's where I keep what stuff I've hung onto through the years. You've been here before. It's the main research facility." Jeffrey tossed him an empty duffel bag, saying, "Bring whatever you want to keep and come with me. It seems Ben's gone on strike and won't do his work unless he can see you."

Jack felt a stir of excitement. This was a break in the boring routine, at least. And he looked forward to seeing Ben.

He moved around the room putting things into the bag—gingerly, for his ribs still ached. There was little to pack. The suits, shirts and ties, the sunglasses, the underwear, even the robe and stitched-skin coat. He started to leave the hats behind, then changed his mind. Jack never could throw anything away.

Jeffrey escorted him down the ramp and into the hanger. It *did* look familiar—but all of these underground installations had taken on a dull sameness to Jack. As they walked into the corridors, his impression remained unchanged. They all looked alike. He figured he must be under New Mexico again, if Jeffrey said he'd been here before. But how could anyone tell his way around such a maze? There were signs on the wall—Level 14 H 36 turned into Level 14 H 35 as they crossed an identical intersecting hallway—but where was the directory? He was reminded of several sprawling urban hospitals he'd gotten lost in and wondered just how many levels there were to this installation. It was not merely an underground base, it was a subterranean *city*. If he ever did want to try to escape, how could he possibly find his way out?

Jeffrey knew where he was going. After several turns that took them through a large common room that was clearly a self-serve cafeteria, they walked into a newer section of halls with a slightly more expensive look to the decor. These halls had carpeted floors rather than tile and textured wallpaper instead of paint. "Living areas," Jeffrey explained. A few moments later he stopped in front of a door numbered 318 and gestured Jack inside. "Your room. Just drop your bag on the bed and come with me. Ben's expecting us."

Ben's room was in another part of the complex altogether, on a hall labeled Level 12 CA 140. While Jack was certain he could find his way back to his own room, by this time he had given up trying to figure out the numbering system.

He would have to learn his way around the place by exploration, if they would allow him the freedom to explore. He wondered if he could get someone to give him a map.

"Lost are you, Jack?" Ben asked mockingly as they stepped at last through his door. This was a palatial suite by contrast to Jack's quarters. To one side Jack saw a small kitchen, its two-person table piled high with goodies. To the other he saw a bedroom with comic books and magazines scattered everywhere. This central living space was colorfully decorated and equipped with every electronic gadget a teenage boy could hope to have at his disposal. There were no windows, however. Jack had really begun to miss windows.

"You'll help him find his way back to his room, right?" Jeffrey asked Ben, who had not bothered to get up from the overstuffed couch on which he sprawled.

"He knows the way," Ben grumbled, picking this information effortlessly from Jack's mind. "But I might take him back down anyway, just to have a reason to get out of here."

"Can't imagine why you'd want to," Jeffrey observed, glancing around. "You've got everything you need. Gotta run. I'll see you again, Jack." Then Jeffrey was gone.

"He will, you know," said Ben as Jack sank deep into a comfortable armchair. "See you again, I mean."

"Oh. Atlantis. Yes, I've already told him that."

"We just don't know if you'll see *him* again." Had Ben picked that out of his mind as well? That tension about ever being able to return home? The boy's voice sounded cynical, even angry. Jack turned to look at him.

"How are they treating you?"

"Look around," Ben gestured. "They've given me everything I could want."

"Except freedom."

"You're the one who keeps saying I want that, not me."

"Then you're happy?"

"I didn't say *that,*" Ben growled. "I'm bored to death."

"I know the feeling."

"You know what I do all day?" Ben went on. "I sit behind a one-way mirror watching terrified people answer questions I don't understand. As they respond, I scrape through their minds, looking for shreds of information or creative possibilities they often don't even know are there. Then I dictate a report to be channeled and wait until the next frightened scientist is brought in. In some ways, Jack, it's worse than reading demons. Have you any idea how petty and uninteresting most people's thoughts are?"

"Only my own."

"Do you know how difficult it is to get them to concentrate—even for just a few minutes—on what's really important?"

"On what's really important to the Fallen, you mean."

"You know what I mean," Ben grumbled.

"Because," Jack went on, "I would imagine their own fears are far more important to them than any creative thinking would be."

Ben peered at him a moment, then got up to get a soft drink from the refrigerator. "So how are *you* feeling?" he called.

"Read my mind."

"I have," Ben said as he returned. "You've figured out what they're doing."

Jack didn't answer out loud. Instead he thought, *Have you told them that?*

Ben plopped back down on the couch. "They know."

Jack thought that over for a few moments. When Ben didn't comment, he at last asked, "So what are they going to do with me?"

"That they *don't* know. They don't know what to do with you."

"How about just slipping me back into time where I belong?" Jack shrugged. "Letting me go on living my life?"

"They can't. You know too much. And you *talk* too much."

"So, I'm just stuck here?" Jack asked. He didn't want to think it, but the thought came to mind anyway: this was Ben's fault.

"I've apologized for all that before, Jack," Ben said without looking at him. "Many times."

Jack regretted the thought immediately. He was reminded again how much easier it is to control words than to control thinking. "I'm sorry I blame you, Ben. I don't mean to. It's really not your fault."

"Oh, right," the boy sneered. "It's God's."

"That's what I have to believe, Ben. That's what the angel told me."

Ben sat up now and looked at him across the garbage-strewn coffee table. "I know. So I've made a suggestion to them, and they've agreed to it. I've told them you'll agree too."

"I will?" Jack said, smiling uneasily. "You know that already?"

"I think so. I think I know you pretty well. I know you're a good listener. As you said, it's hard for people to be creative when they're frightened. They need someone to listen to their fears, and to help them to relax and think. I've suggested to Kundas that you be made the chaplain of this facility."

Jack stared at Ben, open-mouthed, then he burst out laughing. "They *agreed* to that?" he asked, incredulous.

"They see the sense in it, yes. I told them it might tame you down."

"Tame me down, huh?" Jack frowned. "You think that?"

"I said that's what I *told* them. I didn't say I believed it myself. I *do* believe you could help some of these abductees to think more clearly. Then they could go home sooner, and I would be finished with this chore."

Still incredulous, Jack asked, "So you mean the Fallen would let me conduct prayer services or something?"

"Not that," Ben shook his head. "No organized meetings. But I've told them how depressed these people are, and that you could help them feel better by counseling them. They've agreed to let you wander around and listen to people's problems."

"How do they think this is going to 'tame' the Holy Spirit?" Jack argued.

"They don't. They just think they can make some use of it, to relax these kidnapped scientists enough to get some value out of them. I told them you'd agree to do it."

"Why would I want to?" Jack asked, still arguing faintly. Already he was wondering if this might not be his true purpose here.

"Because I knew once I suggested it, you'd begin to believe this must be why God put you into this situation."

Chagrined at the boy's impudence, Jack still began giving the idea serious thought. *What other choice do I really have?* he wondered.

". . . and because I knew you'd realize you really had no other choice. That is, unless you want to be transferred to an UMMO saucer that's going back to pick up bodies from the Stalin's Gulags. That's the alternative Kundas preferred. Of course, they'd sting you again. . . ."

"No," Jack said softly, "I wouldn't want that."

"You see? I'm looking out for you, Jack."

"Would they let me have a Bible?"

"They won't go *that* far."

Jack sat with his hands between his knees, thinking and praying about this unexpected turn. *Lord?* he asked. *Is this it?*

Ben rolled backward to lay again on the couch. "You two go ahead and talk," he mocked. "Take your time."

*Is limited ministry better than no ministry?* It was not an insignificant question, despite Ben's apparent dismissal of it. The Fallen had long used state control of churches to prevent them from being truly effective—the way firefighters set backfires to slow the progress of a really big blaze. But the Holy Spirit would *not* be controlled. . . .

"Good," Ben snapped, sitting back up. "Then that's settled. You can start any time. By the way," he added, "the UMMO suggestion was never a real possibility. They don't want you around."

Jack stood up. "But you do, don't you, Ben?" he said. "Because you, too, need the comfort only the Holy Spirit can bring. Whether you've admitted it to yourself yet or not, you're already a believer. You're just trying to find the confidence to refuse to serve these demons any longer."

Ben held up his hand and whined, "Don't start on that again, Jack. I'm in enough trouble already."

"I'll just keep praying for you."

"Do whatever you want, Jack," Ben murmured. Then he looked up and fixed Jack with a threatening gaze. "Just don't betray me."

But it was too late. Jack already had. There was no way he could do what Ben was asking of him. What puzzled him most at the moment was why Ben apparently hadn't read that in his mind.

# Chapter Sixteen

*Then Calvin was right*

As he bid the boy good-bye and stepped out into the hallway, Jack's heart was pounding. He tried to appear relaxed as he walked casually back to the elevator, but in his heart he was already on the run.

As he stepped into the elevator, his mind was racing. He would go to his room first, to 318 on the level below them, and grab that duffel bag off the floor.

But how? Ben was reading his thoughts this moment. He knew it. He had to be. *Just wait,* Jack told himself. *Jeffrey will be waiting at my doorway with MIBs to take me back to the harvest ship.* "No!" Jack exploded in the empty elevator. "I will *not* go!" But what choice did he have? They would be waiting for him there. He just knew it.

The elevator opened and Jack jumped off, turning to hurry toward his room and grab his gear. No one was waiting for him at his door, but what difference did that make? They would be waiting for him inside, ready to grab him. Or—was it possible? Could it be that Ben wouldn't tell anyone he was running? Or could the boy be waiting for him to get away before raising the alarm? By now Jack had arrived at his door, and he gently eased it open. . . .

*No one's here,* he told himself with quiet elation. *They don't know yet!* He swiftly closed the door behind him, and would have locked it, had there been any locks. *Why are there no locks on these doors?* he asked himself in surprise. *Because security is so tight in this place that no one would think to steal from anybody else?* "Ridiculous!" Jack snorted. The place was full of demons! More like the men in black wanted immediate access to every room, so no one could hide from them! *And how am I to hide?* Jack fretted. *How can I hide from my mind-reading friend?*

There was no time to answer that now. This was the room he'd been assigned, the first place they'd hunt for him. He had to get out, *now.* Jack grabbed his duffel bag and launched himself out into the hall, half-expecting Jeffrey—or far worse, Wesley—to be waiting for him there. But no, it was still clear. As Jack fled down the hallway toward the elevator, he was praying for God to tell him where to go.

Where were the offices in this underground city? He wanted at all costs to avoid them. On what level were the labs where all of those collected bodies were being autopsied, or whatever it was they did with them? He wanted to stay away from those too. Most of all, Jack wondered at the size of this vast, empty complex. Where were all the people it had been constructed to hold? It was like a ghost town—or a ghost hotel. Not that he was really wanting to run into anybody else. . . .

He jumped onto the elevator again and searched the buttons for clues. There were no labels listed beside any of the buttons to tell the purpose of any level. Which way should he go? Up was toward the surface. Wouldn't it make sense that the more occupied levels would be up? Then he would go down. He stabbed a button at random, thinking as he did so, *This is never going to work!* At the same time he felt a wild elation, a sense of freedom of action he'd not experienced since he'd set off for that farmhouse in the snow.

The elevator door opened on Level 22, and Jack stuck his head out to look both ways. Good! This hallway was just as deserted as the one he'd left behind. He jumped off quickly, chose a direction, and started walking, stopping intermittently to check the doors on either side. None of them were locked. None of them were occupied. He turned right, then left, then right again, checking doors all the way with the same result. Finally he choose one of them and plunged inside it, slamming the door behind him and sitting on the floor with his back to it. He needed time to reason out what to do next.

*This will never work,* Jack told himself again. *They're already on the way down to get me.* But they hadn't gotten him yet. . . .

\* \* \*

Jeffrey responded to Ben's frantic summons as soon as he got it. He found the boy's room a wreck, and Ben busy adding to wrecking it further. "Stop it!" he shouted as Ben crashed a stereo against the wall. "I said stop!" he shouted again when the boy picked up a speaker, and lunged forward to grab the boy around the waist and jerk him over to the couch. Throwing him down on it he seized Ben by the collar, shook him violently, and shouted, "What's wrong with you! Speak up! What is *wrong?*"

"I've lost Jack!" Ben shouted back up in his face.

"Lost him? What do you mean, boy?"

"I mean I've lost him! I can't read him—can't see him! It's like he's disappeared from my mental screen—just like that!"

Jeffrey's thin lips curled into a disbelieving sneer. "Just like that, huh? And just how does such as thing happen, hmm?"

"I have no idea!" Ben raged helplessly. "It's never happened to me before!"

"I see," Jeffrey nodded, his manner turning cool. "And have I disappeared too? Tell me what I'm thinking right now."

Ben started to whimper. "You think I'm lying, and you're deciding how you're going to hurt me!" Tears began to roll down the teenager's cheeks, and he started shaking.

"Right so far. And now what am I thinking."

"Now you're frightened that I might be telling the truth, and you know they'll hurt you for it!"

"Right again."

"And now," Ben hastened on, sniffling, "you're wondering how it could be that such a thing could happen, and I'll tell you again, Jeffrey, *I don't know!*"

Jeffrey threw Ben back onto the cushions and stepped away. "This is bad, Ben. This is a real problem." No one could know of this, Jeffrey was thinking. Kundas would kill him.

"*I'm* not telling anybody if *you* won't!" Ben responded as if the words had actually been spoken.

Jeffrey stroked his chin, struggling to remain calm and think what to do next. Search, of course. Starting . . . where?

"The unoccupied areas!" Ben supplied. "That's where anyone would hide—if he's hiding."

"He may not be hiding?" Jeffrey asked, brightening.

"Don't you get it yet?" Ben whined angrily. "I have no idea *what* he's thinking! And it terrifies me!"

Jeffrey looked around again at the trashed suite. "Apparently. Look at all the pretty broken toys. . . ."

"Who cares about all this garbage?" Ben barked, sitting up. "You work me so hard I never get a chance to use any of it!"

That was probably true. Maybe the boy needed some rest. A day off. Meanwhile a quiet, unobtrusive search—a security exercise, he would call it, just to check their level of preparedness. But first he would go look in Jack's room. Jack would have no way of knowing that Ben could no longer read his mind. And if he knew Jack, his friend would either be asleep or writing out questions on his notepad and angsting over them.

"That's just it," Ben grumbled quietly, his eyes staring off into emptiness. "You don't really know Jack." Jeffrey looked at the boy sharply and saw tears streaking his cheeks. Ben looked like he'd just lost his best friend as he murmured softly, "And right now—for the first time—neither do I."

\*   \*   \*

No one came looking for him. Not soon, anyway. He sat with his back to the door for at least an hour, listening intently for sounds of motion in the hallway, hearing nothing. Could it be that Ben was asleep? The boy *had* looked terribly weary. His slave-masters were overworking him. That had to be the only explanation: Ben was out cold. Otherwise he would have told somebody. Ben couldn't just let Jack disappear. The boy was too frightened of his keepers to do that. They would punish him if he tried. Who knows what they had done to him already.

Jack felt a stab of guilt. They would punish Ben in any case, as soon as Jack was missed. Yes, he had betrayed him—*was* betraying him. And to what end? Jack had no plan. He had no real hope of escaping. This was foolishness. Maybe he should just go back up to his assigned room before he was missed—pretend he'd gotten lost or something. Easy enough to do in this vast maze.

No. He couldn't do it, couldn't perform the task Ben had assigned to him, couldn't betray the *Spirit* within him in the way that Ben had asked. And after all, he reasoned, this had already happened. Ben had told him so. If they found him, that was one thing, but he wouldn't just give himself up. That would be an even greater betrayal.

They *would* search. Sooner or later they would come looking for him. What would he do then? He had to think.

Hours later, he heard it at last: doors opening and closing in a nearby hallway, men calling to one another, moving methodically through the corridors—men in black. Jack leapt to his feet, his knees trembling. The urge to run rattled through him, tingling every nerve ending in his body. "Lord," he murmured, "what do I *do?*" He paced the room, ears tuned to every noise. Should he risk a glance out into the hall? What good would that do? If there was no one there, what would he do? Run and call their attention to him? That would be stupid. He paced faster as the sounds grew closer, then fell to his knees beside his duffel bag and jerked it open. The knife . . . had to find the knife. As he jerked it out, scabbard and all, he was thinking over and over again, Fight or flight—*fight or flight.* He pulled out the blade and examined it. Did this mean he was ready to fight? Ready to kill somebody to preserve this brief sense of freedom?

They were coming closer! They were right through the wall! *The back wall,* Jack thought, calming himself. They were one corridor over. He went to that wall and leaned against it, listening. . . .

"Closet—nothing. Under the bed—nothing. Bathroom—nothing." The door slammed.

Another door opened, and Jack leaned in to listen. The cadence was just the same: "Closet—nothing. Under the bed—nothing. Bathroom—nothing." Then that door slammed, and the searcher moved on. He heard this same formula repeated twice more before the sounds faded out. How long would it take them to get to him? He had to move!

He grabbed up his bag and slipped swiftly out the door, then walked as silently as he could in the opposite direction from the way they were going. At the intersection he paused, listening, and his heart quailed. From here he could hear several teams at work, in many different directions. He felt so exposed! *Which way, Lord? Which way?* In panic he fled across the intersection, running quietly down the far corridor, expecting any moment to hear the shouts that would mean he'd been spotted. *Gloria!* he thought frantically of the angel, *are you going to get me out of this one too?* He raced through a large lounge, noticing as he passed that it was equipped with vending machines and a small kitchen. He made a mental note of that and sprinted onward into yet another corridor, aware that the sounds of the search were no longer audible. Could it be they had already searched this section? Was it possible that he'd slipped behind them? He chose another door, bolted inside it, squatted against it, and gasped to catch his breath.

Two things were apparent—good news and bad news. The bad news was that they'd missed him at last, and the dragnet had begun. The good was that they were having to search at all. Ben had obviously alerted the Fallen that he was missing, but it was equally obvious that Ben didn't know where he was. The question now was what to do about it. He stood up and paced this room, a mirror image of the one he'd just left behind, identically furnished. When had this place been constructed? The sixties, by the look of the furniture. Why, he wondered again, wasn't it occupied? Had it once been? Or were these rooms just waiting to be filled with an ever-expanding population of abductees? Who had built it? Government contractors, of course, but what had happened to them? Why hadn't somebody told the media about the huge building project in the desert? Because it was Top Secret, naturally. And there *had* been all those rumors. But what an excavation! Where had they put the *dirt?*

Passing by the bathroom door, he caught a glimpse of a man in black and his heart stopped. Then he gasped in relief. It was his own reflection in a full-length mirror. As he sucked in another deep breath, he seemed to breathe in an idea, and it caused him to go back to the mirror and examine his reflection more carefully. *Why not?* he wondered. After all, he certainly looked the part. After all, how many MIBs would it take to staff a place this huge? Given their apparent absence of any personality, how well would they know each other? He'd been in their presence often, but he'd never seen the slightest hint of any real relationship between any of them. "Why not?" he asked the man in black in the mirror. "Why not just go join the search for myself?"

Not immediately, of course. It was possible that they'd searched this section already and wouldn't be back. But if they did come again—and he felt certain they would—then he was resolved to step outside and start checking rooms himself. He could already mimic the cadence. First, however, he needed to find a place to stash his stuff—*the lounge area,* he thought. Vending machines and kitchens meant food—and trash. Trash cans that were never emptied. But wouldn't they, too, be searched? He would have to take that chance. Checking his reflection once more, he straightened his tie and put on that expression he'd seen on so many MIB faces: deadness. He was a little alarmed at how easily it came to him.

\* \* \*

It was almost too easy. Once his bag was safely stowed, he followed the sounds of the search until he caught up with an active crew. Walking stiffly, eyes dead, he simply asked them, "Where do I start?"

"Where's your partner?" one of them asked expressionlessly.

Jack didn't miss a beat. "On another assignment." He didn't elaborate. MIBs never answered more than the question asked.

The other man didn't blink. The task was boring, and since they'd found nothing yet, it was only to be expected that the search would grow. More hands meant they'd be finished more quickly. "You can work with us."

Jack made no other response than to open the closet door and look in. "Closet—nothing," he announced flatly, loud enough for the others to hear. "Under the bed—nothing. Bathroom—nothing." He knew the drill. For the next few hours he searched alongside his pursuers, and never once did they cast a suspicious glance his way.

"Closet—nothing. Under the bed—nothing. Bathroom—nothing." Slam. "Closet—nothing. Under the bed—nothing. Bathroom—nothing." Slam. "Closet—"

Jack paused. Not long. Half a second, perhaps, then "nothing." He lied. For there was a man hiding in the closet. The man cowered on the floor in the corner, looking up at Jack with a guilty expression. He was about to speak when Jack put a finger to his own lips to silence him, and the man's eyes widened in astonishment, swiftly followed by equally wide-eyed appreciation. "Under the bed—nothing," Jack said aloud without bothering to check, for his gaze was still locked into the man's eyes. He looked familiar. Jack smiled encouragingly, then called out, "Bathroom—nothing. Bathroom break." This followed a pattern already set by his coworkers, and it gave him a moment to step into the bathroom, fish a scrap of paper out of his pocket, and to scribble a note.

*We need to talk. Wait here. I'll be back as soon as I can.*

He left it on the lavatory, flushed the commode, and quickly rejoined his companions, casually glancing at the room number as he did so.

They finished two more corridors, another hour and a half of looking, before one of his comrades announced, "It's dinner time."

Jack had been waiting for this, preparing what to say and how to say it. It was a simple line, and he delivered it with quiet authority. "You two go ahead. I ate before I came down." His expressionless face belied the tension he felt inside. How would they respond?

They responded by going to dinner and leaving him behind to continue the search. When they were well out of sight, Jack walked purposefully to the lounge where he'd left his bag and found that it was still safe in the trash bin. He pulled it out and doubled back to find that room number he had memorized. He was wondering if he would find the man had fled.

He had not. He jumped off the bed when Jack opened the door—then sat back down looking relieved. "I'm not going to hurt you," Jack said quickly in his most comforting voice.

"I know that."

"You do?"

"Of course. You're an angel, aren't you."

"What? No!"

The man looked puzzled. "But God did send you to me, didn't He? To rescue me?"

Jack started to say no again, then stopped himself. Was this *why* he was here? "Maybe so. You think so?"

"That's what God told me," the man said anxiously.

Jack blinked and sat down on the edge of the bed. "Well if that's what He told you, that's certainly good news. I was wondering who He would send to rescue *me*."

The man still eyed him anxiously, then said, "I recognized you immediately, in spite of the black suit. You were the man on the tram who tried to tell us we weren't in hell."

So he *had* looked familiar! Jack studied the man's face more carefully—then remembered. The white lab coat should have been a giveaway. He was still wearing it. "I remember you now. You didn't speak."

"I was terrified. Still am," he added. His hands were trembling.

Jack started to answer that he was, too—then decided against it. Why add to the man's apprehension? "What are you hiding from?" Jack probed.

The man looked shocked. "I . . . I assumed you knew! Weren't you . . . those people you were with . . . hunting for me?"

"Actually," Jack smiled, "I thought they were hunting for me. Since I already had the black suit, I figured joining the hunt was the best way to keep them from finding me. Now I guess it was God's way of finding us both. I'm Jack Brennen," he added, extending his hand.

"Carl Pellian," the scientist responded, shaking Jack's hand self-consciously.

"Good to meet you, Carl, especially good to meet another believer in this place. And I'm guessing you're here because you're an exceptionally bright researcher who has been kidnapped by aliens and brought here to work on God knows what."

"Oh, God knows what, all right," Carl mumbled softly, glancing away. "God knows *exactly* what I'm working on. And they're not aliens."

Jack raised his eyebrows. "You know what they are?"

"You're the one who told me."

Jack smiled wanly and nodded. "On the tram. I wasn't sure anybody was really listening."

"Oh, I was listening all right. It confirmed for me what I already thought—what I already *knew*. And I've spent the last three weeks trying to *keep* from them what I know. So when they told us that they were going to rummage through our minds and then send us back home again with no memory of the missing time, I ran. There are things in there they *cannot* be permitted to know!"

Jack frowned in concentration. "What's your field?"

"Genetics."

"And they have you working on their attempt to extend life indefinitely?"

"That," Carl nodded, "and more. All of us working on the Human Genome Project understand the health obsession that drives the funding. But this cuts deeper. A *lot* deeper. And it's my fault. . . ."

"What is?"

"This . . . discovery I made." Carl shook his head. "I shouldn't have done it. I should have left well enough alone. They can't be allowed to learn it. Believe me, Jack," he said earnestly, "they can't know!"

Jack didn't want to push. He didn't want to ask. He wasn't sure he wanted to know what Carl was about to tell him. But he was absolutely certain Carl *needed* to tell him and had needed to tell someone for a very long time. "Why, Carl?" he asked quietly. "What *is* this discovery?"

Carl Pellian drew in a deep sigh and shifted position on the hard chair. Then he looked at Jack long and hard with an expression that asked, "Can I trust you?" Jack answered by opening his hands and keeping his mouth shut.

Carl finally began. "Do you know anything about genetics?"

"Not much."

Carl nodded. "Most people don't. But you know about DNA?"

"I know it's the blueprint for life. I know there's a double helix of something, amino acids, is it? And that the genes are on that, somehow."

"Genes are segments on the DNA strand. The double helix is connected by nucleic acid chains. There are four kinds of chemical composition on the strands: adenine, guanine, cytosine, and thymine. Adenine and thymine combine, guanine and cytosine combine, and— Are you getting this?" Carl interrupted himself to ask.

"Are my eyes glazing over?" Jack responded. Then he shrugged. "I used to try to teach students how television works, and they'd glaze out on me. They already knew that if you turned the TV on, the pictures would appear, and that was enough for them. I know genetics works. Do I need to know how to understand what you need to tell me?"

"Not really, I suppose," Carl admitted, pondering how to explain. "It's just that—well, let me try this: There are around 110,000 genes in a human body, each controlling various aspects of our shape, size, hair color, eye color, skin color, intelligence, etc. Geneticists around the world have been researching the purpose of each of these genes through the use of a super-sequencer—an electronic tool that can analyze and decipher a million DNA characters a day. Thus far we've mapped the purpose and impact upon the body and mind of about a tenth of those. You may have read that we've found a gene that relates to obesity, a 'fat gene' the media called it."

"I read that," Jack nodded.

"Did you know that we've found the 'levitical' gene?"

"The what?"

"A genetic indicator that links the tribe of Levi, especially prominent in persons with the family name Cohen."

"Really?" Jack said, genuinely surprised. "So, the line of the Levitical priesthood could be reconstituted on the basis of genetic evidence?"

"Theoretically. If we *needed* it, which of course the book of Hebrews tells us we don't. Anyway . . ." Carl paused, getting up the courage to make his real revelation. "I began to wonder if there was some genetic predisposition to *faith*, to being able to believe in God and accept the offering of Christ's sacrifice. Strange thing to pursue, huh?" he asked, obviously embarrassed.

"And . . . ?" Jack prodded.

"I found it," Carl said quietly. He said it with understandable pride—but then he shook his head and buried his face in his hands.

The hair was standing up on the back of Jack's neck. He didn't like this, not at all. "Let me see if I understand," Jack said, trying to paraphrase what he'd heard. "You've discovered that there is a gene that all believers *have* and unbelievers *don't?*"

Carl looked up at him and nodded.

"But it happens every day that people who are unbelievers come to faith," Jack argued, and Carl nodded again, vigorously.

"That's the whole purpose behind evangelism. To call out the called, to tell the truth to everyone, so that those who *can* believe the truth will. The Bible says, 'For faith comes by hearing, and hearing by the word of God.' So they hear, and they grab hold of it, Jack, and the Holy Spirit changes their lives. But some people who hear the message do not believe, regardless of how many times they hear it."

"Now *that's* certainly so," Jack agreed. He'd seen it proven again and again in his ministry. He'd seen it proved in Jeffrey, who had witnessed so much that testified to the power of God, yet still would not believe. "But are you saying they can't," Jack asked, "that they are genetically *incapable* of faith?"

"I'm saying that some are genetically predisposed to reject the message. They don't believe. They're nonbelievers. They're—"

"Not elect," Jack supplied flatly.

"That pushes the conversation out of genetics and into theology. But yes, that's what I'm saying."

Jack gave a long, low whistle. "Then Calvin was right."

"The apostle Paul, really," Carl corrected.

"'For by grace are you saved, through *faith*,'" Jack quoted to himself. "'And that not of yourselves, it is the *gift* of God, lest any man should boast.'" Jack scratched his head, racing with the implications of this stunning idea. Being more practical than theoretical in his theological outlook, his mind ran immediately to applications. "So when we do door-to-door visitation," he smiled, "we could give people an on-the-spot blood test to see if it would be a waste of time to share the gospel with them. Talk about targeted evangelism!"

"It isn't funny, Jack," Carl said gravely, killing Jack's smile. "Especially not now. Not here. Not in this place, when they might come any minute to take me to some room and interrogate me." Jack just stared at him, and Carl went on. "Think it through. You and I both know that the creatures who control this place are demons. They'll do anything to prevent the growth and expansion of God's kingdom. Armed with just such a test as you suggest—or with this information along with a genetic map of every gene of every human on the earth, which may be conceivable by 2005— what's to prevent them from eliminating from our world *any* person with the predisposition to believe? From murdering the 'elect of every nation'?"

"Oh, Lord." It was the only response Jack could muster.

Carl plunged on. "Suppose this! Suppose they could use their influence with government and the courts to somehow categorize this gene as *defective*, maybe not even releasing the true information to lawmakers as to why? Suppose there was a neonatal version of your blood test that allowed them to check for the presence of the faith gene in an unborn child. Is it inconceivable that they might not eventually find a way to have all such 'defective' babies aborted? We're talking about demons here, Jack! Think about it!"

By this time Jack had buried his face in his hands. He'd heard enough, but Carl still wasn't through unloading weeks—perhaps years—of his own guilt-ridden speculations.

"And what about cloning research? That promise of someday being able to offer to parents 'the designer child,' the perfect baby, free of all possible defects. What would prevent them from manipulating the genetic code so that the gene for faith is simply excised out, so that there is *no* possibility of such a child ever experiencing faith? They want to be gods, Jack! They've played at being gods. Now, they literally want to make man in *their* own image, perverting God's creation even further and using human hands to do it!" Then Carl paused and looked down. He examined his palms. "Using *my* hands . . ." he whispered. His face was stricken with guilt.

It took Jack a minute to pull himself together—or rather, for the Spirit within him to rally him enough to respond. "You did this research here?"

"Oh no," Carl said. "I did it in my lab, back at my home university in Canada. I did it and then I destroyed it. Every shred of evidence relating to my pursuit of the topic. I even thought of leaving the field altogether, but it's what I do, Jack, and I have a family to support. *Had* a family," he added sadly. "So I pressed on with other ideas, justifying my grants, angling away from any further pursuit of genetic spirituality. But they found me anyway."

"But not your research."

"Not about this, no. But here's the thing: I've been told that one of these evil creatures actually reads minds, and that before I'm to be returned to my family he's going to read *mine*. I destroyed the records, Jack, but I can't destroy the thoughts." He pointed to his head. "It's all up here. Exactly where that gene is located. Do *you* know any way to keep it from them?"

Jack was still working over the characterization of Ben as an "evil creature" on the order of one of the demons. He could certainly see how Carl would consider him such. And he knew that Ben would effortlessly pluck this idea from the scientist's mind, especially when he saw how eagerly the man was trying to conceal it. "No," he said at last.

"Well *I* do. You say you're not one of their so-called 'men in black,' and I believe you. Why, I don't know, other than that I can just sense the presence of God in you. But you are dressed like them, and I know they carry weapons. If you have one, then do the Lord, the world and myself all a favor, and kill me."

"What?"

"Just kill me. You're surely authorized to do such. Shoot me in the head so that they don't get this knowledge because if they do . . ." Carl couldn't finish his sentence. He just buried his face in his hands.

*Act* now, the Holy Spirit told him. Not in audible speech, not through the appearance of Angel Gloria, but through the still, small voice that had *always* been the Spirit's way of regular communication. And Jack acted. He stood up and announced, "We've got to get you out of here."

Carl looked at him incredulously. "Get me out?" Carl snorted. "There's no getting out of this place for me, short of death itself!" Then he added a plaintive, "Is there?"

"I don't know," Jack said honestly. "I've gotta go see."

"Wait!" Carl stopped him. "Where are you going?"

"Over here to pick up my duffel bag, first," Jack answered calmly as he opened the bag and pulled out the knife. Carl gasped when Jack handed it to him. "It's the only weapon I have," Jack explained. "If they come back here before I do—or if I don't come back—and if you really feel like killing yourself is the thing God wants you to do, there it is. But I'm going to do my best to come back for you."

"What are you planning?"

Jack thought about that a moment, then answered, "Neither of us believe this was a chance meeting. God ordained it. So my plan is to try to figure out what God's plan is for us. I'm certain He has one. But first, tell me everything you know about the upper levels. I'm going to need all the help I can get."

*　*　*

As he rode the elevator up to Level 6, Jack's misgivings began to get the better of him. Was this wise? Was this right? Was this the way God was leading him? Or was he somehow walking into a trap? It still seemed inconceivable to him that Ben could no longer read his mind, even though that was the only explanation that made sense. But even if that was so, he supposed Ben could still read other minds—like Carl Pellian's. If he could, and if he had, then all this effort might be for nothing. For wouldn't he also read Carl's secret and report it to his superiors? Jack had given Carl specific instructions to sleep while he was gone. The man was obviously exhausted by his weeks of anxiety and from the terror of nearly being discovered. He needed the rest. And if Ben were to locate Carl's mind with his formidable gift, Jack wanted the boy to find nothing there but fitful dreams. *How do you escape from a mind reader?* Jack fretted. *By the intervention of God,* the Holy Spirit answered. Jack knew he was definitely walking by faith.

# Then Calvin was right

Stepping out of the elevator onto Level 6 was like passing from a ghost town into midtown Manhattan at the midday rush. Suddenly there were people everywhere, rushing about in obvious haste. It was just as Carl had described and more. There was color here, and Jack was surprised by it, having grown accustomed to beige walls. There were corridors wide enough to bear vehicular traffic. Jack passed the glassed-in laboratory Carl had described to him, where scurrying lab technicians performed innocuous experiments upon the tissues of long-dead humans, working wonders in the name of "progress," which would ultimately be used only to tighten the demons' control on the human race. Jack didn't linger. He went into the marketplace, praying for some direction, some sense of guidance by the Holy Spirit.

No one stopped him. No one even looked his way. It was as if this black suit he wore was a kind of shield. Everyone he approached looked nervous and sought to get out of his way without meeting his eyes. He understood. He'd felt the same way about the men in black. Odd, he thought, how God could use such a symbol of terror to His advantage.

Then he saw Henry Ritter, sitting in a brightly colored waffle dispensary. Jack recognized Ritter as soon as he saw him. It was hard to miss the loud, arrogant redhead with the big red mustache and the gaudy shirts. Henry was seated at a table wolfing down pancakes and washing them down with milk. *There,* the Spirit told him, and Jack acted. He walked over to Ritter's table and sat down without being invited.

Ritter stopped chewing and looked up at Jack with shock. "What'd I do?" he asked fearfully.

*Think cold,* Jack told himself. "You tell me."

Ritter swallowed hard and put down his fork. "Do . . . do we need to go? Does somebody want me? I mean, I thought it was all right if I left today."

271

"You're leaving?" Jack asked quietly.

Ritter seemed to hear the question as interrogation and leaned in to whisper, "No one's going to notice it, I promise! It's just one little airplane on a dirt airstrip! Look, I'm not calling any attention to this place! I just thought I'd take some pressure off you people because I know you're really busy right now and—"

Jack held up his hands in a gesture to slow Henry Ritter down, but instead it cut him off short. He stared back at Jack in unmistakable fear, his face frozen in a guilty grimace, for while Jack recognized Henry Ritter from his first abduction, Henry didn't recognize him—or if he did, he certainly didn't place him as a preacher with whom he'd once shared a conversation on a saucer bound for Tampa-St. Pete. He'd boasted to Jack then of his skill in flying drugs into the country from the Caribbean. The reason for his fear of this man in black now was obvious. Henry Ritter colored outside of the lines, even in his dealings with the Fallen.

Jack played the part of cool interrogator to the hilt. He was certain now that this was the avenue of escape God had provided for them. Carl's life—and his own—depended on his ability to carry off this deception. "So," he said in measured tones copied from his conversation with Wesley, "you've parked a private plane on a landing strip on the desert above this base?"

"It may not even be there!" Henry Ritter protested. "I was going to go up and check on it this afternoon, but I don't have to do that—"

"Why don't you finish your breakfast," Jack suggested with icy kindness. "Then we can walk to your room and talk about this in private."

"I'm through," Ritter said, pushing away his still full plate. "Um, this was my second helping," he gestured over it, then patted his round stomach and pretended to smile.

"Really don't need it anyway, right?" Jack just gazed back at him, and Ritter hurriedly stood up.

Jack let Ritter lead him to a nearby elevator and up to Level 5. He made a smiling, "after you" gesture to Ritter as the door opened, which the man evidently perceived as highly threatening. Ritter led him directly to his door, opened it, and Jack followed him in. There Ritter spun around and confronted him angrily. "Why am I under surveillance? I haven't done anything. I've come when I've been called! Tell me why?"

"*Have* you been under surveillance?" Jack asked quietly.

"Oh, come on," Ritter grunted, throwing himself down into a chair. Jack was glancing around. Ritter's apartment was as opulent as Ben's, maybe more so. The decor was more elegant and the colors more muted. There were wine bottles rather than candy wrappers on the coffee table. "You people are everywhere—of course I know I'm being watched. What I want to know is, why? What have I done?"

"You mean, besides parking an airplane on a—"

Ritter interrupted him with a curse and a plea. "No one's going to *see* it!"

"Were you planning to leave without authorization?" Jack asked.

"No!" Henry Ritter was protesting. "Not without authorization; you know I wouldn't do that!"

"But isn't that *why* the plane is waiting on the desert above us, to provide you a means of departure without resorting to authorized transportation?"

"I've done it before!" Ritter blurted out, then hastened to add, "With permission of course! You could check your records."

Jack's heart pounded as he asked, "The aircraft is fueled and ready to depart at a moment's notice, I take it?"

Ritter gulped. "Yes," he squeaked, his voice box constricted with tension.

Jack took a deep, dramatic breath, then glanced around the apartment dismissively. "Very well," he said coldly. "That's all I need to know." He turned and walked to the door.

"Then I'm free to go?" Ritter asked his back.

Jack paused with his hand on the doorknob. No, he didn't want Ritter to leave, not without himself and Carl on board. Nor did he want Ritter checking with the real MIBs for authorization because of this conversation. Summoning his most authoritarian tone, he looked back over his shoulder and said, "I'll have to get back to you on that. You wait here." Then he was out the door and walking swiftly down the hallway, heading for the relative safety of the elevator.

# Chapter Seventeen

*An open door*

W ake up," Jack said flatly, and Carl's eyes flew open. "Come on. We've got to go."

Carl bounded off the bed and stared at him, as if shocked that he'd actually returned. Jack was busy in his duffel bag, pulling out the other black suit Jeffrey had given him. *The Lord will provide,* he was thinking as he tossed the suit to Carl and went back down into his bag to find a bundled shirt and a tie. "I'm heavier than you, but we're about the same height. Put those on. Quickly." His tone of voice permitted no objection, and the scientist began to do as instructed. Meanwhile Jack dug deeper into the bag . . . and there they were. Sunglasses. Two pairs. He stuffed one pair in his own shirt pocket and passed the other to Carl, who by this time was stuffing in his shirttail. It was a good thing he'd thought to bring everything with him, Jack was thinking—and in that same spirit he began to move around the room, cramming anything he thought might be of use into the bag.

"Where are we going?" Carl asked nervously.

"Better just let it be a surprise," said Jack. The less Carl actually knew, the less Ben might pick out of his brain—*if* Ben was in any condition to listen. After all, the search had obviously proved unsuccessful. Jack was beginning to worry what the Fallen might be doing to Ben right now, but he had to block that out of his mind and focus on the moment. At least he had the assurance that Ben would survive. He had no such certainty about Carl and himself.

As Carl knotted the tie, Jack pointed to the discarded clothes and opened the mouth of the bag. "We might need those. Put them in here." As soon as they were in, he jerked tight the bag's strings and threw it over his shoulder. "Let's go," he said and started for the door.

Carl Pellian, new man in black, suddenly blocked it. He turned his terror-stricken eyes to search Jack's face. "I need to tell you this, Jack," Carl said nervously. "I really don't like surprises!"

"It would just be better if you don't know too much."

"Are we going to Level 6?" Carl demanded. "They know me on Level 6! They'll recognize me!"

Jack laid a hand on Carl's shoulder and smiled reassuringly. "They won't even look at you. Trust me, they'll do their best to avoid your gaze. Try to relax."

"How can I relax? You haven't even told me your plan!"

How could he? Jack still didn't have a plan, only a half-formed notion of somehow using Henry Ritter's innate shadiness to spirit them out of this place. And *spirit* was the right word. Only by the direct intervention of Holy Spirit could they ever hope to succeed. But at least he saw a possibility now, an open door. And he'd had a clear directive from the Spirit to act. They were acting. If this was indeed of God, then God would take that action and work His will through it.

But how much of this did Carl need to know? "Say nothing," he told Carl calmly. "You've seen the men in black—they don't speak, they don't smile, they show no emotion. They're like machines, right? Act like a machine. And follow my lead. You have to understand this," he added earnestly. "We're not alone."

Trembling, Carl threw a glance over his shoulder that telegraphed clearly his thought, *We sure* look *like we're alone!*

"I know what you're thinking," Jack said confidently. "But think of Daniel's three friends in the fiery furnace. They were alone. They had no way out. They had no way of escape. Yet they lived because they trusted God completely. You say we each have a genetic predisposition to believe, Carl—that we, at least, are able to have faith. Time to trust Him, Carl. It's not by accident that we found each other. Our God is able." He pulled one of the pairs of sunglasses from his pocket, opened them, and pushed them onto Carl's face. He smiled and slapped Carl on the shoulder. "You look great, Shadrach. Let's go walk through the furnace."

Jack led Carl to the elevator and summoned it. They rode upward in silence to Level 5, Henry Ritter's level. By the time the elevator door opened again, Carl had either found some courage or his terror had reached such a proportion that it had frozen his face into a solemn mask. Jack stepped off briskly, ignoring those eyes turned to look in his direction. They quickly looked away as Carl fell in beside him, and they stalked purposefully into the hallway. Jack felt a strange elation as Carl matched him stride for stride.

They were going to escape. Jack didn't know how, but he now knew they would. How do you betray a mind reader with the resources to travel in time? Somehow he had managed to betray Ben, and there was no way of doing that. *No logical way.* For once he'd been missed, why hadn't the Fallen simply sent MIBs back in time to interrupt their conversation in the room? Or back further still to prevent them from meeting entirely? Logically, Jack thought, they shouldn't even have gotten *this* far. But they had. The only explanation that made any sense was that God was *preventing* Ben from reading him at the moment and would continue to prevent that as long as necessary to allow them to get out. Through the Guardians, He would also prevent the Fallen from going back in time to change these events—or so Jack hoped. No. So Jack *believed.* As they rounded the corner to walk down the hallway toward Henry Ritter's apartment, Jack was tempted to look over his shoulder to see if the Son of God was not walking in formation behind them. *No need,* he thought to himself. Jack knew He was there.

When they arrived at Henry Ritter's door, Jack pounded on it with authority. It opened immediately, and the frightened man greeted his two black-clad visitors with a stuttered, "I-I-I thought you were never coming back! I've been waiting here just like you—"

"You must get that plane away from here immediately." Jack cut him off, his voice and face utterly deadpan.

Henry Ritter swallowed hard and blurted out, "Right! Oh, of course, right! I'm so sorry! Just wasn't thinking! I mean, *anybody* could spot it just sitting out here in the middle of nowhere, military plane, spy satellite, 'What's that plane doing down in the—'"

"Now," Jack snarled, and Henry Ritter stumbled over the coffee table as he raced back into his room to obey.

"*Yes* sir! Yes *sir!* Just let me grab a few things—"

"Leave them," Jack ordered, taking a menacing step into the room. "You'll be back," he added for emphasis, then bit his tongue. *Say as little as you need to,* he told himself. *Explain nothing.*

"Right!" Henry yelped, reversing himself to come running back toward the door. Jack stepped aside to let the heavy man hustle through it, then glanced up to see Carl waiting in the hall. *Yes!* he thought, smiling inside, for Carl stood as straight and stiff as a marble column, as expressionless as a Buckingham Palace guard.

Sweat beading on his forehead, Ritter turned a circle in the hallway and stammered, "Wh-wh-which way?"

Jack was startled, but he didn't show it. Instead he calmly, patiently, smiled the ironic smile he'd often seen on Jeffrey's lips. "You show us, Mr. Ritter. We're right behind you."

Henry Ritter again had trouble swallowing, but he led the way, taking them down the hall away from the direction they had come. "I . . . I . . . just . . . got a little nervous there for a minute, you see, because—"

"Try not to talk," Jack ordered. He'd been surprised that there'd been no surveillance cameras down in the lower levels and had decided that must be because they were below notice. He felt certain there were cameras monitoring these upper hallways, and he wanted to make as little a scene as possible.

It was a long, brisk walk, and Henry Ritter was huffing and puffing when they finally reached another elevator. This hall was clear as he pressed the button, which Jack found most encouraging. They got on, Jack and Carl stepping toward the back of the elevator, still letting Ritter steer them. With a flick of his eye, Jack noted that *this* elevator went all the way up to Level 0. He never would have found it on his own. *Thank You, Lord,* he thought.

The florid-faced Ritter leaned against the door as he pressed that top button, gasping for breath. He glanced back over his shoulder at them, smiled weakly, then turned to face the front. He'd clenched his fists. Jack noticed they were trembling.

It was so *easy* to imitate the MIBs! They inspired such fear! No one dared ask them for any identification. Did they even carry any? They had unquestioned authority, at least down here. It was the perfect disguise! And, yes, God had provided it. In His own time, in His own way, through Jeffrey, of all people. Jack was amazed.

He was also feeling just a little uncertain. What if these elevator doors opened and a whole squad of men in black stood waiting for them? This was the critical moment, he knew. This doubt flickered briefly in his mind, then his faith quashed it. *Why would they be?* he thought to himself. God was doing this.

This time the elevator opened onto a dimly lit access hall of concrete block, barely wide enough for two men to walk abreast. Henry led them out into it, then stopped. "It's this way, isn't it?" he asked, pointing to the right. Jack looked into the man's eyes. Was he suddenly testing them? Henry Ritter, after all, was a most successful drug-runner, which made him also a very high-stakes gambler. He'd surely had occasion to bluff the hardest-nosed crooks. He wasn't a fool and could not be underestimated.

Jack stared unflinchingly back into his eyes, saying with his look, *We're testing you.* "It's your route," he said laconically. Henry Ritter blinked.

"Right," he said, then he cleared his throat and led them on through this dark maze muttering, "This really is a fascinating system you have down here. Well-designed. Completely safe and secure!" They reached a blank wall, and Henry reached out to flip a hidden lever. "I mean, even if they *did* come investigating my plane, what would they find?" The wall opened before him, and they stepped out into an old mine shaft, illuminated only by the sunlight coming through the mine entrance. "A worthless silver mine!"

Ritter finished, gesturing around. The wall closed back behind them, leaving no trace of its real nature. It looked like any other part of this abandoned shaft. The illusion was perfect. "So you see," Henry was almost pleading as he led them to the light, "it's really nothing! No problem! Besides, I'll never do it again!"

Jack wanted to ask how Henry had found this way in the first place, but instead he feigned disinterest. They had made it to the surface! He glanced at Carl and saw hope on the man's face for the first time. Then he hardened his own features and grumbled, "It never should have happened the first time."

"Right!" Henry said quickly, "Oh, you're right, no question!" The entrance was about thirty yards away, up a steep incline. "I'm just . . . I mean, the area looks so empty! In fact, it's so hard to find I just hope that idiot pilot didn't get the wrong place. . . ."

Jack felt a twinge of uncertainty. What if—but they would be outside, in any case. And God would provide.

Henry reached the mouth of the shaft first and leaned on the planking holding it up, gasping as he looked out into the sunshine. "There he is," he said at last, obviously relieved. Then he looked back at them. "OK. I'll just be on my way, and all of this'll be forgotten, right?"

Jack kept on climbing and now pushed past Henry out into the sun. The sun! Apart from that brief, chaotic moment on the Mayan pyramid he hadn't seen the sun in . . . awhile. He wanted to drink it in, but that would be out of character. Instead he turned around and looked back at Henry, and announced, "We're going with you."

Henry's mouth dropped open. "Wi . . . *with* me? But . . . but *where?*"

Now that was a good question. Jack hadn't thought that far ahead. Where should they go? Should they try to fly to Canada? Jack turned back around to look at the plane still twenty feet away. He saw movement inside it as the pilot, recognizing his boss, scrambled to get the door open and steps down. The words came to him. "I assume you were on your way somewhere else when you were summoned to appear?"

"Huh? Oh. Yeah. We were on our way to Atlanta when these saucers . . . Wooo! That was scary. Were you in one of those ships?"

"Finish your trip," Jack said.

"Atlanta?" Henry said, and Jack just nodded. "Well, that was where I was going. . . ." Henry was walking quickly toward the plane now, stirred by new purpose. "Buddy!" he shouted to the pilot. "We've got passengers." He climbed up into the plane, Jack and Carl following closely behind. It was roomier inside than it looked, with places for six. Two of the seats had been removed, however, doubtless for carrying Ritter's forbidden cargo. Jack tossed the duffel bag behind him and sat in the seat behind the pilot. Ritter pulled up the steps and shut the door, then slipped into the front seat. "Been waiting long, Buddy?" he asked.

"Just got here," the man responded.

"You see?" Ritter said, looking back over his shoulder, "It wasn't even a problem! Fueled?" he snapped at the pilot. He seemed to Jack to be trying to impress them, now that he was back in his own element.

"Refueled in Santa Fe," the man answered, quickly flicking switches and adjusting dials. He too glanced over his shoulder. The last time he'd seen his boss, Ritter was getting into a flying saucer. Now he'd brought two of these frightening beings on *board* with him!

"How are things in Atlanta?" Ritter asked.

"On ice until you—"

"Let's go," he snapped, and he settled back into his seat.

The plane was a Cessna 310. Jack only learned that by reading the trim. It was a two-engine prop plane, and in moments, the pilot had both propellers whirling noisily as they taxied down the sand. The pilot reached for the radio microphone and brought it to his lips, but Jack quickly laid a hand on his shoulder and said, "Don't do that."

"Ah . . . gotta file a flight plan. . . ." the man began. Jack looked a warning at Henry, who took charge.

"We don't want anybody to know we're coming. Fly VFR." Henry looked back at Jack, smiling smugly. "That means Visual Flight Rules. It's a clear day. We'll call the Harts field tower when we're twenty miles out. No problem!"

Jack nodded and settled back into his seat. He glanced over and saw that Carl's face was white. So were his knuckles, so tightly did he grip the armrests. The plane was picking up speed, rushing across the dirt, then they were airborne, and Jack looked out the window to watch the ground recede below them. No problem.

"Woo!" Henry Ritter shouted above the engine noise and fired off a string of curses. "Glad to get out of there, I can tell you! Yeah, that was pretty startling when the saucers came up on either side of us. Wasn't it, Buddy! Never seen a saucer, had you, Buddy? Ha! Yes sir. Been a *weird* trip. A weird trip." He glanced back at Jack and said, "I recognize you now. Saw you walking out of the meeting with your guys around you, only you weren't in your suit. Saw you talking with the television lady before, what's her name? Sherry Lynn Ward. That's right. Yeah, Buddy! She was there too! You were wearing some strange getup. I guess you were in deep cover, huh? Time travel stuff?"

Jack nodded, remaining noncommittal. He saw Carl glance over at him, a strange look on his face.

"I knew it!" Ritter went on, adding a gratuitous obscenity for emphasis. "Had to be. That was some meeting, huh? Especially that ending when they blew up the bug!"

"Mr. Ritter," Jack said calmly, "that action was taken in part to remind people not to speak of confidential matters."

Ritter's eyes flew wide again, and once more he was apologizing. "Oh! Right! Look, I'm sorry! I didn't mean it! You're not going to—"

Jack held up a hand for silence, and Henry shut up. The silence didn't last for long, but it was nice for the duration. It gave Jack a chance to think.

He thought about Ben, mostly. He really hated to leave Ben behind. Still, the boy had now become much more enmeshed in the evil of Ultrastructure, and there really wasn't any choice. Of course he would feel betrayed. Jack was his only comfort—his only real friend—and now Jack had run off and left him. *Ben,* Jack thought, *if you're reading my mind, then you know I'm sorry. But I can assure you, you'll be all right. In fact, when you finally choose Jesus, you'll feel wonderful. I hope to see you again soon. The* grown *Ben, I mean.* Then he leaned over to put his forehead against the window and gaze down at rocks and hills below. To be honest, he was also half-way watching for saucers himself. . . .

\* \* \*

"Get up."

"Hmm?" Ben woke out of a deep sleep to see an angry Jeffrey looming imperiously over him. "What?"

"Get up and tell me where he is." Ben blinked his eyes. "Come on, kid! I know you know!"

Ben gulped and rubbed sleep from his eyes. "But I don't know! I'm the one who warned *you!*"

"Yeah, right!" Jeffrey snarled, red-faced. "You 'warned' me so I'd have half my agents traipsing around through the lower levels, giving him freedom of movement! We think he's linked up with one of the genetic scientists UMMO imported, and now both of them are missing. You'd better let me know where he is, boy, and I mean right now, before Kundas learns of this, or the Ultrarch will hang *us* from the rafters and blow us up! Come on!"

Ben nodded curtly, then set his jaw in frustration, sending his mind out to search again for Jack. Then he blinked and shook his head. Still nothing. "I can't!" Ben shouted in fear and frustration. "I told you before! His mind is just . . . not there!"

"Keep trying!"

Ben concentrated still harder, hunkering down on the edge of the couch—fists, teeth, and eyebrows all clenched. While he searched, he was also fighting the fear he'd been feeling since Jack had first gone missing—fear that his gift was slipping. The one thing that made him special, that made him *worth* something to the horrible things that surrounded him might be gone. But it wasn't that. He could pop into Kundas' mind easily, and did, and saw that Kundas didn't know about this escape, yet. He popped into Jeffrey's mind, then quickly came out of it, trembling at the thought of what Jeffrey would do to him if he failed. Jeffrey didn't trust him. He was going to be punished for this! And he hadn't done anything! *Jack!* he thought fiercely. *Why did you do this?* But he could get no answer.

He finally sighed, looked up at Jeffrey, and shrugged helplessly. Then he dodged aside, for Jeffrey had sought to slap him and he'd seen the blow coming. "It's not my fault!" he shouted as he hopped off the couch and ducked away. But Jeffrey, fuming, came after him anyway, knocking him to the floor and straddling his chest. He was only saved from a beating when another man in black stuck his head in the door and shouted, "Henry Ritter's gone too!"

Jeffrey paused, his fist cocked to strike, and looked back toward the door. "Ritter? How?"

"We guess his private plane. He's done it before," the man added quickly in the face of Jeffrey's icy stare.

"Who authorized *that?*" Jeffrey shouted.

The man shrugged and said, "We've got a search on for the plane. He has to come down somewhere."

"Find him!" Jeffrey screamed, and the man darted out of the room. Jeffrey slumped, then looked around sharply at Ben and stuck a finger on his nose. "Heads are going to roll because of this! And it better not be *mine!*"

"Atlanta!" Ben blurted out, for he'd quickly found Henry Ritter's thought patterns and saw Jack there in Henry's mind. "They're almost to the Atlanta airport!"

Jeffrey leaned back, then got off Ben and straightened his tie. "Good. There's time. We'll pick them up there." Then he slammed out of the room, shouting orders at people down the hall.

Ben crawled back up onto the couch and stretched out on it. "Jack!" he snarled. In all his lonely young days he'd never felt this alone—or this hurt.

*   *   *

Henry had a car waiting near the airstrip, a large black limousine. Relieved to apparently be rid of his guests at last, he asked them where the limo could drop them.

"The main terminal," Jack said flatly, and within a few minutes they were there, the duffel bag thrown over Jack's shoulder. He still had no idea where they were going, but he felt very relaxed. As they walked through the new rotunda toward the security lanes, he longed to jump into the air and shout. They were free! He would put Carl on a plane home to Canada, and he would grab a quick flight to Louisville. He glanced around for a phone.

And stopped walking. Four men in suits approached them, watching them intently. They weren't wearing black, but they might as well have been. They had the look. Jack's spirits plummeted.

Carl Pellian hadn't seen them yet. He stopped walking and looked back at Jack, puzzled. Jack wanted to scream, "Run!" at him, but it was too late. The four surrounded them, flanking them on either side. Carl's eyes widened, then drooped. His whole body seemed to sag. But Jack wasn't ready to surrender. He looked at one of the suits and said politely, "Yes?"

"Come with us," the man responded quietly.

"Why?"

"You know why," the man said, nodding at the two on either side of Carl. They quickly squeezed the man between them, seizing his arms.

"We're in a public place—a *very* public place. Suppose I start yelling?"

The man smiled slightly. "What are you going to scream? That you're being abducted by aliens? Come on," he said to the others, and they started to escort Jack and Carl away.

*Lord!* Jack thought, black despair surging through him. *After letting us come so close?*

He heard her before he saw her. "Stop where you are. I'm a federal marshal, and these two men are under arrest."

The whole group stopped moving and turned as one to look back. The tall woman didn't hesitate, but moved with authority in among them, grabbed Jack's shoulders, and wheeled him around to face away from her. Jack wanted to laugh and cry at once. Instead he gasped in surprise. Trisha Paulson was handcuffing him!

# Chapter Eighteen

*"My guest today . . ."*

T risha whirled Jack back around to face her and stared into his face. The expression that passed between them was of agreement that *she* would handle this. Jack was happy to let her. He was too busy thanking the Lord for having intervened yet again.

"Joseph Brockman, I'm arresting you for breaking the terms of your bail agreement in Mobile." She reached into the pocket of her suit and pulled out the warrant, flashing it in his face then replaced it quickly. "Let's go."

"There must be some mistake," the man who'd been holding Jack protested with a faint smile. "This man is Dr. Jack Brennen—"

"I'm well familiar with Jack Brennen. It's one of Joe Brockman's frequent aliases. Isn't that right, 'Dr. Brennen'?"

Jack lowered his head as if unable to respond. But he also flicked his eyes over his shoulder, seeking to direct Trisha's attention to Carl. He didn't need to. Trisha had already read the situation enough to see that this other man was with him. They were, after all, dressed identically. "And that would make you Haley Fisher," she said to Carl Pellian, making up a name without blinking an eye. "You'll be coming along as well."

"You have the wrong man—" the gray-suited man in black tried again, but Trisha was already reaching out to grab Carl by the shoulder of his black suit and pull him toward her. Carl would have come with her willingly, but the two men who held him wouldn't yield that quickly.

"Let go of him," Trisha ordered them crisply.

"May we see the warrant for his arrest also?" Gray-suit asked coolly.

"I'll *have* that warrant just as soon as I can get to a judge. This man is a well-known drug-runner and a known accomplice of Brockman. And who are *you?*" she said, stepping aggressively toward Gray-suit and pushing her face into his.

The man leaned back from her but still didn't yield. "I'd like to see some identification," he said.

"Fair enough," Trisha nodded, and she whipped out her badge and held it before his face, making sure that he read it closely. "Now you show me yours."

The gray-suited man tried one more time: "We're on a special assignment, and these two men have already been placed under custody—"

"And *I'm* asking by whom," Trisha said, completely unintimidated. "What agency are you with? I'm not a stranger to jurisdictional disputes. I just want to know who I'm dealing with, so you just show me your badge, mister, and we can go to the security office and straighten all of this out. Otherwise—" Trisha took another step toward him and pulled aside the edge of her coat to show him the Smyth &

Wesson riding on her right hip. "—I think we may have a problem."

Gray-suit glanced at the others with him. "I don't think we do. We'll let you take them for the moment and call our supervisors to—"

"I just want to know who those supervisors might be," Trisha said, grabbing Carl by the shoulder of his suit and pulling him roughly toward her. She didn't let go, which obliged him to stand uncomfortably close to her. Trisha didn't seem uncomfortable at all. Her eyes never left those of the gray-suited man. She had a bulldog's grip on the situation, and Jack could only watch with admiration. "Now are you going to show me your identification or not? Because if you're not, I'd suggest you and your buddies run along and let me do my job." She nodded past Gray-suit's head and added, "We're starting to draw a crowd here, which means a security detail very quickly. Then you'll *have* to show your IDs or else show just cause why you're interfering with the actions of a U.S. marshal."

That was enough. In fact, two of the group of four had already started walking away, one toward the doors of the terminal, the other back toward the gates. Gray-suit lidded his eyes, nodded, and gestured to his one remaining colleague. They left the area together, and quickly.

Still clinging to Carl's shoulder, Trisha wheeled around to grab Jack by the arm and propel them both forward towards the offices of the FAA. As she did so, she scanned the faces of those who'd stopped to watch, giving each a hard look that told them to beat it. "Nothing here to see," she warned quietly, and people immediately remembered why they were in the Atlanta airport and got on about their business.

The three said nothing during the double-time walk, although Carl did throw a confused look at Jack. He just smiled and kept pace with Trisha, and Carl seemed to relax.

At the door of the FAA office, Trisha typed a code into the security pad, and it buzzed open. She'd been in here just moments ago, signing the papers that permitted her to carry her gun around the security checkpoints, and the woman recognized her immediately. "Just chance, I guess," Trisha said brightly, "but I happened across two fugitives in the rotunda. I need another pair of handcuffs and a briefing room."

The woman appeared startled but not really surprised. She supplied Trisha with her own set of handcuffs and quickly let them into a room. "Need some help?" she asked, and Trisha just shook her head and pulled Carl's hands behind him to cuff them together. Carl was looking anxiously at Jack, but Jack was too busy stifling a grin to even look at him. Trisha pushed the two men into the room ahead of her, snapping, "Now sit down," as the door was closing behind her.

When it clicked shut, Trisha leaned back against it, closed her eyes, and took a long, deep breath. When she opened them she looked at Jack—and smiled. "Hi, Jack."

"Trisha. Am I ever glad to see *you*."

"I'm glad to see you too. And I know someone else who's going to be glad to see you. Have you called your wife?"

"I'd love to have the chance."

"We'll take care of that in a minute. Who's this?" Trish said, looking at Carl.

"This is Carl Pellian. Carl, this is Trisha Paulson, a long-time friend—and no, I don't think she's an angel, but she's sure acting like one!"

"You want to tell me what this is all about?"

"That all depends," Jack smiled. "Do I need a lawyer? Aren't you supposed to read me my rights?" He twisted his shoulders to wave his locked hands.

"Sorry," Trisha said as she came around behind him to free them from the cuffs. "That was the only way I could think of to get you out of that situation."

"And I'll be eternally grateful," he said, rubbing his wrists as she circled the table to remove them from Carl. "How did you know where to find me?"

"I *didn't*," she blurted, patting Carl on the shoulder comfortingly as the benumbed scientist pulled his hands into his lap and folded them there. "Gloria told me something had happened to you and I was halfway trying to find you, but just now I was on my way to Chicago to arrest this Brockman guy. It's sheer coincidence!"

"Oh no," said Jack, shaking his head. "That was heavenly intervention. But what did Gloria tell—"

"She called me Sunday night when you never came home from church. Told me the whole story—the demon aliens, your previous abduction, the man who reads minds, the whole thing. Pretty weird, Jack. Pretty weird."

"It's at least that," Jack frowned. "Sunday night? *Last* Sunday night?"

"Yep. So I promised I'd check into it, expecting to get a call back that you'd been found in a snowbank or something. Then on Monday morning I got this." She started digging in her suit pockets for the fax that she'd folded away.

"What *day* is it?" Jack asked, still frowning.

"Wednesday," she grunted, finally finding the fax and pulling it out. "What's the matter," she grinned at him. "You lose track of time?"

"You have no idea. . . ." he said, looking across the table at Carl. The man hadn't moved. He was just studying his hands where he'd clasped them before him. He looked shell-shocked.

Trisha folded out the fax before Jack, saying, "This came from somewhere in Louisville. Any ideas who sent it?"

293

Jack scanned the fax quickly. "Carrie Baxter," he murmured.

"No, it didn't come from her," Trisha said quickly, misunderstanding him. "She was in Huntsville. I talked to her Monday evening, and she told me this whole *other* story that blew my mind. Seems she tried to blow the whistle on some enormous cover-up at General Aeronautics, where they were building some kind of space vehicle for aliens. The congressman she gave her information to sat on it, and she figures it got swallowed up in a government conspiracy. Is that who those guys out there were with?"

"No doubt," Jack answered quietly, still puzzling over the fax.

"Did that come from this man Ben?" Trisha asked, pointing at the fax.

"I have no idea," Jack murmured flatly. What would the grown Ben know about Carrie Baxter? All Jack knew about her himself was that he'd seen her on the *Sherry Lynn Ward Show*.

"In any case," Trisha continued, "Ms. Baxter knew nothing about your situation, other than confirming you might indeed have been abducted. I really didn't know what else to do for you, and anyway I was tied up with searching for this Joseph Brockman guy. I flew over this morning from Huntsville on my way to Illinois to try to track him down, and there *you* are, surrounded by the Feds. That's what I took them for at first. Then I just—" Trisha stopped and shook her head before going on "—it was . . . strange."

Jack turned his eyes up to Trisha's and asked knowingly, "What was strange?"

Trisha smiled and half shrugged. "I don't know. I just suddenly got this sense that, Feds or not, they were *not* on government business. And that they were . . . evil. Jack?" she asked, leaning forward to him. "Were those men in black?"

Jack just raised an eyebrow and nodded.

"Whew," Trisha said, sitting back in her chair. "I read about those guys last night on the Internet. Strange business." She looked at Jack and shook her head again. "You're running with some pretty heavy company there. Those guys don't mess around."

"And now *you're* running with them," Jack said soberly. "I'm really sorry I got you mixed up in all this."

"Well, actually you didn't. Your wife did. And besides, when I saw you there, it's just like God said to me 'Go get 'em!'" She shrugged. "So I did."

"If you hadn't, there's no telling where the two of us might be right now. We do thank you."

Trisha leaned closer. "So that's my story. You want to tell me *your* story now?"

As Jack unfolded it for her, Trisha sank back in her seat, astonished. It was utterly incredible. Unbelievable. And after the last few days, Trisha was also convinced it was absolutely true. Occasionally she would glance over at Carl, who still seemed in a daze. Jack left out the nature of his discovery, saying only that it was of major world importance and held frightful implications. Then again, all of this held frightful implications for Trisha. The more she heard, the sicker she felt—and the more powerless in the situation. Still, when the tale was done, she put on the best face she could muster and said, "Well then, I don't know what we can do about this conspiracy thing. But it looks like the next step is to get you home to Louisville and Carl, here, back to Canada."

"I can't go home until I know Carl is safely home," Jack interjected. "It's just something God has told me to do."

"I can hardly argue with that," Trisha smiled.

"There's a problem," Carl said gravely, and they both looked at him. These were the first words he'd spoken since they'd come into the room.

"And that is?"

"All my identification was in that duffel bag."

"What duffel bag?" Trisha frowned as Jack winced in sudden remembrance and clasped his hands behind his head.

"The one we left on the floor of the rotunda when you arrested us," Carl said to Trisha.

She gazed at him, her mouth twitched to one side as if to say "You might have mentioned this before now," then left the room. Jack sighed heavily and laid his face on the table. Carl just kept looking at his hands. After a few minutes of silence he began to speak.

"I need to say thank you to you, Dr. Brennen," he said somberly. "You—and the Lord—have been working miracles of rescue all day long. I feel like Peter let out of prison, I really do. Can hardly believe it. But . . ."

Jack didn't raise his head from his arms. He just turned it back to look up at Carl. "But what?"

"But I wonder what good it's all going to do. I mean, suppose we do get out of this airport. That's assuming she finds my identification, and we do make it past these agents working for the demons. Suppose I do get back into Canada, back to my wife and my school. What then? What's to prevent them from coming and picking me up again? Or what's to prevent this mind reader, whom you seem to know, from simply plucking these terrible ideas out of my head from where he sits?" Carl dropped his chin down onto his chest and shook his head. "In the long run, I'm still thinking my own solution is the only effective way to suppress the knowledge of my discovery."

Jack paused a moment before responding. "You mean your death?"

Carl did not look up. "I mean my death."

Jack sat up then and leaned back in his chair. "A spirit of fear."

"What?"

"One of the reasons I know the evil one is not *entirely* focused on this Ultrastructure conspiracy is that he still interferes personally with each one of us. Maybe he does it through demonic activity, I don't know. But I tend to believe he harasses us each individually. Paul said God did not place in us a spirit of bondage to fear, but a Spirit of adoption. That Spirit that makes us children of God. I think you're listening to the wrong spirit."

"That may be. But look at the *reach* of these creatures! Look what they're able to do! Who can stand against them? They'll take whatever they want, whomever they want, and *do* whatever they want! They're *demons,* Dr. Brennen, and they control the world! We are powerless against them!"

Jack thought a moment before answering, choosing his words. "You may be right about this genetic predisposition to faith. But let me tell you what I know from my own experience. True faith takes practice. And God's been giving us plenty of practice today. Maybe it's all in the way you look at it, but what I've seen today of the workings of God makes me wonder why the demons don't just throw their hands up in despair and quit. Carl, listen to me. Was it by accident that you chose today to act, to respond to the impulse of the Spirit to leave your level and hide? It certainly wasn't by accident that you were hiding in the closet *I* inspected, rather than one of the other guys. You think it was by accident that I happened to meet Henry Ritter today, and the Lord provided us with a back way out of the dungeon and a plane ride to freedom? Or that my friend Trisha—well prepared to face all of this—just *happened* to be walking through the airport at the precise minute that we needed her? You're right, of course. We're not out of here yet. But if God's brought us this far, why do you think He can't continue to deliver us, both of us, together or apart?"

"I know all that's true, and yet . . . why doesn't God just . . . just—"

"You'd like to see some massive intervention by the heavenly host."

"Right! I'd like to see a . . . a spiritual *bomb* blast targeted on that infernal desert hellhole, like He rained down on Sodom and Gomorrah! Or a flood to drown them all out, like He sent in the time of Noah!"

*The flood,* Jack thought. *I was in that flood. Should I tell him? No.* Instead, Jack said, "I know. I've wished for that too. But remember, there are a lot of people down in that hole with the Fallen who don't deserve to be there any more than we did. What I'm trying to say is that I think God wants us to start *using* the spiritual tools He's already placed within us, instead of quailing in fear at the terrible forces ranged against us and pleading for angels to come to our rescue. Genetically predetermined or not, we both know by *faith* how all of this is going to turn out. God's already won. We ought to be living in victory instead of defeat."

Carl was silent, thinking. "You don't know the guilt I feel."

"Yes I do. You think you *deserve* to die for it."

Carl's head jerked up sharply, about to object. But when he met Jack's challenging gaze he just mumbled, "I do," instead.

"For thinking? For being a good researcher? Do you really believe your death will somehow prevent that from ever being discovered in the future? Look, Carl. If what you've found is true, somebody else will discover it again, whether you're alive or dead. Unless the Lord comes first, we'll both die, but isn't the timing of that up to Him?"

Carl buried his head in his hands. "But the horrors it could loose—"

"Are horrible, yes. And I'm with you. I don't want the Fallen to have this knowledge any sooner than necessary. But you told me yourself this Genome Project could be finished in a decade. It may produce all kinds of terrifying discoveries about the way we behave. But Carl. Do you really think God is not *prepared* to handle that?"

Once again Carl was quiet, pondering Jack's words. The door opened, and Trisha whooshed back in, dropping the duffel bag on the table.

"You found it!" Jack grinned.

"Security had it. Picked it up *real* quickly, as soon as they saw it abandoned. This is Atlanta, you know; they're sensitive about that here. They x-rayed it and found nothing explosive in it, and when I told them I needed to impound it as evidence, they gave it to me. So, are we ready?" she asked, handing Carl his wallet.

"For what?"

"To get out of here. The government just bought each of you tickets to Chicago."

\* \* \*

"The woman's name is Trisha Paulson. She's a U.S. marshal out of the Alabama Southern District."

"And what's her connection with all this? What was she doing there?" Jeffrey demanded of the underling who'd brought him this news. When the man shrugged, Jeffrey dismissed him with a wave and turned to Ben. "Perhaps *you* can answer that question for me?"

Jeffrey had ordered Ben to be brought to him in the Central Command of the subterranean city, on Level 4 near the dwellings of the Fallen. This was an area Jack would have remembered had he seen it. It was here that the Fallen clustered together and in the next room that Kundas conducted business.

Ben sat in a chrome-armed swivel chair, swinging himself back and forth, frowning in deep frustration. "I've told you," he snapped. "She's blocked to me."

"Blocked by who?" Jeffrey shouted.

Ben shouted back. "You know by who!"

299

Jeffrey slammed his hand down on a huge, curving desk that overlooked a bank of computer monitors. "Is *everyone* we need to know about blocked to you today? This is getting *way* out of control! You!" he pointed to a man seated at one of the keyboards. "Check the passenger lists of every airline leaving Atlanta for that woman! I want to know where she's going! And *you,*" he said pointing back at Ben, "had better start providing some useful information immediately!"

"I can tell you that Kundas is wondering what's going on in here," the surly Ben replied. "And that right now he's on the way into the room."

As Jeffrey blanched at this news, the door to the Central Command swung open, and Kundas stalked in. Jeffrey whirled to face him, a fawning smile on his face. But from the feverish activity in the room, Kundas knew immediately there was a problem. He spoke in Jeffrey's mind directly, demanding to know what it was.

"There's been a security breach," Jeffrey answered flatly. He knew the words would bring down a torrent of wrath from his master, but he had no choice but to use them. His only hope was in being able to assure Kundas that the situation was still manageable. Under the circumstances that would be hard.

"A security breach!" Kundas roared inside the minds of everyone in the room. "What kind of security breach?"

"One of the scientists taken during the unauthorized action by UMMO has apparently left the complex."

"Left the complex?" said Kundas. The rage in his tone of thought terrified the entire Central Command staff. "Are you saying he simply walked out?"

"Apparently so. Not without help, of course."

"And from whom did he receive this help?" Kundas screamed, giving everyone present a splitting headache.

Jeffrey gripped the base of his skull with both hands, fighting the wave of pain and getting ready to feel worse. "From Henry Ritter, for one, who apparently had parked his private plane in the desert above us—" Jeffrey paused for another outburst, but by this time Kundas was just staring at him, his almond-shaped eyes mere black slits. "—and by Jack Brennen, whom I think you know. Ben's friend." Jeffrey felt no need to mention his own long-term friendship with Jack. After all, he'd had nothing to do with Jack's abduction.

Kundas glared at Jeffrey, then turned to glare at Ben, who sat stock-still in his swivel chair, watching and listening and reading both minds. "So, Ben," Kundas snarled. "Do you know what I'm thinking?"

The boy's only response was to visibly tremble.

"How is it, Ben, that you allowed this to happen? The man was your responsibility, was he not? I think you told me he was not going to be anymore trouble at all, for you could monitor his thoughts and control his activities. Am I remembering correctly?"

Ben continued trembling, reaching around to grasp the back of his own head and opening his mouth in a silent scream.

"And yet, now I hear this man has left us. And taken a scientist with him. Why, Ben? Why this particular scientist?"

Ben couldn't answer. It was apparent to every witness in the room why not.

"Where is he now, Ben? This friend of yours? What's inside his mind?" Kundas suddenly released Ben from the gripping pain, and Ben slumped out of his chair and onto the floor. There he sat, breathing hard, as Kundas rounded the long desk to come toward him. "You're not hurting now," he demanded briskly. "Where is he?"

"I . . . I can't . . . read him. He's . . . his mind is . . . bl-blocked to me."

Kundas peered down at Ben in disgust, but he, unlike Jeffrey, immediately believed Ben's words. Kundas *knew* whom they were truly battling. "Blocked, are you? Worthless boy." Then the Gray circled the desk back to Jeffrey and demanded, "What of Ritter? Is he lost too?"

"We have Ritter," Jeffrey answered quickly. "Took him from his car in Atlanta. He's on his way back here."

Kundas' eyes appeared to grow thoughtful. "Good. He's a valuable man. Valuable contacts. Makes a lot of money. Still, an action like this cannot be tolerated. I will discipline him personally. Now Jeffrey, as my security chief, and the one whom I will hold ultimately responsible for all this chaos, can you give me a straight answer as to where this Brennen and this scientist are now?"

"They were arrested in the Atlanta airport—-"

"Good."

"—but he was taken from our people by a U.S. marshal. A woman."

Kundas seemed to breathe a long exasperated sigh. It wasn't audible, of course, but every person in the room would have interpreted it as that. "And what arrangements are being made to apprehend the three of them?" he asked wearily.

"Sir?" the man ordered to search passenger lists called up to Jeffrey. "I have that. She's on her way to Chicago, and she just purchased two other tickets."

Jeffrey heard the news with relief and turned to look back at Kundas. He was premature in his hope. The Gray had fixed his coal black eyes on him.

"You've disappointed me," Kundas announced. "All of you have. Your timing in this misstep could not have been worse. The Ultrarch has been on a time journey with UMMO and is arriving back this minute. You can all be certain I will inform him of exactly who's at fault in all of this and of what actions I've taken to correct it. Jeffrey. You apparently cannot handle day-to-day operations. Perhaps your best talents lie in field command. I'll let you prove that to me. I have an assignment in deep, *deep* time that may be exactly right for you. And Ben. Since your gift apparently has deserted you— and since only your gift has been of any value—I think it's time that you be discarded." There was total silence. Kundas slowly turned his huge, cold eyes onto every person present in the Command Center. Then the spindly Gray stalked pompously out of the room.

Once he was gone, Jeffrey turned to throw a withering stare at Ben. It was wasted on the boy, however. Ben's eyes stared at the floor and his head was cocked to one side, as if he was listening to a conversation far away and was utterly baffled by it.

* * *

They kept very close to one another on the tram ride to their departure terminal. All three kept gazing around them on the ride up the towering escalator. They checked out every man wearing a suit, which earned them some strange looks back. But they saw no sign of the four who'd accosted Jack and Carl in the ground-side terminal, and they each began to breathe easier. Carl was still concerned about his lack of a passport, but Trisha kept reassuring him that she would help him with the INS. Despite their very realistic concerns, they got to their gate safely without incident

There was no one at the check-in desk when they arrived, so Trisha plopped down in one of the chairs and pulled open her bag. "Here," she said, handing them their respective tickets. "Just in case something happens." She didn't have to spell out what that something might be. They each felt the peril of their situation. Still, at the moment all seemed well, and nothing seemed more inviting to Jack than a talk with his wife. It had been so long!

"Think it's safe to make a call?" he asked Trisha.

"You know these guys better than I do, Jack. I don't think it's safe *anywhere* here. But why should it be any less safe by a telephone? Go call her. I don't want her to have to worry another minute. Besides, I need to run to the restroom."

Jack still carried the duffel bag as they walked back the way they'd come toward the telephones. He was determined not to let go of it again. He was thinking about this as they passed the gaping entryway of an overpriced bar and grill when he happened to glance up at the big screen television inside. He froze, then grabbed Carl and jerked him inside the bar behind him. "What are you—" Carl frowned, then worried, "Are they—" Then Carl's mouth gaped open as he realized what had caught Jack's attention . . . and why.

Jack stared at the big screen television in the corner of the bar. There were few patrons watching; it served mostly as a kind of moving wallpaper, a momentary distraction for bored travelers longing to be elsewhere. But Jack stared at it as if hypnotized. It was tuned to the *Sherry Lynn Ward Show*. It was Wednesday, and he was the featured guest.

"So Dr. Brennen, are you saying you *do* believe in aliens or that you *don't?* I'm confused here." Sherry Lynn Ward's smile was as bright and brittle as ever. Jack's own face looked uncomfortable, as if he would give anything to be elsewhere at the moment.

"I believe there are beings posing as aliens in our society," Jack heard himself say, in that voice he hated so much hearing on tape. "I believe that some very thoughtful, serious people are having encounters with them. But no. I don't believe they are extraterrestrial biological entities, alien travelers from another planet."

Jack groped his way onto a stool and was gripping the tiny table anchored to the floor in front of it. He didn't know what to think. What shook him most was the tiny graphic down in the corner of the screen that indicated this program was live. A number was superimposed on the screen for viewers to call in and ask questions. This was live. How could he be there *and* here?

"Then what exactly *do* you believe about these creatures, Dr. Brennen?"

"I believe they're demonic," Jack on the screen said flatly. He didn't seem to be surprised by Sherry Lynn's rolling eyes, nor by the scornful laughter from the audience.

Carl, too, was mesmerized. Here was Jack sitting right beside him, yet up there on the screen as well. At least, Jack *had* been sitting right beside him a moment ago.

He found Jack standing at one of the windows in the adjoining gate area, staring blankly out the window. "Jack?" he asked. "Jack, I know this is disturbing, but—"

Jack whirled around to face him. His eyes were filmy—his face a chalky white. "Carl," he asked. "What do you know about cloning?"

Carl started to answer one way, then seemed to realize the intent of Jack's question and instead answered, "Oh, I don't think that's a good explanation. You see, a clone would age at the same rate you do—something like a twin. To get a duplicate copy of you at this age, they would have needed to start the clone's life at the same time *you* were born."

"So?" Jack said woodenly. "That's just a time question, isn't it? What problem could that possibly be to the Fallen?"

Carl stared back at Jack, perplexed. "All right—so they *could* do it—*if* they had the technology. But no one has successfully cloned a human embryo—"

"No one has *announced* successfully cloning a human embryo. That doesn't mean it hasn't been done."

Carl's expression didn't change. "You're right again, of course. But that still doesn't explain *why* they would do such a thing!"

"I don't know," Jack shrugged, looking utterly baffled. "To . . . replace me? I guess I *have* been a real problem to them. To infiltrate the faith? Who knows? To have me go on the *Sherry Lynn Ward Show* and make a fool of myself talking about demonic aliens in front of the whole country?"

"Jack, listen. Certainly there must be some other explanation for this."

"None that I can think of," Jack murmured, his voice muted by shock. He turned to look out again at the taxing jets. "Sure does provide a new explanation of why they let us get away so easily."

Carl's face hardened. "That was God's doing, Jack. You convinced me of that yourself."

Jack nodded. His voice seemed far away as he said, "That was before I realized they'd already stolen my *life*."

Though this area was several gates over from their own, they still clearly heard the boarding announcement for their flight to Chicago. Jack took a long deep breath, then stooped to pick up the duffel bag. He saw Carl's eyes suddenly grow wide, and Carl, too, whirled to face the window. "MIBs?" Jack whispered without looking back.

"A different pair. They just passed us," Carl murmured, hunching his shoulders. Then he tossed a furtive glance over his shoulder and added, "They didn't notice us."

"How could they not notice us," Jack whispered, "when we're wearing these identical, standard-issue suits?"

Carl had now turned all the way to watch. "Because they were busy boarding our plane."

Jack blinked. Then he scooped up the duffel bag, and they sprinted all the way back to the escalators.

# Chapter Nineteen

*Yukon quest*

This is inexcusable."

"I know that, Ultrarch," Kundas responded humbly, bowing his thin, gray body double in obeisance. They had been summoned to meet in the Chamber, a large, dark room in the most secure core of the subterranean city. It might as easily have been called the throne room, except that there was no throne, only a high-backed leather executive's chair, in which Ron Pearson now sat. Or rather, Ron Pearson's body. There was by now little left of the man's own personality, so thoroughly had it been dominated by the Overlord. This was the only chair in the dimly illuminated room. Everyone else stood in the Ultrarch's presence—or bowed.

"When I placed you in charge of the Zeta group, it was with the explicit understanding that you would *correct* the mess your predecessor left behind, not add to it."

"I understand that, Ultrarch," Kundas answered, not moving. Kundas knew how to grovel. He'd had long practice at it.

"UMMO? Your opinion?"

The UMMO, standing to the Ultrarch's right, conferred. They were pleased with this turn of events, for with each further stumble of the Grays, the status of UMMO increased. Frustrated for centuries by the Zetans' overwhelming technological edge, UMMO still believed they might yet gain total control of the rich North American territories. The new speaker for UMMO shuffled forward and announced the consensus of the group. "UMMO should handle this."

"I'll decide that," the Ultrarch murmured. "But your willingness is noted. So tell me, Kundas. How had *you* planned to clean up after yourself?"

"We've alerted our people in Chicago," Kundas said without rising. "There is a large contingent awaiting the arrival of the plane. Two others have boarded the plane in Atlanta. They are far better connected governmentally than the woman who interfered. She will be commended for her diligence and given a citation, but she will also be relieved of this case. A vessel has already been dispatched to return the other two to us here."

"And Henry Ritter?"

"Is already here. He is being interrogated at this moment. He is claiming he was duped."

"And in your opinion?"

"I think he was."

"This enterprise has no place for dupes, Kundas. UMMO, your opinion?"

The caucus was brief. "UMMO should handle this."

"Your eagerness is noted," said the Ultrarch, waving them aside. He pondered a moment, then announced, "I've always thought Henry Ritter talked too much. Kundas, you will surrender Ritter to UMMO. Perhaps they can teach him to control his tongue."

There was an excited stirring among the cluster of huge insects in response to this favorable decision. Kundas bowed more deeply, then stood up and waved at one of the men in black who waited in attendance. This was one of Jeffrey's former lieutenants, now elevated to the position of new chief. He left the room, accompanied by Wesley, who was equally pleased with the growing influence of his masters.

"I notice the former chief of your security staff is missing," the Ultrarch continued.

"He has been reassigned," Kundas answered quietly.

"Already. Where?"

"Very deep in time, Ultrarch."

"Was he not also 'duped'?"

"He was not an accomplice in this affair. Nevertheless, he failed. He is a man of talents, a very useful tool. He will be spending a lot of time in another eon, exercising those talents."

The Ultrarch raised his eyebrows, then nodded, accepting this disposition of Jeffrey's case. "Tell me about this researcher who ran."

"There's little to tell," Kundas said. "Just another scientist snatched up indiscriminately in UMMO's sweep." UMMO bristled at this affront, the armor of their shells scraping audibly in indignation. "I'm only telling the truth," Kundas added snippily.

The Ultrarch's eyes narrowed. "And yet you say the mind reader claimed to be blocked from the man's mind?"

"He did."

"Then perhaps there is something useful in the man's ideas that our enemies would prefer we not learn. Make the scouring of this scientist's mind the first priority when he's returned. But first I'd like to speak with this young mind reader of yours. Where is he?"

"He's waiting to see you, Ultrarch."

"Fetch him," the Ultrarch ordered, and another man in black bolted from the room. "Now as to the other runner— this Brennen person," the Ultrarch went on, smiling dangerously through Ron Pearson's lips. "What had you planned for him?"

"He shall be killed."

This time UMMO did not wait to be consulted. The speaker for UMMO stepped forward to speak the mind of all. "UMMO should handle this!"

The Ultrarch turned his smile on the agitated swarm of insects. "Yes. I think the Grays have exhibited far too much lenience with this irritating man. When the vessel arrives from Chicago, Brennen shall be surrendered to UMMO. I want no more trouble from him. Ah! Here's the boy."

Waiting in a room nearby, Ben had heard all the conversation leading up to his summons. He walked into the Chamber with an arrogant swagger, wearing an expression of unmistakable contempt for everyone present. The Ultrarch marked it well. "So, young Ben. You say you've been blocked from reading your friend's mind. Explain yourself."

"I've been blocked," Ben shrugged. "That's all I know."

"Curious," the Ultrarch said, "that you should be blocked from this particular mind at this particular time. Are we to understand your gift is gone?"

"No. I can still read all the minds present. I can read yours."

Ron Pearson's nose flared, and his eyes narrowed dangerously. "Can you, now? And what am I thinking?"

"You've already decided what to do with me."

"And what is that?"

"To take me away from the Grays. To take personal control of all my assignments. To take away my 'toys' and put me in a cell, and to try to make me as miserable as possible."

The Ultrarch's jaws clenched, but still he smiled. "And why is that?"

"Because you think I'm still potentially valuable, but that I'm impudent and spoiled."

"You *are* impudent and spoiled," the Ultrarch snarled. "And I don't like anyone invading my thoughts. Perhaps your gifts are not so important after all. Perhaps they are something of liability—"

There was a disturbance at the door. Wesley walked in, grim faced, and approached the Ultrarch directly. He bent down to whisper in the Ultrarch's ear, causing him to jump from his chair and swing around to face Kundas. "How can Jack Brennen be on a plane for Chicago, when he is this *moment* appearing on the Sherry Lynn Ward program, live from Los Angeles?" Kundas staggered backward, caught totally off-guard, as the Ultrarch railed, "What is the *matter* with you Grays? Isn't she one of ours? Is this open *rebellion?*"

"I . . . had no idea," Kundas pleaded, but the Ultrarch had already wheeled away from him to look toward UMMO.

"With UMMO's assistance, I shall handle this personally! Prepare the craft! We're going to Los Angeles!" He started to stomp from the Chamber, but stopped short when Ben insolently called out, "That's not the one you're after."

The Ultrarch turned around and oozed across the chamber toward Ben, drawing up Pearson's six-foot-plus frame to loom over the boy as he snarled through clenched teeth, "Explain."

"It's all your messing with time, don't you see? You've so corrupted the time stream that you've totally confused your-self—Owww!" The Ultrarch had slapped Ben across the face, hurling him toward the floor. Now he stepped across Ben's body and glowered downward, hands on his hips.

"Can you read the mind of the Jack Brennen on television?"

"Sure I can read him," Ben snapped, rubbing his jaw.

"And yet you said nothing about this."

"I told you. He's not the one you want. He already has memories of an encounter with you, *not* in Chicago, but in Alaska."

"Alaska!"

"East of Fairbanks. He's trying to get the scientist home to Canada in a dogsled."

The Ultrarch started to stomp down on Ben's stomach, but Ben curled into a ball in anticipation. Instead, he pointed down at the boy and menacingly said, "I'll deal with you later. Kundas," he snapped, "put this boy in a secure cell until I return." Then he spun around to look at UMMO, say-ing, "Take me to Alaska!" and stormed out of the Chamber.

The room emptied quickly. The UMMO scrambled after the Ultrarch, followed by Wesley and his crew. Kundas, shaken by the repeated humiliations of this meeting, waved his long fingers at the remaining members of Jeffrey's old group and said, "See to it. Take him out." Then he turned his back to the door and clasped his spindly arms to his chest, seeking to summon back up from inside himself some measure of personal dignity.

The black-suited men lifted Ben off the floor and hustled him into the hallway. He didn't fight them. He didn't need to. He knew their minds. Their chief had been deported to another time. Their supposed leader had been humiliated by the Ultrarch. They had no wish to continue backing a loser, especially when there was another option available. And that option was . . .

As they marched Ben through the corridors another figure fell in with them, a new man Ben didn't remember, wearing wire-rim glasses. Ben automatically dipped into the man's mind and found—

"Baal?"

*Keep silent, you idiot boy!* Baal thought back at him, and when Ben quickly sealed his lips he continued, directing his words into Ben's mind only: *Did you think I was gone forever? Surely you knew me better than that! I may have been ripped from my body but my spirit is intact. Bruised, but intact. If the Ultrarch can ride that fool of a businessman, I can certainly ride this creature. Although he has proved willful at times.*

The man jerked his head around to look at Ben, his blue eyes suddenly wild behind the wire-rim glasses. Ben read the man's unfettered thoughts—briefly—just long enough to learn that he was Randolph Donaldson, and that he was terrified. Then the eyes calmed, and the face smiled, as Baal regained control.

*You see what I mean, Ben?* Baal whined in Ben's brain. *It's been a long time since I've had to do this. It's tedious. You have to watch them every minute. I need a new body, and quickly, and I know just where to get one. Or to have it made. . . . Astra is waiting for us there, and you're coming with us.*

Curious to know where, Ben's mind reached into Baal's to pluck out the location: Atlantis. So. Jack's memory was correct—it hadn't been a dream. And Jack would eventually be there too. Ben felt his jaw where the Ultrarch had slapped him. It still ached—a testimony to Jack's betrayal. Oh yes, Ben thought, he would be giving Jack Brennen a piece of his mind.

*It'll be like old times again, right Ben?* Baal was still saying inside his head. *Unless, of course, you'd prefer to stay and work for Kundas?*

Ben shook his head no and smiled back at Donaldson. They walked directly to the hanger, pausing outside the door to allow the Ultrarch and UMMO ample time to depart. *We'll give them a chance to get well away, right Ben?*

Ben just smiled.

\* \* \*

Trisha waited at the top of the ramp as long as she could—two or three minutes longer than the counter agent would have preferred. He finally tapped her on the shoulder and said, "Ma'am, the pilot's ready to close the door and push back. We can't hold this flight any longer."

She should have gone with them, she was thinking. No, she should never have let them go at all! It was her fault, all her fault! As the man tore off the stub of her boarding pass and handed it back to her, her eyes were still gazing back over her shoulder toward the wide aisle of the terminal. Nothing. She sighed, saw the impatient smile of the steward and forced a smile of her own, and boarded the airplane. She was so tied up in her own thoughts that she took no notice of two men in dark suits, seated in first class. They took careful notice of her.

By the time they were over Tennessee she had convinced herself that she had done the best she could. She had a job to do, after all, and she was doing it. She'd gotten them out of one jam; it wasn't her fault if they'd gotten themselves into another. Still, she was dreading the task she'd set for herself when she got into the hotel that night: to call Gloria and give her a report. No wife would want to hear what she had to relate. How would she phrase it? "I saw your husband in the airport in Atlanta today. Yes, he had been abducted by rogue agents of the United States government. I got him away from them long enough to learn that. But I'm afraid they got him again."

Trisha was still rehearsing that conversation as she walked up the jetway at O'Hare. But as soon as she saw the six dark-suited figures waiting for her at the top of the ramp, her whole attitude changed. *Oh, Jack!* she thought. *I'm so glad you didn't get on this plane! Thank You, Lord!*

They were moving down toward her, their eyes feverishly scanning the faces of the passengers deplaning behind her. Trisha reached into her pocket and pulled out her badge.

*　*　*

"Why Alaska?"

"It's our only option," Jack said wearily. "Trisha can't help us anymore. You've got to get across the line into Canada. I have, rather, I used to have friends there. Maybe I still do. And why should the Fallen look for us there?" Jack paused. "You have any other suggestions?"

Carl did not. Both of them were bone weary from sleep deprivation and the constant shocks of their escape. They were tired of each other, and both running a little short on faith. The decision was made without fanfare.

It had taken some finagling and a big chunk of what remained on Jack's plastic, but he'd finally managed to get their tickets changed to two one-way flights to Fairbanks. They had one more stop to make before boarding: the ATM. Jack didn't hesitate. He took out all that remained of his credit limit. He said nothing about it to Carl, but he didn't expect to be returning home. Let his double figure out how to pay these bills, Jack thought sourly. Maybe the new Jack Brennen would get a good honorarium from appearing on the *Sherry Lynn Ward Show.*

He regretted not being able to call Gloria, but what would he say? "I'm going to Alaska to get killed, have a

315

good life"? She'd probably still be watching the new Jack Brennen on television. Why confuse her?

Carl Pellian still hadn't bought the cloning theory yet. As soon as they were seated, he began chewing Jack's ear about the complexities of such a procedure, trying to keep his voice down so as not to bring stares from other passengers. Not that there were that many close enough to them to hear. They were seated in the middle row of the jumbo jet, and they had it to themselves. "It simply isn't possible," Carl said quietly,

"Why not?" Jack said bitterly. "My secretary was always saying I needed to be cloned so I could be two places at once. Now I have been."

"I'm telling you, Jack, we won't have the technology to do that for another five years!"

"So the Fallen went five years into the future and got it early. What's so hard about that?" He was fishing down in his pocket as he said this, already putting it out of his mind. "Now this," he said "is a real mystery." He pulled out the fax Trisha had given him in the airport. Now he folded down his tray table and spread it out to examine it again. "Who sent it? And why?"

"You already know why," Carl said impatiently. "To get Ms. Paulson to where she needed to be at the proper time."

"But who?"

"Someone the Lord told to do it!" Carl snapped, and he stood up to get a blanket out of the overhead bin. Within moments he was asleep. Jack puzzled over the writing a while longer, trying to link together explanations that made sense. None did.

It was probably because his thoughts kept rolling back again and again to his clone, to this interloper who had taken over his identity. When had they decided to make it? From the very beginning? Was that why he'd been taken back to Atlantis, so that the body technicians of that ancient age could make a perfect copy of him? He hadn't forgotten how perfectly they had matched Gloria's image. Was that a clone too?

But why? Why him? Why had he been picked? Because of Ben, of course. That chance meeting with a frightened boy in San Francisco, to whom he'd tried to be loving and Christlike. It was Ben who had picked him, young Ben. An *angry* young Ben, by the time he arrived in Atlantis, a boy feeling betrayed. How easy it would be for Ben to train Jack's clone in the proper mannerisms, the proper intonations and inflections of speech. Ben had practically lived inside his mind! Ben, who'd seen his every thought, who knew him better than he knew himself.

And yet the mature Ben had never said *anything* to him about any—

"He didn't say anything at all," Jack muttered under his breath, for now he begun to doubt even the older Ben, his own son in the ministry. Had it all been an elaborate con? Had the Fallen placed Ben in seminary so that he could watch Jack and make subtle preparations for sliding the new Jack Brennen into the empty place left by his disappearance? Then that new Jack could do what the Fallen had been wanting him to do from the beginning: to betray the faith from the inside. To use his classroom to teach young preachers to deny the very God they'd come to study, to question God's absolute authority, to water down God's ethics, to ridicule the inspiration of His Word.

High in the sky somewhere over the Midwest, Jack felt as low in spirit as he could ever remember. Lower than he'd felt when he'd first been taken, lower even than when he was hanging suspended inside the black cone. He knew, of course, the prescription for his fears—he'd preached it that very day to Carl. But he didn't follow it. Instead, he went to sleep.

They both slept all the way to Anchorage, waking only to eat whatever was placed before them. Neither of them minded skipping the in-flight movie. It was something about alien abduction.

They changed planes in Anchorage, flying on to Fairbanks in a small commuter jet with a picture of an Alaskan husky painted on the side. That was fitting, Jack thought, for the plan that had been emerging in his mind ever since they'd left Atlanta involved a musher and her dogsled. They arrived in Fairbanks in the early evening, which felt to Jack exactly like morning, and froze as soon as they stepped outside. They took a cab to the only hotel Jack knew, a famous old seven-story building downtown, not far from the Chena River. Jack parted with some of his precious cash for the cab fare. He parted with still more for a room with two single beds. Then he tipped the desk clerk ten dollars to ring the room if *anyone* came looking for them. Nobody knew they were here. Anyone who'd manage to track them had to be from the Fallen.

Neither of them slept well. By 2:00 A.M. they were both sitting up. "You want to talk?" Jack asked.

Carl drew a deep sigh and laid back on his bed. "Why are we here?" he asked.

"I don't know," Jack confessed. "I did what I thought was right at the time. I trusted the Holy Spirit, and I acted. Maybe I was wrong. But here we are. Walking by faith."

"And what next?" Carl asked soberly.

"*More* walking by faith."

"Running blind is more like it," Carl grumbled.

"Maybe. I've done some of that in my life and *called* it faith."

"So how do you know the difference?"

Jack pondered. "The outcome? God's blessing? Hindsight?"

"Ah, yes," Carl murmured. "'The evidence of things hoped for,' whatever that means."

"I think it just means that we can look back and see the evidence of God's hand in our lives, the way He's answered our needs, and believe that He'll continue doing so in the future." *Are you listening to yourself, Jack?* he thought as he spoke. *Is this what you truly believe?*

"And what if we never escape the Fallen and the dogged pursuit of their MIBs?" Carl argued. "Suppose they finally do catch up to us and take us back. Does that outcome prove that it wasn't real faith after all?"

Jack frowned. "No. It just means God's working things out a different way, that we don't see yet. That's 'the conviction of things not seen.'" *Yes,* Jack answered himself firmly. *This is what I truly believe.*

"Yes, but what about things you do see, the things we *have* seen? Things that are wrong, and that God allowed to go wrong."

"Angry at God are you, Carl?"

"Aren't you?" Carl demanded pointedly. "You sounded angry enough on the airplane, talking about your clone. How is God going to work good out of that?"

"I don't know," Jack answered honestly. "What I do know is that I'm going to have to trust Him to do it."

"You think you can do that?" Carl asked. His words had almost a taunt to them. They made Jack uncomfortable.

"I think I'm going to have to try." Jack didn't go on to say what he was thinking—that he didn't expect to survive this trip, and thus he didn't expect to have to deal with that problem. "Isn't that what *you* would do?"

"Yes . . ." Carl said, but the word sounded distant, as if his thoughts had traveled elsewhere. "I've been thinking about what you said in the airport, that my discovery would doubtless be made by someone and that God would be prepared to handle it."

"And?"

Carl looked at Jack, weariness drawing his eyes down at the outer edges. "So why keep on running? If you're right, and they'll discover it anyway, why not just give up and give it to them? If God can stitch it all back together again in the end, regardless?"

That surprised Jack. In fact, it finally made him angry. He got up off the bed and paced the room. When he looked again at Carl, he knew his eyes were blazing. "You'd give up, Carl? We've come this far by faith, and God has miraculously taken care of us, yet you'd give up?"

Carl turned his head away. "I know it doesn't sound very courageous, Jack. But I'm not like you. I've never been taken by these creatures before, I'm not a preacher, I've never met an angel, I don't have a friend who reads minds—"

"What does any of that have to do with living by faith, Carl?" Jack exploded. "You think preachers have a ready supply of spiritual courage to draw on that other people lack? It doesn't work that way. You think only people who've seen angels can truly trust God? Very few people have seen angels, Carl, and yet the Church has continued to grow! Has that happened because God's children have said 'God will clean it up eventually,' and given in to evil? I don't think so!"

Suddenly Carl was wailing, "I can't *do* this anymore!" He buried his face in his hands and whimpered, "I'm exhausted, I'm stressed. What do you want from me?"

Jack backed away from him then, controlling his anger, controlling his tongue, knowing that the evil one was as much present in this room as anywhere—and as much at work. He struggled to let the Holy Spirit speak to him, and through him, and to be evident in him. He sat back down on the edge of the bed, seeking to think clearly and speak truthfully, with love.

"I want for you what I want for myself. To be a disciple. To trust God. To follow Jesus. To not give in, whatever comes. To do all I can, whatever that means. And to not try to do for myself what is God's place to do. That's all." When Carl didn't answer, Jack rolled back onto his pillow, lacing his fingers together on top of his head. "It's a team thing, Carl. God works in this world in marvelous ways and some of those ways are through us. And when we all work together with Him, the world changes."

There was a long pause between them. Then finally Carl said, "You're right, of course." Jack let out a long exhale of breath. He hadn't been aware that he was holding it in. After a moment, Carl went on. "I'm sorry, Jack. I'm not at my best."

"None of us are, *all* the time. Tomorrow I may need you to pick *me* up off the floor. Or out of the snow."

"You haven't told me what we're doing tomorrow," said Carl, almost accusingly.

*Oh well,* Jack thought. *No time like the present.* He shifted position on the bed and said, "I'm going to try to find a lady who gave me a dogsled ride once. I'm going to see if she'll take us to Canada."

"By *dogsled?*"

"At least they won't be able to check the passenger list."

They slept some then. Jack did, anyway.

# Chapter Twenty

*Northern lights*

It was midmorning in Fairbanks, and the sun had just come up. The Weather Channel told them it was twenty below outside. Not bad for a February day, but they sure weren't dressed for it.

Jack emptied the duffel bag on the bed. He wished they still had the knife, but they'd been forced to ditch it in Atlanta. No way they could carry that through a security gate. But Jack did have a small penknife attached to his key chain, and he opened the blade and started cutting the drab green canvas. He cut the circle on the bottom down the middle, then split it up both sides, cutting the bag in half. A little more cutting, and he had fashioned two rough hats, with longer strips of canvas hanging down from the front to tie under their chins. Jack tried one on.

"Looks ridiculous," Carl told him.

"You'll be glad for it when we go outside. Our ears will freeze before we get to the store if we don't have some protection. Here, put this back on." Jack tossed Carl his lab coat, then threw him the third black suit, which had been wadded in the bottom of the bag. Carl put it on over his other suit and the lab coat without question. He was from Canada, after all. He knew the advantage of layers against the cold.

Over his own suit, Jack donned once more the woolen robe he'd worn in a previous century and that smelly garment of stitched-together skins. Strange as it looked, it was at least warm, and he'd once seen a trapper in the Fairbanks airport wearing skins far more outlandish. The boots were warm too. "We need to buy some hats and gloves, first, and you some boots." He pulled out his wallet and counted his money. He hoped they could find some cheap clothes. He'd need to save most of the wad to offer the musher.

"That river is frozen solid," Carl said, looking out the window.

"That makes you one-third sourdough," Jack told him, stuffing his wallet down through the neck of his robe and into his pocket. "You've seen the Chena River frozen. By this afternoon you'll be two-thirds sourdough."

"How?"

"You'll have ridden in a dogsled." Carl shook his head in dismay. "I thought you were a Canadian!" Jack teased.

"Southern Canada," Carl smiled. "What's the final third?"

"You have to see the Northern Lights."

"I've seen them already. I remember when I was a child we used to—"

The telephone rang. Both of them looked at it, then at one another, then Jack snapped, "Stairway!" and dashed out into the hall. Carl didn't argue. He just grabbed up his own makeshift hat and sprinted for the door. The elevator was on the way up as they clattered down the stairs. On the first floor Jack dashed toward the back of the hotel and the kitchen instead of through the lobby. Carl ran right behind him. Surprised cooks dodged aside as the two fugitives hit the backdoor and were outside and running.

The change in their pace was immediate. Frigid air hit their lungs, robbing them of breath. Jack pointed Carl through an ice-covered alley that led to the front of the hotel, and they skated through it onto the main road. Jack paused here and looked back at the large, dark automobile that now sat in the front of the lobby. Its engine was still running.

"Jack!" Carl shouted at him. "What are you *thinking?*"

But Jack wasn't thinking about it any longer. He was already acting, racing up the street to sling open the door and hop into the driver's side.

Carl jumped into the other side and slammed the door, protesting "This is grand theft auto!"

"Yeah, well, they can blame it on my clone," Jack muttered as he hit the gas and they sped up the street. The two men in black came running out of the lobby as they turned the corner. "At least it provides *us* with transportation, and leaves them *without.*"

"We're *never* going to escape these people!" Carl wailed as they crossed a major intersection near the heart of town.

"We have for the moment."

"But they'll call the police!"

"I'd like to hear *that* conversation," Jack grunted. "We'll have abandoned it by the time they do. That is, if—"

"If what?" Carl demanded.

"If I can remember where I'm going."

He knew the general direction and went that way. Soon they were off the main streets and onto a snow-slicked road that was gravel in the summer time. Eventually they would have to stop somewhere and ask specific directions. Jack spotted a small store and skidded to a stop beside it. He left the car running and stomped inside through the snow.

It didn't take long for the owner to identify the musher Jack was seeking, especially when Jack described her to him and handed him a twenty. Fairbanks was a small town, and mushers were semi-celebrities. The man just nodded and said, "That would be Brand McNally."

"Brandy?" Jack asked.

"Don't call her that. She goes by Brand. If you say you've met her, then you should know why."

Indeed, Jack knew why. Although he hadn't remembered her name, he'd never forgotten her personality. She was a tough, wiry little woman with a hard face and a no-nonsense manner. She was the kind of person who liked dogs more than she did people and who regularly dared the winter to kill her. As a favor to a mutual friend, she'd given Jack a dogsled ride one midnight, under a full moon. If anyone could get them into Canada without passing through a border checkpoint, she could. Jack described his memory of her cabin to the store owner, and he nodded and gave him directions. He also offered to sell Jack some warmer clothing—"used, of course, but cheap"—and Jack jumped at the chance. He hadn't really realized that he was shivering.

He bought enough layers for the both of them, and they struggled to get into them with the motor still running. Twenty minutes later they were standing at the foot of a small, snow-covered hill with a pack of dogs baying at them like wolves. That brought Brand onto her porch, along with her shotgun. "Pug! Spark! Judy! Geezer! You shut up!" At the sound of her voice, the dogs quieted down. Then she turned her attention—and the barrel of her gun—on these strangers. "What do you want?"

Jack and Carl didn't move. "You don't remember me," Jack called up to her, "but some years ago you took me for a dogsled ride. It was midnight, and the lamp on your helmet went out, and—"

326

"And I turned you over in the snow, and you almost caught the anchor in your stomach. Yeah, I remember you." She still didn't lower the shotgun. "What do you want?"

"I want you to take us to Whitehorse."

"What?" she yelled down, incredulous.

"I have money!" Jack shouted.

She hesitated. "How much?"

"Look, can we come up there and talk? It's hard to negotiate in the cold!"

"All right," she said, and she jerked her head toward her door by way of invitation. But she still didn't lower her shotgun barrel.

As soon as they took a step up the hill the dogs were back on their feet baying and barking, their chains rattling together as they struggled to get free. "Down!" Brand shouted at them, and once again they were quiet. Jack and Carl climbed the hill quickly and cautiously.

Once inside her cabin Jack took off his toboggan, and the woman inspected his face. "Yeah, I remember you," she said, and she lowered the shotgun and nodded down at it. "Can't be too careful." She stood it against the wall—but still within easy reach—and gestured around. "I'd offer you a place to sit, but—" then she smiled. It was a genuine, toothy smile that flashed for just a minute on her hard features, then disappeared just as quickly.

There was nowhere to sit because there was really nowhere to *be*. The cabin itself was really not much more than a frame built to house and keep warm a gigantic water tank. Bookshelves and storage spaces were built around and under the tank, and a narrow stairway—little more than a slightly angled ladder—climbed up to the loft built on top of the tank. The bed was up in the loft, and the kitchen and a long counter took up most of the space on this side of the tank. The woman shrugged, and leaned against the cabinet. "So what's this about me taking you to Whitehorse?"

"We need to get to Whitehorse. I have cash—"

She held up her hand for silence, and Jack stopped. "The Yukon Quest run, huh?" When she saw Carl's vacant look, she explained, "The Yukon Quest is a race. Not as famous as the Iditirod. Just as hard." Then she looked back at Jack and said, "There are easier ways to get to Canada." When he started to speak she said, "What you *really* mean is that you need to get into Canada without going through customs. Am I right?" She flashed the smile again, and Jack nodded. Then she looked at their empty hands. "What are you carrying?"

"Nothing," Jack told her. "Nothing but ourselves."

She raised her eyebrows, and said, "How much?"

"I have $750."

She leaned against the counter, her arms folded across her chest, casually scratching one arm as she thought. "Whitehorse is a long way. How about if I just get you to a town *inside* Canada?"

Jack looked at Carl. He shrugged and nodded.

"It won't be a fast run. And you'll need parkas. It's OK," she added when they started to protest. "I've got a couple to lend." She scratched her head and said, "Yeah. I could use the practice run. Where's the money?"

Jack reached inside his robe to pull out the wad of bills, then stuffed it back into his shirt. "Can't be too careful," he smiled.

Brand smiled back—briefly. "It'll take me about an hour to get ready. There's coffee on the stove. What about the car?"

"Somebody will be by to pick it up."

"Uh-huh," she nodded knowingly. "Then why don't you *not* park it right in front of my house," she growled. Jack nodded and went out in the cold to drive the car a mile back up the road. He left it locked, with the keys inside, and walked quickly back.

Brand was still preparing. For the next half hour, they watched as she checked provisions, packed gear, and sorted through leather traces for the ones she wanted to use. She ducked back behind the tank, crawled under the tank, made one trip up to the loft and tossed down parkas, then wrapped herself in one and went out to hitch her dogs. There was one long, thin window beside the door, and they watched her as she pulled a sled out of a wooden shed and lined the traces up before it. Immediately the dogs were up, calling to her, begging to go. She loaded the sled, refusing any help, putting the shotgun in place right in front of the high handles at the back. Then she knelt down and talked to each of her two dozen dogs in turn, petting them, checking their paws, choosing one and taking it over to buckle it into the gang hitch, then going back to choose another. By the time she was finished hitching up the chosen ones, all the dogs were in a frenzy of excitement.

Jack and Carl felt mostly apprehension. But there was some excitement between them, too, and Jack was encouraged by a change in Carl's attitude. There appeared at last to be some real hope in his eyes, as if he was finally coming to believe he would actually make it home.

As Brand came back inside, Jack pulled out the money and handed it to her. "Oh," she said. "You trust me now."

"No. You turned me over in the snow once. I just didn't want to be responsible for losing it."

She laughed then and took it, and said, "One last thing before we go. What are your names?" When they looked at each other she said, "I don't care. I just want to know who to holler for if you get lost."

Moments later, bundled up against the cold, the two men were seated in the sled, Jack in front between Carl's legs. Brand pulled loose the anchor—a three-pronged trident bent back in the shape of huge fishhook—and handed it to Jack. "Here. Don't stick yourself with that." Then she stepped onto the back of the sled, grabbed the handles, and shouted, "Mush!"

The team bolted into action, immediately running full speed down the hill, directly between two trees. Jack's heart raced—this was better than any theme-park thrill-ride—then they were onto flat ground and running eastward.

The first fifteen minutes was fun. The next half hour was interesting. After that, the unchanging scenery of snow-covered flats, snow-covered hills, and snow-covered pines became a bright blur. Jack managed to wiggle around and fish his sunglasses out of his pocket, anchoring them firmly behind his covered ears and the tight welt of his toboggan. Despite the glasses, his eyes still blurred. Even though wrapped up tight, his lips still chapped. This was going to be a grueling trip.

Jack may have been dozing when he heard Brand say, almost to herself, "What *is* that?" His eyes flew open, and canted his hips forward to peer over the dogs. A light snow had begun to fall, and he could really see nothing ahead of him. Brand's eyes were apparently better.

"What is what?" he called back to her.

"That . . . thing out there," she said, and by craning his neck he could see she was pointing to the north.

"It's them," Carl said, his voice dead.

And it was. "UMMO," Jack muttered. It was one of the dark, squarish ships of UMMO. They'd been found. But how? *Ben?* he said in his mind. *Are you* that *angry with me?*

"What *is* it?" Brand was screaming now, for it was coming their way, skimming along about five feet over the snow. A moment later it didn't matter what it was, just that it was shooting at them. "What have you gotten me into?" Brand screamed, and she mushed her dogs to run full speed.

The strafing didn't touch them, but only because Brand was able to adroitly turn her dogs forty-five degrees and run under the ship. They all ducked. By the time the saucer swooped upward and turned around to come in for a second pass, Brand had jerked the shotgun free and was firing back. All the time she was bellowing curses, both at the ship and at her two riders.

UMMO's gunners hit nothing on this second pass either, so they opened up with the cannon on the snow in front of the dogs. As the snow parted before them the dogs yelped and jerked away, throwing the sled into a wobble. As Brand tried to fire and turn her dogs at the same time, the sled turned over, running on its side twenty feet before the dogs could pull it no more. Brand slammed the butt of the shotgun down between Carl and Jack and struggled to right it as the dark craft swooped and started back again. Before she could get it back on its runners, Jack wiggled out of his seat and threw himself out into the snow.

"It's me they want!" he shouted, as Brand savagely twisted the sled upright and jumped back on the back. "Go!" he shouted. "Go!"

The woman certainly wasn't staying. In a matter of seconds the dogs lurched forward again and the sled shot away at full speed. "Go on!" Jack called out. "Take him to Canada!" But he doubted if she ever heard him. The UMMO ship was careening back toward them, and Jack was jumping up and down, waving his arms to attract its attention and its fire.

UMMO obliged, shifting direction slightly to come hurtling toward him. Bullets whiffled around him and Jack tossed himself headlong into a snowbank, half burying himself in it. Then he hopped up and began to run.

It was useless, he knew, but he ran. He churned through the snow, pumping his knees high like a hurdler, but he made very little forward progress. He heard the craft swooping back, threw himself flat at the last possible moment, and heard the ship bounce off the snow just beyond him.

*Only a matter of time now,* he thought, but he jumped up to his feet again anyway, and tried again to run, toward the UMMO time craft now, so that at least he could see it coming. *Only a matter of time,* he thought again, noting the irony of his thought. It had always been a matter of time with these creatures. His foot hit a hidden rock and tripped him forward, and he sprawled in the snow, aware that it was already caked on the few exposed places on his body, and that they were freezing—aware that he had completely run out of breath—aware that he was going to die. He pushed himself up on his forearms and looked up, watching the UMMO craft ascend straight upward, preparing to curl over and come back. This time he didn't get up. He just waited.

It wasn't a surprise, after all. He hadn't expected to make it home this time. Apparently he wouldn't be missed, for there would be a Jack Brennen there, filling his shoes. He hated that thought.

Still, Jack thought as he instantly reflected back on his life, he wouldn't have done anything differently. He'd done what he could. He'd lived with purpose. He'd made an impact on people. He'd been faithful. He was ready to go.

All these things Jack Brennen thought as the ship climbed into the sky. Then, behind it, Jack saw something else. Something beautiful. A curtain of multicolored light filled the northern sky, shimmering, waving, an animated rainbow. Or was it the curtains of heaven, glimpsed from the underside? *Aurora Borealis!* Jack thought. *The Northern Lights! Well. So I'm a sourdough at last.* At the very last, apparently, for the UMMO ship had turned over and started its last pass, an inky blot against that glorious, flickering backdrop.

In that moment Jack really didn't mind dying. He was going to die eventually anyway. Did when or where make any difference? He would go to be with Jesus, he knew that, and with those others whom he'd loved who had passed on before him, a list that grew longer with every passing year. Still, he would have loved to have given Gloria a last kiss.

But the UMMO weren't going to kill him. Not just yet. The black ship had come to hover over him, and now he felt himself begin drawn up, out of the snow and into the air. "No!" Jack shouted, fighting against the beam that drew him skyward. "No! Lord, no!" For while Jack was quite prepared to die, he was *not* prepared to live as a slave to the bugs! Suddenly he had plenty of energy back, and he kicked and wiggled and struggled all the way up into the ship like a bass trying to throw its hook. All to no avail. They had him.

He turned his head back to look upward and saw the door in the bottom of the black saucer sliding open to reveal the orange glow of its interior. It looked like an oven door, like he was being drawn upward into a fiery furnace. For a very brief moment Jack threw a glance at the horizon, hoping for the sight of angels. There were none. Jack clenched his jaw and looked upward into that approaching inferno, thinking, *This time there will be no angels.* Then he was inside. The hatchway shut beneath him. A swarm of stinking bugs surrounded him, crushing him between their glistening shells, and carried him upward into the control room.

There sat the Ultrarch. Oh, he looked a lot like Ron Pearson, Jack thought, but that poor man was long gone, trapped inside his body, watching the Overlord steer. And now the Overlord peered out of Pearson's eyes at Jack and smiled with Pearson's mouth—a huge, gloating smile.

"Thought you'd done it, didn't you," he said, his words piercing through Jack's mind. "Thought you'd gotten away. Thought you'd tricked us—*we,* who taught you tiny creatures every trickery! Well look, Jack Brennen! You failed. You have utterly, hopelessly failed. Oh yes, we saw the little doggies running away. Think they'll get far? Think they'll get to the Canadian border? When we can literally be there a minute ago? You *are* persistent, I'll give that to you. I like that in a man. *My* men. And it is because I admire that quality in you that I'm going to make you a very generous offer. But before I do so, please let me make clear to you the consequences you face if you refuse. Are you ready?" he smiled brightly.

Jack just gazed back. An UMMO had gripped him around the chest from behind. He couldn't even move.

"Good," the Ultrarch smiled. "Now, you've been a lot of trouble to us. Far more trouble than we should have allowed. I'm tired of that. So unless you take my offer I'm going to give you to UMMO here to take back to their cone. You've been there, I think? That black, scary hell hive? Yes. First, of course, they'll sting you up full of stingers. They'll do that here, in just a moment. Then they'll take you there and hang you on the wall—alert, awake, aware—and leave you there. Oh, did I mention they'll take you back to the beginning of time, first? Yes. And they'll keep on doing that. Over and over. Whenever you'll think you've almost endured into the present—to THE END you people are always prattling on about—why then, they'll just move you back to the beginning. What's that I see on your cheeks, Dr. Brennen? Why, are those tears? But come on, my friend! Were you really expecting us to simply give you death—and heaven?"

Jack felt the hot tears course down his cheeks. He struggled against the arms that held him bound. Helplessly.

"You see, Jack," the Overlord rasped, "we've *been* there. We've *had* that. You think its absence doesn't burn in our black souls every moment? You think the loss of everything that matters could ever be replaced by the petty pleasures of making you tiny creatures miserable? You think—out of our hatred for you—that we'd actually *give* you that?"

Jack tried to speak but could not. It was as if a tiny hand had reached up from his windpipe into his voice box and clamped his vocal cords together.

"No, no," the Ultrarch sneered. "No dramatic 'Touch not the whatziz whatziz' this time. I haven't finished making my offer. When I'm done, then you can speak, but you'd best choose your words carefully when you have the opportunity. It will be your last. And I have to tell you, UMMO is hungry for you to say no, for they *do* so long to bury those stingers in you. I trust I've made quite clear to you the price of rejecting me? Have I?" he added when Jack made no response.

Jack found he could nod his head.

"Very good. Now this is my final offer. We'll return you, this *instant,* to your wife, your life, your home, your job—all the things you hold dear. All I ask is that while you go about your little religious functions you remember that *I* am your master now. Oh, I don't want you to announce that publicly of course, that would be defeating the whole purpose. Just put in a good word for *all* the diverse worldviews as being equally helpful—and ultimately relative. Encourage people to make up their own religions in the name of 'personal freedom.' Endorse alternative lifestyles as being perfectly legitimate expressions of 'the human spirit.' Cause your students to question whatever they've been taught. And if you should be fired, you can blame it on 'narrow-minded bigotry,' and we'll find you a much more prestigious teaching position at triple the salary. I think you get the idea, Dr. Brennen. Just tell the truth, that the one you've always worshiped is powerless to keep any promises. It *is* true you know. Otherwise . . ." The Ultrarch gestured around the cramped interior of the UMMO vessel ". . . why would you be here? Not so hard to do, right, Dr. Brennen? I promise you, hundreds of churchmen have done it before you, and *very* effectively."

Jack listened to all of this with a rising sense of revulsion. He felt like snakes were wrestling in his stomach, and he wanted to vomit them up.

"Now then. It's your turn to speak. Tell me what I want to hear."

The clamp that had locked together his vocal cords was suddenly gone. He cleared his throat, swallowed, then cleared it again. Then he made the only statement he was capable of making. "The God I worship *is* able to save me. But even if he doesn't, I will never serve you." The clamp was just as suddenly back.

"Oh dear," said the Ultrarch, smiling. "A martyr's speech. Fine then. If it's martyrdom you choose, we'll give you eons of it. UMMO? He's yours."

With evident glee, the two UMMO on either side of the Ultrarch raised up on their hind legs and curled their abdomens forward under their bodies. The sharp-tipped stingers plunged toward him and—

All the power suddenly went off in the craft. The abrupt fall into darkness was exactly as if they'd dropped into the black hole of the time void. Blinded, the UMMO hesitated, then fell backward as the whole saucer shimmied once, then turned over onto its side. There was a sudden scramble and some abortive flight and some indiscriminate stinging among the insects themselves as they panicked in the darkness. And Jack watched it all, for to him it was now bright day. The walls of the saucer had disappeared, and he could see all around him the brilliant glow of the dancing Northern Lights. The multiple colors were swirling, coalescing, taking shape into what Jack believed was a beautiful hallucination. The lights formed two mighty angels, each as tall as the sky itself, and they gripped the ship between them by its squared-off edges and shook it like a toy box.

The UMMO craft stalled. It flipped belly up. It hung there, quivering, dead in the sky, but at an impossible angle. So there were to be angels after all, thought Jack, struggling against the hands that still held him from behind. When he couldn't break free, he just stared open-mouthed at these immense angelic faces, looking back and forth from one side to the other. They were beings of light, pastel in shade, of greens and pinks and reds. But despite the sweetness, the genuine loveliness of their colors, these faces were hard with righteousness, fierce with dignity, chiseled with power. There seemed to be no effort at all to what they did as they stepped apart, twisted their wrists, and cracked the ship in half—as if it were nothing more than a foam plate at a picnic. Then they shook the pieces, scattering their contents across the sky. Jack heard a horrible screech directly above him and looked up to see the body of Ron Pearson plummeting downward. He saw the man's eyes, wide and terrified, and realized the Overlord had already made his exit. Jack reached out to try to grab the man's flailing arms, but they were out of reach. Seconds later, the now-dead body buried itself in the snow a half a mile below. And now, Jack guessed, there would be another summons to appear, another conclave of the Ultrastructure, and upon someone else would be bestowed the "honor" of becoming the vessel of the Ultrarch. For that selfish, sadistic Overlord was out there, somewhere, still.

As was Jack, to his utter astonishment. He was left hanging in the air, untouched in the midst of the flying wreckage, wrestling with the hands that clutched him tight, struggling to be free. Still they held him, as tight as steel bands, and he gasped to see the two gigantic, angelic faces turn to look directly at him—and bow.

At first he thought they were bowing to him and couldn't imagine why. Then he caught on. He managed to twist around to look over his shoulder and knew immediately who it was that held him. He met the eyes of Jesus, and they were the most beautiful eyes he'd ever seen. Jack wept in shame and triumph.

"I've got you," Jesus said, smiling. "I've *always* got you."

\* \* \*

"I've got you, Preacher. Relax. I've got you."

Jack stopped struggling and laid back into the arms of his deacon. He felt another pair of arms circling his feet, and still others digging down into the snow beneath his back and his legs.

"Let's get him to the ambulance," George was saying to the others. "On three. One—two—"

Jack felt himself being hoisted into the air. He opened his eyes. It was night, but in the beams of a dozen surrounding flashlights he could see snowflakes still tumbling from the sky.

\* \* \*

At 10:30 the phone rang again. Gloria pounced on it and almost slammed it through her ear. "Hello!" she barked.

"We've found him."

"George! Is he all right!"

"Half frozen, but we've got the medics here, and they say he'll be just fine. They're putting him in the ambulance right now to run him to the hospital."

"Which one?" George told her, and she shouted, "I'm on my way!" It wasn't until later that she realized she'd hung up on him. By that time she'd already dialed the fire station, which was right around the corner. With a combination of desperation, demands, and pure charm she talked the fire chief into coming to get her. Gloria arrived at the hospital in the front seat of an enormous red pumper.

George was already there, with Brother Henry beside him, and they all hugged on the run as she hustled in the door. "He's all right? They're sure he's all right?"

"He's fine. He wouldn't have been if he hadn't been dressed so warmly."

Gloria wrinkled her forehead. "In—what? He left this morning in his suit and overcoat."

"Well you know," George said with a puzzled expression, "that's what he was wearing when he left the church too. But when we found him in a snow drift he was . . . well he was—"

Gloria stopped walking and looked at him. "What?"

George gave her an I-can't-explain-this shrug and said, "He was dressed up like an Eskimo in sunglasses."

Gloria paused, nodded reflectively, then headed on down the hallway at a trot, yelling back, "Which room?"

Jack was sitting up in bed, but with the covers pulled all the way up to his chin. His nose was red, his ears were red, and he had what looked like goggle lines around his eyes, but he was smiling. Gloria stepped inside the room, saw the fur parka draped over the chair between them, and stopped at it to run her fingers through the fur. There was only one explanation. "They took you again, didn't they?" Jack nodded. "Whew!" she said, letting out a whoosh of breath. "So that's finally behind us!" Then she ran to jump up onto the bed and grabbed him.

They clung together for several minutes, tightening and re-tightening their embrace. Then Gloria popped her head up and said, "I have to call Trisha!" She grabbed immediately for the phone.

Jack fought her for it and wrestled the phone back into the cradle, ignoring her frown. "Don't worry about calling Trisha. Trisha will call you, probably Wednesday night from Chicago."

"Trisha's not in Chicago."

"She will be by then. Honey, it's a *long* story, and I promise I'll tell you every detail. Just not tonight."

Gloria's forehead wrinkled, then she said, "Well, can I at least call Ben?"

"Go right ahead."

Gloria quickly dialed the number she had memorized that afternoon in her worry. She spoke for a few minutes, then hung it up and looked at Jack. "Ben's on his way here," she related in worried tones. "The people he was staying with said about eight this evening he suddenly told them there was something he had to come to Louisville to do. What do you make of that?"

"I don't know. I guess we can ask him when he gets here."

"Ask me what?" said Ben, appearing in the doorway.

Jack looked up and saw him—a man of faith, a man of God—and teared up. "Ben," he said and held open his arms.

Ben came over to the bed and hugged him, hard, then leaned back and asked quietly, "Are you all right?"

"I'm home," Jack smiled. "I guess the question is, am I going to stay home?"

Ben met his gaze. "Are you asking me if they take you again?"

"Oh, I don't think they'll take me again." Jack smiled broadly. "I cause them too much trouble." Ben laughed and patted Jack's hand. As he started to pull away, Jack held him and added, "Besides, you wouldn't tell me if you knew."

Gloria listened to this exchange with growing concern, then said, "I . . . don't know if I want to hear this. I'm going to go check on George and Henry."

As she stepped out of the room, Ben looked back at Jack and said, "She's had a terrifying day. We all have."

"Yes," Jack nodded. "We *all* have. And somewhere out there, I'm still having it." He shook his head, bemused.

"Time overlap?" Ben asked, and Jack nodded. "Strange feeling, isn't it? Where *are* you now, or do you even know?"

"I think I do. But we were in and out so much I . . ." Jack faded out. Then he looked up at Ben. "There *is* something puzzling me—" he began, but stopped himself when Ben reached into his pocket and pulled out a sheet of paper.

He unfolded it and laid it on Jack's chest. It was the original of the fax. "You sent it?"

"Yeah," Ben nodded. "About twenty minutes ago. It was hard to find one of those places open."

Jack looked down at the sheet again, still perplexed. "But how did you know about Carrie Baxter?" he asked, his suspicions growing. "Or about Trisha Paulson, for that matter?"

"Carrie Baxter I read out of your mind," Ben said matter-of-factly. "Trisha Paulson I read out of your wife's."

Jack stared up at him. *Then your gift is back.* He didn't voice it, but Ben replied to it anyway.

"For the moment," he said, almost apologetically. "I don't quite know what to do about it. Happened about supper-time this evening, while we were praying for you. What do you think it means?"

*Just that God heard your prayers—and answered them through you,* Jack thought. *He heard mine too. Don't worry about it, Ben. If it stays, then this time God sent it and will teach you how to use it for His glory.*

Ben nodded reflectively, and Jack wiggled back into his pillow and sighed with contentment. Then he frowned and sat up straight.

Ben smiled and murmured, "The answer to that is *yes,* you still have to go."

Jack moaned. He'd just remembered about Sherry Lynn Ward. And in just a few minutes, it seemed, the woman was on the phone. . . .